THE BLACK BOOK SERIES

SPECIAL EDITION

USA TODAY BESTSELLING AUTHOR
THERESA SEDERHOLT

MURDER BY MISTAKE

Book One
One bomb; the ripples of devastation—endless.
Tick . . . tick . . . tick . . .

Michelina

A week ago, I was a simple high school science teacher, and my biggest worry was making sure that my students got their final project in on time. Now, that is the furthest thing from my mind. Instead, I am in a race to save my life. In my possession is a key my grandfather left me. This key could change the lives of the five New York crime families that run the East Coast. I'm surrounded by the FBI and Mafia families. Good guys. Bad guys; the line blurs. One wrong decision could end so many lives, including my own.

Luca

I've lived my life on a dare—a life where I can do what I want when I want. Whoever gets in my way be damned. When I was assigned to protect her, she had no idea who I was—no one did. I didn't expect to feel anything for her, except hate. Hate for what her family did to mine. Instead, I was beginning to fall in love with her. A forbidden love that could get us both killed or . . . it could land us at the top of La Cosa Nostra.

One wrong decision and it could blow up in our face . . . literally.

DANGEROUS PURSUIT

Book Two

There are some secrets that seep out the sides of even the most confined places. Secrets that get people killed when they are supposed to be protected by them. Secrets that change the dynamics of life as we know it.

Michelina has been a victim of all these possibilities. The only thing she can do is continue to search for answers and try not to get herself killed in the process.

Family can be a wonderful blessing. It can also come at a cost. The more Michelina learns about her family, the larger it grows and may just cost her everything.

Luca is doing everything he can to keep the woman he loves safe and the truth from spreading like wildfire. But when a bullet, meant for his brother, is closing in on its target, instincts kick in, and the truth explodes all around them.

There is one man at the helm of these wicked lies and deceit: Agosto. For years he thought he was doing the right thing. Maybe he was, or maybe he was unknowingly supplying the ammo to have his entire family taken out.

BLOOD VOWS

Book Three

Self-destruction is ingrained into human nature. Each person carries the ability to cause their own extinction in all facets of life. Intervention rarely changes anything because one thing is clear. . .no matter how hard we try to set someone on a new path, their choices will always belong to them.

Save her best friend's life again or save the cousin she never knew she had. That is the dubious decision Michelina faces. She never imagined she'd turn out more like Carmine, the grandfather she hardly knew. He was ruthless, which was reflected in the hoard of enemies that followed him. The blood on her hands won't wash away easily as Michelina gathers her strength to become the head of the Amato family.

The contention between family members begins to fester, as her stepbrother's plans for Carmine's legacy puts not only Michelina's life in jeopardy, but also the life of her closest friend.

A house full of secrets will always be divided.

INFINITE ABSOLUTION

Book Four

The reigns have been handed down to the younger generation, the generation whose ties are connected by deceptions in the past. There's only one man left from the older generation who has been pulling those strings all along: Agosto. Agosto knew all the damage he left in his wake, but he didn't care; he was in competition with a dead man.

He walked away thinking he would have infinite absolution once the love of his life became truly his under the eyes of God. Viviana's love was strong enough to forgive him of his misgivings, he was sure of it. However, Agosto has never been able to understand the love for your child, the power behind such a love...

For some, there is no absolution.

Bern
SWITZERLAND
LIECHTENSTEIN
Innsbruck
AUSTRIA
HUNG.
Klagenfurt
Ljubljana
Zagreb
SLOVENIA
SERBIA
Bolzano
TRENTINO
ALTO ADIGE
Trento
Udine
Gorizia
Trieste
BOSNIA AND HERZEGOVINA
Aosta
Como
Bergamo
Lecco
Vicenza
Verona
Treviso
Venezia (Venice)
Rijeka
Sarajevo
Milano (Milan)
Lodi
Padova
Golfo di Venezia
Novara
Vercelli
Pavia
Mantova
Rovigo
Turino (Turin)
Asti
Alba
Alessandria
Cremona
Parma
Modena
Ferrara
CROATIA
Piacenza
Reggio nell'Emilia
Split
Genova (Genoa)
Bologna
Ravenna
FRANCE
Savona
La Spezia
Carrara
Massa
Forlì
Rimini
Pesaro
Dubrovnik
MONTENEGRO
Nice
San Remo
Imperia
Golfo di Genova
Viareggio
Lucca
Pistoia
Prato
SAN MARINO
Urbino
Ancona
MONACO
Livorno
Pisa
Firenze (Florence)
Arezzo
Siena
Macerata
Porto San Giorgio
LIGURIAN SEA
I.di Gorgona
Perugia
ADRIATIC SEA
Ascoli Piceno
San Benedetto del Tronto
Isola d'Elba
Grosseto
Terni
Pescara
Corsica (France)
I. Pianosa
I. di Giglio
I. di Giannutri
Viterbo
Rieti
L'Aquila
Chieti
Isole Tremiti
Pelagruža (Croatia)
ROMA (Rome)
VATICAN
Lido di Ostia
Frosinone
Isernia
Campobasso
Foggia
Bari
Strait of Otranto
Latina
Benevento
Caserta
Avellino
Brindisi
Napoli (Naples)
Potenza
Matera
Taranto
Lecce
Salerno
L. d'Ischia
L. di Capri
Golfo di Taranto
Sassari
Nuoro
IONIAN SEA
Oristano
TYRRHENIAN SEA
Sardegna (Sardinia)
Cosenza
Crotone
Cagliari
Catanzaro
Isola di San Pietro
Isola di Sant'Antioco
Isole Eolie (Aeolian Islands)
Isola Stromboli
Messina
Reggio di Calabria
MEDITERRANEAN SEA
Palermo
Trapani
Monte Etna
Acireale
Catania
Enna
Caltanissetta
Agrigento
Syracuse
Ragusa
Sicilia (Sicily)
Strait of Sicily
Tunis

MURDER
BY MISTAKE

In loving memory
Vito Batz

My sweet Vito. You were so much more than *just* a dog. So many times, you licked away my tears. For seventeen years you were my ride or die partner in crime. With every move around the country, you took it all in stride. You listened when I needed you to. You tolerated Godiva and taught Sir Winston how to be a gentle friend. You were what all mankind should strive to be like. I miss you every day. Until we meet again. Hugs.

PROLOGUE

Carmine Amato

WE ARE BORN, AND THEN WE DIE. THEY ARE BOTH expected. It's the life we live in between that sets the standards we are willing to live with. Family is everything to me, however, there is always a "but." We all have stories that become memories and before too long, those fade away too. When the book was opened to me, I became a made man. First, I took an oath: the Omertà code that we all must live by. You must be loyal and keep your mouth shut. You must put our Mafia family before your own flesh and blood. All these years, I thought I did just that. However, when they found out about my insurance policy, all bets were off. Having broken the most important rule, I was no longer the trusted one. To save my family, and of course myself, I did the unthinkable—I sang. The first thing I did was stash my books that detailed all the transgressions of the five families. The logs that show where I funneled cash, diamonds, emeralds, and photos that could bring down the United States Government if they got out. Then I gave a sample of what I had to the FBI. They were chomping at the bit to get me to agree to testify against the Mafia. I gave them a list of my terms, which I knew they would agree to. Once the agreement was signed, the fun began. Two years of cloak and dagger. Living in the shadows until it was time. Really, I thought it through and found this was a win for everyone involved ... so I thought.

CHAPTER ONE

Michelina Amato Ciccone

MY NAME IS MICHELINA FRANCES AMATO CICCONE. I WAS born in Brooklyn, New York. My mother, Frances Amato, never married my father. Oh, she had every intention of marrying him. Unfortunately, the Manhattan district attorney had other plans for my father, Nick Ciccone. After spending five years in Rikers Island, they killed my dad with a shank to his throat. My grandfather, Carmine, broke the news to my mom. I was too young to know what happened. All I remember is my mom crying and throwing our clothes in her car. She kept repeating that she would never be under Carmine's thumb. That night we moved out of her parents' house and never moved back. Mom and I moved to Mesa, Arizona. Mom wanted to make a new start, and Arizona had everything she wanted. Life was peaceful until my grandfather, Carmine Frances Amato, died of a heart attack. It is commonly referred to as "the widow maker." After he died, my mom helped my grandmother sell everything they owned and moved her to Arizona. My grandma bought a house near my mom in Mesa. They said it was a new start. I was young when this happened, so I don't have a lot of memories of Carmine. The ones I do have are mostly good. One day he was there and then he wasn't. Neither my mom nor grandmother talk about death in the Amato home. Everyone continues on like it's just another day in paradise. My mom got a job at Boeing where she made some good friends. She never dated or got married. I could never understand why she chose the life she did. I didn't have much of a choice in anything until I was eighteen; I legally took my father's name.

Today mom and I are at Grandma's house, clearing everything out so she can sell it. Grandma's house is in the Red Mountain Ranch community where the neighbors are close and look after each other. Unfortunately, the neighbors can't be there 24/7. Even though Mom's job at Boeing was only two miles away, she realized after the fire department's third visit for a minor kitchen fire, it was time. Mom decided it was best to move Grandma into the assisted living community in the same area as her home, giving her peace of mind. She needs to sell the home and use the proceeds to pay for her care. Mom and I don't really see eye to eye on most things, but I did promise to help her. It's my only Saturday off from work and my best friend Jessica wanted to hang out, but the one thing I learned is that you never turn your back on family, no matter what. Thankfully, Jessica was okay with the change of plans. She used the weekend to go visit her folks in Flagstaff. So, I'm in the den, boxing up books to be donated, when I come across an old composition notebook.

"Mom, look what I found tucked behind some books. I think it was Grandpa's." I hold it out for her to look at, but she waves her hand over it.

"It's nothing, Chelle, just the ramblings of an old man. Throw it away."

"Throw it away. Why would I throw it away? I want to read it. I don't have very many memories of him. Maybe it will give me a better insight to Grandpa."

"Chelle, what's there to learn? He did things his way, and if you went against him, well, let's just say I've never met anyone that could hold a grudge longer than my father."

"You say that like it's a bad thing. You had him your whole life, but

I had so little time with him," I remind her. She looks right at me, but she doesn't see me. Her eyes fill with tears, which is a rare thing for her. What is she remembering? What could be so painful?

"Do what you want with it, but remember, sometimes things are not always black and white. The only place perfect exists is in a delusional mind." She wipes her eyes and quickly gets back to the task at hand … clearing out this house.

"Oh, and Chelle, if you are that interested in finding out more about your grandfather, there are boxes in the attic with all his journals. If you don't want them, then put them out for the trash collector."

I race up to the attic to retrieve his stuff. There are three bank boxes labeled "Carmine's personal stuff." If I open them now, I'll never get done here. Instead, I drag them downstairs and put them in the trunk of my car. When I close the trunk, I stare at it for a moment longer than I should, like inside holds the key to some great mystery. Mom's probably right; they are just the ramblings of an old man. I remind myself the sooner we get done here, the sooner this place can go on the market. I hope whoever buys it finds only happiness and love. Mom thought I would buy it, but the sadness here always outweighed the happy times. When I head inside to give Mom the all clear, I find her crying.

"Mom, what can I do to help?"

"Chelle, there is nothing anyone can do. We live the life we are given and not always the one we wish for." I give her shoulder a squeeze, turn and head back out to my car. She follows closely behind me. "Chelle, are you coming home tonight?" she says as I step closer to my car.

I rent a guest cottage on the grounds of a small estate in Mesa. The owners live in Norway, and, for a very discounted rent, I take care of the maintenance for the main house. I couldn't afford to buy a place of my own, so this worked out perfect for me. Mom was not happy about it. Even though she knows I have my own place now, a beautiful one that I call home, she doesn't care. To her, the house I grew up in will always be my home. I turn around, keeping my composure, making sure my face doesn't give away how annoyed I really am. "No, I'm heading back to my place. Unless you need me?" I put it out there, knowing she would never force me to change my plans.

"There are some things I would like to talk to you about, but I guess they can wait." Her smile fades like a sunset at the beach. The guilt I feel, knowing how hard all this has been on her, makes me wish I could take back my quick response.

"You know, Mom, I haven't eaten yet. How about we grab some dinner before I go home?"

"That would be great, if you have the time."

"Always, Mom. I'll follow you to the Blue Bird diner. That's the halfway point for both of us. I can go home from there."

I get into my car, start it up, roll down the windows, and blast the air conditioner to let some of the heat out of my car. I'm about to pull out of the driveway, but something is telling me to stop. I look in my rearview mirror before taking off and see Mom in her car putting her seatbelt on. She starts her car. Suddenly, there is a tremendous explosion. My car shakes and my back window splinters. I throw my car in park and get out. The heat hits me, taking my breath away. The explosion set off my own car alarm, preventing me from hearing my own screams. I'm trying to get to her, but someone is pulling me back. When I look over my shoulder, I realize it's the neighbor's grandson, Jimmy. *Where did he come from?* He wasn't here a minute ago. I try to wiggle free, but his grip is tight. "Please, we need to help my mom."

"There is nothing you can do for her. When my grandpa heard the explosion, he quickly called 911. The police and firefighters are on their way; they are only a mile up the road." It's still hard for me to hear, but when the flashing lights come into view, I feel hope. Two fire trucks, an ambulance, and two police cars quickly fill the area. The flames get worse as I yell for them to help my mom. The police and an EMT pull me back toward the ambulance, and Jimmy follows. I watch as the firefighters work on the car and the surrounding area, making sure it's not spreading to the house.

"Please, you have to help my mom. She was in the car when it blew up."

"Let the firefighters do their job while I check you over. Can you hear me?"

"You sound muffled, like I have cotton in my ears."

"My partner is going to check your vitals while I check you for any cuts."

"Please, make it fast. I'm fine, but it's my mom," my voice trails off as I see a

firefighter talking to a police officer and shaking his head. Any hope I had that my mom might still be alive quickly fades. The officer approaches me with a solemn look on his face. I push away from everyone and head toward him. The policeman introduces himself, but now my ears are ringing and I'm not sure which is worse.

"Miss, why don't we move back? Can you tell us what happened?" His hand is on my back as he guides me further away from the car. The firefighter follows us, as does Jimmy. I quickly tell him how little I know.

"Was there anyone else in the car?" Knowing full well the answer before he asks, but I guess he has to make sure.

"No, just my mom." My words echo around my head like yelling into a cavern.

"Do you know if your mother received any threats recently?"

"If she did, she never told me. However, my mom tends to play her cards close to her chest. If something happened, I would be the last to know." I didn't tell them she wanted to talk to me about something. What would be the point? I do not know what it was and now I never will.

"What about friends, work, or could she have been in a relationship that went bad?"

"She has or had one girlfriend at work. Her name is Constance Tucchi. She's Mom's supervisor. My mom just switched to the third shift at Boeing. With the sale of this house and the extra money working third shift, it let her spend more time with my grandma at the assisted living community."

"What about financial problems? It's very expensive to keep someone in an assisted living community."

"Are you not paying attention?! I just told you what the plan was." I'm shouting, yet again.

"Please, miss, I'm just trying to help."

"You can start by calling me by my name: Chelle. If you want to help, then tell me, what the hell do I do now?"

"The fire didn't spread to the house. When the investigator is done, you can continue on with the sale of the house. He will let you know when you can make arrangements for your mom. I'm sorry for your loss." He turns and walks away. The firefighter follows close behind, writing notes on his pad. I lean against my car, staring at the smoldering pile of what used to be my mom and her car. *What the hell was that all about, and what do I do now, Mom?* In my mind, I'm asking her, waiting for her to answer … an answer that will never come.

"I can tell you what you won't do. You won't give up. Your mom wanted this place gone. She wanted to keep your grandma as comfortable as possible."

I realize I must have been talking out loud. "Jimmy, did you know my mom?" He hesitates as he drags the tip of his boot in the dirt.

"No, only in passing or when she would come over to talk to my grandpa. I used to keep an eye on your grandma while your mom was at work. She would do the same for me with my grandpa. Look, why don't you come inside, and I can make some coffee."

The little voice inside my head is telling me no. "Thank you, but I think I'm going to head home. I need to figure out what I'm going to tell my grandma when I don't understand all of this myself." I wave my hand around to push my point. He nods and opens my car door for me. For a fleeting second, I'm almost too scared to start my car again. I shake off the feeling and start my car. I let out the breath I was holding, wave to Jimmy and head back to my house.

CHAPTER TWO

I brought Grandpa's boxes in the house, along with the composition book. I don't think anyone would want them, but then again, why would anyone think my mom was a target for violence? She would never hurt a fly. In a matter of seconds, I lost the strongest person I know. I grab a bottle of wine, along with a chilled glass from the fridge, and curl up in my grandpa's favorite chair. When he passed away, Grandma gave me some of his stuff for my place. She insisted I take Grandpa's favorite chair. How strange that this old, beat-up chair always comforts me. What must that say about me? I really want to go to Mom's house. Could there be something there that would explain why this happened? Maybe, but I don't think it's something I should do alone, especially this time of night. Instead, I pour another glass of wine, pick up the notebook, and begin reading. *My name is Carmine Francis Amato. My parents came to America in 1959 from Savoca, a small town in Sicily. That town would later become the filming place for* The Godfather. *After that movie came out, I never talked about going home again. I was only seven years old when I came to America, yet my parents expected me to help wherever I could.*

At seven years old, the only thing I was expected to do was play with my Barbie dolls and stay out of the way. His entire family was part of the New York City working class. They worked hard and played hard, but none of them went to college. I was the first in our family to go to college and actually finish. My mom thought I would become an engineer. Instead, I became a high school science teacher.

My mind wanders back to my mom: the best woman I've ever known. And yet, I felt, in her eyes, I could do nothing right. I push down those thoughts, take another sip of wine, and get back to the book. Each chapter is a block of time. Sometimes it's a month, and other times it's years.

I come from a large family, with seven brothers and one sister. My sister Gina was sick from the day she was born. She was always crying. One day she was there and then she was not. When I asked my mom about it, she would cry, and my dad would yell at me to stop asking questions. After a while, that's exactly what I did.

According to Carmine's list, he was in the middle of the pack. He followed his older brother's and set an example for his younger ones. According to Grandma, the only thing Carmine and his brothers knew were the streets. His older brothers were hotheads, quick with the fists. Not Carmine. He always took a step back to listen to the problem while trying to figure out a non-violent way to end the conflict. However, he wasn't afraid to use his fist if he had to. Some of his brothers died on the very streets they fought to protect. Some of them ended up in jail. Before long, Carmine was the only one left in his family. He met Grandma through the Italian American Civil Rights League. He went for a meeting and, afterwards, he saw her serving coffee and pie. This is where he gives details about his life.

I walked right up to her and asked her to go on a date. She laughed and said, 'I would need to at least know your name before I can decide.'

I took her hand in mine, brought it to my lips and kissed it right before I whispered, 'Carmine.' It's a name you will never forget. She told me her name was Viviana. By the next night, I found myself wanting to marry her. She would have no part of that until I learned to read. I was too old to go back to school, so I went to the local library. With my hat in my hand, I walked up to the desk and when the librarian turned around, I saw it was my Viviana.

'How can I help you, Carmine?' Her smile made me forget why I was there.

'I met someone special, and she won't give me the time of day unless I learn to read and write. I'm too old to go back to school. Is this something you can help me with?'

'I can give you one hour before my shift is over. You must be here at 4 pm every day. The first time you're late, the classes end.'

The very next day, I started my classes. Within two months, I could pick up a menu and order without pointing to the pictures. In six months, I could read books. By nine months, we were engaged. I made many promises to Viviana, and I've kept every one of them. The most important promise was to never bring my work home with me. The dinner table was a time for the family. Finally, when it came to my children, I must always be there for them.

I stare at the book and smile, realizing that I get my persistence from him. Reading meant so much to him and when I could see him, he always pushed for me to go to college. When I was younger, my mom would find excuses not to go to his house. As I got older, her excuses didn't work for me.

Today I wrote my brother Agosto off for good. In my eyes, he is dead. He might be the only brother I have left, but he didn't keep his word. If a man can't keep his word, then he's no man at all. Wow, that was pretty harsh. Maybe that's why he said he was the only one left. Grandma told me once that all the Amato family were dead. There was no one to carry on the family name. I wonder if Uncle Agosto is still alive. Did he have a family? If he is alive, does Grandma know the truth? I take another sip of my wine before I continue reading.

Totally surprised today to learn today that Agosto got pinched. So, that's why he was a no show. He kept his mouth shut, so maybe I can look the other way. Then again, if he was stupid enough to get caught… Wow, I wonder if my mom knew how cold Grandpa could be? I reach for the phone, and

I realize I can never call her again. The floodgates open and my heart breaks. I read some place that everyone grieves differently, and most people say it comes in waves. Maybe it's true since I feel like a wave has hit me like a storm at the beach, knocking me off my feet. After wiping away my tears, I pick up the book and flip to the next chapter. There is only one word—*Death.*

CHAPTER THREE

EATH HAS A WAY OF SNEAKING UP ON YOU WHEN YOU LEAST expect it. When God snatched Arturo, my firstborn, I questioned, 'Why me Lord?' When he took Ettore, my second, and then Dario, my third, I turned my back on him. Why ... why be that cruel?

I shift in my seat and pour the rest of the wine. My mom never talked about her siblings. I do not know how old they were when or how they died. I would think if there were any living family members, my mom would have told me. This explains why my grandmother kind of went off the deep end. Losing three children would send anyone into a tailspin. Unfortunately, tomorrow I have to tell her that her only daughter has died. When I pick up the wine bottle, I realize it's empty. This has to be a sign that I need to call it a night. I get up and head into the kitchen. I toss the wine bottle into the recycle bin and grab a bottle of water, along with some aspirin for my pounding headache. Maybe the wine will help me get some sleep. I take the stack of boxes and struggle to get them upstairs to my bedroom. For some reason, I feel the need to hide them. Maybe it's the events of today that have me a little paranoid. In my closet is a hidden panel. It was here when I moved in, courtesy of the little boy that lived here before me. I quickly stash the boxes, close the panel, and spread my clothes along the pole. I climb into bed thinking sleep won't come, however, when my head hits the pillow, I'm out for the count.

The morning sun is blaring through the open blinds. I wish I would have thought to close them last night, but that was the furthest thing on my mind. I pull the covers over my head, thinking this will help; it doesn't. Instead, I kick back the covers and stare at the ceiling fan going round and round. After a few minutes, I remind myself that I have way too much to do today. I drag my ass out of the bed and head into a nice hot shower. My routine is to wash my hair first, slap on the conditioner and after that, do the shaving and washing. Finally, I rinse the conditioner out and I'm done. Except, today is a different story. I am not in the shower for five minutes when there is a loud banging on my front door, I quickly rinse off, grab the towel and my robe. I wrap the towel around my head and try to get my robe on as I race down the steps. The banging gets louder, and someone is yelling, "FBI!" My cat, Gustavo, chooses now to come out of hiding. I trip over Gus and land on my hands and knees by the front door just as the FBI kicks it open. In all the commotion, I've lost my towel. My wet hair is every which way and I try to pull it out of my face so I can, at least, see past the really enormous feet in front of me. I realize my robe is open and I'm trying to pull it closed as I attempt to gracefully stand up.

"Did you really need to break down my door? You better be prepared to pay for this, mister." I wave my hands around the splintered door and realize my robe has fallen open, yet again. Quickly pulling it closed, I turn and head into the living room. "Since you've given me no choice, you might as well follow me inside!" I shout over my shoulder.

"We are sorry about the door. When you didn't answer, my partner thought you might be in distress."

I turn and look at him, wondering if that bullshit really works. I roll my eyes and head over to the laundry room closet, which is right off the living room. The towels were in the dryer from yesterday. I grab one and wrap it around my head, so my hair is contained. "I hope you are here to tell me you know how my mother's car blew up."

"That's why we are here. But first, my name is agent Cody McJohnson and my partner is Luca Gill. We are part of the organized crime task force for Phoenix." They flash me their badges.

"Organized crime? My mom worked the assembly line at Boeing for twenty years. She just recently switched to the third shift so she can be around more for my grandma. What does any of that have to do with organized crime?" They keep looking at each other and then back towards me. "What do you know that I don't?"

"All we can tell you for now is Carmine Amato died two months ago and since then, everyone is coming out of the woodwork trying to make their bones."

I'm staring at them in disbelief. "Make their bones, what exactly does that mean?"

"The short answer is they are trying to make a name for themselves on the back of Carmine and his family."

"Cody, I think you are mistaken. My grandfather died two years ago, not two months ago. My mom has been taking care of my grandmother all that time. She has gotten worse, you know leaving the stove on type of stuff, so we moved her into an assisted living community, and we are selling her house to offset the costs. Like I said, my mom switched to third shift so she could be around her more." I pull my robe tighter, like some sort of warrior getting ready for battle. Luca steps closer to me.

"Ma'am, maybe you should sit down."

This is where I feel my temper boil to the surface. I try to calm myself before I say anything, but I realize that is impossible. "My name is Michelina, you can call me Chelle, and don't you dare tell me what to do. Now, do you know who killed my mom?!"

"Carmine was in witness protection. He knew once he was dead, Frances wouldn't leave her mother alone in New York. One of his demands was that we relocate him to Arizona. He wanted to keep an eye on his family. It was the only way he agreed to work with us." While Cody is trying to convince me of this, I see Luca looking through his phone.

"I think I would have known if my grandfather was alive all this time."

"The agreement was no one would know. He could keep tabs on his family and we would keep them safe. Two months ago, Carmine had a heart attack and died. It was right before he would have to testify against the largest mafia family in New York."

"Wouldn't it come out that he was alive?"

"We hoped it wouldn't, but if it did, by that time, the damage would already done. As far as the world was concerned, Carmine was dead. Plus, he had so much plastic surgery, I don't think anyone would have known it was him. I have a few videos of him before and after, if you want to see them." Luca passes me his phone. My legs feel weak, so I sit in the chair and hit play.

Watching my grandfather talk about his life of crime, something I knew nothing about, was a total shock. He talks about his only living brother, Agosto. Apparently, he is married and has children that are also caught up in all of this. I press play for the next video and it's documenting all the different surgeries he had. At the end, I would have passed him on the street and never looked twice.

"Was he a free man all that time?"

"Yes, but we brought him in before his heart attack so we could prep him for trial. Unfortunately, that never happened."

"So, do you know who killed my mom?"

"We have an idea, but we aren't ready to discuss that." Cody is not very forthcoming with any answers.

"So, all this time he had a brother that is alive. We have more family. Why would he hide that?" I pass Luca his phone.

"We were hoping your mom could shed some light on that subject." Luca shoves his phone back into his pocket.

"What about my grandmother? How much danger is she in?"

"We have someone stationed in the assisted living community, but honestly, with her fleeting memory, I don't think anyone would bother

her. It's you we are worried about." Luca states so matter of fact, like this is an everyday thing. Which, maybe for him, it is.

"Why would you be worried about me? I didn't know he was alive and prior to that, I hardly knew the man. I mean, yes, he's my grandfather and all, but my mom's relationship with him was strained, so our visits were mainly to see Grandma when he wasn't around. After we moved to Arizona, I was very busy with school. I would visit Grandma when I had a day off from school. By then, he was already dead. Well, at least that's what I thought. So again, I don't understand why you would think I would be in danger."

Luca looks at Cody and then back toward me. "They were after something. That is probably what caused your mother to be killed. We have some agents sitting on your mother's house, waiting for us to bring you there. We would like for you to see if anything looks out of place."

How do I explain to Luca that since I got my place, I hardly go over there? Things between us have been strained lately. I turn toward Cody. "While I'm getting dressed, please fix the door. You can follow me to my mom's house." I don't give them time to argue with me; I turn and head upstairs to my room. I'm feeling grateful that I hid everything in my make-shift Harry Potter room. I think what is really nagging at me is the thought that my mom might have known about all of this. Could that be what she wanted to talk to me about? I quickly get dressed and head back downstairs. They patched the front door up the best they could under the circumstances.

"Let's go before I change my mind." I reach for my keys, but Luca swipes them off of the counter.

"I—*we* would rather you come with us. We haven't had time to go over your car."

"Go over my car! You really believe someone wants to kill me, too?"

"Ma'am—sorry—Chelle, we do not know, but we are not prepared to take any chances."

With my keys tightly in Luca's hand, he holds the door open for me, basically giving me no chance to change his mind. I follow him to his car, but I can't take my eyes off my own. He catches me staring at it.

"Don't worry, Chelle, we will have someone inspect it while you are safely at your mom's house. It will be done by the time you get back home."

"Is Cody coming with us?"

"No, he is waiting for the bomb squad to come and check out your car."

The drive to my mom's house is not far and, as we get closer, I feel the anxiety build up inside of me. We were never really close. She didn't like any of my choices, and I didn't like the way she made me feel. Almost like I couldn't do anything right. Yet, here I sit, still alive, so how bad can my choices be?

My mom's house is in a very quiet community just up the road from her job. We pull into her driveway, and the first thing I notice is the six black SUVs just like the one I'm sitting in. When I get out of the car, I can hear it before I see it: a helicopter circling above us. Luca rushes me inside, muttering under his breath about reporters.

"Chelle, I want you to know we really tried to keep a lid on this."

"Apparently, that's not your strong suit." With my back up against the wall, I lean out the door and look around. I don't think this sleepy neighborhood has ever seen so much action. Luca clears his throat, which brings me back to reality.

"Please stay away from the doors and windows until we know what we are dealing with."

He nudges me along and closes the door behind me. I take a few steps inside, and my whole body is refusing to move. The house has an open floor plan, which is something Mom loved but I didn't. With one big open room, everything must have a place, otherwise, it always looks a mess. There are no hiding spots, which is one reason I love my place with all its quirks. I take a few steps inside, and that's when it hits me. I knew it would happen again, but I didn't think the grief would hit me like a tsunami. Wave upon wave, emotion so raw that I fall to my knees while I fight to catch my breath. Luca squats down next to me as my whole body shakes.

"Chelle, let me help you up." I don't answer him, as my teeth are chattering. All I can do is nod. He helps me to the sofa and grabs a throw blanket for me to wrap myself in.

"Luca, I just don't understand. Why did someone kill my mom? There's no way she had or would want anything to do with what my grandfather did. It doesn't make any sense." My voice cracks and the tears flow.

"I wish I had some answers for you. All I can do now is try to keep you safe while we figure this out. When you are ready, I would like to go through each room with you. I know it is difficult, but if something is out of place or missing, you would be the only one who would know."

I know he's right. I get up and begin the slow process of going through each room, one memory at a time.

CHAPTER FOUR

Y MOM WAS ALWAYS IMMACULATE AND EXTREMELY organized. She would always say, *"If it doesn't have a place, then you don't need it."* Me, on the other hand, would eventually find a place for it even if I didn't need it. Maybe it was my way of challenging her. As I walk through each room, I try to be brave and strong, basically the adult that is needed right now. That's the only way I will find out answers. I know I should have a million questions, but right now I only have one… why? Luca thinks I could be a target, yet I can't wrap my mind around that. I finally stop at my old room and push the door open. The same posters are on the wall and the room looks like time stood still. Nothing has changed and nothing is out of place. When I spin around to leave, my heel catches on a buckled piece of carpet, causing me to fall backwards. When I try to catch myself, I grab onto the only thing available… Luca. I let out a yelp as we both tumble to the ground. When I look up, all eyes are on us.

"I'm so sorry, Luca. I told my mom so many times to get that carpet fixed." He quickly gets up, taking me with him.

"Don't worry about it, Chelle. Does anything look off to you?" He continues on as if nothing happened.

"No, but then again, I really don't know what I'm looking for. Did my mom know her dad was still alive?" I ask. His jaw gets tight as he looks away from me.

"Yes, we have a video of the two of them together. We scheduled a meeting with your mom to go over how much she knew about Carmine's situation and to find out if he gave her anything for safekeeping. Unfortunately, that meeting was today."

"I want to see that video." My voice cracks, but I fight the tears that I feel coming to the surface.

"I can show it to you, but you won't get much from it; there is no audio."

"When was it taken?"

"Two weeks before he died. Prior to that, he didn't have any contact with your mom. Something changed, but we don't know what."

"What did she say when you confronted her about the video?"

He steers me back to the front of the house. "Chelle, we tried to talk to her, but she denied everything. When I showed her the video, she finally agreed to sit down with us. Like I said, that meeting was today. After the events of the last twenty-four hours, it's safe to say your mom either had something or knew something that got her killed."

I want to tell him about the boxes I took home with me, but I feel like I should probably keep my mouth shut until I know everything that is in them and more about what is really going on. "So, do you think she gave me something or told me something that would now put a target on my back?"

"Exactly. Chelle cars don't just blow up on their own. If I'm going to keep you safe, you have to share everything with me."

"Except, I have nothing to share. My mom and I were going to dinner last night because she said she had something to talk to me about. However, that never happened, so now what do we do?" I throw my hands out in question. His brooding stare runs a chill up my spine.

"Now we dig through everything in your mom's life. It had to be big for Carmine to risk coming out of hiding."

"What about me, Luca?"

"That depends on how much you want to help us."

"Help you?! I think your help might just get me killed." I push past him and head outside, only to realize I have no car. "I need my car, Luca. I have to go see my grandmother. I can't let her hear about this from anyone but me."

"For now, I'll take you wherever you need to go, just until the dust settles." He holds his hands up in a gesture to show me he means no harm.

"Fine, for now, but you better not hold anything back and get me my car!" I storm off and quickly head to his car. I climb in and slam the door. By the smirk on his face, he knows I'm watching him as he strolls toward the car with no urgency, gets in, and closes the door.

"Alright, let's head to your grandmother's. I have an agent stationed with her to make sure she doesn't see any television or read the paper. Have you thought about what you're going to tell her?"

"You act as if I've spent no time at all thinking about what to do. On the contrary, I spent the entire night trying to figure this out. I honestly have no clue. I will start slowly and from there I can figure out how much she knows. More Importantly, what she can remember. You know truth vs fiction. Some days she is sharp as a tack and other days she wants nothing to do with anyone. Plus, what if she is having a bad day and nothing registers with her? I know the day-to-day uncertainty of her is what my mom feared the most. It's hard when the roles reverse. You know the parent becomes the child while the child needs to navigate the adult role."

He says nothing, keeping his eyes straight ahead. My mind is racing, and my thoughts are all over the board. Finally, I take a deep breath. "Luca, maybe I should go see Uncle Agosto. You know, introduce myself and tell him I'm not a threat to him or his family. Maybe he will leave me and Grandma alone." His grip on the steering wheel gets so tight his knuckles turn white.

"You can't possibly be that naïve. He might not have been a part of

Carmine's life anymore, but that didn't make him any less ruthless. My money says he's the one who bombed your mom's car."

"Well, if you believe that, then why can't you do something about it?" I jerk my full focus onto him as he drives. He rolls his eyes to the point where it must really hurt.

"Oh, I don't know, maybe because I have no proof. Contrary to what you see on crime shows, Chelle, I can't arrest someone on a hunch."

"Let's face it; it's not you they are after, it's me. If that's the case, then I can help you." Even I can't believe what just came out of my mouth.

"Let's just focus on your grandmother for now." With that, he dismisses me.

CHAPTER FIVE

Agosto Amato

ONE WORD—REVENGE. IT'S THE ONLY THING I HAVE LEFT. THE hate between us started when we were kids. I was the youngest of the siblings. I tried to learn from Carmine, but when I got pinched, he wrote me off for dead. I kept my head down and my mouth shut, but that didn't matter to my brother. Now, all these years later, Carmine became a rat. It's the one thing I didn't see coming. None of us did. It went against everything Carmine believed in. When his son died, I reached out to him and Viviana. I know what it's like to lose a child. It guts you in a way that you never recover from. When I showed up at his son's funeral, he turned his back on me. The level of disrespect was not something I ever expected from him. I walked out that day and didn't look back. When two more of his sons died, I said nothing. That door was closed forever. When my wife Gisele was diagnosed with lung cancer, the doctors suggested we move out of New York. The Mayo Clinic in Scottsdale was at the top of the list for quality care. I knew I had no choice, so I moved my family to Paradise Valley, Arizona. I might not live in New York anymore, but that lifestyle never leaves you. It took a while to adjust to a new way of life but. in time, my family adapted. Two years later, Carmine died from a heart attack. Frances moved Viviana to Arizona. Just like that, my last living brother was dead. From time to time, I checked up on Viviana, Frances, and Michelina. I was told that Viviana was becoming lost in her own mind. Having lost children of my own, I understand how it breaks you. Frances got a good job at Boeing and Michelina graduated from Arizona State University. It seemed they were living a peaceful life in the desert. However, life isn't always what it seems.

If anyone was to tell me that my big brother, who always thought he was better than everyone, would stage his own death and go into hiding, I would think they were batz. You know … bat shit crazy. Yet, here I sit, staring at a video of Carmine talking to the Feds that Gianni, my oldest son, has on his phone.

"Gianni, how is this even possible? You know Carmine always said Omertà above all else; my eyes must be deceiving me. How could he still be alive?"

"Dad, no disrespect, but you know everything I've found out shows that the person Carmine presented to the family was a lot different behind closed doors, starting with his supposed loyalty."

"Where is he now?" I feel his eyes on me, but I can't look away from the video he sent me.

"Pops, the ironic part of this story is that he dropped dead of a heart attack two months ago."

When I look up from the video, I try to contain my rage. "Gianni, how sure are you that he's really dead? I mean, did you see the damn body for yourself?"

"I saw a body, Dad. The thing is, Carmine had a lot of plastic surgery done. I don't think his own family would know him if they passed him on the street. I have some pictures on my phone. If you are done with the video, I can show you."

I pass him his phone and wait. Why would Carmine do this? He passes it back to me and waits for my response as I flip through the photos of a man on a table at the morgue. It could be anybody. Then I get to the photo of Carmine's birthmark. He had a dark spot in the shape of lips on his chest, just above his heart. Our mom said the angels kissed him before God sent him to us. I always thought of him as Cain from the bible stories that our mom would read to us. Carmine always said he was the special one, chosen by God. He let none of us forget how special he was, even if it was only in his own mind.

"If they altered his face, why not remove the one thing that could prove his real identity?"

"You know how cocky he was. He probably left it so he can rub it in your face."

"Did you take these pictures? I mean, you said he died two months ago. Didn't they bury him?" I'm sure he knows where I'm going with this, but sometimes you need to lead your children to come to the conclusion that you already know.

"Dad, I wasn't about to leave this to anyone else. I took the pictures myself. No one claimed the body. The Feds have him on ice, hoping the other families won't find out. They want them running scared, thinking Carmine is going to testify against them. Although my source said they told Frances everything, and she didn't believe them."

"Carmine didn't have a heart, at least when it came to family. If he did, he would have never put them through the pain of thinking he was dead for two years. Add to that how they must have felt when they found out the truth about his real death."

"Dad, there's more and it's not good." Gianni has always been the one to bring me bad news. He knows I want to hear it directly from him. His younger brother will embellish a story, but Gianni is a very fact-driven man. He's a very black and white, by-the-book type of guy. It's good in some ways, but in matters of the heart, it's bad.

"I figured there would be more. Nothing with Carmine was ever easy."

"There was an explosion yesterday. Someone blew up Frances Amato's car with her in it."

I grab the arms of my chair with a white-knuckled grip. The vein at my temple pounds as I feel my neck flush. "Who did this? Gianni, women and children are off limits, everyone knows that. Where was Michelina and Viviana? Are they okay?"

"Apparently, Frances and Michelina were at Viviana's house. They were clearing it out and getting ready to put it on the market. Viviana had moved into an assisted living community closer to Frances's house. Since Frances works the overnight shift, they felt this was the safest and best solution all the way around. Michelina was in her car in front of Frances's car. When Frances started her car, it exploded. Michelina is okay, in shock at seeing her mom die, but okay."

"Who did this?"

"I'm trying to find out more now. Of course, the Feds are all over this."

"Do you think Frances and Michelina knew about Carmine's book?" My brother kept journals his whole life, but he also kept a little black book of every transgression that he was a part of or knew about.

"If they did, no one has said anything, yet. I'm trying to find out more. It looks like Feds have surrounded Michelina to protect her, and Viviana is still in assisted living with the Feds guarding her twenty-four seven."

"Gianni, get a hold of your best men and have them search for Carmine's book. If they find his old journals, they are to come directly to me. Do you understand?"

"Dad, should we be worried about the contents?"

"Whoever has his book holds the power over all the families, so what do you think?" He nods his head and leaves. I pour myself a cocktail that, by doctor's orders, I'm supposed to avoid. Let the damn doctor walk a mile in my shoes and carry the family burden that I carry.

CHAPTER SIX

Michelina

I TOOK IT SLOWLY WITH MY GRANDMA. I WASN'T SURE HOW MUCH she was grasping. She already mourned the death of her other children and her husband. I didn't tell her he died two months ago instead of two years, as they led her to believe. Luca and I head back to the car, but not before he had a private conversation with the agent protecting Grandma.

"Is everything okay?" I ask him point blank.

"I wanted to bring agent Daniels up to speed on what we know about the case so far."

"Which, if I'm not mistaken, is nothing." I realize, even to myself, I sound like a snarky little bitch.

"Chelle, we only scratched the surface when we were at your mom's house. I have a list of questions for you, but I thought I would give you today to deal with the aftermath of yesterday's bombing."

"The best way for me to deal with everything is for you to find out why someone thought it was a good idea to kill my mom. I do, however, have a question for you. What happened from two months ago to last night that made someone take such an extreme action against my mother?" My question causes an awkward amount of silence from him. I wonder if he is trying to piece together what he thinks I should know and holding back the rest. He motions for us to get into the car before he says anything.

"Word got out that your grandfather didn't die two years ago. Somehow, it got out that up until two months ago the real Carmine was living the high life on the Feds dime. We already had hours of video of Carmine giving up many people. What we don't have is Carmine's little black book. Right now, agents are going over every square inch of your mom's house and your grandmother's house. Did your mom ever mention it?" I'm immediately reminded of Carmine's journals that I have hidden in my house. However, I haven't come across a black book, only his memoirs, so maybe I don't even have it.

"I know nothing about that." I try to sound nonchalant, but I'm not sure he's buying it.

"Chelle, if you know anything about it, please tell me. I can't stress the danger that you would be in if anyone thought you knew where it was."

"What is in this book? Is it like the book that Nevada has that list banned people from casinos?"

"It's nothing like the Nevada book. Apparently, Carmine kept notes on everything. From murders to loans. Favors that were owed and why. It could put many people away for a very long time. He always referred to it as his insurance policy."

"How well did you know him?" It's sad to think that this complete stranger, most likely, knew my grandfather better than I could have ever hoped to know him. He smiles as if he enjoys the thought of spending time with Carmine.

"I spent two years of my life getting to know the man. Why he thinks the way he does. I've tried to anticipate his every move even before he would." I raise my eyebrows at this information. "It's not an obsession, Chelle, it's my job." He cocks his head in defense, but gets a faraway look.

"So, what are you, some kind of profiler?"

"Not anything close to that. I'm just a guy that people feel comfortable with and eventually tell me their entire life story."

We sit in silence. My mind wanders to those boxes, increasing my sense of urgency to get back to them to see what I find. "Luca, I need to go home now. I have to call the mortuary and plan a service for my mom."

"I can take you home, but I can't leave you alone. Consider me a permanent fixture wherever you go." He starts the car up and makes his way out of the parking lot and onto the main road.

"Is that really necessary? I've done just fine all this time on my own. I really just need my car back."

He shakes his head and goes back to the silent treatment. My urge to punch him is real. "You can't keep me locked up like a prisoner. I've done nothing wrong!"

"I can if it's the only way to protect you." His words hang in the air like a dense fog.

"Protect me from what? I doubt I'm on anyone's radar. It seems the only one I need protecting from is you." In return, he slams his hand on the steering wheel so hard, I swear I could hear a crack. The rest of the ride is in silence until we pull up to my place and I find half a dozen black SUVs parked.

"What are all these cars doing here?" I ask in an octave I've never heard my voice make before.

"They have a warrant to search your place."

"How are they able to get a warrant if I'm the victim?" When I turn to look at him, he turns away. My mouth goes dry and the anger I feel right now only fuels the raging headache I'm being blessed with at the moment. What if they find Carmine's boxes? Will they be lost to me forever?

"I'm sorry, Chelle, but there is no other way to do this. We need to make sure you are safe."

"How does rummaging through my life keep me safe? All it does is draw attention to me. Maybe no one knew I even existed and, if that's the case, you just blew it all to shit." Again, nothing but silence. He finally brings the car to a stop, and I quickly get out.

"For the record, Luca, I rent the cottage that is on the back end of this property. I'm in charge of monitoring the main house. The owners live in Norway and trusted me to make sure there are no problems. So now what am I supposed to tell them about this?" I wave my hand around the mess for emphasis, not that it matters.

"Well, maybe you don't have to tell them anything. I can arrange for a cleaning service to come in when the search is done."

"Is that even a thing?"

"No, but I feel bad. I'll pay for it."

"Forget it. Just find out when the hell they are leaving. Oh, and I expect you to leave with them." I turn and head inside, hoping he gets the message. Hearing the crunching on the gravel behind me tells me he didn't. To boot, he has the audacity to follow me inside, totally ignoring my request for him to leave. The door frame has been fixed, so at least that's a positive thing. I continue to look around and I notice my laptop is gone.

"Luca, where the hell is my laptop? I need it for work!"

"They will give it back to you when they are done."

I dig my nails into the palms of my hands as I feel my face flush. "That will not work, Luca!" I scream.

"It's out of my control. They are following what the warrant dictates. I'm sure if you let the school know what's going on, they will work with you."

I head into the kitchen and pull a beer out of the fridge. "I would offer you one, but right now I can't even look at you, let alone have a beer with you. Luca, you need to leave." I'm glaring at him as he shuffles his feet. He stops then takes a step forward. I try to take a step back, but I'm up against the counter. He is so close I can feel the heat coming off of his body. Not the Arizona dry heat that feels like your head is in an oven. This is different and extremely uncomfortable. He traps me when he grips the counter with a hand on each side of me. He leans in so close I think I might pass out.

"Chelle, let me put this so you will understand. Under *no*

circumstances will you be on your own. You will *not* try to ditch me. You will go *nowhere* without me. My one job is to protect you, that's it. If something happens to you, not only will I be unemployed, but it would be the first ding on my record, so don't fuck this up for me," he says through his teeth, clearly trying to keep his composure, or what's left of it.

"So, it's all about you. Glad you cleared that up for me. To think I almost thought you cared." I push his arm away and head upstairs. "I'm going in the shower, since I didn't get to finish it this morning. And no, you *can't* come with me." I yell over my shoulder.

CHAPTER SEVEN

Luca

WHAT THE HELL DID I GET MYSELF INTO? I'M NOT A babysitter. I didn't go through months of training for this. It took everything I had to get into the FBI's organized crime unit. I didn't mind when I had to babysit Carmine. He at least had some significant stories he loved to share. This one, she is nothing but tits and ass. I mean—a science teacher—could this be any more boring? I hear the door behind me and spin around just as Cody steps in.

"Where is she?" He asks as he hands me a folder. I open it to find grainy photos of Michelina walking toward her car with boxes.

"When is this from?" I'm honing in on the boxes, trying to figure out the writing on the front of them, but I can't figure it out.

"Last night, Luca. A drone caught this right before the bomb went off. She has no clue how close she came to lights out. She's hiding something."

"Do you have any idea what's in the boxes?"

"Of course not, but it helped us get the warrant to search this place. You've been with her the whole time, right?"

"Yeah, until a few minutes ago when she went upstairs to shower." I make my way upstairs but turn around when I hear the water running. "Water is still going. Can you make out what it says on the front of the boxes?"

"No. When we enlarge it, it gets too grainy."

"If we were watching this, then chances are, so is everyone else who wanted Carmine dead."

"My point exactly, Luca. When you were held up for months with Carmine, what did he say about the book?"

I think about how much I want to share with him, with anyone. I became pretty close to Carmine. The first thing we are told in training is don't get attached. However, they never met Carmine. "He talked about his books. He said he kept journals though-out his life, but those are separate from the black books. That's what he referred to them as. The black books list every favor owed and why. There are account numbers for all the different families. He also listed all the money transactions that he was involved with throughout his entire life. Carmine didn't believe in computers. He wanted everything in black and white. After he said that, he laughed, but I do not know why. I take it you found nothing here?" I climb a couple of steps and take a moment to listen. "The water stopped. We should talk about this later." I don't wait for an answer. If he found something, he would have gloated about it.

Michelina

The nerve of this man to think that he can just root himself into my life. And yes, I have a damn life and he will not ruin it. I still need to go through Carmine's stuff, but not while Luca is here. Maybe I can get Jessica to come over and be a distraction. However, first I need to make sure no one found the secret storage area. I turn on the water in the shower, so Luca won't bother me. When I head into my room, I look around and notice all my drawers are open, which means hands were all over my stuff. The thought sends a shiver up my spine. When I open the closet door, I can tell they have moved my stuff. I hold my breath and move the clothes to the side. When I open the panel, the boxes are all there, untouched. At least I know they are safe. I grab some clothes and head back to the shower. I need a plan to get the hell away from Luca. My earlier thought that Jessica can be a distraction is sounding better and better. I quickly finish in the shower and take a seat at my vanity. Before anything, I need to get a message to Jessica.

> Me: Hey, can you come over tonight after work?

> Jessica: I just heard about your mom on the news. I wish I hadn't gone away this weekend. I feel terrible that you've been going through this alone. I can come tonight. Is there anything you need me to help with?

> Me: Bring the wine and I will tell you everything when I see you.

She gives my text the thumbs up. At least I know she will have my back. I turn on the blow dryer, but my only focus is staring at my closet door. I wish I had a more secure place to hide the boxes, but I have to be thankful the FBI didn't find them during their raid. When I think about it, my blood boils. I'm the victim, yet I'm being treated like the criminal. Which brings me back to wondering what *exactly* did my grandfather do? I throw on my clothes and head downstairs. It's time I sort this out. When I enter the room, Luca and Cody stop talking.

"Cody, I hope you brought my car back. I need to plan for my mother's service."

He looks toward Luca and then back towards me. With his hands shoved in his pockets, he smiles. I'm not falling for it.

"I brought your car back. There was no problem with it. Until we get to the bottom of who killed your mom and why, Luca and I will take turns staying with you."

"No, absolutely not. I don't know why anyone would want to kill me. You can't tell me why my mom was murdered, only that you think it involves my dead grandfather. I don't know what you think my grandfather did for a living, but as far as I know, he was in construction. How does that get someone blown up?"

Cody walks towards the kitchen and drops my keys on the counter. "That, Michelina, should be cause for alarm. If he was just a construction worker, as you like to think, then why would he have been in protective custody? Why would someone blow up your mom's car with her in it? Why are all eyes on you now? You can't possibly tell me that after we leave, you'll be totally comfortable going out that door, sitting in your car and turning the key."

"Maybe it was a murder by mistake. Don't you watch crime shows? You know that stuff happens all the time," I throw out there. Luca rolls his eyes and I really want to smack him. He steps closer and with my back against the counter, there is no place for me to go.

"You really have no clue what your grandfather did for a living? I find that very hard to believe that you could be that clueless, even for a science teacher."

"What the hell is that supposed to mean, Luca?" I shout, only inches from his face. I hope he can feel the heat radiating from my body, and not the desert heat that's everywhere. He backs up, putting his hands up in disgust.

"Cody, you deal with her. I'm done." He turns away, mumbling under his breath.

"There is no dealing with me, Cody. You brought me back my car; thank you for that. I'm having company tonight, and there is no reason for either of you to be here."

"Luca and I will stay outside in our car all night. We won't disturb you, but we also won't leave you alone. Maybe while you wait for your company, do an internet search on your grandfather. I think you will find it most interesting."

"Thank you, Cody. I will take it under advisement. However, everyone knows you can't believe what you read on the internet. Besides, the FBI took my computer, so, even if I wanted to find out more information, I can't." I head to the front door and hold it open. He finally gets the point and leaves with Luca following behind him. I slam the door behind them and double bolt it. There are two hours left before Jessica arrives. I head back upstairs, eager to dig more into Carmine's world.

CHAPTER EIGHT

Michelina

AFTER A QUICK SHOWER, I STILL HAVE AN HOUR OR SO BEFORE Jessica gets here. I take the next journal out of the box and curl up on my bed.

The death of my son, Arturo, brought all the rats out of the woodwork, even Agosto. He paid his condolences to Viviana and the rest of my family. Agosto is a big man and most kids, hell—most people—are afraid of him, that is everyone except Frances. She walked right up to him and offered him a handshake. This makes me smile, but also makes me sad. There is so much about my mom that I don't know, however, I can totally picture her doing this. Fighting back the tears, I check the time and continue on.

I watched him kiss Viviana on each cheek. He has always showed her respect. Me, however ... not so much. Maybe there is just too much bad blood between us, since I was the one who turned my back on him. I had to for reasons unknown to him. I knew if I didn't, it would only be a matter of time before they pitted us against each other. He would have gotten an order to kill me, and I would have gotten the same. I took the decision away from him. That's probably the only good thing I would do for him. Realistically, I did it for my mom. I wouldn't want her to have to choose sides. Now we all pay the price. It sounds like Agosto wanted to continue family relations, but Carmine didn't. What did Carmine mean by reasons unknown? This brings me back to what mom said about Carmine holding a grudge.

I didn't see Agosto until months later when I found out his son Salvatore was murdered in front of his house. Just like he came and paid his respects to me and my family, I went to the viewing for Salvatore. Agosto and his wife, Gisele, had four children. Gianni is the oldest followed by Geno, Salvatore and their only daughter, Daniella, who died from leukemia at three. With her boys surrounding her, I stepped close and took her hand. "Gisele, I'm so sorry for your loss." After kissing both cheeks, I stepped back. When I looked over toward Agosto, I saw the pain that was etched on his face. I decided to be the better man and offer him my condolences. There was a line of people and I fell into place. When it was my turn, I extended my hand. Agosto gripped it tightly and pulled me close. "I nostri figli, essendo sei piedi sotto terra, livellano il campo di gioco." He dropped my hand and turned away. I wanted to shoot him right there, but I'm the older brother. I had to keep it together.

I quickly bring up an app on my phone to translate it. Roughly translated, it means, our children being six feet under the dirt levels the playing field. Wow, how cold and cruel, and to think—I'm part of this family. All they know is violence. Now I'm second-guessing if learning about my family would make me happy. Maybe Mom keeping all of this from me was actually a good thing. I hear the bell ring. I glance at the clock and realize Jessica is here. Time seems to stand still when I'm in Carmine's world. I quickly put the book with the others, throw on my jeans, and head downstairs. When I open the door, Jessica is standing there with two Venti coffees.

"Did my bodyguards stop you?" I blurt out without thinking.

"If you mean the hot-looking FBI guys, yeah. If I would have known about them, I would have come over sooner." I take one coffee and close the door behind her.

"I didn't notice. What I know is they are not going away anytime soon. They want something from me…"

She holds up her hand, stopping me in midstream. "Well, if you hold out, will they stay longer? I mean, Chelle, that one guy with the dark hair and bruiting face, yeah, I would totally do him."

I nearly spit my coffee out. "Jess, I'm very busy trying to deal with everything that happened, and just trying to stay alive that I didn't even notice."

"I call bullshit. Anyway, what do they want from you?"

I want to tell her about Carmine's journals and how he faked his death, but if what Luca says is true, I don't want to put her in danger. "Let's forget about that for now. I need to get everything regarding my mother handled. I do not know where to start. Please, Jessica, I need your help." I can feel my chin quivering. She pulls me into a hug, and I cry. The flood gates have opened, and I don't think it will ever stop. It finally hits me: I'm alone in this world.

Luca

It wasn't easy, but with a lot of hard work, I finally earned my way onto the Carmine Amato case. Now Chelle is going to blow it all to shit. I was so close to getting the coveted book. The book that would finally let me go home. Better yet, it would put me on top. Carmine had to drop dead before I could get my hands on it. At first, I thought Frances had it, but now I'm pretty sure she didn't, so that leaves Chelle. "Cody, while I was stuck babysitting Chelle, did you find anything at Frances's house that could lead us to the book?"

"Like I said—nothing. Maybe we can get a warrant for the big house."

I shake my head. "You know we don't have cause. Hell, getting the warrant for Chelle's house and car was on thin ice."

"Which reminds me, Cody, did you get the full report back on her car?"

"Hell yeah, and you won't believe what's in it. You know the story about Frank "Lefty" Rosenthal's car?"

"Yeah, the manufacturer of the car put a metal plate under the driver's side of the car. Some kind of balance issue. What does that have to do with anything?"

"Chelle's little shit-banger car has a metal plate under it that was put in after market, which is not like the plate under Rosenthal's car that was done by the manufacturer."

"What the hell, Cody? Why would the sweet and innocent science teacher have her car reinforced with a steel plate?"

"Maybe it wasn't her that did it. Maybe it was something that Carmine did before he died."

"If that's the case, why wouldn't he do his daughter's car, too?"

"Luca, don't forget he died suddenly. Maybe he didn't have the time."

"Maybe, but I guess we will never know." I put my hand up, shielding my eyes from the setting Arizona sun, and stare at her car.

"Luca, you were with Carmine more than any of us."

I put my hand up, stopping him before he can even ask his question. "I might have spent more time with him, but he kept everything to himself. Whatever he was planning died with him that day."

I turn around and go back inside before the heat gets the better of me. Cody quickly follows. I use my lock-picking skills to get inside as quietly as possible.

"I thought she wanted us to stay outside?"

I turn toward Cody and hiss, "She can bite me for all I care."

CHAPTER NINE

Agosto

I'VE MADE SACRIFICES. SOMETIMES VERY DIFFICULT ONES, BUT IT'S always for the good of the family. Once Gisele died, I took steps that, to this day, only a few would ever understand. When I took the oath of Omertà, they became my family before anyone, including blood. Carmine and I were in different families, otherwise, I would have had to bow down to him. That would never happen. The speed at which he became a made man was astonishing. Bad enough I was always behind him, but I know for a fact he tried to block me at every turn from moving up the so-called ladder. By the time the early eighties rolled around, Nevada became my dumping ground of choice. I used Arizona as my stopping point since it was a quick round trip from Arizona to Nevada. Who would have thought that years later Arizona would become my home. My persistence prevailed; besides the fact I pulled off some hits that no one thought possible, including my brother. In the end, I made my way to the top, however, like everything else, time takes its toll. Before you know it, things are being done differently and you're too old to change your ways. My

Geno is a prime example of this. He is my second-born son, a techie, as the youth of today call it.

There is a knock on the door. I look up at the camera that Geno insisted I have. Speak of the devil—it's him. I get up and head toward the door. When I open it, he rolls his eyes and shakes his head. "What did I do wrong now?" I ask, knowing that without even trying, I exasperate him daily. At least, that's what he tells me.

"You are supposed to use the buzzer under your desk to let people in. Dad, you need to follow the security measures I have in place," he tells me for, what seems like, a thousandth time. I wave my hand in the air as I head back toward my desk, but not before I stop at my bar and pour a glass of Sambuca. I add three coffee beans. There are many ways to have it, but this is the way my father always had it. Three beans representing health, happiness, and prosperity. In life, I've had it and lost it. We all have. I sit behind my desk and slowly sip my drink, waiting for him to give me a daily update on all the families.

"Dad, we have an enormous problem: climate change."

I nearly choke on my drink. "You can't be serious, Geno. What the hell does that have to do with us? You know I don't believe in that shit."

"Well, you better start believing. The surface of Lake Mead has been steadily dropping. It's been this way for years, however, with climate change the amount of rainfall has significantly decreased. Add to that the higher demand for water, and it's a problem. I won't bore you with all the technical stuff, but the bottom line is two barrels with bodies inside have come to the surface, and there will probably be a lot more."

"I wasn't the only one who used it as a dumping ground, so why is it just my problem?"

He grips the front of my desk and leans in, only inches from my face. "Have you forgotten Uncle Carmine and his books?! He has it all and when more of them surface, we are all screwed."

"Kind of like the dead guys in the barrels." I can't help but laugh at the irony of it.

"Laugh all you want, but you know this is going to come back and bite us all in the ass."

"Don't worry, son. I have a plan in place to fix all of this. I've had it for a while," I assure him.

He sits down and runs his hands through his hair. Finally, his eyes lock onto mine. "Dad, it's only Gianni and me left. When are you going to share it with us?"

"When the time is right; now out." I wave my hand. He gets up to leave and stops when he gets to the door.

"I pray to God that you know what you're doing."

With that, he walks out, slamming the door behind him. If only he knew I pray every day, hoping I did the right thing. When your child dies from a disease like my Daniella did, you know you are helpless. I prayed, begged, and even offered myself to God if he would let Daniella live. In the end, the world moved as it was intended, and my Daniella gained her wings. However, when Salvatore died a violent death right in front of my house, I knew I had to do something. I can only hope that the choices I made were enough.

Luca

"Cody, it looks like they are in for the night. Why don't you bring me up to speed on everything you found out today," I say, trying to keep my voice empty of any emotion.

"An amateur definitely put together the bomb. The bomber pieced together different signatures from some famous bombers. Typical of an amateur. It surprised our guys it didn't go off sooner."

"What made them think that?" This really piques my curiosity.

"Chelle and her mom were loading up the trunks of both cars. With all the jostling, it could have set the bomb off."

"When you were at Frances's house, did you get a feel for what Chelle was like as a child?"

"I did, but where are you going with this?" Cody stares at me, barely blinking, not even an uncomfortable twitch.

"Stop trying to profile me, Cody. I'm not the one under surveillance here. I'm just trying to understand her better, so maybe I can figure out where Carmine's stuff is. We saw from the drone that she put some boxes in her car. Where are they? She came directly here after the bombing, yet you searched this house and found nothing. So again, where are they?"

"I think she had to stash them in the big house and, without a warrant, we are not getting in there."

I really want to get into that house, but I need to do it alone. If I find the book, I need to do it without Cody breathing down my neck. I was so lost in my thoughts that I never heard her friend Jessica come down the steps.

"Aren't you supposed to be outside for the duration?"

"Aren't you supposed to be consoling your friend for the duration?" I snap at her. This gets me the *what the fuck is wrong with you* look from Cody. I know I should just shut up and play nice, but sometimes that's not in my wheelhouse.

"If you must know, I came down to get some more wine. I wasn't expecting anyone to be here." She holds the bottle up in front of me as her eyes slowly roam my body. Part of me wants to pop open that bottle and get this party really going. The other part reminds me I'm working, and my goal is to get the book, not the girl. Although, it wouldn't be bad to have both. She stands there hesitating, but in the end, being a good friend wins out. She shakes her head and makes her way upstairs nice and slow so Cody and I can watch her tight, little ass.

When she is finally out of sight, Cody grabs my arm and whispers. "What exactly would you have done if she would have said yes?"

"We would have had a hell of a good time, my friend."

CHAPTER TEN

Michelina

Before Jessica left, she made all the arrangements for my mom. I need to go to the mortuary and complete the arrangements once I have a date. She also put together an announcement of my mom's death. All we have to do is add the time of the service and then she will send it out. After she left, I remembered to email my boss. I let him know Jessica was handling the arrangements and she will let him know when the service is. Before I get another journal out of the hiding place, I check the lock on my bedroom door. Quickly, I collect the next journal. I rub my hand over the cover and wonder what new discoveries I will find in this book. Carmine dated this one 1982. The earlier ones had no dates, but I could figure them out. I want to know more about my mom and dad, even if it's only from Carmine's point of view.

Carmine

The eighties were turbulent times in New York City. Top guys were getting killed. One of the top guys was John Gotti. The press labeled him the Teflon

Don. He conducted his business out in the open. However, nothing he does illegally ever seems to stick. Eventually, he paid the price, they always do. Even Capone got locked up for tax evasion. Going in, I knew this life doesn't always allow for a long lifespan. However, I decided a long time ago I was going to have an insurance policy. Everything I hear or see goes into the book. I've even been able to get photos. Senators with hookers and drugs. The more I gather, the more insurance I have. I want nothing to do with drugs. However, when the money started rolling in from the distribution, everyone looked the other way. Once you start with it, there is no turning back.

Every crew has their thing. They have to do something to bring in the money they are supposed to funnel weekly to the top cappos. My crew does high jacking semi-trucks. The I95 corridor is a gold mine, not just for me but for the drug cartels making a daily run. They use the best hookers and bring the drugs up from Miami. The drugs come up and the money goes down. If you value your life, you never bother them. For me, it's all about the product, anything from fur coats to lobsters. Given the opportunity, everything has a price, especially since the alternative is a gruesome death. The higher up you move in the family, the less you have to do. The people under you do all the work and you just collect. I paid my dues and now I'm at the top. The bad thing is, everyone at the top has to get knocked off. It's usually every ten or fifteen years you have to clean house. Otherwise, people get complacent and that's when the trouble starts.

I slam the book closed. I can't believe this is my grandfather. How could I not know any of this? He talks about murder like it's no big deal. My stomach knots and I want to hurl. My mom's words are swirling around in my head like a whirlpool. *The ramblings of an old man.* Did she know, and that was her way of sheltering me from the truth? With a deep breath, I open the book again. It's like a train wreck I can't look away from.

Today that heathen, Nick Ciccone, came to me and asked to date Frances. My daughter could do much better than him. I watched him leave and waited for him to show his hand, knowing this was far from over. As predicted, the next day, I found him standing before me in my study.

"Sir, Frances and I are in love and would like your blessing to be wed."

That's when I knew the rumors were true. My beautiful Frances was going behind my back with Nick Ciccone. For that disrespect alone, I said no and threw him out of my house. Viviana tried to plead their case, but I wouldn't hear it. Instead, I did what any other self-respecting father would do: I had him arrested. I figured after a month, Frances would forget about him. I got two months of the silent treatment. I didn't care. Finally, Frances came to my study with Viviana, holding her close. I had a feeling I knew what was coming, or so I thought, but I let Frances speak.

"Daddy, I'm pregnant. Nick and I want to get married. We need your approval and your help to get him out of jail. You know he did nothing wrong... I'm pregnant."

I waited, counting the beats of my heart. It filled part of me with rage. The other part of me wanted to tell her it will be okay. I stepped closer toward her. "What is it you think I can do for you now? You are nothing more than a common whore, Frances." With my eyes focused on Frances, I didn't notice that Viviana had come closer to me. Her hand swung so fast, connecting with the side of my face. I was stunned into silence. My beautiful wife, who would never hurt a soul, reached back again and, with her tightly balled fist took a second swing at me. I grabbed her wrist in time and twisted it until she fell to her knees. When I let go of her, Franes dropped to her knees next to her. I watched as both women held each other, crying and shaking.

"Frances, you can stay here and have your child. I will take care of both of you for the rest of my life. However, under no circumstance will you have anything more to do with Nick Ciccone. Do you understand my terms?" My voice bellowed, almost bouncing off the walls of my small study.

"But Daddy, he is my baby's father. I want my child to have his name. To know him and love him like I do."

"Help your mother up and get out of my sight," I replied, ignoring my daughter's sobs as she helped my wife up. I glanced quickly at my wife, but she didn't meet my eyes. Viviana is a passionate woman; however, her passion has never turned to violence, especially toward me. I know the chord I struck was inexcusable in her mind. She was protecting our child, I understand that. I just hoped she understood that I needed to protect her, too. Once they were

gone, I made the call. I wasn't expecting to be blindsided by my family. They left me with no choice.

What call? I frantically flip through the remaining pages, but they are blank. Damn it, this book ends here. I'm about to look for the next book when my phone rings. The caller ID says unknown. Normally I would flag it as spam and delete it, but I've got a strange feeling in the pit of my stomach. I slide the bar across the face of the phone.

"Hello."

"Trust no one. I'll be in touch soon."

The phone disconnects and I'm staring at a blank screen. I realize I'm shaking. Is it fear of what the caller said or the fear of finding out who my grandfather really was? I look at my watch and realize if I don't do my daily swim now, I'll be late meeting Jessica. After quickly storing the book, I throw on my suit and head out back like normal, except really cautious about everyone around me, including the FBI.

CHAPTER ELEVEN

Luca

After Jessica left, as promised, Cody and I spent the rest of the night outside. He stayed in the car all night. I opted for a chase lounge by the pool. Carmine talked about his only grandchild all the time. He wanted to have a large presence in Michelina's life, but Francrs blocked him. Carmine was such a big presence and from what I've learned so far about the girl, maybe he would have been a good part of her life. Unfortunately, we'll never know. Sometimes he wanted to talk off the record. Honestly, I never had a problem with that. He always said, "Luca, you're on the wrong side in life. You could have been my right-hand man." I would laugh and thought *if you only knew*. The sliding glass door opens and Michelina steps out. She drops her towel on the chair and works her way down the pool steps. I'm hiding behind my shades, pretending I'm doing something on my phone. She slowly lowers herself into the pool, trying to act like she is not putting on a show for me. She takes off her bathing suit top and tosses it on the chair next to me. I stay still and say nothing. She does a couple of laps and then tosses her bathing suit bottom on to the chair.

"I usually do my morning swim in the nude, but I didn't want to make you feel uncomfortable, Luca."

I get up and crouch down in front of her, tilt my head towards her face and brush my lips over hers. Getting a taste of her nearly makes me forget the truth. The truth about me, the truth about her, and why taking this any further is forbidden. It could be deadly for both of us. I shake those thoughts from my head and get back to reality. "I don't have a problem with it at all, however, you need to finish up here. We have to head over to my office. Apparently, a creditable threat came in on you. My boss wants to put you in Witness Protection. I'll meet you out front." I don't wait for an answer; I turn and leave Just missing the water she splashes my way. I can't help but laugh.

Michelina

After retrieving my suit, I head inside. Luca just took all the fun out of my morning. Well, at least what I thought would be fun. All night long, Jessica could not stop talking about Luca and what a fine ass he has. By the time she left, it was all I could think about. I thought I could have some fun this morning, but surely, I'm not his type. Maybe he's gay. I mean, it wouldn't surprise me. By the time I get outside, Luca is pacing by the car and Cody is messing with his phone.

"Sorry it took so long. I started my morning swim later than usual." I stand there with my dark shades on and take a long gaze up his tall, buff body. Does he know? Probably. Do I care—no. He doesn't move and neither do I. Cody keeps clearing his throat, but neither one of us moves. The heat coming off of him is intense, even for an Arizona summer morning.

"Excuse me, but when you are both ready, we have appointments to keep."

"I think Cody needs you to move out of the way and let me get in the car." I smirk. He takes a step to the side, reaches back, and opens the door for me. "I'm more than capable of opening my door as long as you're not standing in the way."

"Are you going to fight me every step of the way?"

"If I said yes, would it matter?"

"Not at all." His voice is deep and raspy, which takes my mind to all kinds of places it probably shouldn't go. I climb into the backseat and he slams the door with so much force that Cody nearly jumps out of his seat.

"The first stop is the mortuary. The district attorney came through and gave the go ahead to have the service for your mom. Did your friend finish setting everything up for you?"

"Cody, why do I need the go ahead from the district attorney? It's not like they arrested anyone for the explosion that killed my mom," I remind him, not that he needs reminding.

"We had to make sure we could bring in enough people to keep you safe."

"Like you kept my mom safe?" Before Cody can answer, Luca turns in his seat and pulls his glasses down. His eyes are as dark as coal.

"We gave Frances every opportunity to work with us. She flat out refused. She thought we were crazy. I guess it's safe to say we weren't." He puts his glasses back on and turns around.

As much as I want to lay into him, I hold back. It's hard to fight when you don't have the entire story. We pull into the parking lot, and I barely wait for Cody to bring the car to a stop before jumping out and heading through the front door. Luca races in behind me and nearly knocks me over.

"I'm trying to keep you alive, Chelle. Why do you have to fight me?" His hands grip my arms so tight that I flinch from the pain. "I didn't mean to hurt you. I don't want you to end up like your mother."

"Take your excuses someplace else. You should have kept her safe." I don't realize I'm yelling until the director steps out of his office, glaring at the two of us.

"Hello, you must be Ms. Ciccone. I'm Travis Rittenhouse. Your friend Jessica said you would be by this morning. Why don't you come into my office, and we can go over everything." He opens the door wider and waves me through.

When he waves for Luca to come, I hold my hand up stopping him. "You can wait outside this door." Mr. Rittenhouse face pales as I slam the door in Luca's face.

"Ms. Ciccone, I promise you are safe. My family has owned this business for over thirty years and anyone that has come here recently was already dead."

I'm staring at him, and I lose it. Another bout of hysterical crying ensues.

"Oh my Gosh, Ms. Ciccone, I was trying to make you feel safe. I'm sorry."

"Please call me Chelle. I know you meant nothing by it. Her death was very unexpected. Then again, it's not like anyone expects their mother to be blown up." His face turns a shade paler as he passes me a box of tissues. What I would much rather have right now is a shot of whiskey and something to turn back time. I pull myself together and ask Mr. Rittenhouse to go over the arrangements with me. By the time he is done, I'm feeling better. We set everything for Friday. That gives me three days. Before I leave, I send Jessica a quick text with the last details. My mom had only a few close friends and co-workers, so this should be fairly simple and small.

I leave the office expecting to see Luca outside the door, but Cody is there instead. "I thought Luca would be here," I furrow my brows, "not that it matters. Just surprised, is all," I offer him an explanation even though he hasn't asked for one.

"I wanted to talk to you for a minute," he says in a serious tone. "Luca did everything he could for your mom. She fought him every step of the way. Even though he's not responsible for what happened to her, he still feels guilty. I know he can be a prick but take it easy on him."

"Why did my mom fight him?" I pull the strap of my purse higher on my shoulder in an aggressive manner. I don't know why I'm bothering to ask any more questions; no one seems to have any answers and it only gets me more frustrated.

He rocks back and forth on his heels, hesitating. "Look, I don't know what kind of relationship Frances had with Carmine. Maybe he kept the mafia part of his life hidden from his family. The only thing I know is she kept referring to him as a foolish old man."

Those words, combined with what I read about my grandfather, are racing through my mind. I stop moving so quick it causes Cody to nearly knock me over.

"What is it, Chelle? Do you know something?"

"No, Cody, they kept me in the dark about so much, I don't know what to believe."

"Maybe things will become clearer after your mom's service." As we head to the car, I can only hope the books will bring more clarity than a service honoring the dead.

CHAPTER TWELVE

Agosto

WHILE I WAIT ON THE NEWS FROM GIANNI, I WALK AROUND my cactus garden. There is a lot of beauty in the desert if you open your mind to it. I might have come here for my wife, but I stayed for the lifestyle. Every few days I refresh my inground feeders I have for the many quail birds that come into my garden. They have always fascinated me. The birds mate for life and both share equally in the parenting duties. We can learn a lot from these birds. When I look up, I see Gianni has finally gotten here.

"Pop, sorry I'm late. I was waiting for confirmation from the mortuary. They set the service for Frances on Friday. Will you be going?"

I walk over to the bench and sit down. I tap my hand on the seat next to me for him to sit. "How much do you think Michelina knows?"

"The FBI has flanked her since the explosion. Even if she knew nothing, I'm sure by now they filled her in."

"The question is: how much will she believe?" I mindlessly toss some cracked corn towards the feeders for the quail.

"Are you thinking of going to the service?"

"I never had a problem with Frances. Besides, Viviana will be there. Out of respect for her, I will go. I expect you and your brother to be there, too."

"I'll let Geno know. What if our presence stirs the pot, though? Viviana is in and out of reality, and Michelina probably doesn't even know we exist. So, how do we handle that?"

"I will handle it. You and Geno will pay your respects and leave."

"And you? What will you do?"

I say nothing because it is between Viviana and me only. I get up and head inside, leaving him to tell his brother what I expect.

Michelina

We leave the mortuary and I decide to go home. I need to wrap my mind around everything. More importantly, I really need to get back to Carmine's books. I think the answers I need are right in front of me. When we pull up to the house, I hesitate. Luca turns toward me and slides his glasses down. "Chelle, is there a problem? You said you wanted to go home."

"Where will you both be?"

"Well, our job is to keep you safe, so if you are staying here, so are we."

"Look, it's a hundred and twenty degrees in the shade. I'm not cruel; you can stay inside, but only in the living room." I don't wait for an answer. I get out and head toward the door, but Luca stops me.

"We need to do a sweep of the place before you can go inside."

"Is this really necessary?" He cocks his head to the side and gives me a smirk. The man is infuriating. "Fine." I toss him the keys and wait with Cody by the car. He's in and out in under ten minutes. Of course, everything is okay. I stop by the kitchen and grab a bottle of water before making my way upstairs.

I take out the next journal, hoping they are in order. I need to find out what Carmine did, and why he felt he had no choice.

Viviana is not talking to me, and Frances is very emotional. I'm the one who must keep a clearer head. I'd rather my daughter hate me than finding out Nick already knocked up another girl. He has at least one son that I know of. Where there is one, there is always more. Instead of working his way up the food chain, he thought he could take a shortcut to the top. That privilege is earned, not given freely. He's a player and set his sights on my daughter, hoping to get to me. He will never get that close to us again. I only hope that one day my family will understand why this had to be.

The realization of what I just read hits me like a wrecking ball. I have at least one half sibling. The urgency to find out more is even greater now. My phone rings and I nearly jump out of my skin. Caller ID unknown again. I slide the bar across. "Hello."

"You do not know, do you?"

"Who are you, and what do you want from me?" I question through my teeth, trying to keep my voice down, yet forceful. A sinister laugh rings in my ear. I want to hang up, but something is telling me not to.

"Everyone wants one thing from you, the only thing that is keeping you alive. You need to trust me. I'll help you get all the answers you are searching for."

"Why should I trust you and not the FBI?" I glance at my bedroom door as if that will stop Cody and Luca from hearing me. The laugh is louder, like something out of a horror movie.

"Well, you see where the FBI got your mother and your grandfather. We will talk again soon." He hangs up, his words weighing heavy on my mind. Maybe trusting the FBI is not a good thing. When I mentioned to Luca that maybe I should contact Agosto, he was quick to shut me down. I had let it go, but maybe now I should at least look into him. There is a knock on my door, causing me to jump once again. If this keeps up, I'm going to die of heart failure before someone has a chance to murder me.

"Just a minute." I shout out as I stash everything back in the closet. When I open the door, I find Luca standing there with my laptop.

"Sorry to bother you, but I remember how important this was to you. Since the tech team was done with it, I figured I would bring it back to you." He passes me my laptop, but his eyes are darting around the room.

"Thank you. Was there something else?"

"No, I'm downstairs if you need anything."

I close the door and listen for the creaking stairs to know he left. The first thing I do is fire up the laptop and make sure everything is still there. I'm not sure if the FBI put some sort of program on here that monitors what I'm doing, but Luca said to search the internet on my grandfather. I figure I can at least do that. Only popular or polarizing people actually have a page dedicated to them. At least, that's what one of my students told me, that and the fact being an influencer is her destiny. I put in Carmine's name and hit the search button. It only takes a few seconds for the page to fill. I feel my heart pound in my chest as I read about his life. The list of crimes they accused him of is mind blowing. How could there be so much about my grandfather that I never knew? Why wasn't my mom honest with me? Maybe that's what she wanted to talk to me about. Unfortunately, I'll never know. Maybe she knew what was in the journals, and since I would not throw them away, maybe she wanted to prepare me for what I was about to find out. Sadly, all I can do is speculate. I put my father's name in a search and the only thing I get are pay sites that will get you the records, which are public anyway. I decide to put Agosto's name in the search. Wow, his profile is worse than Carmine's. Probably because he is still alive, and Carmine is not. It has a picture of him, and it says he lives in Paradise Valley. I snap a picture with my phone before I close it down. My phone pings, letting me know I have a new message. When I look at it, I see it's from Jess. She attached a copy of the announcement for my mom's service. She placed it everywhere she and I talked about. Three days from now, it will be interesting to see who shows up and what they want from me.

CHAPTER THIRTEEN

Luca

Cody and I are watching the early morning sunrise when my phone pings.

"Anything good?" Cody asks.

"The information on the service went out. We have three days to find that book before the service."

"I think it will be very interesting to see who shows up. Luca, do you think Agosto is going to make an appearance?"

"He'd be a fool not to. From what I learned, spending over two years one-on-one with Carmine, he really hated Agosto. I would love to learn more. Why wouldn't you?"

"What happens if we never find the books?"

"There will probably be a lot of bloodshed with so many people looking for them." I put my phone away and say no more. The less said, the better.

"You know, eventually, Luca, we are going to have to let the next team watch her. I've got to go home, shower, and check in with my wife."

"Pop the trunk for me." I get out, go around back, and pull out my to-go bag. It's a requirement that we always have it with us. I pull Cody's out too and toss it to him.

"Don't worry, I'll talk to her about using the guest bathroom to freshen up. She should come out soon for her swim." I open the gate to the yard and see her standing there with two cups of coffee.

"Wow, why the change?" I ask, surprised as hell.

"Look, I'm under a lot of stress, and I know I wasn't very nice. I'll try to have more patience."

"Thank you. Would it be okay if Cody and I take turns freshening up in the guest bathroom? Normally, a second shift would relive us, but I promised you I would keep you safe, and that's what I'm going to do."

"Come inside and I'll show you where everything is." We follow her inside, where I tell Cody to go first, and I'll keep watch. I view this as the perfect time to pump her for some information.

"So, Chelle, now that you have your computer back, did you look up Carmine?" Her face pales at this question.

"Yes, and you were right. He was a terrible man. Unfortunately, that's not the man I knew. I was wondering if you could find out more information about my father. I have some information that I can share with you. However, my mom never said much about him. The only thing I know is he died in prison."

"So, your mom keeping secrets from you is nothing new?"

"Apparently not. I wrote down what little I have." She quickly pulls a slip of paper out of her back pocket and passes it to me. I notice her hands are shaking as I take the paper from her. "I'll see what I can come up with. In the meantime, I think we need to discuss your mother's service."

"What's there to discuss? You were there when we completed the arrangements."

"Yes, but now we need to go over security. For starters, there will be a lot of high-level mobsters, for lack of a better word. They will all want your ear. Not literally, although, I wouldn't put it past any of them. They will leave your grandmother alone for two reasons. One: she is not in good health, and two: wives and children are off limits."

"Tell that to my mother, Luca. Besides, if that's the case, then why come after me?" Her eyes darker, and her cheeks flushed, no doubt from the anger and rage she is feeling. Before I can answer, Cody comes down the hall letting me know that I'm up. "I'm going to head into the shower. We can talk about this when I'm done."

I grab my to-go bag and head into the bathroom. I put the paper she gave me in my bag. I don't need to look it up; I know everything there is to know about him. Someone violently killed him on Carmine's orders. Another one of those confessions that Carmine told me during his interrogation. One that he confessed he regretted. He would give me little pieces of what he thought was wisdom. One of the first things he said to me was, *"Luca, a poor decision in a split moment can't be undone."* What she doesn't know is that she has an older half-brother that lives in New York City. He is in the life. Carmine never said if he knew where the kid was and how ironic it was that the kid ended up under the control of Agosto's family. I don't believe in coincidence and neither did Carmine. I'm sure somehow, some way, given the chance, Agosto would want to take him under his wing. If for nothing else, to rub salt in the wound. The question is, how much do I tell her? I take a quick shower while I mull this around for a while. I quickly finish up and head into the living room, but only Cody is sitting there.

"Hey, where did she go?"

"She said she had a headache and went upstairs to lie down. I spoke to the chief about the memorial, and he said they have the entire place wired for sound and video. If anyone tries to make a move on her, we've got it covered."

I pull water out of the fridge and have a seat across from him. "How much do you think she really knows? I mean she seemed visibly shaken today after she looked up Carmine on the internet." I keep mulling it around in my mind if I should tell him what she asked me to do.

"Look, Luca, maybe they kept her in the dark for plausible deniability."

"Even if that's the case, she is a smart girl. I would think she would have put two and two together."

"We can't sit here and play Monday morning quarterback. For her safety and the safety of everyone around her, we need to help her find the book." For once Cody and I agree, even if it's for different reasons.

"Look, Cody, when you were in the shower, she came to me and asked me to help her find out more about her father. Apparently, her mother told her very little about him." He gets up, walks to trash and tosses his water bottle. He hesitates, saying nothing. "Cody, what's the problem?"

"It's very difficult to say nothing when she is clearly struggling with everything. We have some information that could give her some sort of peace."

"We also have information that could get her killed, so what's the solution?" Before he can answer, Chelle comes down the steps, grabs her purse and heads toward the front door.

"Where are you going?" I blurt out a little too harshly.

"I got a text from the mortuary. They need a picture of my mom for the service. She had a really pretty picture of herself sitting on the steps of our brownstone in Brooklyn. I know where it is at her house, so I'm going to go get it and drop it off before the service."

"Well, where you go, we go." I grab my keys and we head out, giving me time to think about how much I should tell her about her father.

CHAPTER FOURTEEN

Michelina

Cody and, especially, Luca are being extra nice to me today. I sit in the back seat and let my mind wander, reliving Carmine's words about my dad, my eyes glaring at Luca's reflection in the rearview mirror. How much did Carmine tell him? How much is he hiding from me? Better yet, who the hell keeps calling me? I have Carmine's journals but, like my mom said, they are nothing more than the ramblings of an old man. Stories about his family, not a detail book on who did what to whom. I would think if there was something like that, my mom would have told me. I keep hearing that voice over and over in my head: *Look where the FBI got your mom and Carmine.* We come to a complete stop, and I realize I'm back at my mom's house. I take a minute and gather my thoughts before I head inside.

"Luca, is the FBI done with this place?" I ask over my shoulder as I walk through the door.

"They finished up a little while ago. They came across some legal papers that they put aside for you."

When I head into mom's office, I see her strongbox is open with all her legal papers stacked neatly beside it. I know she had a will and an insurance policy, but they are not with the papers. She paid off the house, however, I never asked her how she got it paid off so soon. I know she didn't have a car loan. We purchased our cars together. Same cars and same colors. Mom gifted me mine for graduation. Like everyone else in Arizona, silver cars are a dime a dozen. I find the picture and stare at it for a bit. I'm not sure who took the picture, but they took it in happier times. She was younger and living in Brooklyn. She had just come back from spending the day at Coney Island. Her cheeks are pink from the sun, and she looks so happy. I can't remember when I've ever seen her like that. I put the picture in the strongbox along with the legal papers and make my way back outside.

"I'm ready. Before we go to the mortuary, I need to go home first. I have a nicer frame that I want to put the photo in." They both agree and drive me to my house. When we get there, I bring the strongbox into my bedroom. I rummage around in my closet and find the box with my extra frames. It was a teacher's gift that I put away, hoping I would find the perfect photo for it. When I open the back of the frame to get the photo out, there is a key and a note.

Michelina,

If you are reading this, then I'm no longer with you. If you found your grandfather's journals, then you know what a bastard he was. You have to be wondering why on earth I continued to be a part of his life? Honestly, I stayed because of my mother. The day she stood up for me and he smacked her to her knees, I saw pure evil, but I could not leave my mother alone with him. When I thought he died, I finally felt free. Free of the horrors I lived with. Then one day, I thought I saw him. How could that be? He was dead! The face was unfamiliar, yet, there was a familiarity about him. He drew me in to him like a moth to a flame. I didn't want to be, but I couldn't stop myself. For once in my life, I let my gut rule and not my heart. I followed him for days until I saw him at the country club he frequently visited. He had a shirt on that revealed his birthmark: lips that look like a kiss. That day, my entire world turned upside down. He saw me running into the parking lot and came after me. He grabbed my arm with such force and spun me around. I told him I knew who he was, and he laughed. I asked him how he could do this to us. He said the only regret he had was you, Michelina. He wanted a relationship with you, however; he knew I would never allow it. For that, he felt I should rot in hell. When I turned to leave, he held my arm even tighter. "Frances, you can hate me all you want, but I did what I thought was best for Michelina, for the entire family."

"What you did was have Nick killed. How is that best for us, for her? She grew up without a father."

You couldn't see him for the bastard he was. He already had a son with someone else. Loyalty was not his thing. I did what I thought would keep you both safe. Look, before you go, I need you to understand something. I always loved you. I might not have shown it in a way you needed, but everything I did in life was to protect my family. It's all I have left.

All you did was drive a wedge between us. That's when he pressed a key into my hand and a piece of paper with the name of a bank and a number. He told me whomever has the book has the power and to guard it with my life. He let go of my arm, turned, and walked away. It was not even a week later that the FBI informed me he really died this time… the widow maker. The FBI quickly pulled me in, asking me for Carmine's black book. I said nothing. I only knew their side of the deal they had with Carmine. They continued to watch my every move. I have since moved everything that was in Carmine's box to a safe deposit box of my own. Actually, it's the box you went with me to set up. I know I took you to the bank under false pretenses, but I didn't want to drag you into something you knew nothing about. However, after I started reading the book, I knew you needed protection. Please remember to trust no one. I will always love you.

Mom

With my fingers clenched tightly around the key, it feels like it's burning through to my soul. I'm just a simple high school science teacher that has been forced into a world I only thought existed in the movies, and not the Christmas in July movies that I love to watch. I take the key and the letter and put it with Carmine's journals. My head is spinning, but with a few deep breaths, I pull myself together. I need to get this picture to the mortuary. When I open my bedroom door, Luca is standing there. I panic, nearly jump out of my skin at the sight of him.

"What are you doing lurking outside my bedroom?"

"I wasn't lurking. I came to let you know the mortuary will close soon, so if you want to get the photo over there today, we need to leave now." His face shows no emotion. It never does. As he steps to the side, I pull the door closed behind me.

"I'm sorry. We are all a little jumpy right now. I was thinking maybe we should make the service closed to family only. That way we know it will be very small with no worries about car bombing or whatever else you are expecting." I head downstairs with Luca on my heals.

"Chelle, that would defeat the entire purpose."

"What purpose is that? My mother was murdered, or have you and your FBI friends forgotten that?" Cody is waiting by the front door for us. I head toward him, but he doesn't move. Instead, he puts his hand on my shoulder and looks directly into my eyes. For the first time, I realize he has a calming effect on me, whereas Luca makes my blood pressure rise in a very unhealthy way.

"Chelle, we are trying to catch the person who murdered your mom. If you hide away, he or she will have the chance to either slip away never to be seen again or plant another bomb in your car."

"Cody, I get it. However, no one's ever said why they bombed her car. I mean, if she had the book, why kill her before they got it?" When I look at the two of them, it hits me like a brick between my eyes. "Oh My God, that bomb was for me, not my mom. They murdered her by mistake!" I feel my body sway, and Cody quickly guides me to a seat while Luca gets some water.

"Chelle, you said yourself that you and your mom have the same car, same color and you bought them together. Odds are it was a mistake."

"So, what you are telling me, Cody, is that the service is to see who wants to come back and finish the job?"

"He only gave us small parts to keep us hanging on. He was a master showman, like the puppet and the puppeteer. Unfortunately, his time ended abruptly. Now it's up to you to find the black book."

"What are you going to be doing?" I ask Luca.

"Trying our best to keep you alive."

With the picture clutched to my chest, I stand up and we get on our way.

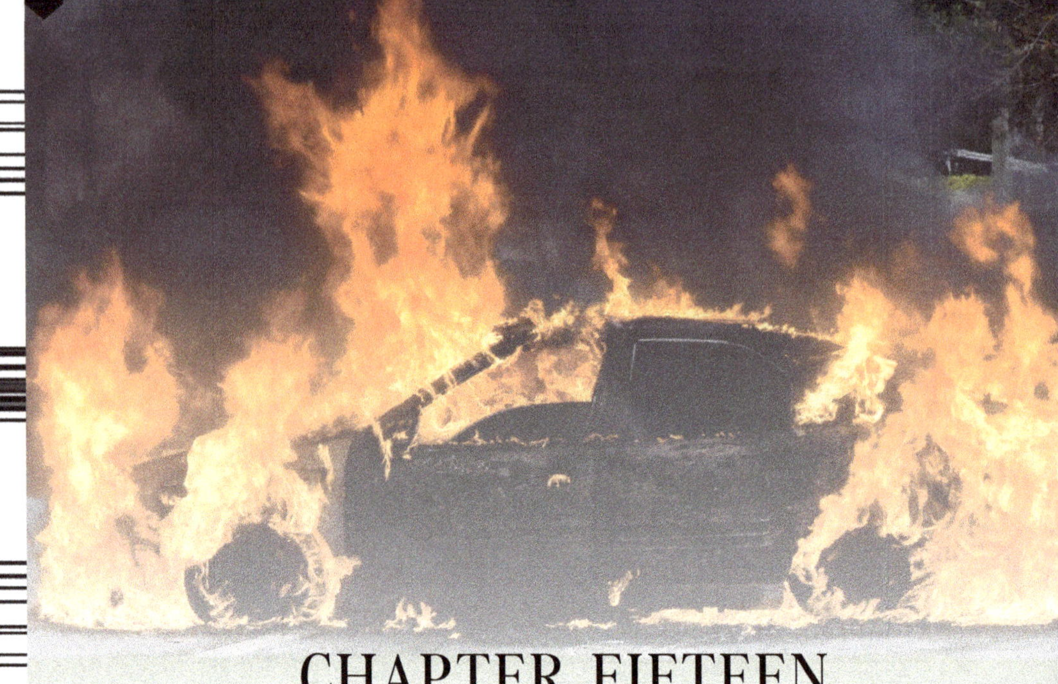

CHAPTER FIFTEEN

Michelina

IT'S THE NIGHT BEFORE MOM'S SERVICE AND I'M SCARED—TERRIFIED is more like it. The more I read the journals, the more shocked I am. I asked Luca, if possible, to please find out more information about my father. What I really wanted to ask him is if he could find out about any siblings I might have. I can't tell him I read it in Carmine's journals, and I'm not sure how to go about finding out any more information. Sitting on the floor in my closet with the key my mom left me pressed so tightly in my hand that my knuckles turn white, I wonder if she knew my father had other children before me? Was she so in love that she didn't care, or did she think he was her way out? An out that totally failed. Did she steer me toward Carmine's journals knowing I would question her about siblings? What does my grandma know? How much can she retrieve from the dark place in her mind that she retreats to? What if I ask her; would it do more harm than good? I push my thoughts aside and pull out another journal.

I knew I needed to start my black book when John Gotti began moving up the ladder. He was the fresh face of the mafia, one that would eventually change history. They considered me the level-headed leader, which was some-thing Gotti wanted no part of. I monitored the five families and tried to keep everything flowing smoothly. However, Gotti was a force to be reckoned with. A powerhouse that could flip on a dime if you fucked with him. He knew I started my book. Hell, everyone knew. They just hoped a long-standing friend-ship would keep them out of it. When Gravano turned state's evidence, it re-enforced my decision to create the book. It became more about protecting me and my family, even if they wanted nothing to do with me. Frances used Michelina like a weapon against me. When I would ask her to bring Michelina over for Sunday dinner, she would always decline. She would only come over when I wasn't home, so Michelina could visit with Viviana. One day I asked Viviana to talk to Franes, to see if she could change her mind. Viviana said she didn't want her grandbaby around someone with a black heart. After that, I stopped asking.

I can understand why my mom felt she didn't want me around him, but I would think my grandmother would have tried to broker some sort of peace. Then again, I don't know all that he put them through. I'm will-ing to bet he left a lot out of these journals. My phone rings and startles me. Caller unknown—again. I slide it to answer.

"So, you are really going through with it tomorrow? Apparently, you really have a death wish."

I take a deep breath and slowly let it out. "You act like I have so many options when, in reality, all I have is a dead mother that I need to lay to rest. So yes, I'm going through with it. I need closure. Maybe you should come and show yourself to me instead of the constant veiled threats."

"Careful what you wish for, little girl."

There is a click, and the line is dead. Well, that didn't work, or maybe it did. It's not like I'll know if he shows up tomorrow. I pick up the jour-nal and continue reading.

The higher up the chain, the more people try to hide stuff from me. Eventually, it all comes out in the wash. My brother Agosto thought he could hide his big secret from me. I knew, I always knew, but I played the game to see where it would lead. In the end, I'm a father and given what I know now,

I can't say I wouldn't do the same to protect my son. When the timing is right, I will eventually let the cat out of the bag but, for now, I will keep his secret.

Damn it! That's it; this journal ends on a cliffhanger. I put the journal back in the box and open up the next box. I need to know what Carmine had on Agosto.

Today my past hit my future when Nick Ciccone's oldest boy came to see me. I normally wouldn't bother with such nonsense, but he is a twelve-year-old boy wanting to know about his father. He walked into my club like he was a big man, not the little boy he really was. When he stepped closer to my table, he pulled a gun out of his coat pocket. Butch, my right-hand man, wrapped his enormous arms around the kid, practically squeezing the life out of him. I got up and took the 22 away from the kid and ordered Butch to let him breathe.

"Son, I'm going to forget what just happened here. You are a kid and shouldn't be threatening adults with a gun. What is it you think I did that would send you here wanting to kill me?"

"You killed my father. My mom said you did. Why?"

"Son, your mom is mistaken. Your father died in prison, and I had nothing to do with that. What would make your mom tell you such terrible stories?"

"She said my dad messed with your daughter and he had to pay for that. Why? I have nothing because of you."

"It's not because of me, it's because of your father. What is your name?"

"Nick Ciccone Jr."

"Well, Jr., you can do two things: you can go through life blaming everyone but your father or you can accept the fact that your father did a lot of bad things. He wouldn't have been in prison if he wasn't guilty. The choice is yours. I will do nothing to you today. I will keep the gun and if you ever try this again, I can guarantee you, you won't be the one left standing."

Butch walked him out, and I sat there holding the gun, thinking about everything that happened with the kid's father. Looking back, I would still do the same thing. It's not the fact that he knocked up my only daughter, it's the fact he did it thinking he could get in favor with me. If he had done his research, he would have known that on a good day, I dislike most people. Knocking up my daughter was not the way to make me like you.

Wow, so now I know I have at least one-half brother and his name is Nick Ciccone Jr. Maybe that's who keeps calling me. Maybe I can find him if I register with one of those DNA sites for people looking for relatives. Then again, he could be dead if he followed in my father's footsteps.

The rising sun is creeping through the blinds, and I realize, thanks to these journals, time has gotten away from me. I quickly pack them back up and head into the shower. Today is going to be a hard day. Not just because I'm saying goodbye to my mom, I will have people coming at me from all over, people I don't know, people that might want me dead. But I have to figure out an excuse to stop at the bank, so I can retrieve what my mom left me in the safe deposit box. It's got to be important since she hid it.

CHAPTER SIXTEEN

Michelina

WHEN I GET DOWNSTAIRS, THE COFFEE IS ALREADY BREWING, and Cody and Luca are standing next to the pot. "You realize staring at the pot will not make it brew any faster, right?" I raise an eyebrow in amusement. Just as the dripping slows, Luca takes the pot out and pours each of us a cup. They drink it black, but I have to put an acceptable amount of creamer in mine. Guilty pleasure for sure.

"Chelle, we need to go over the procedure for today," Luca tells me as he pulls out a chair for me to sit.

"Well, I thought we are going to get my grandma and then head to the mortuary. Or do you have something else planned?"

"That is the general plan. You are not to leave with anyone. We have a black limo for today. If anyone tries to give you something, you are not to accept it. I will be in the front left corner and Cody will be in the back right corner of the room. If something is off, look at one of us and we will step in. We have agents all around the outside of the building. There is no graveside service, but afterwards we will head to All Saints Catholic Church where Father Dominick will hold a private mass for your mom.

After the mass, we will head to your mom's house for coffee and pastries. The only thing I need you to let me know is when you will want your grandmother to be taken back to her residence. Did I leave anything out?"

"You made all these arrangements?"

"I would like to take credit, but no, Jessica helped set everything up. She knew it was just too overwhelming for you. You have a great friend. You're very lucky."

"I know she is a great friend, but I don't think I'm so lucky, otherwise my mom wouldn't be dead."

He puts his coffee down and pulls a chair out, sitting himself very close to me. "Look, I understand you are dealing with a huge amount of grief, and they kept you in the dark your whole life about the true identity of your grandfather. However, you are very lucky. The more I think about it, the more I'm sure that bomb was meant for you, not your mom. Someone wanted to blow up your car and scare Frances into turning over the book. Now it's you who has a bullseye on your back. You're still alive, Chelle. Take the wins where you can."

I let Luca's words sink in, not knowing how to handle everything that has been thrown at me in the last seventy-two hours. I'm scared where this day will lead me. Will my half-brother show up? Will I even know who he is? How many siblings do I have? What about Agosto? How much danger will there be if he shows up? Even more worrisome is my grandmother. What will she remember and what will she share with me? How is she going to react to the people she sees, people like Agosto? Will she remember him or will seeing Agosto send her spiraling down a dark place in her mind?

"Thank you, Luca, you too, Cody. I appreciate your compassion and help through all of this. Before we head to pick up Grandma, I need to stop at the bank. My mom didn't believe in online banking, so I have to deposit money in her account to cover her bills. Also, I can't find a copy of her insurance policy or her will. I know she has a box at the bank. I had to be with her when she opened it. If I remember correctly, she put all of her and Grandma's legal papers in it. Once everything is settled, I can close her accounts. It shouldn't take me too long. If we leave now, I will have more than enough time to stop before we pick up Grandma." I get up, pick up my purse and head toward the front door, leaving them no room for debate.

The car comes to a stop outside the bank just as it's opening. Luca jumps out first and opens my door. "I'm perfectly safe going into the bank." He says nothing but stays one step behind me. When I stop abruptly, he nearly knocks me over.

"I will just stay in the corner until you are done."

"Don't you think that will raise some suspicion?"

"If need be, I can flash my badge."

I close my eyes and take a deep breath and slowly exhale. Being this close to him messes with my thoughts. "Look, I need to talk to the manager about my mom's stuff. I don't want to be looking over my shoulder at you." He reaches his arm around me, pushes the door, and holds it open for me. I throw my hands up, gesturing my frustration before stepping into the bank. Luca sits in the waiting area as I sign in and request to speak to the manager. When she comes out, I explain my mom has passed and I need to do some banking. Her name is Emma, and I only met her once when I came here with mom to do the safe deposit box. Her eyes look over toward Luca and back toward me.

"Why don't we go into my office, and we can get started?"

I follow her into her office, and she quickly closes the door behind me. I'm still in Luca's eyesight. She motions me to sit and instead of taking the seat behind her desk, she sits next to me.

"Michelina, I was very upset to learn about your mom's passing. She was not just a customer; she was a friend. I'm probably overstepping, but if something is wrong, and I didn't ask, I could never live with myself. Are you safe? Who is that man? Should I call the police?"

Her questions are quick and unsettling, exactly what I thought would happen. "Thank you for your concern. He is with the FBI and is making sure I'm safe. My mom has a safe deposit box I need to get into. I will also need to know what automatic withdrawals my mom had on her accounts. I want to clear all that up before I close them." Nodding with understanding at the situation, she gets up and goes behind her desk and pulls up stuff on her computer.

"All your mom's accounts are joint accounts with you only, except for your grandmother's account. That one has the three of you as authorized signers. You are the only one listed on the box with your mom. Would you like to access it now?"

I take a steady breath. "Yes, please." She grabs her keys and leads me to the back of the bank. I can feel Luca's eyes following me. After we each use our key, she takes the box and brings it to a private room, places it on the table and steps out, closing the door behind her. The box is bigger than I expected. I open it and there are six ledger-sized leather books. They remind me of what accountants used to use in the old movies. I remove them and find two black velvet bags underneath. One has uncut diamonds, and the other has emeralds—big ones. Next, there are bundles of cash. The bills are old, and I wonder if they are no longer in circulation; will they still be good? Finally, there is my grandmother's will and my mother's will, along with an insurance policy for both of them. I put the wills and the policies in my bag and put the rest back in the box. It is the safest place I can think of. Before I put the ledgers back, I open one of them. I really want to see what was worth killing over. Attached to the inside cover is an envelope. Inside the envelope there are photos of people in some really horrible sexual situations. I don't recognize the people until I get toward the end, and I see a former president dressed as a baby and his wife is whipping him. I nearly throw up, thinking I voted for this man! Each entry has something to do with a favor or debt that is owed. I close the ledger and put it back in the box. When I open the door, Emma is waiting for me. She puts the box back and we each use our key to lock it.

"Thank you for your help, Emma. I wanted to let you know there is a celebration of life for my mom later this afternoon." I jot down the information for her and she gives me a hug before I leave. My mom had more friends than I realized. I walk at a hurried pace through the lobby and directly out of the bank. I don't even wait for Luca. He catches up to me outside and opens the car door for me.

"Did you get everything you needed?" he asks in an urgent voice.

Totally ignoring him, I climb into the back seat and hold up the papers. "What did you think I was going there for, some book you keep telling me about that I don't even believe exist? Like I said earlier, this is what I went for: the insurance policies for my mom and grandmother and their wills." I pull the envelopes out of my bag and wave them before I put them away. That shut him up and the rest of the ride to pick up Grandma is in total silence.

CHAPTER SEVENTEEN

Michelina

WHEN WE GET TO THE ASSISTED LIVING, GRANDMA IS dressed and waiting for me. I'm reminded of how beautiful she is. Her slim-fitting, black dress and long string of pearls really accent her beauty. She has her rosary beads wrapped around her hands. She has a beautiful lace veil that drapes over her shoulders. When I would take her to mass, she would wear a smaller one that she called a toquilla. When we had the funeral for Grandpa, she wore the full one that she has on now. There is a sadness in her eyes, and it breaks my heart. A mother should never outlive her child.

"Grandma, I know today will be difficult, but I will be beside you the entire day." We head out and I feel like the weight of the world is resting on my shoulders. However, for my grandmother, I would do anything.

When we pull up to the mortuary, Jessica is waiting outside for me. I'm thankful for our friendship that has stood the test of time. We have been friends since middle school, which is the most turbulent time in anyone's life. She steps next to Grandma and slips her arm in hers and we go inside together, where we find the director Travis Rittenhouse waiting for us. I hold out the photo, passing it to him.

"Thank you. I spoke with Father Dominick, and he has the private mass set up for 2 o'clock. After the mass, I let him know you did not want a receiving line. I will lead everyone into the rectory, where there will be refreshments. All Saints Church is just up the road, but I figured if we send people over about 1 o'clock, that would give them enough time to get settled in. As you can see, there is an abundance of floral arrangements. I sent about the same amount to the church." He waves his hand around as if I needed his help to notice all the flowers. The smell is overpowering. He leads us to a few empty chairs that are separated from the rows of chairs for people who come to pay their respects. It's like a receiving line at a wedding, only there is nothing joyous here. We get Grandma settled in her chair. Jessica stays with her while I walk around looking at all the flowers. There is a pedestal with a guest book on top for people to sign. I might know a half-dozen people, but judging by the flowers, there will be more than that showing up. In the corner is a large spray of white roses shaped like a heart with a silk banner that says *Rest in Peace.* When I get closer, I see there is a card. It simply reads *Agosto.* My hands shake as I try to put the card back. Right now, I've seen enough to last me a lifetime. When I turn around, Luca is behind me.

"Is there a problem, Luca?" His stare cuts right through me.

"Problem? Not yet. However, I want to give you a quick heads up where we will be and what happens before we go to the church."

He hurries through the positioning of the agents. We are to wait until everyone is gone before we attempt to go to the church. I nod my approval and sit back down with my grandma. I just want this to be over.

The doors open and people slowly start coming in. Her supervisor, Constance Tucchi, is the first one through the door with a small group of people. They are wearing shirts with the company logo on them. As they come up to us, my grandmother sits very stoic, looking straight ahead. Constance kneels down in front of my grandmother.

"I'm so sorry for your loss," she offers. Grandma says nothing, she doesn't even blink.

Constance turns toward me, offering her condolences. She informs me that a few of Mom's workers could come between shifts. The others sent a card. She hands me the card and I pass it to Jessica. It's not something I can deal with right now. They offer their condolences and move on. Is this what I'm supposed to do? My mom is no longer here to help me, and I feel my heart breaking all over again.

There is a steady flow of people, none of whom I know except for Grandma's next-door neighbor. His grandson helped me that horrible night. He is here to see Grandma. He talks to her, but she says nothing. I'm getting nervous. Maybe this is too much for her. She moves her hand down to the next bead on the rosary. That's when I realize she is not saying anything because she is praying the rosary. As I sit here watching all of this, my mind wanders. If I was to die tomorrow, other than Jessica, who would show up? Why would they show up? I know it is a sign of respect, however; I think I would rather have people present in my life while I'm alive rather than showing up when I'm dead. That to me is respect.

I keep scanning the crowd, thinking surely, I would recognize a half-brother. Maybe he might even look like me… nothing. I have no clue what to do with all the stuff in the safe deposit box. I can't carry it all out at once and even if I did, what would I do with it? My initial thought was maybe I could sell the books, but after taking a quick look at what's in them, it could get me killed. Oh, and let me not forget the diamonds and emeralds. I really want to tell Jessica everything, but I can't put her in danger. I mean, Luca keeps reminding me I have a bullseye on my back.

More people come in. The men are in suits and the woman are in too-tight dresses. Summer in Arizona is not the time for suits. They come in pairs. For people who don't want to draw any attention to themselves, they stick out like a sore thumb. It's nearing the time to move to the church for mass. Mr. Rittenhouse is very good at staying on task. I could use someone like him as my teaching assistant. After all the stressing and planning, nothing has happened. No one that resembled me has shown up. No one that resembles Agosto showed up. Once the room is empty, Luca comes over and kneels down in front of Grandma.

"Ma'am, I have the car out front and ready to take everyone to the church. If you don't mind, I'm going to help you now."

I'm watching him with her and he's like a totally different man. He's respectful and kind. Who is this guy? I get up while he helps her up, watching as he guides her to the waiting car. When I look at Jessica, her eyes are wide as she shrugs her shoulders. Obviously, just as surprised as I am.

The short ride to the church is silent. We are the last to arrive, which is the way Father Dominick wanted it. Luca is still helping Grandma to her pew. There are more people here than there were at the mortuary. When we get to the front, I turn my head and that's when I see him—Agosto. There is no mistaking him. Our eyes lock and it's like looking into my grandfather's eyes. Jessica is waiting for me to sit. She looks around to see what is distracting me. She sees him but does not know who he is. With a gentle nudge from her, I turn around and sit down.

Father Dominick begins but I find it hard to concentrate on the mass. I want to introduce myself to Agosto and ask him a million questions. My mind is racing through everything I read about him in Carmine's journals. I remember the last part about the secret and it's like someone pulled the emergency brake while speeding downhill. My chest tightens as I fight off the wave of anxiety. When the mass is over, Father Dominick takes Grandma and me into his private sanctuary. He guides her toward the chair, and I take a seat next to her.

"Viviana, Frances was a beautiful child of Christ. She loved the church and helped us every Sunday. She spent her free time with us, and I am thankful. I'm so sorry for your loss. I'm here for you and Michelina anytime." He turns and smiles at me. I knew my mom went to mass every Sunday. I didn't know how involved she stayed after I made my confirmation. Grandma still says nothing. She stares straight ahead with a blank stare. I'm so worried about her.

"I think I should get Grandma home. Clearly, today has been too much for all of us."

"I agree. I will make your apologies and have the car brought around back for you. No one will fault you for wanting to get her home." He gets up and leaves. When I help Grandma up, I realize how frail she really is. I pray I won't be doing the same thing for her anytime soon. When I get her outside, the car is just pulling up. Father Dominick opens the back door and helps Grandma in. I take the seat across from her, grateful this day is over. As the limo pulls away, there is a knock on the roof. The tint on the windows is very dark, so I can't see anything. The limo stops, the doors unlock, and the door opens. Agosto climbs in, closing the door behind him. He presses a button on the door panel and says, "Drive." As the car moves, I feel the blood drain from my face. My instinct is to throw myself over my grandmother so I can protect her. As I unbuckle my seat belt, Grandma turns toward Agosto and smiles. What the hell.

"It's been so long, Agosto. How are you? How is your family?"

I feel like I'm in some sort of time warp. She is lucid and smiling.

"We've had our difficulties. No different from yourself, I suppose. I was very sorry to hear about Frances. Our families have experienced so much unnecessary loss."

She closes her eyes, and I notice a tear trailing down her cheek. "I know who you are, and I hope, out of respect for my grandmother, that you will leave us alone." I don't know where I find the courage to be so bold with a ruthless killer only a few feet from me.

"Viviana, I have some private business with Michelina. Would it be okay if we take you home now?" Slowly she nods her head yes. We travel in silence. I can feel his eyes on me the whole time. I try not to look at him. My focus is on my grandmother. The car finally comes to a stop, and someone I've never seen before opens the door. We are in front of the assisted living community. I turn toward Agosto and honestly, I'm not sure where I find my courage, but I lean in, my face so close to his. "I need to bring her inside and make sure I get her settled in… alone."

"I would expect nothing less from you."

With that, I get out and help Grandma inside.

CHAPTER EIGHTEEN

Michelina

MY HEAD IS SPINNING. I HAVE SO MANY QUESTIONS, YET I CAN'T let anyone know that I have the books. The biggest question is where the hell are Luca and Cody? They've been up my ass since this whole thing started and now, they are nowhere to be found. When we get into her room, she squeezes my hand.

"Come sit for a moment." Now?! Really?

"I rather stand. I'm a little nervous right now."

"Don't be. Agosto was always the good brother. I think if I would have met him first, I wouldn't have given Carmine the time of day. They say hindsight is always 20/20, and it was never truer in this situation. Be honest with him and he will not hurt you."

"People change, Grandma. You don't know the man he is today. You're remembering the man he was all those years ago." She kisses my cheek and gives me a hug.

"You need to go. He is the one with the answers you are looking for."

"Wait, how do you know what I'm looking for?"

"Michelina, you wear your heart on your sleeve. Besides, I'm the one who put those boxes in the attic."

She walks over to the door, opening it for me. I have to trust her and my instincts. I head out the door and the limo is still waiting for me. Maybe in some random universe, I really believed I would walk out the door and this would have all been a dream. I open the door and I climb inside.

"Hello, Agosto. Nice to make your acquaintance, I think." He laughs, and it puts me at ease. The car beings to move and I do not know where we are going, nor do I feel the need to ask.

"I wanted to get to know you after you were born, but that was not an option afforded to me. However, I have been following everything you've been doing. That being said, I know you are in possession of Carmine's black books, as he liked to call them. You also have his journals. If you give them to me, I can guarantee you your safety. If not, all bets are off. As we speak, there is a ten million dollar bounty on your head. You see how easy it was for me to get to you today? That is nothing compared to what they want to do to you."

"Who are they?"

"Every person my brother has something on. Plus, anyone who wants to move up within the organization. Look, what they did to your mom was a mistake. Sadly, that bomb was intended for you. It was supposed to send a message to Frances. I could stop the attempt on Viviana, however, I did not get to Frances in time."

"Someone wanted to hurt my grandmother? She's a sweet old lady who would never hurt a soul." My hands are ice cold, and a shiver runs up my spine. He presses a panel, which slides open, and pulls out a bottle of whiskey along with a couple of glasses. He pours me a glass. As I reach for it, my hand shakes so badly, I'm afraid I'll spill it.

"This is the life I was born into. We all were, Michelina."

"No, you might have been born into it, but what about your children?"

He becomes silent and turns his head away from me. "You do not know the sacrifices I've made or the price I paid."

"Uncle Agosto, I know more than you think." He arches an eyebrow in sardonic inquiry at my words.

"What exactly do you think you know?"

"I know your brother was not very nice to you. I know about your daughter dying from leukemia and your son gunned down in front of your house. Your wife died of cancer. Should I continue?" Maybe it's the whiskey that is making me bold.

"Answer this, please. Were you happy teaching high school science?"

"Mostly, yes. However, like any job, there were difficulties. Why?"

"Why would you want any part of this life? You have the opportunity to walk away from it all a very wealthy woman. Your safety and Viviana's safety guaranteed."

"Like my mother's safety? Look, I will take it under advisement. What happened to my FBI detail? Did you do something to them?"

We sit quietly for a long time. Finally, the car comes to a stop.

"You think you know everything there is to know about me, but you couldn't be further from the truth. My brother turned his back on me. In his mind, he probably justified it. I never could. When my daughter Daniella died, it hit all of us very hard, especially my wife, Gisele. Then with my son Salvatore being gunned down right in front of my house. My wife was the one who found him. My sons, Gianni and Geno, followed in my footsteps. I never wanted this life for them, but you can't tell your children what to do."

"Why are you telling me all of this?"

"You need to understand the sacrifices that were made. Not just by me, but by Carmine and our wives. If those books get out, there will be bloodshed for sure. Do you want to be responsible for that?"

I let his words sink in, but something is off. "What is it you're not telling me?"

"I have another son; one no one knows about. He was conceived after Gisele passed away. When I found out about Carmine's books, I knew it was only a matter of time before he gave the information about my son to the family. Carmine was obsessed with my life. He would bend over backwards to find out everything in my life. Then he would try to use it against me. Is there a chance Carmine left it out of his book, maybe? Did I trust my brother enough to take that chance? No. To protect him, I staged his death and changed his name. As far as anyone else is concerned, Matteo does not exist anymore. If this information gets out, his life could be in danger."

"Again, Agosto, forgive me but why are you telling me this? For all you know, I could be just as ruthless as Carmine and sell your information." I was expecting rage but what I got really shocked me. He laughed.

"Michelina, you are a babe in the woods. If I really thought that you had the guts to do that, you would never make it out of this car alive."

"Where is he now?" I ask. He taps on the privacy glass, and it slowly comes down.

"Michelina, say hello to your cousin Matteo."

The man turns around and I'm looking at Luca. My mouth hangs open, and I feel like the world is spinning out of control. "Luca … Matteo is your son? All this time, you've been hiding this from me. Luca—Matteo—or whatever the hell you go by. If you were so worried about your identity, and you thought I had the books, why didn't you just tell me? What if it's not in the books?" I throw whatever's left of my whiskey in Luca's face, swing the door open and get out while I still have my sanity.

CHAPTER NINETEEN

Michelina

I TAKE OFF RUNNING LIKE MY LIFE DEPENDS UPON IT, WHICH IT quite literally does. That realization lets the fear invade my rational thinking, or what's left of it. My whole life I've been fed a plate of lies. In one week's time, a car bomb, meant for me, blew my mother up. I find out my grandfather was a big-time mafia Don. I have a safe deposit box filled with stuff that's probably going to get me killed. Then there's the half-brother I never knew about. How many other siblings do I have? The FBI agent protecting me that turns out to be my cousin, a cousin I shared an intimate kiss with! I'm sure I'll be going to hell for that one. I'm a simple high school science teacher. A week ago, my biggest worry was making sure my students got their final projects in on time. Now, that's the furthest thing from my mind. I stop running, look around and realize I'm right back where I started, the back parking lot of All Saints Church. Running toward the gated community, I find a low-enough wall, climb it and land at the feet of Luca, the man that was supposed to protect me. The very man I've been running from. The man who is my cousin.

"Chelle, was all this really necessary? You know I won't hurt you.

If that was my intention, I could have done it a million times over." The smirk on his face is far from reassuring.

"If that's the case, why didn't you tell me from the beginning who you really are?" I'm bouncing from one foot to the other, feeling the adrenaline surge through my body.

"Get back in the car and let's finish talking. I promise I won't hurt you." He opens the door for me, and I see Agosto sitting there smiling. He outstretches his hand. I know I've got no choice. Putting my hesitation aside, I climb into the limo, praying I'm doing the right thing.

"Welcome back, Michelina. Here is a fresh whiskey." He passes me a glass I decline, needing to keep a clear head and pull a bottle of water out of the cabinet in front of me.

"Agosto, I'll be honest with you; I'm sure by now you've figured out I have some of Carmine's journals, but that's all I have. Honestly, I'm not ready to part with them. You need to understand. My family kept everything from me. Reading Carmine's private thoughts are the only window into my family's past. You can't expect me to just give them to you." I bite the inside of my cheek, trying to focus on the pain and not the lie.

"You must understand the danger that comes with anything involving my brother is huge. The urge you have to know more might be the very thing that gets you killed. I don't think I could live with that. If anything happened to you, it would be the nail in Viviana's casket." His voice is suddenly hard and laced with a coldness I don't remember hearing it earlier.

"That might be so, but I think we are at a stalemate. I will not give in to your demands." He double taps on the privacy glass and, without a word, the car moves. My heart is in my throat and my palms begin to sweat.

"You look alarmed. I can assure you that you are safe with me."

"Where are you taking me?" my voice barely above a whisper.

"Home. Let me clarify that. I'm taking you to my home. You will be safe there and it will give us a chance to get to know each other."

"Luca—I mean—Matteo already searched mine and my mom's. They found nothing."

"Going back to my house has nothing to do with finding the books. I'm an old man and I'm tired. I thought it would be a good time for you to meet the rest of your family. You are not alone anymore, Michelina."

His words tear at my heart. I've been feeling so alone. How could he know? "Can I ask you a few questions?"

"Of course. I will do my best to answer them."

"Why did you say I nostri figli, essendo sei piedi sotto terra, livellano il campo di gioco to Carmine?" His face pales at this question. He gets a faraway look and I wish I knew him better, so I could tell if this was normal or if I hit a nerve.

"How much do you know about that time in our lives?"

"Probably not as much as you think. I know the death of a child is devastating for everyone." He draws in a deep, harsh breath. Slowly exhaling as his eyes meet mine.

"You say you want answers, but are you sure you can handle them? This life might seem fascinating when you're on the outside looking in, however, living it day-to-day can kill you. Why do you think you don't see many people my age in the business?"

"Answering a question with a question is a diversion. Please remember I'm a high school teacher who has seen a lot. I'm not that easily scared away. You want me to trust you, well, you need to offer me the same respect and trust me. So, how about you answer my question? Why did you say that?"

"Carmine was responsible for my son Salvatore's death. He swore on our mother's grave that he wasn't, however, there was too much proof and it was all directed at him."

"What if he was telling you the truth? What if the information they gave you was to drive a wedge between the two of you?"

"What you don't understand, Michelina, is there was already a wedge between us from our childhood. Carmine was a smooth-talking liar. He knew about the hit on my son and never warned me. He was just as guilty as the bastard that did the deed. After that, all bets were off."

"If he knew, I can't imagine he wouldn't tell you what was going on, or at least warn you."

"You are looking at this through the eyes of a granddaughter who wants to believe only the good things about her grandfather. No one was perfect, least of all Carmine. We were both trying to climb the ladder and stay alive. Instead of being a brother and a friend, he undermined everything I was doing. If you are not careful, Michelina, you are going to get yourself killed. Is he worth falling on your sword for?"

Right now, I have a need for information, not just to keep me alive, but to find out more about any siblings I might have. Agosto is the only one with all the answers. With an empty feeling in the pit of my stomach, I find the courage to ask him the one question I really need him to be truthful with me about. "I have a question for you." He smirks as if he knows what's coming. Hell, maybe he does. "Do you know how many siblings I have and where they are?" At that moment, the car comes to a stop and the door opens.

"Let's talk inside over an espresso." He exits the car and a man I've never seen before is offering me his hand. *Where the hell is Matteo?* I swat it away and glare at him as I get out. The smirk on his face does not go unnoticed.

"Agosto, where is Matteo? He was driving when we were at the church."

"I have kept his real identity secret, even from his brothers. When this is over, I will bring him home where he belongs."

While I'm following him, I take in my surroundings. They built the house on the side of a mountain. It is understated elegance. "Do you live here by yourself?" He opens ornate iron gates that lead to a beautiful courtyard filled with many beautiful flowers and cacti. "Did you do all this yourself?" I ask in amazement.

"Yes, well, with the help of my gardener, Joseph. He knows what I like and finds it for me. The Arizona desert is not kind. Come inside where it is cooler."

I follow him through the massive double doors. The first thing that hits me is the view. No matter where I look, there are mountains and desert painted sky. I want to say crime pays very well, instead I opt for, "You have a beautiful home, Agosto."

"Let's take our coffee out back by the pool. It's turning into such a beautiful night."

He leads me through the house and out back where there is an amazing negative edge pool. It looks like it's falling off of a mountain. I lean over and stretch to see where it goes, and I hear Agosto laugh.

"You won't fall. I laugh, Michelina, because everyone that comes here for the first time does the same thing. Come sit with me."

When I turn around, they already set the coffee up for us. How the hell did it just appear? He pours us each a glass of Sambuca and drops three coffee beans in it. He passes me a glass, holds up his glass and says, "Health, wealth, and happiness."

"I always thought that was only in the movies."

"Traditions sometimes get played out in the movies. However, most of the time, they don't get the true meaning. Some things cannot be taught with words. It's feelings that get lost along the way. Salute." He holds his glass out in front of him and swirls the liquid. The three beans swirling around are mesmerizing. My grip on my glass gets tighter and, for a moment, I want to do the same thing, but the beans would probably fly right out of my glass. I take a sip and wrinkle my nose, keeping my thoughts to myself. I glance at Agosto to find him smiling.

"So, you want information from me about any siblings you have? What makes you think you have any?"

"I told you I have Carmine's journals. He mentions a half-brother. After reading what he thought about my father, it made me wonder." He just slowly sips his drink before he pours what's left in his espresso.

"You have a half-brother: Nick Jr. And a half sister: Gemma. Nick is in the business. At one point, he set out to kill Carmine, but he was only a boy and didn't think it through. In a moment of weakness, Carmine let the boy go. He lives in Brooklyn and runs his own crew. He does well for himself, even though he never got to avenge his father's death. Gemma lives in Scottsdale. She is a very talented sculptor. I have a few of her pieces here. She is also under my protection. Michelina, the more you dig into his journals, the more trouble you are in. Do you understand what I'm telling you?"

The news is overwhelming. I really thought what Carmine wrote was just the ramblings of an old man. "I get it, but I can't stop reading them, even if it means I'm going to, as you say, fall on my sword. Did Carmine have any other children that I don't know about?"

"No. Carmine was a bastard, but he never stepped out on Viviana."

When he talks about my grandma, his entire demeanor changes. "You sound like you love my grandma."

"What if I do? It's too late now. Carmine got to her first. That ship sailed a long time ago. Now I watch over her and make sure she is safe and comfortable. When you get older, life changes. You realize love comes in many forms. The lust from our youth is gone, and that's when we realize what true love is." He finishes his coffee and gets a melancholy look. After this conversation, I can't picture him as a cold-blooded killer. He seems like a sweet old man. There is a knock on the door before the sliders open. Two men come in and I literately lose my breath. Dark hair with chiseled good looks. All I can picture is my best friend Jessica drooling and describing their rock-hard bodies in *great* detail, like she did with Luca. The cousin I kissed ... the same man I found myself attracted to.

"Michelina, I would like to introduce you to my sons: Gianni and Geno."

Quickly, I stand up and offer my hand out to shake. They take turns pulling me in for a hug.

"We've heard a lot about you. Happy to finally meet you," Gianni states.

"Thank you. Nice to meet you both. Will you be joining us for coffee?" I ask, like I'm the hostess here.

"No, Geno and I have some stuff to take care of. We didn't want to leave without meeting you. We look forward to getting to know you."

They each hug me again before they head out. I'm left standing there speechless.

"Michelina, come with me for a walk. I want to show you something." Agosto stands up, takes my hand, and leads me through a wrought-iron gate. He says nothing as we make our way to a shady bench. He sits and waves his hand for me to do the same. I don't know why he brought me here. He's quiet and I feel out of place.

"This is my cacti garden. I have feeders set up in different areas. Every day, I sit here and watch the quail. If you sit here and remain really quiet, they will come to the feeders. They are so used to me now that some of them come right to my feet."

"My mom has—I mean—had them at her house."

"Michelina, people can learn a lot from them. They are loyal and have one mate for life."

"I have so many questions for you," I blurt out. This all just seems surreal, like I'm in a weird dream. I feel like I need to get my answers before I wake up.

"Of course, you do, but are you sure you really want to know everything?"

I sit quietly for a bit, thinking about all the unknown that has been thrown at me in such a short time. The quail comes around him as he tosses some seed. He offers me some. I look at him and realize I walked through this door and there is no going back. No matter what happens, I am ready for it all.

"Agosto, I was born into this mess. For me it was not a choice. That being said, I feel like I can't walk away from this. Therefore, I'm ready to learn everything." We both sit quietly, watching the quail peck at the food. I finally made a decision, on my own, that I'm at peace with.

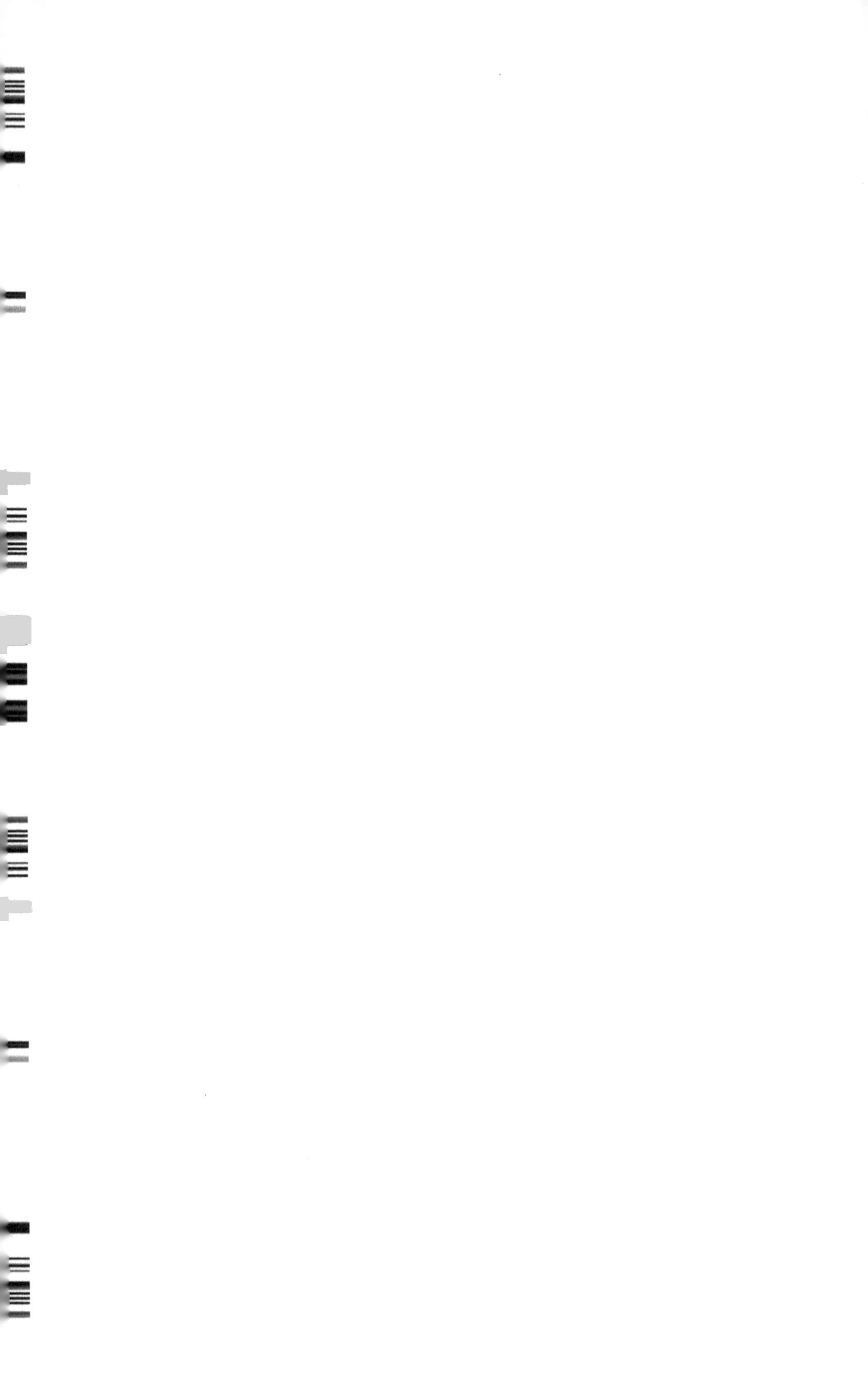

DANGEROUS
PURSUIT

This book is dedicated to everyone who never gave up.
Who never gave in to the pain and the sadness.

You are strong.
You are beautiful.
You are different.
You are proud.
You are brave.
You be you.

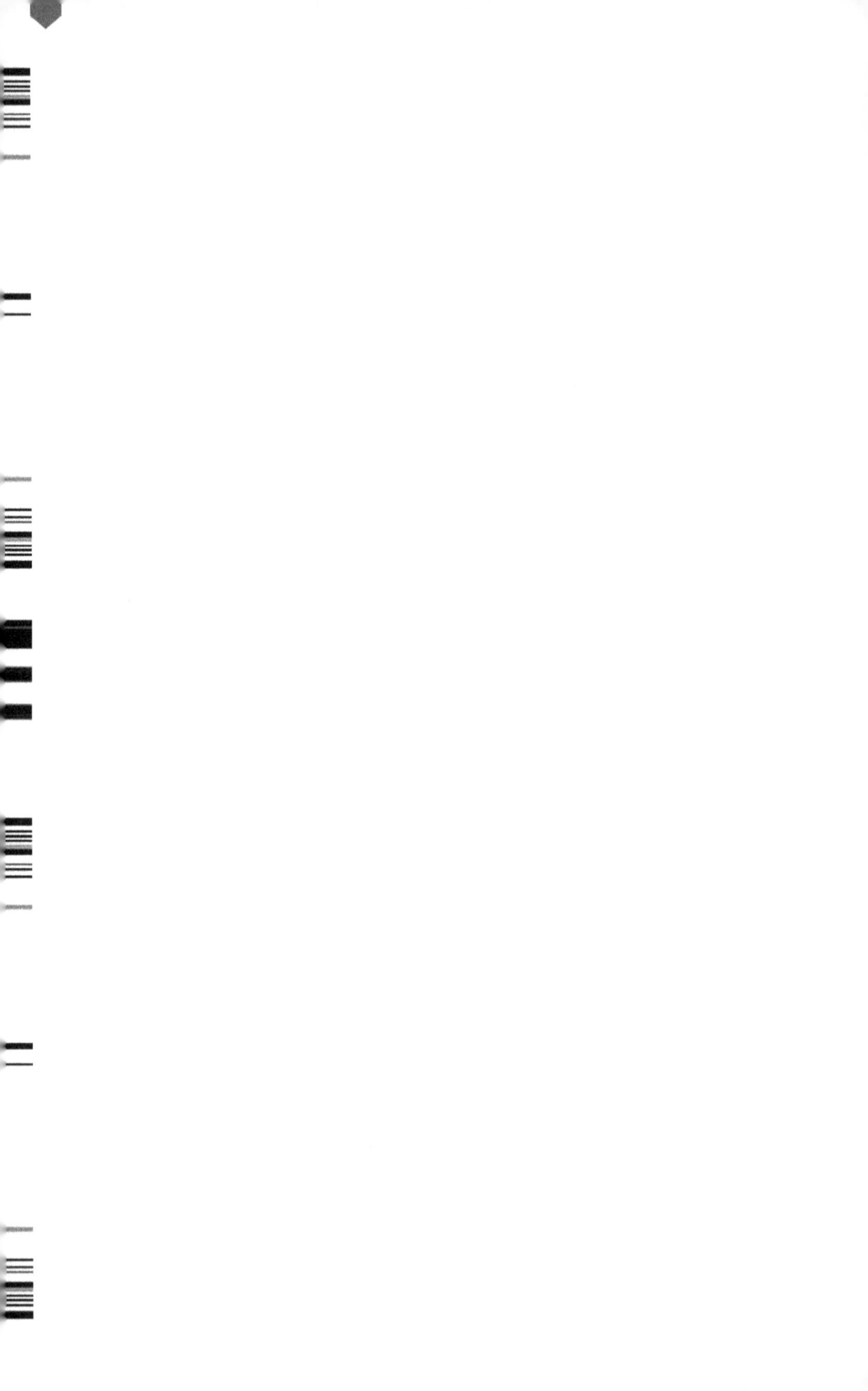

CHAPTER ONE

Agosto

AFTER TALKING WITH MICHELINA TODAY, I REALIZE SHE IS A lot like Viviana: strong willed and fiercely independent, yet she has a vulnerable side that she tries not to show. She thinks she is ready for everything. In reality, she might not be able to handle the truth about the family—her family. She did not choose this family, God did. I can only warn her so much. Some things in life must be learned by experiencing them.

Every Sunday I go to mass, after which I go to the cemetery to put flowers on the graves of my loved ones. When I'm done, I pick up two coffees and go see Viviana. Some days her cognition is better than others. One of her caregivers would always let me know when Frances left, so I would not run into her. Not that it mattered to me, but I knew Frances wanted no part of the family. It's not Sunday yet, but with everything that happened today, I want to see for myself that she is okay.

The ride to Viviana's is quick, even with the stop to pick up pastries for the staff. My driver Fernando follows me in, his arms laden with pastry boxes from Viviana's favorite Italian bakery shop. I find Viviana alone in her room. Her face lights up when she sees the pastry box.

"One or two today, Agosto?" She smiles when I hold up two fingers before she can even finish asking.

"Viv, I really think they are making the Sfogliatella smaller every time I go pick them up." I set her coffee down and put her pastry on a plate for her. Every day I wish things could have been different. Now I settle for what I have with her in the present: a lifelong friendship and respect that can never be broken.

"Agosto, why are you here tonight? It's not Sunday already, is it?"

"With everything that has happened today, I thought you might need me." I shrug. She closes her eyes and a tear escapes that she quickly wipes away.

"What happened with Michelina today? She was scared but don't let her fool you; she is very tough."

"I took her back to my home and introduced her to her cousins. She was surprised," I fill her in. She becomes very quiet. Finally, she puts her coffee down and looks at me like she is searching for something.

"Did you tell her about Nick Jr. and Gemma?"

"She flat out asked me Viv; I had no choice. Besides, *she* told me about Junior. Apparently, it was in Carmine's journals. Personally, I wish you would have listened to me and burned them when you had the chance."

"That would have been best for you and even for Frances, but that would not have been the best thing for Michelina. I can sit with her all day long and tell her stories about Carmine. She would believe them, yet she would only hear my side of things. Giving her those books lets her learn about him in his own words." She picks at her pastry, letting me contemplate her words.

"We've all embellished our stories to make us sound like stand-up men. I'm sure Carmine did the same, so how much of the truth do you think she is getting?"

"She is a very smart girl. She takes nothing at face value. By the time she is done, I don't think she will be too happy with him. She will come to that conclusion on her own."

"I hope you're right."

"I usually am. Did you tell her about Matteo?" she asks. My jaw tightens at the mention of his name.

"I did if for no other reason than to show her I trust her."

"Give her time. You have to remember . . . so much was thrown at her. On top of that, my sweet Frances died right before her eyes. That is something she will never forget." She closes her eyes, and the tears fall. I get up, lean in and kiss her cheek. She says nothing as I leave the room. I pray that losing another child doesn't push her permanently into the dark corners of her mind.

Michelina

Luca took me home and Cody was waiting for him. I went inside, basically ignoring both of them, however, I could hear Cody screaming at Luca for ditching him. I'm not sure what he told him to calm him down, but it worked. When I pull my phone out of my purse to call Jessica, I realize it's been on silent all day. There are numerous text messages and voicemails from Jess. I'm not sure what I'm going to tell her, but I really need to talk to her. I'm about to call her but she beats me to it.

"Hey, before you go all postal on me, I left to take Grandma home. As you can imagine, the day was too much for her. Thank you for covering for me with everyone."

"Chelle, what the hell is going on? I know you're upset about your mom but there is more to it than that."

I'm shaking and crying. The words are not coming. "I'm sorry, I'm a blubbering idiot. I need you, Jess."

"I'm on my way right now. Don't do anything stupid. I'll stay on the phone with you till I get there."

"No, I rather you concentrate on driving. I'm okay, just get here." I hang up and stare at my closet, wondering if there are more answers behind that door or more questions? Is my need to know greater than the pain of what I'm finding out? I wipe away my tears and head downstairs to let the guys know that Jess is on her way. They are both in the living room, messing around on their phones. No one looks up or acknowledges me.

"Jess should be here any minute." Still nothing. "Hello, are either of you even listening to me?"

Luca slips his phone into his pocket. "Heard you; Jessica is on her way. We will be down here if you need anything. I hope you don't mind but we are starving. I'm going to cook for all of us. I'll make sure I make enough for four."

"I have food that you can cook?" I'm shocked, knowing I hardly ever go food shopping.

Cody finally puts his phone away, gets up and heads into the kitchen. "Honestly, Chelle, I figured you didn't have time to get food in the house so after the service, I went to Sprouts. It's only a mile up the road from here. I know you went with Luca to take your grandma home. I didn't think you were going to be gone that long."

I look over to Luca and quickly look away. "Thank you, Cody. Let me know what I owe you."

"Not a big deal, you've had enough to deal with today."

There's a knock on the door and Cody steps in front of me. He checks the peephole and lets Jess in. I'm trying to hold back the tears as she wraps her arms around me. "Come on, Chelle, let's go upstairs."

CHAPTER TWO

Michelina

M Y HEART IS TELLING ME TO PROTECT JESS, NO MATTER WHAT. However, my head is telling me to let her know what I've gotten myself into by no choice of my own. We sit on the edge of the bed, and she takes hold of my hand.

"Chelle, you know you can tell me anything. I will protect you and keep your secrets—always."

"I don't want to put you in danger, Jess. Look what happened to my mom. There is a lot you don't know." She shakes her head and squeezes my hand even tighter.

"You are my best friend. Chelle, my ride or die, so maybe you should put all the shit aside and let me help you."

I get up and pull her with me. "It's more like a show and tell." We head into my closet, and I open the secret door. Her eyes are like saucers when she sees the room behind the wall and all the boxes of books.

"Chelle, what is all that? Why do you have it hidden in this secret room? I have so many more questions." In her excitement, her voice rises, and I have to shush her.

"Jess, no one knows about this, well . . . almost no one. They are my grandfather's personal journals. My mom was going to throw them away, but I took them instead. I thought how cool it would be to learn about my family's history directly from my grandfather's thoughts."

"Okay, so why all the cloak and dagger stuff?"

"Let me get my laptop and I'll show you." When I go back into my room, I double check that the door is locked. On top of everything else, I can add paranoia to my resume. Although, I have good reason to be. I grab my computer and go back into the closet. Jess has the journal marked number one open. She must be very engrossed in what she's reading because I startle her when I touch her shoulder. "Are you okay?"

"I don't know. The little I've read makes me think he was not a very nice man."

"Wait, it gets worse." I pull up his profile on the internet and pass my computer to her. As she is reading, her mouth falls open.

"He was a killer?!"

"Wait, Jess, there's more." I open Agosto's page and turn the computer back toward her. She reads it but then slams the laptop closed.

"You are nothing like these people. Are you sure about all of this? I have so many questions."

"I'm sure you do. Let me start with this tidbit—the bomb that killed mom was meant for me." I take a deep breath before I continue while fighting to hold back the tears.

"So that's why you have the FBI living with you. Do they know who did it?"

"That's just it, there are so many people that it could be, they can't even narrow it down!"

"Is the answer in one of these boxes?" She waves her hand around them to stress her point.

"No, these are just his personal journals. What everyone is looking for are Carmine's black books. He kept records of every mob transaction. He kept account numbers and passwords for all the money he laundered. There is also blackmail material about some very influential people."

"So, if these are not the books, then why target you?"

"Because they think I know where they are." I take a moment and close my eyes. It's now or never to tell her everything. "Before you ask, I have to tell you that knowing all of this could get you killed. Are you sure you want to know?"

"Like I said, Chelle, you're my ride or die. Best friend and teaching partner. We walk this walk together."

"I don't know what I ever did to deserve a friend like you." I quickly pull her in for a hug. "I have everything hidden away. The night my mom died, I think she was going to tell me everything, but she never got a chance." My tears start again, and I can't stop them. The grieving process is strange. There are moments when I can think about my mom and remember how much her laughter could fill a room. Then I remember she's gone forever, and the damn explodes. How will I ever survive this?

"So now what?"

"For now, I continue to read the journals and figure out this man. Then maybe I'll know what my next step should be."

"Pass me the ones you've already read so I can get up to speed while you continue reading. If anything jumps out at me, I'll make notes." I pass her the stack. She goes back to book one, where it all began. I pick up where I left off, the realization that I have siblings.

Carmine

Today, Agosto came sniffing around Viviana. Does he think I don't know that he's always been in love with her? Why is it that the losers in the world try to get to the women in my life? When I asked Viviana what he wanted, she said nothing and waved me off. I said, "I know he's sniffing around here because he wants to be with you. Go ahead, Viviana, go be with him, but if you do, it will brand you a whore just like your daughter."

"Carmine, you're being ridiculous. He lost his wife after a long illness.

He's your brother just seeking friendship." She continued to brush off the idea with me.

"This is what I mean, Viviana. What kind of man wants to be just friends with a woman? Don't answer, I'll tell you. Agosto is nothing more than a pussy sniffing putz!"

"It's so nice to know that's what you think of me and your daughter." She got up and walked out, never saying another word to me on the subject.

I sit behind my desk and watch the birds that come every day to my feeder. One bird has a broken beak. I thought for sure it would die. In life, there is no mercy. However, today, another bird came to feed the bird with the broken beak. I don't know why my family has always had a fascination with birds. In Sicily, my father and grandfather raised homing pigeons that were used in World War II. When we moved to New York, most of our neighbors raced pigeons they kept on the rooftops. I always thought it was a strange hobby, but maybe it was a way for the men to get away from their wives. That is where I first learned about taking bets and keeping book.

As a young boy, I would follow my father everywhere. My brothers were always off playing, but not me. I needed to learn if I wanted to get anywhere in this new world we were living in.

I lost my train of thought. Butchie stopped by to bring me this week's collection, updates, and some sad news. Butchie's an enormous guy with hands the size of baseball gloves. He grew up working in his father's butcher shop, which is how he got his name. I'm not sure why, but all Italians have nicknames. Maybe it's from having so many kids they can't keep track of who's who.

Anyway, today he had diamonds for me: harder to trace and easier to barter with. He seemed happy with this news as he poured them out of a black velvet pouch and onto my desk, but there seemed to be something else. There's always something else with him. So, I asked him.

"Before Nick died in prison, he had a few conjugal visits with the daughter of Jack Grassi, a capo in the Lucchese family out of the Bronx. He knocked her up and also has a daughter named Gemma," he informed me.

"You see, I called it, but I'm always the bad guy." I threw my hands up in the air. Butchie had a somber look on his face, so I asked him what gives.

"It was a difficult birth with a lot of complications. Carmine, the mom, didn't make it. Jack's family is raising her."

With this, I pulled out a bottle of bourbon, two glasses, and poured us each a neat one. This is never the kind of news to relish about.

The journal ends with heartbreaking news. When I reach for the next journal, Jess gasps and grabs my arm. "Chelle, you have a sibling."

"Two: a half brother and sister." I pass her the journal I just read. She looks at it like it will burst into flames.

"Are you going to look for them? I can help you."

"Agosto already knows where they are."

"How much does he know about them and about these books?" She waves her hand over the large stacks.

"He knows everything, Jess. When I took Grandma home today, he went with me. After we dropped her off, he took me to his house. I also met two cousins." Well three, if I count Luca, but we need to keep that secret.

"You're just telling me this now?"

"There is a lot more, but I'm overwhelmed right now. I think we need to finish these and then move on to the next step."

"We have a next step?" Jess asks with a quizzical brow arched above her left eye, which is something I've seen many times over the years.

"We will just as soon as I figure it out." I pick up the next book and start reading.

CHAPTER THREE

Viviana

I'M SO RESTLESS TONIGHT. I'VE HAD VERY LITTLE SLEEP SINCE Frances died. I'm worried about Michelina, not her safety but her emotional well-being. She is all I have left in the world. When Frances came to me to tell me Carmine was still alive, she thought she was telling me something that would break me.

When I met him, he was so different, or at least I thought so. According to Agosto, he was always a bastard. I believed there was a good person deep inside of him until the day he called Frances a whore and smacked me so hard I fell to the floor. That's when I saw the real Carmine, the pure evil Carmine. After that, there was no looking the other way anymore. When I close my eyes and think back to the day Frances came to me and told me everything she knew about her father, a father she thought was dead but, in fact, wasn't. I feel the bile rise in my throat. Why would any parent do that to his child? Although I think deep down inside, I knew he wasn't dead. Let's be realistic, I don't think the devil himself wanted Carmine. The scene plays out like a movie reel in my mind. A reel that is stuck on repeat.

I'm sitting on the sofa going through some old photographs. I want to make a scrapbook for Michelina. Frances walks in and sits next to me.

"Mom, I know you are making this book for Chelle, but I don't want her to think Carmine is a wonderful man. She already has him on a pedestal."

"Maybe you should share all of his journals with her. Let her make up her own mind."

"Mom, he's not dead. I saw him today—in the flesh. He's had all kinds of plastic surgery, but I knew it was him."

"I'm not surprised, Frances. Only the good die young. He'll probably out-live all of us. Did you confront him?" I'm not sure why I asked her. Frances is not one to sit idle when she wants answers.

"Of course, I did. At first, he laughed in my face. After that, he handed me a key and a piece of paper with a bank name on it. He told me whomever has this has the power. He said he did everything to protect his family. After he left me standing in the parking lot, I went to the bank. Sure enough, there was a safe deposit box with my name on it. I'm not sure how he did it, but he was always resourceful. After reading his journals and realizing what was in the safe deposit box, I concluded Carmine was always out to protect himself; family be damned."

"What are you going to do with all the stuff he left you?"

"Did you know what was in the box, Mom?"

"Yes, I did. I watched Carmine over the years accumulating all his 'insurance,' as he liked to call it."

"For now, I moved everything to another bank. I'll take Chelle with me and have her added to the box. I don't know what to do with all of it."

"Keeping it will be a double-edged sword. It's your insurance to keep you and Michelina safe. However, if someone wants it, which I'm sure there are plenty who do, it will put you and Michelina in danger. You could turn every-thing over to Agosto. He will keep you safe."

"How do you know that? Have you been in contact with him?"

"I've never stopped, Frances. When I realized how jealous Carmine was of him, I decided to keep my relationship with Agosto to myself. I'm sure your father knew, but he did nothing about it." I left it at that. Only she could

decide what she wanted to do about the stuff she had hidden. Now she is dead, and without warning, everything has landed in Michelina's lap. I wish Frances would have told her my sweet Michelina the truth. I was so proud of her when she told me she wanted to teach high school science. She said she wanted to change the world even if it was just her little corner of it. Frances, on the other hand, wanted her to be an engineer. She told her being a teacher in today's world is a very dangerous profession. In the end, everyone follows their own path in life.

The ringing phone snaps me out of my daydream. I walk over to the nightstand to pick it up. The screen says caller unknown. "Hello."

At first, I hear nothing. I'm about to hang up when I hear a very deep voice. "Your granddaughter is not listening to me. She is not safe. Tell her to give me all of Carmine's books. Before you say you do not know what I'm talking about, think about what I did to your beloved Frances. I'll be in touch."

My body begins to shake uncontrollably. "No!" I yell out and try to catch my breath. I grab the photo that's always on my night table. It's a photo of Frances, Michelina, and me. I clutch it to my chest. The room begins to spin, and my world goes black as I hit the floor.

Michelina

There are only four more journals before I reach the end. Sadly, I don't want it to be the end. I want to know it all—no—I *need* to know it all. Knowing will be the thing that keeps me alive. When I open the next journal, two photographs fall out. One is a black-and-white photo of a family gathered around a kitchen table. They are laughing and seem so happy. When I turn it around, it lists all the people in the photo. It's Carmine's brothers and surprisingly, his sister. His parents and grandparents. So much has happened to this family, but this right here is from a happier time. The other photo is a color photo of Carmine with all of his children. My mom was so young. When I turn it around, it says it was

Easter Sunday 1970. I run my finger over the photo. My mom isn't smiling. Actually, no one is, well, except for Carmine. I flip open the journal and it picks up where the last one left off.

Today, as I look at old pictures and reflect on my life, I realize life isn't always what we think it will be. I thought I was building an empire to leave for my sons. However, realistically everything will land in Frances's lap. Viviana always treated Frances like she was a fragile doll. She is anything but fragile. Out of all my children, she is the one who is most like me. Why couldn't she be accepting of my life? I admire the relationship Sammy The Bull has with his daughter. Why can't Frances be like that? She should embrace the lifestyle she was born into, a lifestyle I worked so hard to give her. In the end, I will leave her everything I've accumulated over the years. I would rather leave it all to Michelina, but Frances has built a protective wall around the child.

Prior to my first meeting with the FBI, I wanted to put some things in place to keep what's left of my family safe. Apparently, Michelina carpools to work. This was not her week to drive. Once she was out of sight, I had one of my guys take her car and reinforce the undercarriage with steel. She will never know anything was done to her car. Doing this makes me feel like I've kept her safe. Unfortunately, I can't get near Frances's car. For now, I'm off to meet with the FBI and set some ground rules.

The realization hits me hard that, if he would have been able to do to my mom's car what he had done to mine, Mom would still be alive.

CHAPTER FOUR

Michelina

MY PHONE RINGS. I GRAB IT AND SEE THAT IT'S THE NURSING home calling.

"Hello."

"Hi, I'm looking for Michelina Ciccone."

"This is her. Is everything okay with my grandma?"

"This is Cathy, your grandmother's nurse. She had a fall tonight. She was by herself and unable to remember how she fell. Her vitals are stable though, and there is no indication that she has hit her head or broken anything. We did alert her doctor. Right now, she is a little agitated. We gave her a prn to help with that. However, she is asking for you. Is there any way you could stop by today?" she asks.

"I'm on my way," I answer quickly. Jess was already packing up the books and putting them away while I was receiving the information about the fall. I take the two pictures I found and put them in my pocket. I'm not sure why I feel I need to, but I do.

"I'll drive you, unless your bodyguards, for lack of a better term, have to drive you."

I grab my jacket, open the door, and find Luca standing there. "Are you trying to give me a heart attack?"

"No, the agent at your grandmother's just called to let me know she fell. I came up here to get you. Cody is already in the car." He looks at me, then at Jess and back at me. Why can't he just ask whatever he wants to ask?

"Yes, Jessica is coming with us. She happens to be great with Grandma." When I pull the door closed, he shrugs and steps to the side to let us pass. They already searched the room and found nothing. Although I wouldn't be surprised if he has someone come over to search again while we're gone.

The ride to the assisted living is in total silence. In my mind, I keep seeing the people in the photographs. My mom, so young and so care-free. Grandma looks different—happy , but then again, the picture is before any of her children died. The car finally comes to a stop, and Jess and I hit the ground running. Luca stays close behind us. We get to her room and step inside. That's when I see him sitting in the corner, his hat in his hand. . . Agosto.

"Why are you here?" I whisper through gritted teeth.

"I told you Viviana and I have a mutual respect; a friendship that has stood the test of time. The staff tells me if anything happens or if she needs anything. Right now, the doctor has her sedated. She received a phone call tonight and then passed out. Geno is working on figuring out who called her."

I look back and see that Jess is just outside the door with Luca. "You need to know I'm not alone here. If you have a problem with that, then you should leave now. If you need me to, I can distract Jessica while you slip out of the room." In the dim lighting, I can still see a small smile on his face.

"Michelina, you are very kind to an old man, but there is no rea-son for me to slink away into the night. As I said, Viviana is my oldest and dearest friend. If anyone else has a problem with that, they can slink away into the night."

"I'm sorry. I meant you no disrespect. I just don't want any drama. Do you know if she broke anything?" Before he can answer, Jess steps into the room with a nurse that looks familiar. Her name tag says *Cathy*. It hits me; she is the nurse mom always called *chiacchierona Cathy*, which in English means chatterbox. My mom had nicknames for all the staff. She would teach them to Grandma. Mom thought it helped her to remember names. I fight the wave of grief I feel washing over me.

"Hi, Ms. Ciccone. I'm Cathy, the one who called you. She was settled in for the night when she got a phone call. I don't know what was said, but she yelled *"no,"* and fell to the floor clutching the photo that she keeps next to her bed. I was outside her room with the med tech. It was slow, so I was helping her distribute the nightly meds. I got to her quickly." Now I know why she is chiacchierona Cathy. I want to yell at her to just get to the point.

"So, did she break anything?"

"Oh, no sorry, she broke nothing. The doctor didn't attribute it to the phone call. He thought it was from the anxiety she has been through the past few days. He gave her something for that and wants her to rest. Can I bring anyone something to drink? She's probably going to be sleeping through the night, but you are always welcome to stay."

"No thank you. We'll only be about five more minutes. Thank you." I smile. She nods her head and reminds me to call her if I need anything before she leaves.

"Jessica, on second thought, I am going to stay the night. Luca, can you take her home?"

"No, I'm staying with you. I can have Cody take her home." He looks at Agosto and then quickly looks away. Agosto gets up, walks up to Jessica, and introduces himself. I'm praying she doesn't lose her shit since she was just reading about him in Carmine's journals.

"Jessica, I'm leaving now. It seems Viviana is in expert hands. I can drop you and Cody off." Agosto offers her his arm like a gentleman caller and not the cold-blooded killer he is. How is it that I'm thinking all of this is okay?

"Chelle, I'll go back to your place and wait for you. I'll get back to that project for class that we were working on." One thing about Jess: she is quick with the bullshit, and sounds so convincing, I really believe we are working on a project. I pass her my house key and watch them leave together. I must really be nuts to think it's okay. Luca's hand rests on the small of my back, which takes my mind off Jessica walking down the hall with Agosto.

"Chelle, she is safe with him, I promise. I don't believe what the doctor said about anxiety. Whomever called her really spooked her, don't you agree?" I'm chewing on my bottom lip, a habit I broke long ago is back with a vengeance. Luca gently strokes my face. His touch stops my chewing. He leans his face closer to mine, and I realize he's about to kiss me. I quickly back up and his hand falls to his side.

"Luca, you better sit down." He looks apprehensive but finally gives in. I close the door and pull a chair close to him. "Since the night of my mom's death, I've been getting those same phone calls." His face gets flushed, and I swear I can see the vein in his neck pulsing.

"You're just telling me this now?! Do you know who it is? What did the person say?"

"Peppering me with questions is not helping the situation. It's a man. I can't tell much from his voice, except I don't believe he's an older man, like a senior citizen. Every night, they became more intense. Like everyone else, he wants the books. He said you can't protect me and that only he can. He used the bomb as an example. I think he might have been the one to plant it." He gets up, laces his fingers behind his head, and begins pacing. I'm waiting for the onslaught of questions, but they never come.

"Chelle, we need to tell Agosto all of this. He needs to know when the calls came in and what was said. He will give it all to Geno, and maybe we can get to the bottom of this."

"What if Agosto is the one behind all of this? I know he's your father, a father that went to extremes to keep you safe, but that doesn't take away the fact that he is a killer."

"If you really thought that you wouldn't have sent your best friend off into the night with him. You also wouldn't allow him anywhere near your grandmother."

Grandma stirs. Her eyes flutter open. She takes my hand and looks from me to Luca. She says something, but I can't hear her. I move in closer. "Grandma, you're safe," I whisper.

"Michelina, you can trust Agosto." She closes her eyes and is asleep again.

There is a tap on the door before it opens. Cathy pops her head in to check again if we need anything. Trying to stifle my yawn is impossible as I tell her we're fine. I sit back down in Grandma's recliner chair next to her bed and take her hand in mine. Luca heads over to her couch and stretches out on it. I say a silent prayer for everyone's safety before I drift off to sleep.

CHAPTER FIVE

Jessica

CHELLE IS MY OLDEST AND DEAREST FRIEND. I WOULD DO anything for her, which includes sitting in the back seat with an old man who is a cold-blooded killer. The scary part is, I didn't think twice when he offered to take me home. It's only now that I'm questioning my decision. I sneak a quick peek at him, and he is staring at me with a smile on his face that makes him look so innocent, so kind. However, I know otherwise.

"Jessica, is there something you want to ask me?"

It's rude to say nothing, but I don't know what to say. "Look, I'll get right to the point. I know who you are. I know about your brother, Chelle's grandfather."

"I thought you were going to get right to the point?" He smiled as if he could read my thoughts.

"I'm trying to do just that. Chelle just lost her mom. Her emotions are raw. So much is being thrown at her. Now she is worried about her grandmother. She found out a lot of bad crap about her family and, on top of that, someone is trying to kill her. I know Chelle thinks she can handle all of this, but I'm here to tell you she can't. I know nothing about all this gangster crap. What I do know is I want this to end now before she gets hurt." His smile is gone, and his face is void of any emotion.

"Jessica, first, '*Gangster crap*' is just downright rude. Michelina didn't ask to be born into this family. However, at the end of the day, there are still choices to be made—tough ones. I'm trying to make these choices easier for her and Viviana. I can assure you I only have Michelina's best interest at heart. It comes down to trust. I've given her an olive branch and I expect the same from her. If you really are her friend, you will help her with the tough decisions that lie ahead of her. You will have to support her choices even if you don't agree with them. I can assure you this is not a game."

"I'm sorry, I didn't mean to be rude. There is so much to handle, and we are all overwhelmed."

"That's why I told Viviana that I would help her granddaughter any way I can. I had to trust Michelina with some very important information. Information that could get someone I love very much killed."

"Why would you do that? You don't even know Chelle. Don't you think whatever it is you told her is putting even more pressure on her?" I realize I've raised my voice, which could be another reason for him to think I'm rude.

"I had to show her I trust her, and she can trust me. Information in the right hands can be a powerful tool."

"Honestly, what's going to happen next to Chelle?"

He opens the bar and pours each of us a drink. "Do you really want me to be honest with you?"

"You don't know me. I'm not Willy Wonka; I don't sugarcoat anything. I expect the same in return." He takes a sip of his drink and smiles.

"Sadly, she can never go back to her previous life as a teacher. There is too much danger around her. Before Carmine died, his word was gold. He was destined to rise above all the families. Now Michelina holds that power and everyone who wants it will be gunning for her. As her best friend, you need to encourage her to accept the protection I'm offering her."

"I can't tell Chelle what to do. She will forge her own path in life. She's not a follower. However, knowing Chelle, she will learn from the mistakes of others and try not to make the same ones."

"That's all we can ask for. In the meantime, I would like to put some protection on you."

"I don't think that's really necessary."

"That's what Frances thought."

The car comes to a stop and Cody opens the back door for me. "Thank you, Agosto, I appreciate your honesty." Cody offers me a hand as I get out of the car. I watch it disappear, knowing there are a lot of tough decisions that are going to have to be made, just not tonight.

Cody and I head into the house. He does a walk through to make sure everything is okay. Agosto's words replay in my head: *Chelle can never go back to her old life as a teacher again.* I grab two bottles of iced tea from the fridge and pass one to Cody. I motion for him to sit with me in the living room.

"Jessica, why do I feel like I'm about to be interrogated?"

"You're not. I just want some advice. You've been around these types of people, whereas I haven't. It seems logical to ask you."

"I'll do my best. What do you want to know?"

"Is Chelle safe? Is someone going to murder her like they did her mom?" He nearly chokes on his tea.

"I'm not at liberty to disclose much, however, with Luca watching her every move, she is safe for now. To what extent, I don't know. Maybe this will clear it up for you. Frances thought she was safe. Women and children were always off limits. That gave them more freedom than the men. However, that is old-school thinking. Luca tried to get through to Frances on this, but she wouldn't listen to him. The fresh blood in the organization doesn't care about traditions or honor. It's all about drugs and sex. That's where the money is."

"So, in reality, she's not safe. What about me? Agosto wants to put protection on me. Is that really necessary?"

"If Chelle has what everyone thinks she has, then no. She is not safe, and neither are you."

I can feel the blood drain from my face. "What if she got rid of whatever everyone thinks she has, would she be safe then?"

"The short answer is no, Jessica; the damage is done. Carmine saw to that when he let it be known what he had hidden away. You can't put Pandora's evils back in the box."

"It sounds like Carmine was a very selfish man."

"It's not for me to judge. All I can do is tell you the facts. You need to decide what you are willing to live with on your own." He gets up and tosses his empty bottle into the recycle bin. He double checks the lock on the door.

"Thank you, Cody, for your honesty. I'm calling it a night." He gives me a quick nod before pulling a magazine out of his duffle bag that was next to the sofa. I wave as I head upstairs. Now, more than ever, I'm intent on finding out everything I can about Carmine and Agosto.

CHAPTER SIX

Luca

CHELLE RECLINES BACK COMFORTABLY IN HER GRANDMOTHER'S chair next to her bed. She takes her hand in hers and she keeps stroking it. The simple movement is mesmerizing, and soon she falls asleep. When I look at her, I don't see a woman who is harboring secrets. I see a beautiful lady trying to make sense of all that has been thrown at her. My training tells me I'm not supposed to feel anything. However, it's not that easy. How do you shut off these feelings? For fuck's sake, she's, my cousin. I have a mantra I keep repeating in my head. *"She's your cousin, she's in danger, and everyone around her wants her dead. Stop thinking with your cock, Matteo. Protect her no matter what, even if she can't get out of her own way."* That's what I keep reminding myself. She stirs and her lips slightly part. I feel things I'm not supposed to. Why is this happening to me? The vibrating of my phone pulls my attention away from her. I pull it out of my pocket to see that it's Cody; perfect timing.

"Hey, is everything okay over there?" Is how I greet him.

"Yeah, Jessica is upstairs, and the house is secure. She asked me a bunch of questions, mainly if they are both safe."

"Did you reassure her?" I ask. Chelle stirs, so I step outside the room.

"Luca, I told her the cold hard truth: yes, they are in danger. That even if Chelle gave up the books, they would still be in danger. It's out in the world who Chelle is and, by association, who Jessica is, which put a target on her back, too."

"How did she take it?"

"Jessica is like a dog with a bone. I don't see her walking away from any of this, not without Chelle. You know and I know that's never going to happen. How is Viviana?"

"She is resting comfortably. Chelle is by her side. I'll check in later but call me if you need me." I hang up and look inside the room. Both of them are still asleep. One more call to make before the day starts. Of course, he picks up on the first ring, he always does and never says hello.

"Is everything okay?"

"Dad, everything is status quo, which is far from okay. What happened when you took Jessica home?"

"She is a tough lady, for sure. Has Viviana woken up yet?"

"Not yet. It's still early, but I'm sure they will both be up soon. Did you talk to Geno yet?"

"It's way too early for him to be up and about. Did something else happen?" he asks. I can't hide anything from my father; he always knows when something's up. I hate delivering news over the phone, but today I have no choice.

"Yes, I spoke to Chelle last night. She's been getting the same phone calls. She felt like he could be the one who planted the bomb." I hear a bang and a low rumbling growl, which I know from experience is not good.

"She just told you this now?! Where the hell were you when all this was happening?"

"Look, I'm doing my job, which is keeping her alive and getting the books. I can't help it if she hides things from me. I can't be up her ass twenty-four-seven. I told her I would let you know and maybe Geno could look at her phone. It's worth a shot."

"Did she at least agree to that?"

"Yes, once Viviana gets up and Chelle sees everything is okay, I'll bring her by the house. Will that be all right?" It's a fine line I'm walking right now. My brothers don't know about my existence.

"No, I told you I'm not saying anything until we have secured the books. Honestly, I know Michelina has them in her possession, so as long as she does, your secret is safe. Once I have them, I will let your brothers know everything. Have Cody bring her here and maybe you can work on getting information out of Jessica." He hangs up before I can protest. I hate letting Chelle out of my sight, but I really need Geno to look at her phone. When I go back into the room, everyone is still asleep. I pull a chair in front of the door and try to close my eyes for a bit. Now if I can just get my brain to shut off.

Jessica

I've finally caught up to where Chelle is in Carmine's journals. My head is spinning from all the dark, evil stuff that was considered acceptable. What I really want to do is get Chelle and run as far away as we can. According to these journals, running is never a good idea. You can't run from the past. Everything eventually catches up to you. Chelle's alive today for two reasons: Carmine had her car reinforced with a steel plate and the bomber was an idiot. Chelle and Frances had the same car down to the color and year. One exception, Chelle has a sticker on her rear window that gets her into the school parking lot. One thing Mesa did to secure the schools is put gates up at all the school parking lot entrances. If the car doesn't have a sticker, it can't get past the gate. It wouldn't have taken a lot of research to figure that out. Carmine talks about Agosto like he is an idiot who couldn't find his way out of a paper bag, yet Carmine is dead and Agosto is not. I put everything away for now and head into the shower. I'm sure once Chelle talks to Grandma and sees she is okay, she will want to come home and get some rest.

Viviana

When I open my eyes, I find Michelina has a tight grip on my hand. She is sleeping so peacefully. This is probably the most rest she has had since Frances died. Sometimes, it's so hard to turn off my mind. In those times, I turn to prayer. Michelina would always tease me about my being able to whip out my rosary beads at the drop of a dime. It's those beads and my prayers that I find comfort in. I had to turn to something when we were living with Carmine, or I would have lost my mind. Michelina stirs as I incline my head so I can sit up. She slowly opens her eyes.

"Good morning, Michelina. When did you get here?"

"I got the phone call last night letting me know you fell. I dropped everything and came right over. How are you feeling?" she answers as she presses the button on the recliner to get herself in a seated position, as well.

"I'm sorry that they called you. I'm fine, nothing that a few aspirins can't fix."

"I know about the phone call. I've been getting them, too."

I try to keep my reaction at a minimum as I ask, "What did he say?"

"He kept warning me that I was next, and everyone was after Grandpa's black books. I shouldn't expect the FBI to protect me. Every time he called, he sounded more agitated."

"Why didn't you say anything about these calls?" She looks at me for a long moment before taking a deep breath. "It's okay, Michelina, you can tell me."

"Who was I going to tell—the FBI? We all know how well they protected Mom. Are you mad at me for hiding this?"

"I could never be mad at you. The FBI wanted to protect Frances; however, she never believed the threats were real."

"So, there were more threats?"

"Yes. I told Agosto when they first started happening. I'm not sure what he did, but they stopped for a while. They started again right before I moved in here."

"So, you knew about all the stuff that Grandpa had and the danger that went with it. How could you go along with any of this?" She pulls her hand from mine, and I feel a lump in my throat.

"Michelina, for years I watched Carmine collect stuff. It's not something I could talk to him about. When he hit me for protecting Frances, I learned to shut my mouth and bide my time. Was it the right thing to do? At the time, I thought so. I had no one to turn to. I'm an only child and by then my parents had passed. Agosto begged me to leave. He said he would protect me and, at one point, I really considered it, but I could never leave Frances behind."

"I'm sorry you felt so trapped," she says through tears that escape down her face. I try to wipe them away.

"Times were different then. You are looking at all of this with the eyes of the world today."

"So, what should I do? I have all the journals and, of course, everything else stashed safely away."

"Leave the stuff where it is. It's too dangerous to move anything. However, you can trust Agosto. I promise you he will always look after you. He trusted you with his secret, a secret that could get his son killed. That's not something to take that lightly."

"So, you know about that, too. Did my mom know?"

"Oh, heavens no. Until he told you, I was the only one who knew. We suspect Carmine knew and put it in one of his black books to blackmail Agosto with later, if he needed to. I don't think Matteo knows who told Carmine."

There is a knock on the door. The nurse comes in, followed by Luca. His smile is warm and reminds me of Agosto all those years ago.

"Michelina, I'm going to be fine. I think you need to go do

whatever you need to get all this resolved. I'll be right here waiting for you." She leans in and kisses my cheek.

"I love you, Grandma."

"Me too, Michelina." I watch her leave with Matteo. I reach into the pocket of my housecoat and pull out my rosary beads. This is where I find comfort.

CHAPTER SEVEN

Michelina

Everything Grandma told me is racing through my mind, trying to connect the dots with all my own memories. The line between my memories and Carmine's journals is getting blurry. On the ride back to my place, I opt to sit in the front seat next to Luca. Quickly I put on my sunglasses, so I'm able to look at him without him thinking I'm staring at him. I turn in my seat so I'm facing him. "I have questions and, frankly, I do not know when it will just be the two of us." He slowly smiles, never taking his eyes off the road.

"I don't know how much information you think I have. If anything, I think you know more than I do."

"You have to be honest." There's that smile again and, for the first time, I notice a dimple.

"I'm ready; you have twenty minutes before we get to your house."

"Do you have two dimples?" I blurt out. He throws his head back and laughs.

"You mean to tell me of all the questions you could ask me that's the first one you come up with? Yes, I have two and when I shave, I have a cleft chin. Do I get bonus points for that one?"

"No, you don't. This is really a two-part question. How long were you with Carmine? How do you think he found out who you really are?"

"I was alone with Carmine for two months. When he started getting plastic surgery, Cody came into the picture. As far as the second part of your question, very few people know who my dad really is. I have an idea how Carmine found out, but I haven't been able to prove it, yet."

"When you find out, will you kill him or her?" At this, he hits the brakes so hard the rear of the car fishtails.

"Chelle, I'm not a killer. That part of the family is left to Carmine and my dad. Look, I'm not proud of what he's done, but I have learned that if I want my family, they come with baggage, and I have to accept that." He begins driving again. We are lucky, at this early hour, the traffic is light.

"However true that is, it's still very sad. I guess I have to do the same thing. Who do you think is making these phone calls?" I inquire.

"If I had to bet, I would say your brother, Nick Jr. He runs a crew and would love to move up the ladder. Personally, I don't think he will get any further within the family."

"It sounds like you've met him, have you?"

"Yes, I have. He never made it out of high school. He relies on his crew for everything. They take advantage of him. He either doesn't know or doesn't care. If you're thinking you are going to have this wonderful family reunion, think again. That stuff is for made-for-TV- movies, not the real life." He is so cynical, but I say nothing.

"Is Jessica safe?" I carry on with my interrogation.

"She is only safe when she is with us. The people coming after you would probably use her as bait. Just like you were used for bait. Did Viviana say anything more about the phone call she got?" I feel a knot in my stomach over this question.

"She did, but nothing useful to figuring out who it is. The demands sounded the same. Chances are it's the same person."

He's tapping his thumb on the steering wheel and it's putting me in a trance. He pulls into the driveway, and I finally avert my eyes from the tapping.

"How do I protect her? Please don't say give them what they want, and they will go away. You and I both know that will never happen."

"We have options. I just need to think them through before we do anything. For now, we let Geno look into the phone calls and we stay in the house as much as possible."

"Do you think Grandma is safe?"

"Agosto cares deeply for Viviana. He will move Heaven and earth to protect her. When you're ready, Cody will run you over to Agosto's house to meet with Geno."

"Why aren't you taking me?"

"Agosto felt it would be best if Cody takes you."

"I'll go along with it for now, but I don't like it." I get out of the car, slam the door, and head into the house. Jess is in the kitchen, cooking and chatting away with Cody. The smell of bacon instantly reminds me I haven't eaten since yesterday afternoon.

"Jess, I'm starving, and it smells amazing." I sneak up behind her and snag a piece of bacon. She smacks my hand, and I feel like a little kid again.

"Breakfast will be ready in less than five minutes. Can you put the coffee into the carafe and put it on the table, please and thank you." She always tells her students please and thank you. She believes she might be able to instill some manners in even the worst students. I wash up and pour the coffee into the carafe and brew another pot. We all gather around the table and for a moment, however brief it may be, I feel like I've got my life back. As Jess says grace, a wave of *what the hell am I going to do now?* sweeps over me. I take some small breaths and try to push back against the wave.

"Jess, after breakfast, I need to take a quick shower and run an errand."

"Great, I'll go with you." I didn't have time to protest her decision. Luca's stare is so intense, I put my hands up as if to say I have no choice. I'm not sure he is buying it but maybe it will be a good thing.

"Excuse me, I need to make a phone call." I grab my phone and head out back for some privacy. Agosto answers on the first ring. He never says hello. I don't know why this bothers me, but it does.

"Agosto, I'm coming with my phone for Geno to look at, and I'll have Jessica with me. I know you wanted me to come with Cody, but that will not work. I won't leave Jessica behind. Hell, she is putting her life in danger because of my family. The least they can do is make her feel welcome."

"Are you done?"

"Yeah, I think that's everything."

"That's fine. Luca can stay outside with Cody. You will both be safe with me. I'll see you soon."

Just like that, he's gone. I head back inside just as Luca gets a text message. No doubt it's from Agosto. He says nothing, however, his jaw ticks and his cheeks are red. It's probably safe to say he is pissed off with the new plan.

"Jess, thank you so much for cooking. After breakfast, I'll head into the shower and then we can head out."

"I'm glad you're finally eating something. Where are we going?"

"Agosto's house." There is an awkward silence in the room. We all quietly go back to our food. The air is so thick you can cut it with a knife. Jessica drops her fork, hitting her plate with a bang that makes us all jump.

"Now that I have everyone's attention. Why are we going to Agosto's house?" Jessica calmly asks.

"His son is some sort of techie guru. He needs to look at my phone."

"What are you not telling me, Chelle?" Her voice has gone up quite a lot. Cody and Luca are sitting across from me. They put their forks down, look up at me. All eyes are on me now . . . *no pressure.*

"Okay, I've been getting phone calls similar to the ones Grandma is getting. Agosto wants to look into it, that's all. I'm going to jump in the shower now." I hurry upstairs before anyone can question me further.

CHAPTER EIGHT

Agosto

WHEN FRANCES CAME UP WITH THE IDEA TO MOVE VIVIANA into assisted living, I immediately vetoed it. I offered to have nurses on hand twenty-four-seven. She wanted no part of it. I dare not tell her I wanted to move Viviana in with me; she would have blown a gasket. Now Frances is gone, and Viviana's needs have been left to Michelina to figure out. I've thought about it, and I decided to talk to Michelina about moving Viviana in here. If she says yes, it's only one hurdle. I will have many others to clear, starting with my sons: Geno and Gianni. They know I'm very close to Viviana, but they have never questioned me about her. She has always been a love I can only have from afar. Our timing was never right, but that didn't mean we couldn't be friends.

I have kept so much from my boys, mainly for their protection. Early on Matteo wanted me to tell his brothers about his existence, I couldn't. I don't think I could go on living if I lost another child. Geno and Gianni is what kept me living after my wife and two children died. When Matteo's mom died of breast cancer, I thought it was time to bring him into the fold. Just then I got a note in the mail, putting me on notice about Matteo, *"It is only a matter of time until your bastard child will pay for your sins. They always do."* That one note sent me into a tailspin. Even though it wasn't signed, I blamed it on Carmine. With Matteo's mom dead, it was the perfect time for me to stage his death. After that, the rest was easy. I always wondered if Carmine wrote it in one of his books or his journal. Was he holding on to it, ready to use it as a weapon against me? The bigger question is: how did he find out? One way or another, I'm going to get to the bottom of this. I step outside to feed my quail. They help me clear my mind and organize my thoughts. I'm not out here for five minutes before Geno comes out to see me. He takes a seat on the bench next to me.

"Dad, I know you don't like to be bothered when you're out here, but I have some information for you. I was able to back trace the call that Viviana got. It came from back east. I'm trying to narrow it down now."

"I think it could be Nick Jr. or someone close to him. He is based out of Brooklyn, so maybe start there and work your way backwards. Apparently, Michelina has been getting the same menacing phone calls. She is coming by today with her phone, so maybe you can look at it. Oh, and Geno, if it is Nick, no one but me gets that information, understand?"

"Of course, Dad. Why did she wait until now to say something?"

"Geno, how the hell would I know? Today's generation marches to their own drummer. When she gets here, why don't you ask her? By the way, her friend Jessica will be with her," I drop that little bombshell. I knew the moment I met her, she was his type: strong, beautiful, and determined. If nothing else, today is going to be very interesting.

"I know you have a lot of security around Viviana, but maybe she needs something different."

"What would you suggest?" I'm surprised he has brought this up. None of my boys have ever said a word about her, at least not to me.

"Gianni and I were talking about it and what about turning the pool house into a place for her to live? She would be safe and would want for nothing. It would be another reason for Michelina to accept her family."

"I don't think using Viviana as a tool is going to go over well with Michelina."

"I didn't mean it like that, Dad. You know I would never even suggest such a thing. I just think it would be better for Viviana. I know you tried when Frances was alive, and she just about blew a gasket. Things are different now . . . you're different."

"I promise to think about it." It's all I can offer right now. He gets up and leaves me in peace with my quail.

Am I really that different? I don't think who I am on the inside has changed. Maybe I've mellowed, but that comes with age. I'm sitting at the top now, something I worked my whole life for. Now that I'm at the top, it's nothing like I thought it would be. Maybe it's because I'm old now; I'm looking at the world differently. I fought very hard to get to the top. Now I'm fighting just as hard to stay where I am without dragging my sons into it. I head back inside, knowing the girls will be here soon. I need to snap out of my mood and focus on the problem at hand. As I pass the pool house, I stop and stare at it. Could I put Viviana there? Should I offer her a few rooms in the main house or is that pushing my luck? Would she even want to be so close to me? So many questions, but now is not the time for dreaming. When I get inside, I make my way into the kitchen. I want to let the staff know we are having guests and for them to prepare a light snack. However, Geno has beaten me to it. He is telling the staff exactly what he wants and where to set it all up. With everyone's back toward me, I clear my throat, so they know I'm in the room.

"Dad, I thought you would want to have something to offer everyone when they got here. I didn't mean to butt in."

"It's fine, Geno." Just as I finish my sentence, the doorbell chimes and the cameras comes to life. "Our guests are here. Why don't you show them in, and I'll finish letting the staff know what I would like served." He gives me a nod of agreement and leaves. I follow suit as soon as I finish with my requests.

When I enter the room, I hang back for a few minutes to watch. You know a lot can be said for keeping your mouth shut and your eyes and ears open. Just as I figured, Geno is hanging on Jessica's every word. There is an old saying *"you don't shit where you eat."* It's vulgar but very true.

"Hello again, Jessica . . . Michelina. I hope Geno will be able to help you with the calls you are getting. Going forward, I'm here to help and protect you. Please let me know if this happens again. Michelina, how was Viviana when you left?"

"She was resting comfortably. I think it helped that I was there when she woke up."

"Have you given any thought as to her continued care?" I ask her as gently as possible. She looks at me like a deer in the headlights.

"I thought she was going to stay where she is. Is there a problem I should be aware of?"

"I wanted Viviana to come and live here, but your mother wanted no part of that. I would still like her to live here. At least I know she will be protected all the time. She never has to want for anything, and I will have a private nurse here for her. Do you think that's something that might work for you?"

"Agosto, it's not about what works for me, it's what works for Grandma."

"In the meantime, I will continue to keep the layers of protection I have on her in place." She nods and slowly smiles. I let her get back to working with Geno. While they are occupied, I excuse myself and head out to see Viviana.

CHAPTER NINE

Viviana

After Michelina left, the doctor came by and said I should take it easy today. What does he think I do all day in here? It doesn't get any easier than this. I'm about to head into the dining room to get something to eat when there is a knock on my door. Agosto comes in with a basket and a blanket.

"Well, this is a surprise. I didn't expect to see you until after mass on Sunday."

"It's a beautiful day, and I thought we could have a picnic before it gets too hot." I laugh but suddenly stop when Agosto's smile slowly fades. "Do you mind sharing with me what's so funny, Viviana?"

"I was just thinking if we got down on the ground to have a picnic, we would need the paramedics to get us back up." Now we are both laughing. I take his arm and we make our way out of my room to a round table in the solarium. I don't know why I'm nervous. We've been best friends for years. He's taking his time setting everything up. Finally, I can't take the procrastinating any longer. "Agosto, why are you stalling? You have something on your mind. You know you can ask me anything."

"You were always the smartest lady I've ever known. Okay, here goes nothing. I know we talked about this when Frances was alive, and she was adamant that she needed to do what she felt was best for you. I thought maybe you could move into my house or even the pool house, if that was more comfortable for you."

"I remember when you asked Frances. She was very upset and felt I was going from the frying pan into the fire."

"Is that how you felt?"

"No, she never understood you or our relationship. When I tried to explain it to her, it only made her angry." I reach for his hand. Oh, what I would do to turn back the hands of time, knowing what I know now.

"What about now that she is no longer here?"

"Let me think about it. I'm not saying no, but I'm not saying yes. Right now, I want to make sure my only grandchild is safe."

"Did Frances ever explain why she felt the way she did? Was it something I said or did?"

"You are Carmine's brother. As far as she was concerned, it might have been different fruit from the same tree, but the same blood flows through your veins." He runs his finger around the rim of his wineglass. I'm not sure if he's hurt or mad, maybe a little of each.

"So, I never had a chance. I've dealt with prejudice my whole life. However, I never thought I would have to deal with it from my family." He sips his wine and passes me a plate that he filled with antipasto.

"Agosto, our ship sailed a long time ago. I love our friendship for what it is. I have no desire for you to change who you are. I never did. Now, let's put this all aside and tell me what's going on with Michelina? Just so you know, she told me today about the phone calls."

"I wish she would have said something sooner, but I'm just glad she is opening up to me. She wants help, and she is willing to let me help her. As you know, that's really half the battle."

"I know you said you wanted to wait to tell the boys about Matteo, but I really think you need to tell them now rather than later."

"Why? Not telling them might keep him safe."

"You can't possibly think that. Not telling them is keeping you on top of the pedestal they have you on." He's quiet for a bit, no doubt processing what I've said.

"I wanted to wait until I found out who told Carmine. Do you think it's in his journals or possibly one of his black books that everyone is after?"

"I didn't finish reading his journals. When Frances came over and saw what I was reading, she went ballistic. She threatened to burn them. I begged her not to. I told her they belonged to me, and I would dispose of them when I was ready. That's when she moved them into the attic. She knew I couldn't climb up there. It was her way of calling it a win for herself."

"As you must know, Michelina told me she has them and has been reading them. Do you think I should ask her if I could read them?"

"This is very unusual, Agosto. You usually take what you want. What changed?" I ask, giving him a small, impressed smile. He takes a sip of his wine, probably thinking about how much he wants me to know.

"I don't think anything has changed, Viviana. The books are yours. You are encouraging Michelina to read them."

"They are filled with your brother's private thoughts about his family, which includes you. You know he's never had a nice thing to say about anyone, least of all you. The only reason I've encouraged Michelina to read them is so she doesn't keep him on a pedestal where he doesn't belong. Why don't you ask her if he says how he found out? She will tell you the truth, of that, I'm sure."

"Let's forget about all this for now. I brought your favorite dessert." He puts everything away and pulls out a pastry box.

"Agosto, you spoil me." He opens the box, and it's filled with miniature pastries. He carefully puts them in the middle of the table. Next, he pulls out a thermos filled with espresso. Two demitasse cups, a sugar cube and lemon rind for me, and a little Sambuca for him. These are the memories I will hold near and dear to my heart.

"Michelina said you took Jessica home last night. I'm glad you got to meet her best friend. They are thick as thieves. I wouldn't be surprised if she already knew all about you."

"Jessica is nothing like Michelina. She is very protective of her friend and, in no uncertain terms, let me know it. She came with Michelina to my house today. I think Geno is smitten with her."

I can't help but laugh. "You are showing your age, Agosto."

"That's why I rely on you to keep me informed of all that I'm missing." I don't tell him that some days I'm more confused than others. It's his visits that keep me grounded. I can't image my life without him, yet when I was told Carmine died, I mourned him like I was supposed to for the appropriate time. Where did that get me? Lied to and deceived by the very person I was supposed to trust. I vowed I would never put all my faith in any one person again. Yet here I sit, contemplating what my next step with Agosto should be.

CHAPTER TEN

Michelina

WE FINISH UP WITH GENO, AND I PRACTICALLY HAD TO PRY Jessica away from him. I've never seen her like this before. When we pull up to the house, she barely waits for the car to come to a stop before trying to get out. I grab her arm and pull her back next to me. "Jess, we have to wait for the 'all clear.'" I barely get the words out when there is a loud noise and the front window splinters. I feel something whiz past me. When I touch my cheek, it's wet. I look at my hand and see that it's blood. I look down at my chest and find is blood and brain matter all over me. None of it is mine. My instinct to protect Jess kicks in. I pull her down to the floorboards with me.

"Everyone, stay down!" Luca demands, his voice almost savage. He gets out of the car, but Cody is not moving. He can't move. They blew the back of his head off and it's all over me. There is more shooting. Then it gets really quiet. It feels like we are waiting forever to hear anything from Luca. The passenger rear door opens, and Luca is on his knees.

"I don't see anyone, but I'm not taking any chances. I've called for backup. They should be here any minute."

"I hear a helicopter."

"Stay put until I give you the 'all clear.'" The helicopter is getting louder. My body is shaking. My hold on Jess gets tighter. The sound of the helicopter blade is slowing down. I hear a lot of muffled yelling, I think. Finally, Luca comes into view. He's no longer on the ground in front of me, instead, he's helping us out of the car.

"Don't look back. Let's get inside." Finally, inside the safety of my home, I collapse to my knees, shaking. Another FBI agent is talking to Jess. The paramedics come in and when they look at me, they rush over to see where I'm hurt. "It's not my blood," I manage to say. Luca has a tight grip on my hand.

"Will you let me take you into the bathroom and get you cleaned up?" He waves away the paramedics. My teeth are chattering so hard I can't talk. I nod and, in an instant, he scoops me up and carries me into the guest bathroom. He puts me down and I sit on the edge of the tub.

"I'm sorry about Cody. I remember him saying he was married. Did he have any children?" I cry.

"Don't go there, Chelle. You're in shock and the last thing you need is to pile on some useless guilt. When we joined, we knew what could happen." He ties my hair up, takes a wet washcloth, he begins cleaning me up.

"Do you know who was shooting?"

"No, but I don't think they were shooting at you or Jessica. I think Cody was the target."

"What would make you think that?" I feel my head pound.

"The shot was a one in a million. It by-passed you and blew off half Cody's head. If you were the target, the shooter just had to move two inches to the right, and you would be dead. No one wants you dead, at least, not yet. Not until they find the books. The best thing you can do is nothing. That is what's keeping you alive right now. We need to insulate Jessica more and I'm thinking we could stash her at Agosto's house."

I look down at my shirt and then back up toward Luca. Without missing a beat, he unbuttons it. "You have a theory why Cody was the target, don't you?"

"I do, but I don't want to go down that road until I ask some questions. For now, let's just concentrate on keeping you and Jessica safe." He takes my shirt off and tosses it on the floor. He lifts my chin and our eyes meet. "I promise you I will keep you and Jessica safe." He lightly brushes his lips over mine. I feel like I'm going to pass out.

"Breathe, Chelle, everything will work out." After he finishes washing me, he takes off his shirt and hands it to me. I can't take my eyes off of his chest. I reach my hand out and place it over his heart. His skin is hot, and I can feel his heart pounding. Dear God, I'm going to hell for what I'm thinking.

"You might want to put my shirt on before you go back into the living room. The FBI and the forensic team are still here."

I put his t-shirt on and open the door to find Jessica standing there. My face turns a lovely shade of beet red. "Are they done taking your statement?" I ask her, trying to sound like all of this is no big deal.

"Yes, they are ready for you." Her eyes keep looking at Luca's naked chest, and I'm feeling a pang of jealousy.

"Luca, your bag is still in the guest room." That was my way of letting him know to get a shirt on so Jessica can stop drooling.

When I step into the living room, there are three agents. I walk right up to them, acting like I'm not afraid, like this is an everyday occurrence in my life. In reality, I want to throw up. "I don't know what you think I can tell you. As soon as the shot rang out, I pulled Jessica to the floorboards and saw nothing." Luca is back in the room fully clothed.

"Hello, Michelina, my name is Agent Robert Conti. You can call me Bob. I'll be part of the team protecting you and Jessica. I know this is a very difficult time, so I will try to be quick. What can you tell us about the phone calls?" My eyes dart toward Luca and he gives a slight nod.

"How did you know about them?"

"Your friend Jessica mentioned it to me. She said your grandmother got one, too. What did the person tell you?"

"Not much. I mean, he never said his name. He gave some veiled threats, and that's about it."

"We will need your phone to backtrace the calls. We can also tap your phone in case he calls again." I glance over to Luca and he gives another encouraging nod. I pull my phone out of my back pocket and pass it to Bob.

"Please try to get it back to me as quickly as possible. If you are done with me, I would like to go upstairs and lie down." When I turn, I see a man sitting at my dining room table with a lot of machines in front of him.

"That's all for now. Luca and I will be down here if you need anything." He heads over to the dining room table and hands the man my phone. Jessica has already made her way upstairs. I grab two bottles of water and as I pass Luca, he takes my arm. His grip is firm and hot. He says nothing. His eyes are so intense. He finally loosens his grip and I continue upstairs. I was hoping to finish Grandpa's journals tonight, but after everything that happened, I just want to take a sleeping pill and escape it all.

CHAPTER ELEVEN

Luca

WHILE ROBERT IS WORKING WITH THE TECH ON CHELLE'S phone, I step outside for some privacy. Part of me wants to call Agosto and tell him what is going on. The other part of me thinks he already knows. He could be the one that put all this in motion. I told Agosto months ago that I thought it might have been Cody that told Carmine my real identity. Cody was around Carmine just as much as I was, except for the two weeks that I was alone with Carmine. They pulled Cody from another assignment. I later found out that he was investigating Agosto. If he found out, he could have been the one to tell him. Agosto said he was looking into it. Did he find out something? Why wouldn't he tell me? My phone rings. I look down at it and see that it's Agosto calling me. A chill runs up my spine.

"Hello, did you hear what happened today?" Is how I answer.

"Yes, I need you to know it wasn't me. I would never take a chance like that with you in the car. You've got to know this is a set-up."

"For a hot minute, I questioned it. I'm sorry. I should have known better. They assigned Robert Conti to replace Cody. He took Chelle's phone and gave it to their tech. Jessica told them about the calls." I can hear him let out a slew of obscenities.

"Don't worry, I'll get it handled. You need to advise Jessica to shut up. Are you and Michelina okay?"

"I'm okay. She is pretty shaken up. I'll talk to Jessica. Honestly, I was busy helping Chelle when they spoke to her. I never had time to tell her not to say anything."

"You said Michelina was okay. What did she need help with?" He asks in an agitated tone.

"She was behind Cody when it happened. Chelle was covered in his blood. I needed to get her cleaned up. I was afraid she was going to go into shock. I give you my word, she is okay."

"I'll have a new phone waiting for Michelina when she visits Viviana. Which better be soon. I don't want her hearing about any of this on the news." He ends the call without a goodbye. He is pissed and I can only hope it's not at me.

Michelina

When I open the door to my room, I find Jess sitting on the floor, crying. I race over to her and pull her into a bear hug. "Hey, we're okay. Stop crying or you're going to make me cry. We both can't fall apart at the same time."

"How the hell have you been dealing with all of this on your own?"

"I haven't been, Jess; I have you and Grandma to lean on."

"Someone was trying to kill us, Chelle. How can you take that so lightly?"

"I don't take any of this lightly. For the record, though, we were not the target—Cody was."

Her pale blue eyes hold a puzzled look.

"Why would anyone shoot the FBI agent?"

I close my eyes, hoping for a way to tell her without giving away Luca's secret. "It took a very skilled person to make that shot. I felt the bullet whiz past me, Jess. Besides, if I die, the location of the books and stuff that everyone wants dies with me."

"So, these journals are really just a log, for lack of a better term, of family history through Carmine's eyes. Why aren't we going through the ones that everyone is looking for?"

"If we brought the stuff out into the open, there would be no need to keep me alive—any of us—for that matter. I need to make sure Grandma and you are safe, so everything must remain hidden."

"Let's finish reading his journals. Maybe by then we will have formulated some sort of plan." Jessica gets up and heads to the closet. I quickly follow. We pull out the boxes and get back to work. I remember the two photographs that I stuck in my pocket and pull them out. I was going to give them to Grandma, but I forgot. Now I'm glad I didn't. Why have reminders of the past . . . a painful past, at that.

My mind wanders to my mom. I'm starting to understand everything she went through. How she fought to keep us alive. That's why she never mentioned to anyone that she had the stuff. Plus, she had to take care of an aging mother, try to keep a gangster at bay, try to be there for me, all the while working full-time. Talk about a juggling act! Now she's gone and I have so many regrets, so much guilt. I know that's common when grieving the loss of a loved one. If I would have known everything before she died, I would like to think I would have done things differently. Maybe that's just a dream. I pick up the next journal and begin reading.

Carmine

Today I met with the FBI. When you are constantly being watched, it's actually easy to arrange. It was a very simple meeting. It was with a lower-level flunky. His name is Luca Gill and there was something very familiar about him. I shrugged it off and handed him three pages from one of the black books, along with two photographs. The first one is of a supreme court judge having sex in chambers. Normally, I would think it was no big deal. However, he was having sex with two men. Most people look the other way except a supreme court judge is held to a higher standard. Is it right? It's not for me to say. The other photograph was a United States senator in bed with an under-age girl. They were both covered in blood. The girl was dead, and the senator was passed out. I also gave him the information about the dead girl and the location of her body. I'm sure her parents would want to know. Giving up this type of information shows them I have a heart, no matter how black and cold it might be. Luca sat quietly looking at everything, asking me some questions, until he got to the kid. It's like a wall came down . . . hard. Two days later, a deal was brokered. I know Luca didn't have the authority to do the deal, but I liked the kid. There was just something about him I couldn't shake. When he came to me to present the deal, I could tell he was nervous. One corner of his mouth kept twitching. Hell, it's probably the biggest thing he has ever done in his career at the FBI. It's not just "here's the deal: take it or leave it." For me, it's the negotiation; it's like a dance with a beautiful woman. You know you're going to get laid, but first you want the chase. My hands sliding down her back, resting at the small of her back. Bringing her close so she can feel the hardness that is waiting just for her—the dance.

"Put your nerves aside, Luca, and tell me why I should take your deal?" I asked him.

"There is a bounty on your head. We can protect you." His reassuring voice was not so reassuring. For some unknown reason, I want to take this kid and mold him into a ruthless capo.

"Maybe we should forget about this. Let me teach you about the real world. Let's see how far you can go with my guidance."

"You sit here and say you want to mold me into a mini vision of you. Why the fuck would I want to do that? You're the one sitting here today asking for my help." I threw my head back and laughed. This is when the kid proved to me he's got the stones for this business.

"Okay, kid, let's negotiate. Everyone who's anyone will recognize me, so I'm gonna need plastic surgery."

"You want that, then you have to testify."

"I'm not a rat kid. I'm just a man who was smart enough to keep very detailed records."

"Any way you slice it, you're a rat. You won't have to be in the courtroom, we can video record it. Do that and you get the surgery."

"You drive a hard bargain, kid. Fine, but I want to live out the rest of my years here in Arizona. You know I have a brother here. Maybe I should look him up." The kid didn't move. His stare was cold as stone. Could I have hit a nerve?

"We will explain the rules in detail when you get your contract. The biggest one is, if you go into the program, you can't have contact with anyone from your past life. Carmine, do you understand these rules?"

"I don't do contracts. My word is my bond. I will seal the deal with a handshake. If that doesn't work for you, don't let the door hit you in the ass on your way out." I put out my hand. He looked at it, then back up at me. He firmly gripped my hand and shook. Just like that, he made the deal of a lifetime.

I might not do contracts, but I keep detailed records of everything that's been said and done in my lifetime. My own personal insurance. There's a lot to remember these days, and I'm an old man.

CHAPTER TWELVE

Agosto

T HE FACT THAT MY SON QUESTIONED WHETHER I HAD ANY PART in the events of today makes me sick. Never in my life would I put him in jeopardy. If anything, I've gone to great lengths to keep him away from this life. When he turned eighteen, he looked so much like me, I knew I had to do something. That was when I told him all about my life. What I did to survive. Things I was not very proud of. Things that were done out of desperation. I had to tell him he had two brothers, and it was safer for him if no one knew who his father was. Then I dropped the last bomb. I told him why it would be in his best interest to have plastic surgery. Carmine was alive then and jealous of my sons. He was responsible for Salvatore's death. He knew and did nothing. That made him just as guilty, as if he was the one who slit Sal's throat. After Matteo went and did his own research, he came to me and said he would only do a few minor corrections. I felt that something was better than nothing. As he got older, he took on more of his mother's looks, plus a full beard did the trick. Unless, of course, we were standing next to each other. When he graduated college with his degree in Criminal Justice, I was proud of him. When he joined the FBI, I was hoping for a desk job. Unfortunately, he is so much like me, I knew he would never do that. The last thing I ever expected was for him to get assigned to the organized crime division. I still prayed every day that no one found out who he was. Things were going okay until one day he asked to meet me. When he showed up, I could tell he had something big weighing on his mind.

"Dad, they gave me the chance to work on an enormous project. I'll probably just be a gofer, but to be a part of this so early in my career, it's an amazing opportunity." His voice, giving away his excitement.

"What's the assignment?"

"They have put me on the Carmine Amato case." Those words sucked all the air out of the room.

"What is the assignment and why would you accept it knowing who he is?"

"I can't refuse an assignment. That would cost me my job. I can't go to my boss and say, hey I'm going to sit this one out since Carmine is my uncle. Like I said, I don't think they will have me doing much. I had no choice, so I went along with the program. He's turning, Dad. Carmine is a snitch."

So now I know what Carmine's intentions are. Now I'm being tasked with keeping secrets and lying to Viviana, my oldest and dearest friend. Sometimes the lines of that friendship blur. What is truth and what is reality?

I put the memories aside and head out in search of Gianni. When I want privacy, this house is too small. And when I want my sons, they are never around. Gianni's first love is cooking, so I always check the kitchen first. Sure enough, he is just getting started on tonight's dinner. "Are you at a stopping point?"

"I was just about to sauté the garlic. What do you need?"

"Did you hear about the shooting today?" His face pales, and he shuts the gas off on the stove.

"No, was anyone hurt?"

"Cody McJohnson, one of the FBI agents protecting Michelina, was shot in the head. Everyone else is fine." The color begins to come back to his face.

"Why shoot him?"

"Maybe it's some sort of warning or maybe it's the person making the phone calls, letting us know he's not going anywhere. Where is Geno? I want to follow up with him on that?"

"He's chasing down a lead. Maybe for the safety of everyone involved, we should move them in here."

"In theory, that sounds good, but we can't expect everyone to give up their life, hide them away in the name of safety. Gianni, all that does is make them a prisoner."

"Dad, before you do anything, let me look into all of this and see what I can find out." He takes the pan and puts it in the sink before heading out of the kitchen. I guess dinner can wait.

Gianni

Seeing my father visibly upset by today's turn of events really threw me for a loop. The man is never shaken, always calm and levelheaded. I need Geno to help unravel this mess before someone else gets killed. He's probably locked away in his office. Sure enough, that's exactly where I find him.

"Hey, did you talk to Dad yet?"

"If you mean do I know about the shooting, yes. Jessica texted me asking if I have any leads on the caller." He doesn't look away from his computer.

"Can you please stop what you are doing so we can talk? This is not like you, Geno, what the hell is the problem?" He takes a deep breath and turns his chair towards me.

"The problem is, I finally meet someone who holds my interest past five minutes, and she is probably going to get herself killed and I don't think there is a damn thing I can do about it."

"What makes you think you can't do anything? Let's bring them here this way we know they are both safe. Hell, it's more than the FBI is doing."

"I thought about that, but as long as Chelle hangs on to those books, nothing will change. I mean, why would she even bother holding on to them? It's not like she was in this life and knew what they meant or what they could give her. What's her end game?" He has a mini bar behind his desk. He pulls two beers out of the fridge and passes one to me.

"Gianni, did Dad have any suggestions?"

"No, I think Dad's focus is on Viviana. He mentioned he was thinking of asking her to move in here. There is more than enough room for everyone. He says it's for her safety, but he wanted her to move in when Frances decided she was moving Viviana to the assisted living. Maybe if Frances would have agreed, she would still be alive today."

"Monday morning quarterback doesn't solve the problem we are facing. Why don't we both go to Chelle's place; we can have an intervention."

He gets up and tosses me his keys and grabs his laptop. "You need to drive. I've almost got the information I need on the caller. If my sources are correct, Chelle is not going to like the answer."

With my interest piqued, we head out to Chelle's place and hopefully, by the time we get there, Geno will have some answers.

CHAPTER THIRTEEN

Michelina

Carmine

Months, that's how long I had to spend under the watchful eye of the FBI. You know, they say it's a small world. Well, today it got a little smaller. Luca brought in his new partner, Cody McJohnson. He took one look at me, and I thought he would pass out. Not from my plastic surgery, but from the fact that we know each other. He's my right-hand man, Butchie's nephew. A while back, Cody got into some gambling debt that he couldn't get out of. He needed it quietly cleared up. If the FBI found out about it, he would lose his job. If his wife found out, he would lose his balls. In steps Uncle Butchie to the rescue. The only reason I know about it is Butchie likes to run his mouth. All he could talk about was how great it will be to have an FBI agent in his back pocket. I told him he was already in your pocket since you are his uncle. However, he still had to brag.

Oh my word . . . Cody—my Cody—dead Cody. I wonder if Luca knows this? Maybe this is why he was murdered. I look over toward Jess, ready to tell her what I just learned, but she is engrossed in what she is reading. I don't want to interrupt her, but then I realize she's been crying.

"Hey Jess, why are you crying?" She quickly wipes her tears away.

"I'm so sad for Viviana and Agosto. It's clear Carmine knew they had feelings for each other, yet he laughed it off. He even went so far as to make fun of them. Having met Agosto and reading about him in these journals, I can't wrap my mind around the fact that he is a killer. People have suffered at his hand, yet I wish they could see the side of him I've seen. Does this make me a bad person that I have empathy for him?"

I take a few minutes to wrap my mind around everything she just said. I remember Luca telling me how much Agosto cares for my grandmother. Why is it so hard for me to see this?

"Jess, you are not a bad person. I've been so focused on Carmine that I really didn't realize there was a relationship between Viviana and Agosto. I was so focused on me I forgot what my grandmother had to live with, what she is still living with. Thank you for making me see these things."

There is a knock on the door. Jess pushes everything into the closet and closes the door. She runs to the bed, jumps in, pulling the covers over herself. I open the door, see Luca, and quietly slip out.

"Sorry, Jess is sleeping. What's up?" He looks over the stair rail before passing me two new cell phones.

"Agosto had these phones dropped off for you and Jessica. He doesn't want you to use your old phones. Make sure you turn the power off on the old ones before you turn on the new ones. He was going to have them waiting for you when you went to see Viviana but, with everything going on, he didn't want to wait."

"I would ask why, but I'm sure it would be a waste of time. I have something I need to share with you. Cody was a mole. Don't ask me a million questions that I'm not prepared to answer right now. Just know that he was a mole and if he found out your true identity, that is probably how Carmine found out."

"Cody was my partner when we had to babysit Carmine during his plastic surgery days. We would take turns watching him. I could swear that my stuff was gone through, but I could never prove it. I don't carry anything with me that has my birth name, but I never felt comfortable with him. This answers a lot of questions. Can you, at least, tell me how he became a mole and who he worked for?"

"Carmine's right-hand man, Butchie, was Cody's uncle. Cody was into some heavy gambling debt that he couldn't get out of. Butchie made it all right and boasted to Carmine how he now had an FBI agent in his back pocket. Luca, I'm to the point where I don't trust anyone." He holds onto my shoulders and rests his forehead on mine.

"Chelle, I just found out that the justice department is sending over a few agents to talk to you. They are probably going to make you an offer. They want the books and whatever else you have. They know you have them, and they will try to force your hand. Whatever you do, don't give in. If you do, I can't protect you and neither can Agosto." He presses his lips to mine. I know I shouldn't, but my heart is racing. God, forgive me; I want this man. I slightly part my lips and let his tongue dance around mine. He is intense, passionate, and strong. As he wraps his arms around me, I feel my knees go weak. I fist his hair and hold on tight, wanting all of him. He lifts me in his arms, and I wrap my legs tightly around him. I feel his rock-hard cock slam against me just right. "Oh, dear God, I need more, please." I don't care who hears me. I throw my head back, about to scream out with pleasure, when the doorbell rings. He stops and I want to die. My orgasm is dangling in front of me like one of my cat's toys. "Noooo you can't stop. I need you not to stop. Do you understand what you're doing to me? The state you are leaving me in!"

"We can't do this. I need to have some self-control, Chelle." Before I can answer, he pulls me off of him and places my feet back on the ground.

"Chelle, Robert must have answered the door. I can hear Geno and Gianni downstairs. We need to get them out of here before the Justice Department agents get here." He heads downstairs and the only thing I can do is follow.

When I get downstairs, I hear Robert tell them I'm not accepting visitors.

"Robert, these men are my family. I'm more than happy to talk to them. I would appreciate it if you gave me some privacy. You can hang out in the yard with Luca." Luca narrows his eyes at me as he goes outside with Robert.

"Hey, guys, what's going on?" Geno takes a seat on the sofa and urges me to do the same. Gianni, however, is standing.

"I know you got the new phones that Dad sent over. We wanted to make sure you knew what they are capable of. Geno, you can tell her about the phones."

"Chelle, your old phones had some questionable software on them. Now I have a mirror of your phone, so when you get a call, try to keep them talking. I can do the rest remotely. Dad told us about Cody. We think you and Jessica should move into our house. You've been there, so you know it's like Fort Knox. No one is getting in or out without us knowing it."

"Since I saw you last, I learned Cody was a mole." Gianni crouches down in front of me, he takes my hands in his and squeezes.

"Chelle, this is all the more reason you are not safe here."

"What about my grandmother?"

"Dad is with her now. He is letting her know it's really for the best that everyone is under one roof."

I can't get Luca out of my mind. What will happen to him? "I need to talk to Agosto and my grandma before I do anything. Oh, and apparently the Department of Justice is sending some Agents over to persuade me to turn over the books and and offer me protection."

"Let the watchdogs here know you are going to see your grandmother. I'll make the arrangements."

Before we can do anything, Jess comes down the steps, her eyes fixated on Geno. "Jess, I was just coming upstairs to get you. We are going to see Grandma."

"Is she okay?"

"Yes, I have a few things to go over with her." I make my way to the sliding glass doors and let Luca know we are leaving. We head outside. I really don't want Robert to come with us, but he makes it known we go nowhere without him. Luca and Robert are in the front seat, and Jess and I are in the back. We head to Grandma's place with Geno and Gianni following close behind us.

CHAPTER FOURTEEN

Viviana

A GOSTO WOULD COME EVERY SUNDAY AFTER MASS. HE ALWAYS brings the pastry and espresso. Lately, he is coming every day, sometimes twice a day. This afternoon he sits in the chair in the corner of my room with his hat in his hands. He is a troubled man carrying all my troubles with him. I motion for him to pull his chair closer to mine.

"Agosto, what's wrong? I can't help you if you don't tell me." He puts his hat down and takes my hand.

"I want you—no—I need you to move out of this place and into my home. Before you tell me your answer, I need to tell you a story." He brings my hand to his cheek and closes his eyes for just a moment.

"I won't judge you if that's what you are afraid of, you know that."

"I know. Today, Cody McJohnson, one of Michelina's FBI body-guards, was shot and killed. Michelina is fine. She should be here shortly. Viviana, I'm going to insist that Michelina and Jessica move into my house. I need to make sure they are safe. I received word that now there is a ten-million-dollar bounty on Jessica's head. My men already thwarted off one attempt on her life. The feeling is to get Michelina to give up what she's hiding, they need to get to Jessica. In no way do I want to pressure you into making this decision. I need you to know all the facts before you do." Before I can say anything, there is a knock on the door and Michelina comes in with Jessica and Agosto's boys, including Matteo.

"Hi Agosto, I was wondering if you could give me a few minutes alone with my grandma, please." He ushers everyone out of the room and pulls the door shut behind him.

"Michelina, are you here to talk to me about moving?"

"Yes, I am. I know this is not the first time this has been brought up. What would you be comfortable with?"

"I'm sure Agosto would make me comfortable. I understand from him that he wants you and Jessica to move in, too. Are you okay with that?"

"I think it will work fine for now. I'll let him know and I will get the paperwork started for your discharge." She gives me a hug and I'm feeling calm for the first time in a long time. She leaves and a few minutes later. Agosto comes back in.

"Viviana, is there anything that you would like me to have waiting for you? Nothing is too big or too small."

"You know me, Agosto, I'm a very simple lady. I want my family safe and happy. That's all I've ever needed." He sits in the chair next to me and takes my hand.

"Viviana, are you ready for this adventure? I feel like I've waited a lifetime to be under the same roof as you."

"In some ways we have, Agosto, but there are some things I think you need to understand."

"Tell me everything, Viviana, hold nothing back." His grip on my hand gets a little tighter.

"We are a lot older now. Our quirks are more pronounced. There will be days that my memory is not what it used to be. I need you to accept that it is what it is. Please don't try to force the memories. If they want to come, they will. My granddaughter is all I have left, and I need you to promise you will protect her, even from herself. If for some reason

I'm not there, keep her safe and love her like she is your own. The biggest request I have is don't blame her for anything Carmine did. She didn't choose him as her grandfather." He lets go of my hand and pulls my chair so close to him that our knees touch.

"All those years ago, I knew you were the one that I was supposed to be with, the one that I never had a chance with. I stood by you through all the stages of our lives. We helped each other through the death of our children and spouses. I never gave up on us. I expect nothing from you that you're not already giving me." He gently rests his lips on mine. I've come to realize that love comes in many forms. It's like the changing of the seasons. Embrace each one like a new beginning. He pulls back and I stroke my hand down the side of his face. A face that has weathered every storm.

"Agosto, I'm ready for you to take me home." There is a twinkle in his eyes. Maybe it's just me seeing what I want to see, and that's okay. I believe I finally found some peace.

Luca

Sometimes, doing the right thing is difficult. I don't want to give up the little bit of control I have, but she's not a prisoner, she's a victim. If she declines FBI protection, I'm pulled off of this case. Besides, the DOJ has every intention of taking over this case. She steps out of her grandmother's room and Agosto goes in. At this moment, I want to take her in my arms and tell her everything is going to be okay. I'll make it okay for her. Instead, she pulls Jessica aside to let her know what the plan is, a plan I'm not a part of. At this point, the only thing I can do is let her go.

"Luca, is there someone at the FBI I need to talk to about this?"

"I can take care of it. However, the DOJ was coming over today and, like I said earlier, they will probably want to take over the case."

"Jess, where did Geno and Gianni go?"

"They said they were going to get everything ready at their house. So, is it true that we are moving, Chelle?"

"It's the only way we can all be safe. Once everything blows over, we can move back. In the meantime, I filled out the paperwork here for Grandma's move. Agosto said he is going to handle all of her stuff moved. So, the only thing left is to pack up some stuff and grab all of Gustavo's stuff, including his favorite bed. That cat probably has more stuff than I do." While Chelle is giving out orders, which seems to be her way of keeping calm, I've inched my way closer to Robert. With his back turned, I still can't hear anything he is saying.

CHAPTER FIFTEEN

Michelina

W HEN ROBERT PULLS UP TO MY HOUSE, THERE ARE THREE black SUVs, which is standard issue for most government agencies. Our car barely comes to a stop before the men and women coming out of the SUVs surrounded it. Jessica and I are completely surrounded. "Who are you and what do you want from us?" I'm trying to remain calm, but my voice cracks.

"We are with the Justice Department. We would like to talk to you about Carmine Amato. It's boiling out here. Can we go inside?"

"It's not like I have a choice, now do I?" Jessica and I head inside with everyone else following behind us. Robert has a sickening smirk on his face. This has to be who he was talking to.

"My name is Calum and I'm here on behalf of the Department of Justice. I think at this point, we will take over and the FBI can leave."

Robert still has a smirk on his face. I can't tell you how hard I'm trying not to punch him in the face. "Robert can leave, but Luca stays."

"If Luca stays, then so do I," Robert chimes in.

"Guess what, Robert, this is my house. You seem to forget that I'm not a prisoner or a criminal. I'm a victim. The bottom line is: I don't trust you. So, Robert, please leave. Hell, all of you leave." I might sound all brave and tough but, in reality, my insides are quivering.

Calum opens the door and turns toward Robert. "You heard the lady. Your time here is over." Robert's face turns red, and he storms out the door.

Calum turns toward me. "See, Michelina, I'm willing to work with you. I want to keep you and your friend Jessica safe. Turning everything of Carmine's that you have over to us lets you put all this behind you. You can go back to teaching and it will be like nothing ever happened." *What an ass.*

"Calum, you just shot yourself in the foot. You're either a total idiot or you have no regard for my life or Jessica's. Do you even know what you are dealing with? I can never go back to teaching again and neither can Jess. That part of our life is closed for good. Going back could put my students in danger. But that doesn't seem to bother you. Apparently, everyone thinks I have something of great importance to some terrible people. They went so far as to blow up my mother's car with her in it. Again, you seem to think it's no big deal, that I can go back to a normal life. My mother is dead. She is never coming back. She will miss everything in my life and I will miss all the milestones with her, but, again, you think I can go back to a normal life. As they say in *Die Hard*, "Why don't you wake up and smell what you're shoveling?""

I walk over to the front door and hold it open. "Please take your men and leave my home now. I have nothing for you, and I want nothing to do with you or your agency."

"Ma'am, you are making a big mistake, a mistake that could cost you your life."

When the last one leaves, I slam and lock the door. "Jess, why don't you go upstairs and start packing our stuff? I need to go over some stuff with Luca." She heads upstairs and I curl into the sofa. Complete exhaustion hits me. Luca pulls two bottles of water out of the fridge, passes me one as he sits next to me.

"Luca, I do not know what to do next."

"If you don't trust me enough to tell me what you know, how do you expect me to help you? Look, I know you have his journals somewhere in this house." At this, I raise my eyebrows. "Don't look at me like that. I'm not an idiot. Those journals mean nothing to anyone but you. It's the black books that you're hiding. Those are the ones that could get you killed."

"Don't look at you like what? Like maybe you were here just to spy on me. That maybe almost jumping into bed with you was your plan all along. Fuck the girl and get the books?" In an instant, his hand is around my throat, pressing me back on the cushion. His lips roughly on mine, pressing hard for entry. I want to resist him. He's my cousin for Pete's sake, but all reasoning escapes me. I part my lips and, in an instant, our tongues are doing a slow dance. His hand around my throat slides down to my breast. Of all the days, to not wear a bra. He's making a swirling motion around my nipple with his thumb, which is so hard it's almost painful. I want more, so much more. I have so much pent-up frustration that started this afternoon. Slowly he pulls back, our lips breaking the connection. He sits back and our eyes meet. I want to scream. Why the fuck is he doing this to me twice in one day?

"Chelle, I'm not an idiot. I already know where you have them stashed, and that's fine. At least they are safe. So, I don't need to fuck the girl to get the books. Unlike a quick fuck, when and if I decide to take you, the books will be the furthest thing from your mind. Trust me, It will be something you will never forget."

"You're my cousin, low on the tree of life, but still. . . Maybe we should get back to the problem at hand. Once you drop me off at Agosto's house, what will you do? It's not like you can stay with me." It's when I say those words, I realize I've become very attached to him. I'm falling hard and fast for him. I don't know how to stop it or if I even want to.

"I'm not sure. I'm going to meet with Agosto later. I know he's worried about my safety but, honestly, I can take care of myself. I need him to acknowledge my birth right. A man can't live his entire life in the shadows and expect to have a good outcome."

"Can I ask you something?"

"You don't need permission, just ask." He takes my hand and gives it a reassuring squeeze.

"Why do you think Agosto handled everything with you the way he did? I'm trying to understand the man more than what Carmine talks about or my Grandma's memories of him."

"Honestly, I think a lot of it was the fear of losing another child. Growing up, I thought my father traveled for business. I did not know what he did for a living, nor did I know he had another family, that I had another family."

"How did you find out?" I pick up my water bottle and struggle to get it open. He takes it, opens it and gives it back to me. Is he stalling or is this too painful for him?

"My mom got sick. One day she went for a mammogram, and she was told she had stage four breast cancer. Until that point, she wasn't sick a day in her life."

"How old were you?"

"I was fifteen. By my sixteenth birthday, she was dead. Before she died, she told me everything about my father and his other family. Agosto is a widow, so it never made sense to me why he kept us hidden. I understand it now but try making a fifteen-year-old understand that. Even on her deathbed, she defended his decision about keeping me a secret. In the end, hospice helped keep her comfortable as much as they could until she died. Agosto and I were by her side until the end. After we settled everything, I thought I would go live with him, instead I was sent away to an expensive boarding school."

"Wow, I think my respect for Agosto just dropped a few levels. Why would he do that?" I'm learning about a different side of Agosto. I wonder how much of this my grandma knows.

"When I graduated high school, again I thought this is the time he will claim me as his son. After the ceremony, we went back to my dorm, and that's when he told me I had to get plastic surgery."

"Wait, you had plastic surgery?"

"Chelle, if you keep interrupting me, I will never finish the story. Like I said, he came to me asking that I have surgery. I looked a lot like him in his younger days, and he claimed it would keep me safe. I agreed to some minor stuff, my nose, which I never liked and an eye lift."

I grab his chin and turn his head to the side. He takes my hand off of his chin and nips my finger. "There are no scars, but I would love to see what you looked like before the surgery." He lets out a laugh.

"This is also when he dropped the bomb that he planned for my staged death. He had a whole new identity ready for me. He didn't give me a choice, Chelle. That's when I became Luca Gill. Anyway, I went off to college and got my degree in Criminal Justice. I joined the FBI right after graduation. Within a few months they put me on Carmine's case. I was very junior, basically a gofer. It's because of Carmine that I got promoted so quickly."

"Carmine did something good?"

"Yeah, although now I realize it was for all the wrong reasons. I was bringing in food for everyone and he asked questions about me. After that, he refused to talk to anyone but me."

"Didn't you find that odd?"

"Chelle, my whole life up to that point was odd. I know when Carmine said he would only talk to me, Cody got really pissed off. They brought him in as the senior officer, but Carmine wanted no part of him. Maybe Carmine and Cody already knew who I was and all of it was a very well-staged act."

"What did Agosto say when you told him about your assignment?"

"He went ballistic. If he couldn't acknowledge me as his son, then why would I give him any say in what I do?" He moves closer to me but never lets go of my hand.

"I think the answer as to what you do next is sitting right in front of our faces. Demand he accept you as his son. It's your birth right. You have brothers that have the right to know who you really are. There is nothing to be ashamed of. I will be with you every step of the way."

"I'm not ashamed, but at this point, I'm not sure that I want to be sucked into his inner circle. If I do that, there is no going back."

"Only you can make that decision. I'm going upstairs to pack. Whatever you decide, I will support you no matter what, but you need to decide sooner rather than later." I give him a quick kiss and head upstairs.

CHAPTER SIXTEEN

Agosto

T HEY SAY IF YOU WAIT LONG ENOUGH, YOUR DREAMS WILL come true. At my age, it's like playing russian roulette waiting around for that to happen. Today I got lucky. Now let's see if my luck holds out. I'm nervous about bringing her home. Let's face it, I'm an eighty-year-old man who has no time for this nonsense. I look over at Viviana and she is nervously fidgeting with a thin silver rope bracelet.

"Viviana, what kind of bracelet is that? I've never seen you wear it before."

"It was a gift from Frances. It's called a Saint bracelet. When I'm nervous, I'm supposed to run my fingers along the rope and when I get to the metal saint, I'm to stop and breathe. It's supposed to remind me to relax, God is in charge. You never saw it because I usually only wear it when I go out."

"I know you are nervous, but don't worry, we will take everything at your own pace." I take her hand in mine and pray I can finally make her happy. She has lived through so much heartache, she deserves to finally be happy. When Frances was alive, she was a roadblock for me. Not that I wanted her dead, but she tried to stop Viviana from having any relationship with me. The heart wants what the heart wants, and no one should stand in the way. We pull up to the house and I ask my driver to stop. I want to show her everything. Quickly, I help her out of the car and through the iron gates into the courtyard.

"You always loved to garden. It's exquisite." She smiles up at me.

"Thank you. There is so much to show you, but I don't want to overwhelm you. I have a three-room suite set up for you. We can get to that later." We stroll toward the backyard. It's my favorite spot and I hope it will become hers too. When I open the six-foot wall to wall sliders, I hear her gasp. As crazy as this sounds, it makes me proud. "It's amazing, isn't it? We are actually tucked into the side of Camelback Mountain. I didn't think it was possible.

"It wasn't easy, and it took a long time to complete, but I look at it as a work in progress. Come around the side of the house with me. I have something special I want to show you." We take it slow, and I hold her arm in the crook of mine as we make our way to my bench.

"So, this is the bench you always talk about. It's nice to see it in person."

She sits down, and I put some bird seed in her hand and take the seat next to her. "If you wait long enough, the quail will come. They love it here as much as I do." We wait and, sure enough, they come around her. She laughs with delight as they take the food she offers. She turns toward me and takes my hand.

"Agosto, thank you for sharing your life with me. Over the years, I know so much has happened, yet you've always kept your word. You promised me you would take care of me until your last breath. I know what's been said about you and Carmine. While everything about Carmine is true, I know what they say about you can't be. I only know kindness." She leans in and kisses my cheek. I've finally found peace.

Michelina

I feel bad for Luca. He's been in limbo for so long. When he is with Agosto, he is happy, always trying to please him. Let's face it, every child wants their father's approval. I get he's trying to protect him, but at what cost? When I get upstairs, I find Jess asleep on the closet floor, clutching a journal. It doesn't look like we are going anywhere right now. I pick up the journal I was reading and continue where I left off.

Carmine

Some things can be hidden away, other times people turn a blind eye. No matter how hard I try, I can't look the other way. We might be the last two standing, but this kid, Luca, looks like my older brother, Belini, at that age. He was one of the first in our family to die on the streets of New York City. I just had to know. So, I said to him, "Hey, kid, where are you from? Who are your parents?"

"My name is Luca and what business is it of yours?" he answered real snarky like.

"You look familiar, like we could be related or something." His face paled and I knew I had my answer.

"Hey kid, I mean Luca, you don't have to answer since you already did. Don't give up your day job." I couldn't stop laughing. Good old respectable Agosto, planting his seed everywhere. It has to be him. We are the last two standing. At least I'm faithful. I might not want her anymore but, like I said, at least I'm faithful. Doing the mental math, I'm sure Gisele was dead by the time Agosto hooked up with the kid's mother. Why hasn't Agosto claimed this kid as his own flesh and blood? Is he afraid I'll go after him? I had so many questions, but I doubted the kid will answer. It was worth a try, though.

"Hey Luca, where's your mom?" I asked casually, not bothering to look up at him. Instead, I was acting as if I was really perusing my newspaper. I had already read it from front to back that morning. He told me that she died when he was fifteen and kindly reminded me that it wasn't really any of my business, but he had nothing to hide. Yeah . . . I bet.

"Where's your dad?" I continued.

"Why all the questions about my family, Carmine?" He seemed to be really getting hot under the collar at this point. I told him I thought we should get to know each other better since we'd be spending so much time together while I recuperated from surgery. This is the beginning of building trust between two people.

"My dad is also deceased." His stare was so intense. He tried not to look away first, which if he had, it would have meant he was lying. I gotta give the kid credit; he's got a big set of balls to go toe-to-toe with me and not back down.

Wow, so he didn't need anyone to tell him. He figured it out on his own, with the help of Luca. I want to tell Luca what I found out, but maybe it's better if he doesn't know. It will not change anything. His father is alive and hiding behind the self-imposed threat of danger rather than telling his family that Luca is his son. I take a few breaths and continue reading.

I've been faithful to my wife. It's the one thing my father taught me. Even though our relationship was over many years ago, I never wandered. I've had many opportunities to do so, but my father's words always played in the back of my mind. "A man is only as good as his word." Agosto was sniffing around Viviana for years, even though he knew she was married. Now, I'm wondering about this kid's mother. Maybe I'll have Butchie look into it.

It sounds like Carmine will not let this go. Jess stirs and her eyes flutter open. "Hey, sleepy head."

"How long have I been asleep?" She bolts upright, looking around.

"Only for a couple of hours."

"I thought we were packing up and moving to Agosto's house?"

"There is no rush. Grandma is already moved in. We are safe here with Luca."

She quietly stares at me for a moment.

"Chelle, what's the story with him? Don't say nothing. I'm not an idiot. I know there are things about him you're not telling me. Eventually, I'll finish reading these journals, and by then I'm sure I'll know everything, since it seems Carmine loved to talk not only about himself but everyone he's ever met."

"You're right. There is a lot in these journals, and this is just Carmine's personal stuff. This is not what everyone is after. This is what I'm after—the truth about the man. For so long, I had him on a pedestal. I think if I would have known all or even part of this, I would have come to a much different conclusion about the man. These books have changed my life forever. They've made me rethink my past. The worst part is, if I would have known any of this, maybe my relationship with my mom would have been much different. On top of my mounting grief, I harbor so much guilt. I will never have the opportunity to make things right with her. That, Jess, has shattered my heart into a million pieces." The emotional roller coaster I've been on has just come to a screeching halt. Finally, I let my heart feel all the ups and downs. All the missed opportunities I had never had with my mom. The dad I never knew and the extended family I'm now forced to accept with no questions asked. I wrap my arms around myself like a protective armor, bow my head and let the tears fall.

CHAPTER SEVENTEEN

Michelina

After my meltdown, Jessica helped me box the books up and pack a suitcase. I need to talk to Luca before Jess reads any more of these journals.

"Chelle, I'm going to take a quick shower before we have to go. I promise I won't be long."

"No worries, take your time." This gives me a perfect opportunity to talk to Luca. I head downstairs and find him sitting on the sofa. Gus is curled up in his lap, enjoying all the attention he's getting.

"I see Gus has made a new friend, probably for life." He looks at me and for the first time, I see sadness in his eyes.

"Gus and I had a wonderful conversation, even though it's one-sided."

"I've had many of those with him. I'm at a crossroads and I need your input. In Carmine's journals, he talks about when he met you for the first time. He figured it out pretty quickly that you are Agosto's son." At this, he stops petting Gus.

"You need to stay out of my personal business, Chelle. It's only going to get you hurt. By all accounts, my life is a mess and it's only going to get worse. I could never live with myself if something were to happen to you."

"Jessica has been reading the journals. She is going to get to the part about you soon. How are you going to handle it?" I'm putting the ball in his court. I will not tell her she can't read them.

"I guess it's getting to where I will have no choice but to confront Agosto about him dragging his feet."

Before I can say anything, my new phone rings. I turn the phone toward Luca, showing him the screen—unknown caller.

"Put it on speaker and try to keep him talking."

As I hit talk, he starts his timer. "Hello."

"So, Michelina, you don't take direction very well. I don't want to hurt anyone, but you are kind of giving me no choice here. Did you forget what I told you about the FBI? Oh, and did you really think that old bastard was going to keep you safe? Keep your precious grandmother safe? Tick. . . tick. . . tick. . ." My heart is racing. I can hear a pounding in my ears. Luca is waving his hand for me to keep talking.

"Look, Nick, I know it's you. Why don't we meet and talk about this. After all, you are my brother." He lets out a guttural roar that is so filled with hate I almost drop the phone.

"You are not my sister! You are nothing more than a bastard child. It's because of you my father is dead."

"If you really feel that way, then why didn't you kill Carmine when you had the chance? Let's face it, Nick, you've got no fucking balls." I can't believe what just came out of my mouth and by the look on Luca's face, neither can he.

"I guess it's time for me to finish off Carmine's wife." He ends the call. Luca gets up, and with his back toward me, is already on the phone with Agosto. I can't catch my breath. Jess races down the stairs and sees me struggling to breathe. She grabs the rescue inhaler out of my purse and shoves it in my face.

"Use it, now." I take a few puffs and I feel my lungs letting the air in. Luca drops the phone and drops to his knees in front of me.

"Are you okay?"

"Asshole, she has asthma. Were you going to let her drop dead before you got her inhaler for her?"

"I didn't know she had asthma. Chelle, can I do anything?"

"Black coffee helps," I answer. He heads into the kitchen and quickly comes back with a steaming cup of coffee. I take a few sips and feel my body begin to calm down.

"I just made it right before you came down,"

"What did Agosto say?"

"They know it's Nick, but the signal is bouncing all over. He's using a scrambler. Your grandmother is safe. He said she was resting. He sent Gianni to pick up Gemma just in case Nick has any other ideas. Why don't you both get your stuff and I'll drive you over to Agosto's house." I don't want to give him a hard time. I know this is eating him up inside. I get up and head upstairs with Jess following behind me. When we get inside, I see she has the boxes of books piled on the bed. She grabs my hand and gives it a squeeze.

"Chelle, I don't know how you are keeping it all together. I give you a lot of credit. I packed up all the books. Even though you've been keeping them hidden, I think it would only take a small fire to send this place up and you'll lose everything. Like you said, these are not the books they are looking for."

"I have another suitcase that is bigger. We could probably fit them all in there, and that would make it less conspicuous. I can put my clothes in with yours and put all our toiletries in a tote I have." I pull out the suitcase from under the bed and we put the books in it. When I get to the last box, under the very last book is an envelope addressed to me in Carmine's handwriting. I open it and a small red horn charm falls out. I pick it up and open the letter.

Michelina,

I hope Viviana shared all my journals with you. Your mother didn't want you to have them, but knowing your grandmother as I do, I'm sure she put up quite the fight. I have always tried to have you in my life, but your mother wanted no part of that. What a shame that is, so my only way for you to know who I really am and why I did what I did was with my own journals. When the time is right, I hope Frances will share with you everything that made America great for us, for me. In the meantime, please always wear this Cornicello. It will keep you safe. No matter what anyone tells you, I loved you with all my heart.

Carmine

The letter drops from my hand as I look at the charm. "Jess, how did this get in the box?"

"I bet you it was when your mom was getting the house ready to go on the market and she had all kinds of men coming in and out of here. Plus, the roofers were here for days. It had to be one of them."

Everything she says makes sense, but I still feel a shiver run up my spine. "Let's finish up and get out of here." I slip the charm in my pocket and toss the letter in my suitcase before closing everything up and dragging them downstairs.

CHAPTER EIGHTEEN

Luca

THE GIRLS COME DOWN THE STAIRS WITH TWO SUITCASES AND a tote. "It doesn't look like you packed enough stuff," I say with a sarcastic tone to my voice. Jessica rolls her eyes as she puts her small suitcase by the door. Chelle is halfway down the steps with a huge, bright red, rubber suitcase. I climb the rest of the way up to help with her suitcase and I nearly fall down the remaining stairs. "What the hell do you have in here, a dead body or something?" Before she can answer, it hits me: these are Carmine's journals. When I get to the bottom of the steps, I grab my keys off the counter and head outside, dragging the suitcase behind me. I hit the trunk release on my key fob and instead of the trunk opening up, there is a massive explosion that knocks me off my feet. The girls come running to help me, which is the last thing I need right now. "Get back inside and lock the door now!" I yell.

Quickly, I pull my gun and use the suitcase for makeshift shelter as I drag myself back toward the house, dragging the suitcase along with me. I can hear the muffled sound of sirens in the distance. I can't be sure no one is watching. The afternoon sun is making it hard to see anything. I stay huddled behind the suitcase by the front door. Since the emergency services are only two miles up the road, it doesn't take too long for police cars and fire trucks to come barreling down the driveway. I really can't hear anything as the police approach me with guns drawn, yelling something. I hold up my up gun with my finger off the trigger in my right hand and my FBI credentials in my left.

"I'm FBI on the job. I can't hear anything. The bomb went off when I was next to the car." One cop holsters his weapon and crouches down next to me. The other cops keep their weapons drawn and begin a perimeter-type grid search.

"Is there anyone else here?" he yells.

"Two ladies in the house that are under my protection." I must be yelling because he leans back. The men that were doing the search give the "all clear," which allows the paramedics to come to my aid. I try to tell them I'm fine, but they won't listen. The door swings open, Chelle and Jessica try to help me up, but the paramedics stop them.

"I'm okay. My hearing is coming back. I'll be fine."

"Sir, you might have a concussion. We need to take you to the hospital."

It will be a cold day in hell before I go to a hospital. "Really, I'm fine. Big red took the brunt of the explosion. And look not a mark on her. This could probably be a great endorsement for this suitcase." I put my hand on top of the suitcase to steady myself while the officer helps me get up off the ground.

"If you don't want to go to the hospital, that's your choice. However, my captain has informed me that he just got off the phone with your boss, and they are sending over their own technicians to work the scene. We are supposed to keep everything secure until that time. If you want to wait inside where you'll be more comfortable, I have no problem with that."

"Thank you, I'll be inside if you need anything." Jessica puts her arm around my waist and helps me inside while Chelle drags big red into the house and closes the door. I make my way to the sofa and sit down. I shoot a quick text to my boss Peter letting him know I'm okay and as soon as

I get my hearing back, I'll call him. Chelle hasn't moved. She's staring at the closed door with her arms wrapped around her waist. She's shaking and that's when I realize she's crying. I'm such an ass. She's probably re-living her mother's death all over again.

"I'm calling Agosto. All of this is out of control," she says with a voice that is quivering. She pulls her phone out of her back pocket. "Chelle, no!" I shout. "I need to be the one to call him, please." Right at this mo-ment, I want to pull her into my arms and tell her everything will be okay but, realistically, I can't. She spins around and her face is bright red. The tears are running down her cheeks. She holds up the phone and stomps over toward me.

"Make the fucking call now or I will. I can't live through another death. I don't care that he's my half-brother. I want the bastard dead now!" She tosses her phone into my lap and heads into the kitchen. She grabs a bottle of water, pulls a bar stool out from the island, turns it around, sits down and stares at me. Message received. I make the call.

"There was an explosion. My car blew up, but I wasn't in it yet." I don't put it on speaker. I'd rather keep it a one-sided conversation.

"The girls are fine. They were in the house."

"I'm okay. I've got a headache and some ringing in my ears. Nothing a few aspirins can't fix. Can you send someone to pick us up, please?" There is silence on his end, and I get it. In his world, there is no us and there probably never will be. "I would appreciate it if you could drop me off at my place, since it was my car that blew up. Of course, I'm sure the girls will be safe at your home." There is no goodbye, I just hang up. Chelle comes over and takes her phone back. If I look at her, I will see hurt. "I'll be okay." When I finally look up at her, her eyes are filled with such sadness, it breaks my heart.

There is a knock on the door. I pull my gun, head to the door, and look out the peephole. It's Geno and Gianni with the police. I holster my gun and open the door.

"Can you please tell this cop that we are here to pick up our cousin?" Gianni demands.

"That's true officer, they are here to pick up the ladies. Thank you for checking first." I close the door and Gianni is glaring at me.

"How the hell did you get here so fast?"

"Not that it's any of your business, but after the call from Nick we decided to come and pick up Chelle and Jessica ourselves."

"Dad said we are to drop you off at your place first. Is everyone ready?" Gianni is almost demanding while Geno is quietly staring at Jessica.

"Yes, we are ready." Jessica puts Gus in her tote bag while Chelle makes sure she has his food and a few toys, along with his favorite bed. I was going to help with the luggage, but it seems they have everything under control. I just follow suit. My head feels like it got hit by a Mack truck right now, so I'm happy to hand over the reins for the moment.

Geno is driving, so I give him my address.

"Wow, you live in Scottsdale. That's not that far from us." I want to scream *because your father put me there*, but of course I can't say anything. So, I divert the conversation away from myself.

"Do you have any leads on Nick yet?"

"We tracked him to Arizona. He's actually been here for a month. It's safe to say he's been watching everyone the whole time. Now we just need to flush him out. We'll get him."

I hope for everyone's sake he does, and sooner rather than later.

CHAPTER NINETEEN

Michelina

WATCHING LUCA WALK AWAY WAS PROBABLY ONE OF THE hardest things I ever had to endure. I needed one more look at his face. A face that I've etched into my memory. In my mind, I'm screaming at him to look back. Even if he did, I wouldn't know, since Geno practically flew out of the parking lot. I want to scream at the top of my lungs, *"he's your brother asshole!"* However, I can't. They trusted me with the secret and maybe letting the world know could cost him his life. I keep telling myself he will be okay, but my heart is telling me otherwise.

"Gianni, did you know he lived this close to us? I mean, I wonder why he didn't say anything sooner?" Geno glances at Gianni in the review mirror.

"Gianni, what is the status on Nick and Gemma?" I ask, trying to get the focus off of Luca.

"There's nothing to worry about, Chelle. I picked Gemma up earlier. She is waiting for us at the house. She's excited to meet you. Plus, we are hoping she will lure Nick out of whatever fucking hole he's got himself into."

"So, you already told her about me?" I ask. He half turns to face me. The look on his face is one of agitation.

"Of course, she already knows about you. When Dad found out about her, he found her and took her under his wing. He might hate his brother, but she is still part of the family. Chelle, I know it's only been you for so long, but you need to realize you have family and, in our world, family is everything. Your family will always come first and, unlike your grandfather, you never go against them."

"If that's the case, then I don't have to turn whatever Carmine left me over to the government. I could use it to help run the family." He looks at me and then bursts out laughing. I don't find any of this amusing.

"Chelle, I love your sense of humor. Seriously, though, you know you're a woman and that could never happen. Hell, look what they did to your mother, and she wanted no part of this life. To survive in this business, you have to be ruthless. You can't wear your heart on your sleeve. I don't think you have a vicious bone in your body. Besides, you've got to have a pair of balls."

"That's all well and good, Gianni, but guess who is holding all the cards right now—me, a woman." Before he can answer, we pull up to the gates of my new home. For now, at least. I pull Gus a little tighter against me and pray I'm doing the right thing.

Nick

I want what's mine. It's my birthright. That bitch thinks she can keep me away from it. She will be very sorry. I'll continue to pick off her loved ones right in front of her face. Frances got what she deserved. If she didn't fuck my father, none of us would be in this position. I will fight anyone and everyone to get to the top. Part of me wishes I would have killed Carmine that day in the bar, but this actually works out better for me. I will kill his granddaughter and take my rightful place at the top. My vibrating phone brings me back to the here and now. Caller ID says it's Gemma.

"Hey, sis, what's up?"

"When were you going to tell me you're in Arizona?"

"And you know this how?" She is quiet for a moment, and that's how I know.

"Agosto, I'm actually at his place. He wants you to come in, Nick. He says he can help you."

"The only thing he will do is help himself to what's rightfully mine."

"How do you figure it's rightfully yours? You're not even related to Carmine. It's all his stuff, stuff that would have gotten him killed if he lived long enough."

"Because of Carmine, our dad is dead. He took that from us, all because his precious Frances got knocked up. Dad only went with her to climb his way to the top. If he would have let Frances marry Dad in the end, everything would have been left to Dad and, ultimately, me."

"Who is filling your head with this garbage?"

"It's not garbage. Mom told me. She said she's the one who told Dad to sleep his way to the top. She told me that Dad hated Frances, but Mom pushed him into it."

"And now Frances is dead. You settled the score, Nick."

"It will never be settled until Michelina is dead. As long as she's alive, she carries a part of Daddy with her, and I hate her for that." I hang up the phone and toss it on the counter. I'm in a small efficiency motel in Apache Junction, which is an older part of Maricopa County. This is where people go to get lost in the real world. I'll stay until I make Michelina suffer. This is where I'll stay until I finally decide it's her time to meet the devil. Someone like her will end up in Hell, for sure.

Gemma

I need to find Agosto and let him know what Nick said. I don't want to see anyone get hurt, least of all a sister I never met. This house is enormous, but I know he likes to sit outback while having a nightcap. Sure enough, that's exactly where I find him.

"Hey, Agosto, can I join you?"

"Of course, Gemma, you never have to ask. Would you like a nightcap?"

I take the seat across from him. "No, I'm good. I just spoke to Nick. He's filled with rage. I've never heard him talk like he did about our parents and Michelina. After talking with him, I believe he's the one who had Frances killed. He really hates Michelina and talked about making her suffer. I tried to tell him to come here and let's work it out, but he wants no part of that. All he wants is his brand of revenge."

"Thank you for trying, Gemma. He's very hurt and blames everyone but the person he should blame: his father. Nick tried to take a shortcut to the top, a very stupid one. In the end, he paid the price for it."

"What are you going to do?" I ask just as the door opens and Geno, Gianni, and two women step outside. I know exactly which one is my sister. She looks a lot like my father. I get up quickly and introduce myself.

"Hi, I'm Gemma. You must be Michelina. You have our dad's dark eyes and hair."

"Yes, I am Michelina. Everyone calls me Chelle. This is my friend Jessica."

I want to shake her hand, but she has a cat in her arms. Maybe it's for the best. I need to take it slow. There is an awkward silence that encompasses the entire room. Agosto gets up and looks around the room before his eyes settle on Chelle.

"It's time for this old man to turn in for the night. Chelle, please walk with me." She passes the cat to her friend. Agosto puts his arm out for Chelle to take and they head back into the house.

CHAPTER TWENTY

Michelina

"THANK YOU, AGOSTO, FOR RESCUING ME FROM THE awkwardness in that room."

"Don't you mean meeting your sister for the first time?" He slyly smiles.

"I'm assuming Grandma had no problems getting situated here?"

"We spent a lovely afternoon in the garden, after which we had an early supper. These last few days have been exhausting for her, for all of us, really. But there seems to be something else weighing on your mind. Do you want to talk to me about it?"

"Yes, I only know the man that stands before me now, so I have nothing to compare it to. You talk about love and family, yet Luca is shunned upon by the very man that claims to love him." He stops walking and opens the door in front of us. It's an elaborate office that, in some way, reminds me of the oval office at the White House. I step inside as he follows close behind me.

"Please have a seat on one of the sofas. I will get us a drink and we can talk."

"Thank you. Just water for me, please." He pours himself a drink, taking his time before having a seat next to me.

"What makes you think I have shunned him? I give him the same support and love that I give all my children."

"I would like to give you the benefit of the doubt. However, his brothers have no clue who he really is. He should be able to take his rightful place within this family . . . his family. You started out saying it was to protect him and maybe all those years ago it was, but what's your excuse now? Just this week alone, someone tried to shoot him, and his car was blown up. He's an FBI agent who has more than proven he can survive. What's the real reason you won't acknowledge him as your son?" He swirls his glass, watching the ice roll around. Finally, he takes a sip and puts it down.

"You are very outspoken and to the point, Michelina. I've been protecting him for so long, maybe it's all I know."

"Excuse my language, but I call bullshit. You were afraid Carmine would find out and use it against you, but I read most of his journals and I have to tell you, he knew almost from the first time he met Luca. He said Luca looked like his older brother Belini." Agosto's face pales at this.

"That's why I insisted on plastic surgery. What else did my brother say?" his voice trails off. Part of me wants him to read the words for himself, but I'm not a cruel person. Seeing it in black and white makes it very real.

"Not much more. Even he was wondering why you never claimed Luca as your son."

"When his mother found out she was pregnant, I wanted to marry her, but she refused. She did not want her child to grow up in the type of environment I lived in. I went along with it, mainly because I lost a child to this violence I'm surrounded by. Honestly, I didn't think I could live through it again. By the time his mom was near the end of her life, Matteo knew I was his father, but she still wouldn't marry me or let me give him my name. After that, it just became easier not to upset the apple cart."

I let his words sink in. Finally, I find the courage to ask some of the tough questions. "Are you afraid of what Geno and Gianni will say?"

"Yes. For so long, it was just the three of us. I don't know if telling them would bring us all together or drive a wedge between us. Michelina, I can't—no—I won't be pushed to choose sides. It's easy to play Monday morning quarterback when you're not in the middle of it."

"On the contrary, I am in the middle of it. I'm being forced upon two half siblings that I know nothing about. Well, except that my half-brother probably killed my mother. He blew up Luca's car, almost killing him. He threatened me and my grandma. I wouldn't doubt it if he shot Cody, so yeah, I'm living the nightmare here, Agosto." He gets up and puts his glass on the bar in his office.

"Michelina, I think it's time for me to turn in for the night." I get up and slip my arm through his. We head back into the hall toward his room.

"I don't mean to be sarcastic, Agosto, but time is not my friend. The more we just sit on things, the worse it gets." We stop in front of his door. He opens the door and turns toward me.

"Michelina, the older we get, the faster time goes by. Besides, how much worse can it get? You already have everything you need. The bigger question is, how will you use it?"

He kisses me on the cheek and heads into his room, closing the door behind him. I'm stunned by his words. Does he expect me to tell everyone who Luca really is? Does he think I should give him all of Carmine's stuff that's in the safe deposit box? That stuff is the only thing protecting Jess and me right now. Giving it away is a death sentence. I decide to go back downstairs, get Jess, and settle in for the night.

Luca

Having my brother open the car and practically tossing me out really pissed me off. I get he has no idea who I am, but this just proved to me that even if he knew, nothing would change. Agosto is grooming Geno and Gianni to take over his business. I was never part of that equation. Maybe my mom was right when she said to go my own way. I was really too young to understand any of it, but now I get it and it's not good. When I met Chelle, I knew I should resist her. She's my second cousin. There has to be some rule about that. When she was in my arms, I knew I should stop, but I couldn't. That's when I came up with the idea that I should treat my feelings for her like the steak of the month club. However, she made my blood rush in a way I only get when there is danger. There has to be a way to get close to her inside the walls of Agosto's estate. If I was a real prick, I could just go up to the front door and announce that the love child has come home to claim what's his. I'd be dead before I step over the threshold. I mean, they would have to split everything three ways. That's a lot of money and power to lose. For now, I'm going to sit tight until I can talk to Chelle alone. I'm not a patient man, but I'll wait if I have to if it means I get Chelle.

CHAPTER TWENTY-ONE

Michelina

T
HIS HOUSE IS SO MASSIVE I NEED A ROAD MAP TO FIGURE IT out. Jessica and I have adjoining rooms. I leave her reading the journals while I take a long soak in the biggest tub I've ever seen. I'm not in here long before the door swings open and Jess comes running in.

"When the hell were you going to tell me?" I've never seen her this angry with me.

"Tell you what?"

"About Luca."

"Shhh, keep your voice down."

"Chelle, this house is so big, there is no one around for miles. Why would you keep such a thing from me? You know what this means— you're cousins." She throws the words out there like they are going to repel me.

"Even though sometimes I think I'm going to hell, I have scruples, Jess, just not when it comes to him. Besides, I already looked it up and second cousins can get married in all the states. In Arizona, first cousins can get married, but they have to wait until they are sixty-five."

"That's so you don't grow a third eye, Chelle. Let's put all that aside for now. Do his brothers know?"

"No, outside of Agosto and Luca, only Grandma and I know. Tonight, I tried to convince Agosto to tell his son's, but he made up all kinds of excuses."

"What are you going to do?"

"I do not know, but I'm open for any suggestions."

"If you have a picture of Belini you could leave it around, so Geno or Gianni will find it and maybe they will realize Luca is related."

"That's a stretch, besides I don't have a picture. Let me get out of the tub and we can finish reading the journals." I wave her off, get out of the tub, and wrap myself in a warm towel. I walk into my room and find Jess on the floor with all the journals.

"Have you thought of what you are going to do with all these journals when you are done reading them?"

"No, not really. I mean, part of me wants to keep them, and the other part wants to destroy them. Funny thing is, this is my family's history and as much as I want to burn these, I realize if history is gone, then we are bound to repeat it. If it's always here front and center, it will make us think twice. At least, that's the way I look at it."

I sit next to her and pick up the next journal. "Since you are all caught up to me, would you like to take turns reading it out loud?" She lets out a laugh and I cock my head and try to figure out what the heck is so funny.

"Chelle, you are always in teacher mode. Next, you'll have me raising my hand. Besides, what if someone is listening?"

"I wish someone was. Maybe then the truth will come out." I feel the lump in my throat and fight the urge to cry.

"On a more serious note, do you think we will ever go back to teaching?" Every time I think about this, my heart breaks a little more.

"Honestly, no, that part of our lives is closed. I'm sorry you got mixed up in all of this. Maybe this is why my mom had so few friends?" I open the journal and start reading first.

"Today I started testing out my unfamiliar face. I went to Las Sendas Golf Club. It's in the community that Frances lives in. I played eighteen holes and afterwards I had a late lunch. The restaurant is always busy, but the food is good, so it's worth the wait. When I was finishing up, I saw Frances come inside to pick up a to-go order. Our eyes met, but then she quickly looked away. I would think a daughter would know her father no matter what, but maybe I'm wrong. She picked up her order and left, never looking back at me. Maybe this new identity will actually work out." I grab the water bottle sitting on the floor between us and take a sip when I finish.

"I wonder how long he hid in plain sight? Did Luca say how long he was with Carmine?"

"I believe it was months. Luca tried to warn my mom he was alive, but she didn't believe him."

"Chelle, we really need to talk about Luca."

I wave my hand thinking I'm dismissing her, but Jess is not easily swayed. "There is nothing to say. After today, I realize I need to formulate a plan for us."

"What do you mean *after today*?"

"Jess, if you weren't so fascinated with Geno, you would have heard what Gianni said. The bottom line is: we can't go back to work. I need to turn everything over to the *men* because we basically have no brains, in case you weren't aware of this. You know tits and ass are only useful for putting out when the men want it." I try to calm my rage. They don't ever want to understand that women stopped living in the stone age a long time ago.

"Chelle, I can see the wheels turning. I'll back you up, but will it mean that I won't be able to see Geno anymore?"

"That depends on a lot of different things, Jess. I'm exhausted, though, let's call it a night and we can pick this up tomorrow." She gets up and heads toward the door.

Research: it's what I've always done best. I push the journals aside and pull out my laptop. It doesn't take long for me to find out everything I need. Next, I need to sit down with Luca alone and have him help me iron out all the details. My biggest obstacle is trying to be alone with Luca. Tomorrow, no matter what happens, I must find a way to get to him. For now, what I need is sleep. I shut down my computer and call it a night.

CHAPTER TWENTY-TWO

Luca

MY APARTMENT IS QUIET—TOO QUIET. I CAN'T GET THE LOOK on Chelle's face out of my mind when Gianni practically threw me to the curb. In his eyes, I'm the FBI . . . his sworn enemy. It's been ingrained into the minds of the family at a very young age. They can never associate with law enforcement. How will they feel when they find out the truth? Their brother—me/Matteo—is what they despise the most in life. Agosto is always quoting a Sicilian proverb. "He who is deaf, blind, and silent will live a hundred years in peace." Of course, it sounds better when he says it in Italian. At the end of the day, a snitch is a snitch and maybe that was the straw that broke the camel's back between Agosto and Carmine. I think with all the animosity that was between them their whole life, they didn't stand a chance at getting along. The most they could hope for is to not kill each other.

I pour myself a neat bourbon and prepare to drown myself in this wonderful brown liquor and try to forget about Chelle until I get a text from my boss, Peter Gander.

Peter: Hey, tomorrow make sure you get your ass in here for a debrief.

Me: Is this really necessary? You already know what happened. My car blew up. Which means I'm going to have to Uber it.

Peter: It's necessary and leave the attitude at home.

I grab the bottle, put Ed Sheeran's gut-wrenching song "Eyes Closed" on repeat and prepare to drown my sorrows.

Michelina

Sleep was restless. However, I was able to figure out a plan to see Luca. Maybe even go over some options for our future. The entire plan revolves around my grandmother. After a quick shower, I get dressed and head out on the guise that I need coffee. Which, in reality, is true. After some searching, I find the kitchen. There is a hot pot of coffee on the counter, but no one is around. I fix a cup and make my way outside. Sure enough, I find Agosto and Grandma in the garden, enjoying a cup of coffee. I need to get her away from him so I can get her help.

"Good morning, everyone. It's such a beautiful morning, so I thought I would have my coffee in the garden. What a surprise to see you both up so early." I can lay the bullshit on when I have to. Agosto doesn't know me well enough yet, but Grandma knows something is up. I'm never this chipper in the morning.

"Agosto, if you don't mind, can you get me a fresh cup of coffee, please? We were talking so much that now it's cold." She holds out the cup for him, basically not giving him an option. He gets up and heads inside, and I pull a chair close to hers.

"Michelina, what's wrong?"

"I need your help. I need to get away from here without being tracked. Maybe we could run an errand together."

"That's fine, but he will never let us go off on our own without a bodyguard. I think I have a solution that will work. You follow my lead. Oh Michelina, this is very exciting. Probably the most excitement I've had in years." I'm floored. But if she can pull it off, why not? Agosto comes back with the coffee and Grandma makes a show of enjoying it.

"Agosto, I have a doctor's appointment later today and Michelina needs to come with me. We won't be long. It's a follow up appointment that I forgot all about."

"If you're sure I can't take you, then I can at least have Geno drive you."

"That will be great and Agosto, when I get back, we can have that game of scrabble you've been promising me." He gets up and helps her out of her chair. She takes my arm, and we head inside. When we get to her room, we go out on her little patio off her bedroom.

"Thank you for going along with this. I need to see Luca, and my every move is being watched. For all I know, they bugged everything. Do you have a doctor's appointment today?" She smiles at my question.

"Well, my dear, I do now. Besides, I've been meaning to give my friend George a call."

"Wait, who is George?"

"George is a doctor. He comes to visit his son where I was living. He plays a great game of pinochle."

"Oh, are you sure he will go along with this?"

"Of course he will. His dad has a thing for me, but he's not my type." Maybe it's me or maybe it's just wishful thinking, but Grandma really seems to be in the here and now.

"I'm going to have Jess come with us. With Geno driving us, she will be an excellent distraction. Oh, and one more thing, I'm going to need your phone."

"Are you sure? It's very old. Not like the phones that everyone else has." She passes it to me. I open it up and pull out the battery to get to the sim card. I pull that out and hand her back the phone.

"Didn't you know flip phones are coming back in style, Grandma?" She pulls me into a hug and, for a moment, all the world seems right again.

"I'm going to get ready and let Jess know what the plan is. I'll be back in thirty minutes. Oh, and Grandma, what kind of doctor is George?" She giggles and I have no idea why.

"He's an OBGYN." Now I'm laughing. She always had a great sense of humor. We go back inside, and I head off to fill Jess in on the plan.

Jess and I get Grandma then go to find Geno. The look of surprise on his face is not lost on any of us, including Grandma. George's office is near the Scottsdale airport. It's not a commercial airport; it caters to corporate flights. Jess was flirting away with Geno so much that he almost missed our turn. When we pull up to the office, I get out and help Grandma out. Geno turns to get out, as well but Jess puts her hand on his thigh. He pauses.

"Jessica, I've got to go inside with them. I'm not supposed to let them out of my sight. Those were my dad's orders."

"Well, Geno, I don't think there is any reason for you to go sit in a gynecologist's office, do you?" His face turns bright red. He looks at Grandma and I didn't think it was possible, but his face gets even redder.

"Ma'am, what would you like me to do? I want to make sure you are safe and comfortable."

"I'll be sure to tell Agosto how accommodating you've been. You can wait here with Jessica." She gives him a wink. And with that, I shut the door and we take off slowly, arm-in-arm.

"Grandma, I'm going to need your phone now." She passes it to me as she tells the lady at the front desk that she is there to see George. There is a sign on the glass at the front desk with the Wi-Fi code. Even though it is a flip phone, it still has Wi-Fi. I quickly sign in and it works.

"Do you have an appointment?"

"No, please tell him that Viviana Amato is here to see him." The woman looks baffled, but she goes in the back, hopefully, to find George.

We are not even waiting five minutes when a very tall, handsome man with speckled gray hair comes out. He opens the door for us to come in, but first he gives Grandma a big, long hug. I wonder if his dad looks anything like him.

"You must be Michelina. I've heard so much about you from Viviana. Please come into my office." He guides us down the hall and into his office. It's nothing fancy, but it's what I need for some privacy.

"Thank you, George, for seeing us on such short notice. My grandmother and I have been through a lot the past couple of weeks."

"I heard about Frances. I'm sorry for your loss. I was out of town when it happened."

I'm not sure why he felt like he needed to tell me that. It's not like I was expecting him to come to my mom's service.

"Excuse me, I need to use the restroom. Grandma, you can get started. I'll be right back." George points me in the right direction. I follow the path down the hallway and into the restroom. I pull out Grandma's phone and call Luca.

"Viviana. Is everything okay?"

"I didn't realize you knew Grandma's phone number?"

"Chelle, are you okay?"

"I'm fine, but I need to talk to you. I went to great measure not to get caught."

"Do I even want to know?"

"No, but I have a plan and I think it will work."

"Chelle, if it involves me telling Gianni and Geno who I am, the answer is no. They already hate me. Besides, Agosto should have manned up years ago. It's too late."

"Luca, do you trust me?"

"Yes," he says without hesitation.

"Good. Now, let me put my plan into motion. It will only work if we are a team. Agosto is old and wants to pass his business to his kids. He will never acknowledge you as his son. Partly because he is embarrassed by what his sons would think. Plus, he knows they would never accept you as one of them. That would mean that they'd have to split everything three ways. It's never going to happen. I'm stuck with all of Carmine's blackmail material. If I give it to Agosto, there is still a bounty on my head because I know what's in it. The only logical conclusion is we take the stuff, and we set new rules to reign over all the families. You need to find a way to get me away from that house so we can go pick the stuff up together." I'm met with silence. "Luca, I really miss you. I've got to go before someone comes looking for me." I hang up before he can answer and head back to George's office. I can hear the two of them laughing before I go inside. She is having fun with this, but we can't stay here forever. I knock and open the door.

"Well, it sounds like you're having a good time."

"It was nice to catch up. However, I've got to get back to work and, Viv, I've been practicing my pinochle game. Let me know when we can get a game going." He gives her a kiss on the cheek and walks us toward the front desk. No one questions us as we head outside into the blazing heat. I take Grandma's arm and guide her toward the car. The closer we get, I realize that Jess and Geno are very busy with each other, too busy to realize we are back. I knock on the roof and try not to laugh. I can hear Jess asking where her bra went. This ought to be interesting.

CHAPTER TWENTY-THREE

Luca

WHEN I SPOKE TO CHELLE YESTERDAY, SHE SAID SHE HAD A plan, but so do I. First, I need to get a car. Second, I need to have that meeting with my boss. Finally, I need to convince him that Chelle is all for working with the FBI. If I can do that, it will give us some breathing room. When I get to the office, my boss Peter is waiting for me.

"Don't say a word, Luca, just follow me," he bellows. We head into the conference room where Robert Conti is waiting for us. I had a bad feeling coming here and seeing Robert makes it worse. I make a beeline to the coffee machine, grab a cup, and sit down.

"Good morning, Luca." Robert's voice is strained, and his icy glare makes the hairs on the back of my neck stand up.

"Morning, Robert. Peter, I submitted my report yesterday. It was pretty straightforward, so I'm not sure what else you want from me."

"Robert here seems to think that you made sure Michelina and Jessica called off all the protection that the FBI and the Justice Department will offer."

"I guess Robert can't talk for himself. Why the hell would I do that, Robert?" It is all I can do not to choke this asshole.

He turns his chair toward me, leans in so that his face is only inches from mine. "Because your father wanted you to."

"You have no idea what you're talking about. I don't need to listen to this." I get up, pushing my chair back so hard it flips over.

When I'm almost to the door, I hear Peter yell, "Stop, Luca! We know Agosto Amato is your biological father." I freeze. A million things are running through my head. Starting with—*how the fuck could he know that?* "Come sit back down, Luca. You need to tell us everything. Start from the beginning and leave nothing out."

I'm busted. The one thing I was afraid of coming out has. I turn and go back to my seat. Robert has a smirk on his face like the cat that swallowed the canary. "What difference does it make who my father is?"

"Is that how you got Carmine to turn?"

"I had nothing to do with Carmine flipping."

"What's Agosto's end game?" I sit silently, letting his words hang in the air while I try to wrap my mind around all of this.

"I don't know anything. I only found out he was my father when my mom died. His answer to all of that was to ship me away to boarding school and then college. If you think he's going to trust me or bring me into the fold, you are sadly mistake. Hell, he won't even tell his other kids I exist."

"If that's the case, then how did you get Carmine Amato to flip?"

"Carmine hated Agosto. Anything Carmine did was for the sheer pleasure of pissing Agosto off."

"What about Cody? How did he fit into all of this?"

"Apparently Cody was a snitch. Carmine's right-hand man, Butchie, was Cody's uncle. Before you ask, I didn't find this out until after he was murdered." I drop that bomb in Peter's lap. Robert looks at Peter, then turns back toward me.

"Is there anyone involved in all of this that isn't connected?" Robert spews those words with such venom. I shrug my shoulders and keep my mouth shut.

"Relax, Robert. I think Luca might be able to salvage this for us. Does Michelina know who you are?"

"No, as far as she is concerned, I'm just an FBI agent, that's all." For my plan to work, they have to think she was not in on any of this. I want them to think I can convince Michelina to work with the FBI. Now that they know who I am, I'm not sure if working with them is a good idea.

"Do you think you could get her to work with you to bring down Agosto?" Peter asks.

Robert jumps up from his chair and heads toward the door.

"Robert, get back here, now." He freezes at the sound of Peter's words. Finally, he turns around and looks from Peter to me with such hatred in his eyes.

"Look, Peter, you might trust Luca to tell you the truth, but I don't. I wouldn't be surprised if he's already working with Michelina. Don't forget, I saw the two of them together. They aren't fooling anyone, least of all me. I want no part of this." He turns and leaves. This time, no one is stopping him.

"Okay, Luca, it's just us. Tell me, what are you going to do to make this right?"

"Look, Peter, Robert makes it sound like Michelina and I are involved. I mean, she's my cousin, for Christ's sake." If he's buying it, I can't tell.

"Maybe you could use that to your advantage. Do you think you can convince her to at least continue with FBI protection?"

"As I see it, there are a multitude of problems here, starting with Viviana Amato. Yesterday she moved into Agosto's home. Michelina and her friend Jessica also moved in. It will be very difficult to get them away from Agosto. Let's add to that Michelina's jackass half-brother who is trying to kill her and most probably killed her mother. That would be the same jackass that threatened Viviana. Nick Jr. is the reason everyone moved in with Agosto. Maybe this is why Agosto has looked the other way when it comes to Nick Jr."

"What if we have Michelina arrested?" This right here is a desperate man. I take a deep breath and shake my head.

"Why would you do that? Don't you think that would only add fuel to the fire?"

"Do you have a better idea?"

"Actually yes, I do. It's pretty elaborate but with the right help I think we can pull it off." Now would be the time to put my plan in motion. I think I can trust him. After all, he is the head of the Arizona FBI. I've never hesitated in my life yet, right now, I can still feel all the hairs on the back of my neck standing at full attention.

"Luca, I can understand your hesitation, but you know whatever you tell me will never leave this room. The goal has always been to keep Michelina safe and retrieve Carmine's black books. If you can get Michelina to give you the books, then there would be no reason for anyone to hurt her. You know, no matter what happens, we have to get Michelina out of there and away from Agosto. If we don't, she will never be safe, and that includes Jessica and Viviana."

I push aside my doubts and formulate my plan with him to get Chelle alone. If I can pull this off, I'm pretty sure Agosto will never announce to his family that I'm his son. I think I've finally come to terms with that. If he didn't want me when I was a young, vulnerable kid, then he doesn't deserve me now that I'm an honorable, trusting man.

CHAPTER TWENTY-FOUR

Michelina

H EARING LUCA'S VOICE YESTERDAY ERASED ANY DOUBTS I MIGHT have had about the plans I'm making for us. I could have told him over the phone, but I needed to see his face. That's the only way I will really know that he's all in. I'm on Carmine's last journal. I've come to realize so much, not just about the man, but about myself. Having strength to stand up for what's right when no one else will is powerful. Today, I realize I'm the person with the power.

Carmine

Today I finally found out who Luca is. I knew all along that Agosto was his father, but Butchie got proof from his nephew Cody. Today I tried to talk to Frances one last time. I know I will have to disappear forever, but before I do, I want her to know how I feel. Not just about the family, but about things I've done . . . things I should have done and said. I spoke to Luca about it. He was adamant that I needed to stay away. He said I could put her in more danger than she already is. I thought about all he said, however; I needed to listen to my gut. To whomever is reading this, the best advice I can give you is to listen to your gut. I survived a lot of bad things because I listened.

This makes me so sad to think he wanted to talk to her, maybe even explain why he did what he did, but she never gave him the chance. Reading these journals and seeing for myself what damage all these secrets have caused, I never want to live with any regrets. When Carmine smacked Viviana, everything changed. Everyone's life changed from that one incident. My mother lost a man who she thought was the love of her life. She never married. She never got to experience all the milestones that come with growing old together with someone. Grandma despised Carmine and turned toward the one man that could fill Carmine with so much rage that he would relish in the pain Agosto went through when losing his wife and son. And then there's me, poor Michelina, the girl whose father was a mafia wannabe. A man who I don't have any respect for. I mean, how could I? He slept with the boss's daughter, knocked her up, thinking he was on the express train to the top. In reality, he made the worst mistake of his brief life. I turn back to the last few pages of his journal.

Against Luca's advice, I went to the La Sendas Golf Club every day. I thought if she recognizes me, then I will try to tell her everything. If she doesn't, I will finally let it go. I went all different times to the club. Sometimes I swear I could feel her watching me, but I never saw her. One day I finished up my game, went into the locker room and changed into my street clothes. I was heading out of the club when I heard a gasp. I turned and saw her, the shock on her face right before she took off running. When I caught up to her, I grabbed her arm with too much force and spun her around. Her eyes filled with tears, and she was yelling, "I know it's you, Daddy; I saw your birthmark. You didn't even try to hide who you really are." She wanted to know how I could do all of this? All I could do was laugh, which wasn't what she wanted to hear. I said, "Frances, I have only one regret in my life. I wanted a relationship with my granddaughter, and you wouldn't allow it." I damned her to Hell because of it. Looking back, I probably was a little harsh. I tried to explain that everything I did was for my family, but she wanted none of it. She cursed me for everything I did to stop her from being with Nick. She even blamed me for his death. At that point, I knew what I had to do, what my gut was telling me to do. She was irrational and there was no more talking to her. I pressed a key and a piece of paper with the name of a bank and the number of the safe deposit box. I told her whomever has the book has the power, so guard it with your life. Then I turned and walked away, never looking back. I went back to my apartment and Luca was waiting for me. He threatened to kick me out of the program if I ever pulled that shit again. I smiled, knowing I would never need to see her again.

That's it, there are no more entries since he died right after this one. I put it back in the box and stack it in the closet with the others. There is no need to hide them anymore. It doesn't matter if someone reads them. I really don't think anyone can truly understand the depth and depravity of Carmine Amato. My phone rings. I grab it and see that it's the mortuary that handled everything for my mom's service. I answer.

"Hello, Michelina, this is Travis Rittenhouse. I handled your mom's service."

"Yes, I remember. I don't remember if I thanked you. Everything was so crazy at the time. You did a wonderful job and made a difficult day a little easier."

"Thank you. I'm calling because you left in a rush that day and I still have a small box with some of your mother's belongings here. When would be a good time for you to pick them up *today*?" He emphasized the word today as if it has a special meaning.

"I can come today at one o'clock, if that works for you."

"That would be perfect. See you then." He hangs up and I'm left alone to overthink what could he possibly mean and what could I have left there? I decide to leave my room in search of Jessica. Since she made all the arrangements; she might know what we left behind. This time when I go in search of the kitchen, I find it much quicker. Jess is at the table with Geno and Gianni.

"Jess, where is Grandma?"

"Out in the quail garden with Agosto."

"I got a call this morning from Mr. Rittenhouse, the director of the mortuary. He said there was some of Mom's stuff left behind that I need to pick up today. Do you know anything about that?" She finally pulls her attention away from Geno and looks at me like a deer in the headlights.

"No, I don't remember leaving anything. Do you want me to run over there today?"

"No, I told him I would come this afternoon."

Gianni puts his coffee cup down and turns toward me. "There is always construction on that end of town. If you have to be there by one o'clock, you will have to leave about noon. I'll drive you over there myself." His smile is almost sinister. He knew the time, and he made damn sure I knew he listened in on everything. No way was I getting out of here by myself, but the lack of privacy is still irritating.

"If you want, Geno and I can come, too."

"Thank you, Jess, but I brought you here to keep you safe. Until they catch Nick, I think it would be best if you stayed here. You can monitor Grandma for me."

I pour a cup of coffee and excuse myself from the kitchen. I need to talk to Grandma before I go. The house has so many doors that lead outside that I keep getting turned around. It's almost like the doors are for a quick escape, except the house is built into the side of the mountain. Finally, I find Grandma alone, feeding the quail.

"Good Morning, I thought Agosto was out here with you?"

"He had to go inside to take care of some business. He said he was hiring a nurse to come in daily to check on me. I don't think I need that, but I learned a long time ago to pick and choose your battles wisely. What's troubling you today? You seem so anxious."

"I have an errand to run today, but I'll be back later and then you can teach me how to play pinochle."

"Did you need me to come with you?" I wish I could take her, run away and never look back, but thanks to Carmine and, in part, Agosto, that can never happen.

"No, I'll be fine. I wanted to check on you before I left, in case you needed anything." Before she can answer, Agosto is back. He seems a little irritated. I wonder what he knows? I have no time to figure it out. With a wave goodbye, I head inside so I can get my bag and, of course, Gianni to leave.

CHAPTER TWENTY-FIVE

Luca

TIME SEEMS TO TICK BY SO SLOWLY. I REALLY NEED TO BE ALONE with Chelle to explain my plan. Not the one that Peter has planned. Having Chelle work with the FBI will only cause more problems. She and I need to work together. I know my window of opportunity will be small, but I have to try.

Peter picks me up and, as promised, he is alone. Unfortunately, I know he has a few discreet people stationed at the mortuary. It's what I would do. "Have you figured out how you are going to pitch your plan to her yet?" I try not to show my disgust for what I think he might be planning.

"Luca, you're going to be the one pitching the plan. I mean, you got her grandfather to turn. I'm hoping the apple doesn't fall far from the tree."

Inside I'm laughing, knowing how much she despises Carmine and now it seems Agosto has landed himself on that same list. "I'll do what I can. However, if it comes from you, she might listen."

Peter keeps glancing around as we pull into the parking lot. His focus is clearly on what's going on around him. We finally get out of the car and walk up the path to the side entrance of the building. Peter pulls a key out of his pocket and unlocks the door.

"Well, that's convenient. Where is Rittenhouse?"

"He loaned his government the use of this place. He's a genuine patriot and wants to do whatever he can to help. You should take notes from him. Rittenhouse even left all the lights and monitors on for us."

It's best I don't get into a confrontation with him. Hopefully, by the time this day is over, Chelle and I will be on our way to a safer life. . . together. There is a chime from the front door. I look at the monitors and see Chelle walk in alone. I walk out to the vestibule alone, leaving Peter in the office. Looking around, I glimpse Gianni outside. I knew he would not let her come alone. Besides, Nick Jr is still out there trying to kill her. He'd be a fool if he let her go by herself. All I need to do is lock Peter in the office and we can head out back.

"Where is Mr. Rittenhouse? And why are you here?" Her eyes fix on mine, and I know she gets it. This is our way of getting the hell out of here. All we need to do is pick up the stuff and head out of town. Our lives will change forever.

"Why don't we go in the back to pick up the stuff Rittenhouse left for you?"

Chelle walks beside me and as we pass the office, I see it's empty, no Peter. I freeze and pull out my gun. "Stay behind me, Chelle." For once, she doesn't fight me.

We get to the back room, and the door is ajar. I see Peter on the floor in a pool of blood. Chelle is looking over my shoulder and when she sees him, she yelps.

"Luca, I know you're out there and you have Michelina with you. There is no way out, so you might as well come in and let's talk about it."

"Luca, Gianni is out front. I thought we were going to make an escape out back. That sounds like Robert."

"It is, my boss Peter is the man on the floor. I'll go in and deal with Robert. You should go back out front and have Gianni take you as far away from here as you can get."

"No, I'm not leaving you. Besides, you don't know that I would be any safer with Gianni."

"Come on, Michelina, stop making us wait. Oh, did I say us? Your brother is here, and he wants to finally meet you." She is up against my back, and I can feel every muscle in her body stiffen. I hear the chime of the front door. "Chelle, you in here?" Gianni calls out. I turn so her back is now up against the wall. I see Gianni coming toward us with his gun pointed right at me.

"Chelle, what the fuck is going on here? Luca, did you set her up? Typical fucking FBI," he grumbles. He takes a few steps toward us and that's when I see Robert through the open door. His gun pointed at Gianni.

"Well, isn't this nice. Nick, you have to see this. We can get two brothers for the price of one." I feel the blood drain from my face and a lump in my throat. Nick steps into view and gets his shot off first. It doesn't matter who my father is. I do what they have trained me to do. I jump in front of Gianni, get a few rounds off, and take the bullet that was meant for him. All I hear is Chelle screaming and as my eyes close, I see her take the gun from me. Darkness consumes me. Voices fade and all I feel is cold . . . very cold.

Michelina

Watching everything getting played out before me was like slow motion. I grabbed Luca's gun and just kept firing. Gianni picked up where I left off and eventually, the shooting stopped. I'm all over Luca, feeling for a pulse. He has one, but it's faint. I apply pressure to the wound and pray. That's what my Grandma always taught me. When you need him the most, he will be there for you. Well God, I really need you now.

"Chelle, why would he do that? He took a fucking bullet for me. Why?"

"Because he really is your brother. Agosto has a lot to answer for, but

right now, you have to help me save him. We can't let him die... please."
He stares at me for a few seconds and then bends down, scoops him up
and we race to the car.

"If we wait for an ambulance, he will die before they get here. Get
in the back with him and keep putting pressure on the wound. We are
going to Banner Heart Hospital since it's the closest." I do as he says as
he speeds through the streets.

He gets us to Banner in what I'm sure is record time. The emergency
staff is at the car and getting him on to a gurney. "He is an FBI agent.
Please save him." I don't know why I felt I had to let them know that.
Maybe they would work harder to save him? I know that's not rational.
I know they don't judge anyone coming through the door. They whisk
him away so quickly. I collapse in a heap on the floor. I'm staring at the
blood all over me. A nurse runs up to me and is trying to ask me questions. I can't focus. I look at the nurse and another wave of tears come.
"I never got to say goodbye. I never told him I love him. My world will
always be filled with all the things I never said to him."

"Are you hurt? Is any of this your blood?"

I look down at my hands covered in his blood. "It's not mine. My
heart is breaking. You can't get any more hurt than that." I curl into a ball
and cry. The nurse tries to move me, but Gianni comes over, lifts me up
and carries me to a chair.

"I know you're in shock, but you need to tell me the truth."

I open my eyes and look at him. "The truth is something Agosto
should have told you years ago. I blame him for all of this." He doesn't
press me any further. Instead, he gets up and gets some wipes to clean
my hands.

There is a clock on the wall, and I watch the hands moving around
it. With every tick, I'm wishing that we could go back and have a do-over.
Unfortunately, those things only happen in fairytales.

The emergency doors open, and Agosto comes running in with
Geno and Jess. At this moment, I have never hated anyone as much as I

do him. Jess pulls me into her arms, but I can't cry anymore. I can't feel anything but fear of the unknown.

"Gianni, what happened? You were supposed to keep everyone safe!" Agosto yells at him as if it's his fault.

Gianni gets out of the chair and steps up to Agosto. His face only inches from his father's. "No Dad, I was supposed to keep Michelina safe. I didn't know Luca is my brother or that he would take a bullet meant for me." Geno pulls Gianni back, nearly knocking him over.

"What the fuck are you talking about? He can't be our brother; he's an FBI agent—the lowest of the low."

"Enough! Please stop fighting. I will explain everything later. Right now, I need to find out what's going on. I can't lose another child. God please, not my Matteo." He finally addresses him by his given name and acknowledges that he is his son. He sits down in the chair next to me and begins to pray. I see this man for who he is, and I finally understand why Carmine hated him. Hours go by without any word. Finally, a nurse comes over and tells us that the doctor wants to talk to the family about Luca's status. When we all stand up to go, the nurse states only one or two at the most. Agosto steps forward. "I am his father. I will go with Michelina." I jump up and follow them into a small room where Dr. Arif is waiting for us.

"Your son was very lucky. If the bullet had gone one inch either way, we wouldn't be having this conversation. He lost a lot of blood and coded once on the table. My team was able to bring him back. He is going to recover, but it will take some time. Right now, he is heavily sedated. He is in the ICU. It's late right now and you won't be able to see him until tomorrow. I would suggest everyone go home and get some rest, but I don't think you will. If your family can donate blood, that would be helpful. Do you have questions?" He is rather abrupt and to the point. If I had to choose a good doctor or a great bedside manner, I would go with the brilliant doctor.

"Thank you for saving my son's life. I will make sure we all donate blood."

The doctor leaves and I'm left alone with Agosto. "Do you see what your secrets and lies have done? No more. Do you understand me?"

"Yes, but it will not be easy. There is more to it than you know."

"What I know is Luca never felt wanted by you. Like you were ashamed of him. He worked so hard to please you and you turned your back on him. If it was up to me, I would cut you out of our lives for good, but Luca is a better man and I'm sure he wouldn't do that." I open the door and head back to the waiting room with the others. They quickly gather around to hear the news. At first, I thought Agosto would fill them in, but he sits in a chair and says nothing.

"It was touch and go, but he is a fighter. He's not giving up and neither should any of you. Geno, maybe you should take your father home."

Agosto shakes his head no. "I'm not going anywhere. I need to see Matteo. I have to explain things to him, to all of you."

I stare at Agosto, and he's sitting there with his hat in his hands. I'm reminded he is just a man, a man who has brought out the worst in people. A man who wanted to rule the underworld. Now he's just an old man living with his secrets and lies. I'm reminded that he and Carmine were cut from the same cloth.

BLOOD
VOWS

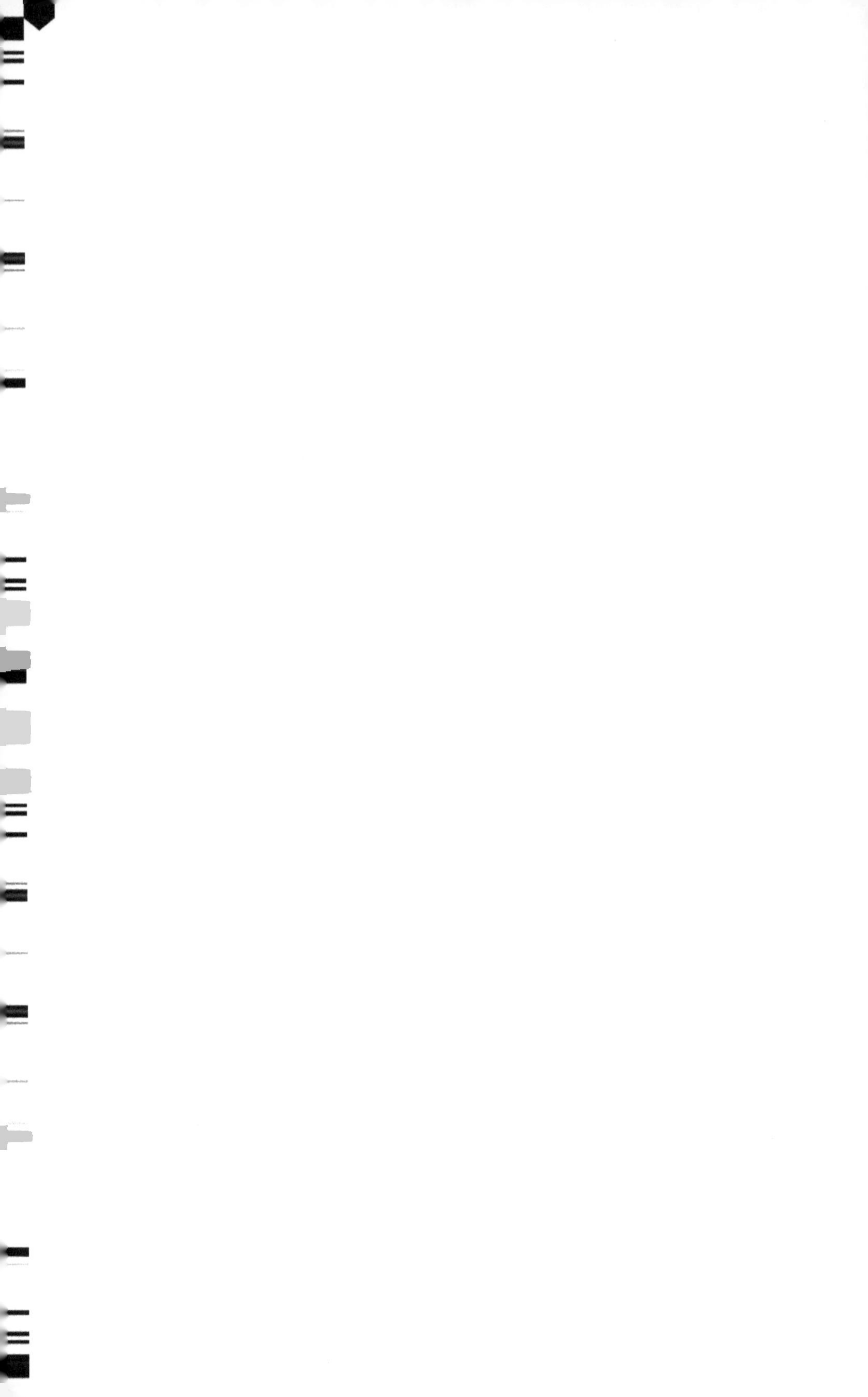

CHAPTER ONE

Michelina

It's been an endless week. Luca had a bleed that had to be corrected. He ended up staying in the ICU longer than we thought. Visiting with him is very limited. I've had to split my time with Agosto. Part of me didn't want to, but I knew Luca would never be mean to him. I haven't left the hospital since the day everything happened. Jess has brought me clean clothes and toiletries. I call Grandma every day and update her on his condition. I thought she would defend Agosto and his decisions when it came to Luca, but I was surprised that she didn't. She warned Agosto years ago that what he was doing would not end well.

Today they finally moved him out of ICU and into a private room. He went for a test and should be back soon. Gianni is here. He comes every day. He sits with me while Agosto goes in. I haven't let anyone in to see Luca yet, not even Gianni, and he hasn't asked. The new head of the local FBI came by, but like the others, I turned him away.

He comes around the corner in his wheelchair. He is laughing and so is the tech pushing him. To think a week ago, I thought he would be lost to me forever.

"Hey beautiful, it makes my day when I can see you smile." I feel my face flush. Gianni comes around the corner with iced coffees from Starbucks. He freezes when he comes face to face with Luca. The tech pushes past us and brings him back to his room.

"I'm sorry, Chelle. I thought I could drop off the coffee before he came back."

Before I can answer him, the tech lets us know Luca is all settled in. "I guess there's no time like the present. If you upset him, you will have to leave." He follows me inside. I give Luca the coffee and he slowly sips it. His eyes are not giving anything away.

Gianni steps closer to the bed and puts his hand out. "Thank you for saving my life." Luca shakes his hand and just shrugs like it's no big deal.

"Can you tell me exactly what happened? I don't remember much."

Gianni pulls the chair closer and sits down. "I thought Chelle was taking too long. When I went inside is when I saw you with your gun drawn. I pulled mine and pointed it at you. I really thought you were the one that was threatening Chelle. Then I heard Nick's voice just as he pulled the trigger. I turned, but he got a beat on me. You jumped in front of me."

"Did Peter die? I remember seeing him on the floor in a pool of blood."

"Peter Gander, Robert Conti, and Nick Jr all died that day."

"Why was Robert there? Did he really hate me that much?"

"He was working for Nick. I'm sorry to say the FBI is a lot more corrupt than you can ever imagine."

"I guess we need to talk about the elephant in the room. I remember Chelle yelling that we are brothers. It was never my intention to hide anything from you, Gianni. I was following Agosto's wishes."

"He finally told Geno and me everything. You never should have been put in that position. You saved my life. That's something I could never repay."

"I'm not looking for you to repay me. However, Chelle and I have a plan. It's big and will change the organization forever. You can be a part of it, or you can move out of the way. The choice is yours."

He gets up and grasps Luca's hand in a shake again. "We are family, Luca. We have to come together and show a united front. If there is fighting within, the walls will crumble."

For the first time, I think our plan will really work and possibly change the course of history.

It's been three days since Luca and Gianni had their talk, and the hospital is finally discharging Luca with strict instructions for continued physical therapy and plenty of rest. Good luck with that one. As much as I would like to believe the danger is over, I'm realistic to the fact that taking out any of the Amato family is a feather in a wannabe's cap.

"Luca, while we are waiting for your discharge papers, I have a few things I want to go over with you."

"It must be troubling you since you keep fidgeting with your bracelet." He smirks. I look down at my hand and realize he's right.

"Like my grandma, I have always fidgeted, so my mom gave Grandma and me a silver cord bracelet with a tiny saint medallion. It helps keep me calm. It's silly to some, but it helps give me clarity. Anyway, we need to talk about your living arrangements." His grip on the wheelchair gets so tight, his knuckles turn white.

"I just assumed I would be going to my apartment and hoping you would come with me."

"Agosto wants us to come to his house. Of course, it's under the guise that we are only safe there. He also threw out the fact that Grandma and Jessica are staying there."

"Chelle, forget about what Agosto wants, I want to know what you think we should do?"

I crouch down next to the chair and pull one of his hands loose. "Part of me agrees with him. It makes sense to keep everyone together for now."

"Then why do I hear a *but*?"

"Luca, I'm still pissed off at Agosto for the way he handled all of this, aren't you?"

"Don't you mean handled me, and how he was ashamed or embarrassed by me? I'm not ready to live under the same roof with any of them and be all *kumbaya*. I want to go back home, my home. I would like for you to come with me, but I understand if you can't."

"You can't be alone, Luca. I'll stay with you and go back and forth to check on everyone else. Eventually, we are going to have to come to some sort of agreement if our plan has any chance of working." He grumbles but doesn't give in. The nurse comes back with his discharge papers, and we are escorted out to the curb where Agosto is waiting.

"I thought I would give you a ride back to the house. You know . . . to show you where everything is." He's standing by the car with his hat in his hand. I have yet to understand the hat in hand thing. I'm going to ask Grandma about it.

"Agosto, I'm not ready to take upon the entire family. I need time and I would like to take it at my own pace. I mean no disrespect. For now, I'd like to go back to my apartment and get some rest."

"At least let me drop you off, since neither of you have a car. After that, we can take it at a pace that you're comfortable with." Agosto's driver opens the back door and Agosto offers Luca his hand. Luca accepts the help, and once we are all in, we head home.

CHAPTER TWO

Luca

A S WE HEAD OVER TO MY PLACE, I REALIZE CHELLE HAS never been inside my apartment. The only time she saw it was from the outside when Geno practically kicked me out of the car. When I needed clothes to go home in, Agosto sent Jessica to buy some. I'm not nervous about having her in my home, it's just that I'm a minimalist. I live by the motto "less is more." Not everyone can appreciate that. Whenever Agosto would visit me, he would make remarks. *"Why are you living like a man with no money? Let me have someone come in here and set this place up like it should be."* After a while of me not answering him, he finally gave up. Today he might start up all over again. Not for my benefit, but for Chelle's.

"It's still not safe for you both to be without any protection. If you keep insisting that you want to go to your apartment then, at least, let me put someone there for your protection." Agosto's words are strained. For the first time, I notice how all of this has taken a toll on him.

"Agosto, I appreciate you wanting to protect me. However, I think we will be okay. I need a few days at least to hopefully stop feeling like a mule kicked me in the chest." That seems to do the trick, at least for now. Finally, we pull into my complex. Each building has three floors. My place is at the top. It's times like this I would have appreciated an elevator. When we get to my front door, Geno, Jessica, and Gianni are waiting for us. Jessica has Chelle's cat, Gus, in his carrier, along with his bed and a bag that I'm sure is filled with toys.

"We know you need rest but wanted to welcome you home. I promise we won't stay long," Gianni says with apprehension in his voice.

"It's fine, but I'm not sure how much of a mess it is," Agosto gruffs under his breath.

I pass Chelle the key, and everyone heads inside behind us. I turn toward her and she's smiling. "What?"

"It's so you. A place for everything and everything in its place, well, until Gus starts exploring." As if on cue, he lets out a wail. Jessica opens his carrier, and he takes off.

I make my way over to the recliner and sink into it. I think I might have let out a little moan when my ass sunk down into my chair. Everyone is awkwardly looking anywhere but at me. I look at Chelle and she gives me a slight nod. She gets it.

"Okay, everyone, as you can see, he's tired and needs rest. Thank you for bringing Gus over." As Chelle ushers them to the door, Agosto tries to talk to her about having food sent over. She politely declines and finally, they are gone.

"Ugh, I thought they would never leave. Luca, I'm limiting everyone and everything until you are back on your feet. I know you're not a child, but you don't have the strength to stand up for yourself right now, so I'm doing it." Knowing she is protecting me does something to me.

"Thank you, Chelle. I don't think I could have stood up to Agosto if you weren't here. It's not that I can't; I've done it my whole life. I'm just tired."

"It's a beautiful view from up here. Why don't we sit out on the balcony, and I can make an early dinner. We can even watch the sunset if you're feeling up to it."

"Chelle, you don't have to wait on me hand and foot. I can manage." Her hand flies up, dismissing my declaration of independence.

"Luca, it would be best if you just follow the program. The last thing you want to do is piss me off. Now, let's go get comfortable outside."

Without arguing, I follow her lead. The view of the valley and mountains is spectacular. I settle down on the double chaise lounge and close my eyes, listening to the sound of the birds and the wind in the trees. My eyes flutter back open, and I realize I must have fallen asleep for a bit because it is now dusk. Chelle is snuggled next to me in the crook of my arm. I knew buying these would be a great investment someday. I mindlessly try to pull her closer and wince with pain. Her whole body stiffens.

"Not one of my better plans," I surmise.

"No, it's not. Are you ready to eat something?" She stares up at me.

"I don't think I have any food in the house." I wince more from embarrassment now. She pulls away from me and gets up.

"An orange and one rotten banana does not cover all the food groups. Honestly, I didn't figure you had any food here. I ordered in. I have everything set up inside."

We head inside and the table looks like something you'd see on onc of those home makeover shows. "Where exactly did all this come from?"

"Neiman Marcus has the best customer service ever. They have a wonderful cafe, and they brought all the extras."

"I'm not sure how you did it. I'm lucky when the laundry service remembers to pick up my stuff."

"It's all in how you approach it. I think I learned that when I started to teach science. I mean, let's face it, most kids that like science are far and few between. They want to get the minimum done so they can pass and graduate. It's my job to make it interesting, to make them want to come back every day. Like I said, it's all in the approach."

We sit down to eat seared salmon filet, jasmine-orange hazelnut rice, shaved brussels sprouts, pomegranate molasses, and butternut squash. I must have been hungrier than I thought since I cleaned my plate. "This was great, Chelle, thank you."

"We need to go over our plans and figure out which would work or maybe merge the two of them. I'm not stupid. I know there is still a price on my back and now on yours, too, Luca."

"The way I look at it, Chelle, we have two options. The first would be to turn everything over to Agosto. He is the top Don, and it would be a level of respect. However, that would mean we would have to stay under his protection. I know, like you, I will never be able to go back to my job. No matter how much I denounce my family ties, no one would trust me."

"I agree with you. And what is the second option?"

"We turn everything over to the Feds and walk away. Total identity change, you know, take up residence in Idaho and become farmers," I throw out there. She laughs, not the reaction I was expecting.

"I'm sorry, but just the thought of us as farmers is more than I can handle. I have another plan that I think might work better. We get Agosto to open the book to me. I know it's a first for a woman. With you as my partner, it might work. I know as far as the family is concerned, that the whole FBI thing has put a stain on you, but with Agosto's backing, it might work. I have Carmine's stuff hidden and I'm not afraid to use it."

"How are you going to get Agosto to go along with it?"

"Luca, that's where you come in. He owes you big time. We don't give Daddy any options. If he wants to be a part of your life—our lives—he has to pay."

"It would be a first, for sure. How do you think Gianni and Geno are going to react to it?"

"Gianni might go along with it. Geno has his head so far up Jessica's ass, he doesn't even know what day it is."

"How did I miss that?" I jerk my head back and ask.

She's trying so hard not to laugh, but she can't hold it in any longer. "You might be the big, tough FBI guy, but when it comes to matters of the heart, you're clueless.

"Now you need to get to bed. The first day out of the hospital, and you're not following orders."

I would love to get lost in all things Michelina, but unfortunately all I really can handle is sleep and plenty of it.

CHAPTER THREE

Agosto

I BROKE MY SON. IT WAS UNINTENTIONAL, BUT I HURT HIM IN A way no father should hurt his son. How do I right the wrong, not just with him, but with Geno and Gianni? I let my fear get the better of me and now they all might be lost to me forever. I find that I am isolating myself in my garden with my quail more and more. Today the Gambel's quail are gathered around with their babies. Sadly, like their parents, they will fall prey to the laws of nature. Much the same in life, I guess.

I hear rustling and look up to see Viviana coming out to join me. I get up, take her hand, and lead her back to my special bench. "Viviana, you look beautiful. What brings you out here so early in the morning?"

"I missed you yesterday. By the time I got back from my follow-up appointment with the doctor, you had already retired for the night. What happened with Luca?" She squeezes my hand.

"As you know, everything I did for my children I thought I was doing to protect them from this life. Unfortunately, it had the opposite effect. They are all in it up to their eyeballs, including your granddaughter." I pass her some seeds for the birds. The babies come running over first and then the parents. They are so trusting, which is probably why they have such a brief life.

"Agosto, I had no illusions about how this would all play out. I told you from the beginning to tell the boys the truth. For such a strong and powerful man, sometimes you can be very foolish." She pats my knee then closes her eyes, taking in a deep, cleansing breath.

"Do you think we are being punished for the plan we put into motion?" I hold my own breath, hoping that's not the case.

"No. You know that saying, '*we make plans and God just laughs?*' Well, I think that's where we are at now."

I take her hand back in mine and she gives it a gentle squeeze. "Frances wasn't supposed to die. We were supposed to be together. Michelina was not supposed to fall in love with her cousin. My boys were not supposed to stop trusting me. I can do many things, Viviana, but I can't watch my family fall apart."

"Maybe that's what it's going to take to bring them together. I talked to Gianni for a bit yesterday. He's finding it hard to deal with everything that has happened. That someone he hated because of his job, not because of the man, took a bullet that was meant for him. That's hard for anyone to wrap their mind around. Add to that he finds out at that same moment that the man is his brother, that's big. Give him time, Agosto."

"I'm an old man. How much more time am I supposed to give him?" She doesn't answer me, instead she takes more of the seed and goes back to feeding the quail.

"Maybe it's time for you to call a family meeting," she finally offers.

"What would I say that I haven't said already?" I shrug in defeat.

"We would tell them everything, Agosto. No more secrets and lies. That's what got us in this mess in the first place."

"I'll think about it."

We continue to mindlessly feed the birds, neither of us saying another word.

Jessica

Michelina never came home last night, not that I thought she would. Never in a million years would I think our lives would turn out this way. We are headed down a dangerous path, yet I don't want to stop. There is a rush that I could never explain.

I roll on to my side and look at Geno sleeping next to me. His body is so amazing. I trail my fingers down his back. How could one man be so perfect? My fingers are no longer trailing down his back. I reach around and stroke his cock. He's still asleep, yet he's hard. I leave a trail of tender kisses before making my way to his cock. When he rolls onto his back, I crawl between his legs. His skin is so soft, with a subtle hint of citrus. He wears Tom Ford Mandarino Di Amalfi. It's amazing, and it makes me heady. When I kiss the tip of his cock, he moans. Slowly, I part my lips and take him in my mouth. He's warm and silky. It doesn't take long for him to move his hips, keeping in rhythm with me. He arches his back, forcing me to take him deeper. I want nothing more than to keep going, however, if I don't slow down, this will end before I even get started. When I release the hold I have on him, he lets out a long low guttural objection. "Don't worry, I'm not done with you." I whisper as I brush soft kisses up his chest.

"Jess, quit teasing me. I want you now."

I straddle him and remain high on my knees. Slowly I come down and as I do, he guides his cock inside of me. I love to be on top, in total control. "Geno, you feel amazing." In an instant he flips me over and any control I thought I had is now gone.

"You thought you were going to do whatever you wanted, and I would just abide by it. You're a very funny lady. Now here is how this is going to play out. I'm going to fuck you every which way I want and when I'm done, if there is anything left of me, you can have it." His movements are so fast and so smooth. His touch ignites a fire deep inside of me. It's nothing that I've ever felt before. Something that I don't want to end. Just as I get to the point where my orgasm is about to take over my rational thinking, he stops.

"Jessica, you see, when you give yourself fully to me, every day can be like this. Do you want me to continue?" It's a game of orgasm denial that he's playing. A game I've fallen prey to, and I don't want it to stop.

"Yes, Geno, please don't deny me," I beg, something I never thought I would do after everything I've been through. I don't care. I want it—no—I need it. He moves again. At first, his pace is slow and steady. He pulls back and slams hard into me. I'm screaming so loud I lose my voice. He lets go of my wrist and puts a hand under each knee, pushing them up. He is pushing his cock so hard into me, I feel like I might split in half. That's when my orgasm comes to the top and I can no longer hold back. I fist the sheets, arch my back and let the waves of pleasure overtake me. My whole body shakes. Finally, he is slowing down and I'm able to catch my breath. When I open my eyes, his face is only inches from mine. His smile is amazing. Hell, he is amazing.

"Now, Jess, isn't that a great way to start the day?"

"Oh, it's wonderful. I don't think I will be able to walk for a few hours, but it is fantastic." My voice is raspy. He rolls over and manages to tuck me into his side where I fall back to sleep, totally satisfied. I feel ready to move forward with my life, a life with him.

CHAPTER FOUR

Luca

I'M STILL A LITTLE SORE, BUT I'LL BE FINE. I WAS NEVER ONE TO PLAY the pity card. I wanted to make love to Chelle last night, but I was lucky if I could keep my eyes open past eight o'clock. At least when I woke up, she was curled up next to me.

I'm a five am guy. Nothing I do ever changes that. In need of the bathroom, I gently make my way out of bed, handle my business, and then head to the kitchen for coffee. Arizona sunrises are some of my favorites. It's like the calm before the storm. With my coffee in hand, I settle on one of the lounge chairs with a blanket and enjoy the peace.

I can't stop thinking about Chelle's plan. Do I really want to be a part of this family? Honestly, I don't know. What I do know is I can't walk away and never look back. I know she won't leave her grandmother. All my life, I've only wanted my father to accept me. Now that he was forced to do that, it didn't seem right. If he wasn't forced to, I think he would have never brought me into the family, his family. It will always be his family. When I think back to my conversations with my mom, I realize how much wisdom she had. Even while she battled cancer, she would always take the time to guide me. One of the last things she said was, *"Mateo, don't fall prey to anyone. Just because they need you, they might not want you. Keep your eyes open and learn the difference."* Not a day goes by that I don't think about her and miss her greatly. Part of me thinks she would tell me to stay and fight for what's rightfully mine. Yet as a parent, she would want me safe. Being safe means leaving all of this behind, including Chelle. She will never leave her grandmother and I would never make her choose. I hear the sliding glass door open and Chelle comes out with a fresh cup of coffee for both of us.

"Thank you. I was too comfortable to get up and get another one."

"Exactly how early do you get up? I thought I was early at six am to do my swim, but you already had one cup of coffee and it's only six-thirty."

"I'm a five am guy. It started when I went away to college, and it's never changed. I find it's quiet at that time so I can think and get a lot done." I lift the throw blanket and she slides in next to me. It feels so right.

"Have you figured out what you want to do about your family?"

"I'm very conflicted. Part of me wants to take you and leave. You know, become a nobody in Nowhere, USA. The other part of me longs for a family. A true family in every sense of the word. I want my father to want me in his family. Not for any other reason. I wish you could have known my mom. She was so wise and kind." I smile at the thought of her and bring my mug up for a sip. Chelle's running her finger across a small rope bracelet on her wrist. She does this when she is nervous or scared. It makes me sad that it's probably because of me. There is a medallion and every time she gets to it, she stops, takes a deep breath, and slowly exhales. "I know your bracelet is to help you, but you have me now to help keep you calm." She laughs, and it's beautiful, much like her.

"Why didn't your mother push to marry Agosto, especially when she found out she was dying? I mean that would have given Agosto no choice but to acknowledge you as his child."

"Whatever her reasons were, she took them with her to her grave. I could spend a lifetime trying to figure it out but, in the end, it's all just speculation."

"I hope you understand, Luca. I can't run. Not just because of my grandma, it's me. I've never backed down from a challenge, and running away is the coward's way out."

"What about self-preservation?"

"Everyone has a different version of it. This is mine. I'm staying. I will fight to the death if I have to. I'm not looking for us to run the organization the way it is today. I'm looking for a change. Is it a pie in the sky way of thinking, maybe, but I know running away is not me, so I don't have any other options. I will support you in whatever you decide you need to do."

"As long as I pick your plan." I didn't mean it to come out as harsh as it did. I try to apologize, but she puts her finger on my lips, stopping me.

"Don't, I get it. I'm going to get ready to talk to Agosto. Let me know what you decide." I watch her leave and say nothing. I know I have the biggest decision of my life to make, but I'm still on the fence as to what I should do. I close my eyes and try to give my mind a rest.

I feel the heat of the blazing son on my face and my eyes flutter open. Instinctively, my hands come up to rub the grogginess away. I must have fallen asleep. I grab both of my mugs off the side table before heading inside. When I get inside, I find I've been asleep for hours, not minutes. So much for starting my day off caffeinated. Chelle is gone but she left a note on my bedside table.

Luca, only you can make this decision. I will back you one hundred percent no matter what you decide. You know where I am.

Chelle

Damn it. I throw on a pair of shorts and a t-shirt and call for an Uber. When I get outside, Agosto's men are waiting.

"We are supposed to watch you and take you wherever you want to go, so you might want to cancel your Uber."

"How did you know?"

"Your car blew up man. Of course, you would call for a ride. Besides, if I were you, I wouldn't be starting my own car anytime soon." I want to say something about his attempt at humor but opt not to. It's not going to get me anywhere.

"Please take me to Agosto's house."

"To your dad's house, we go."

I stare at him for a minute, my feet not moving. "How did you find out who my father is?"

"Man, I don't think there's a person alive who doesn't know. You took a bullet for Gianni. No one just does that out of the kindness of their heart."

"I'm an FBI agent; that's what I do," I say casually. He shrugs and finally steps to the side so I can pass. As we make our way to the car, it seems strange to be on the receiving end of the protection. I'm not leaving without Chelle, so I guess it's time to embrace who I am. If I don't, I could end up like Frances . . . dead.

CHAPTER FIVE

Michelina

I HATED LEAVING LUCA ALONE, BUT I DON'T WANT HIM TO MAKE A life-altering decision because of me. Besides, I really need to talk to my grandmother before I do anything. As usual, I find her in the garden with Agosto. He's constantly up her ass, which makes me wonder if there is more to their relationship than I'm aware of.

"Good morning, Michelina. I'm so happy to see you. How is Luca? Is he with you?" He strains his neck, trying to see past me. I want to yell; *don't you mean your son?* Fuck, he can't even bring himself to say those words. I remind myself to smile and nod through gritted teeth.

"When I left, he was sleeping. I'm sure you understand right now what he needs is rest."

"Of course," he answers solemnly, "I'm sure you want to visit with Viviana. I'll head back inside, but please stop by my office before you leave." It was not a request; it was a demand. I'm starting to learn the lines for him are blurred. I watch him leave and take the seat next to my grandma.

"Michelina, you are very troubled. Is everything okay with Luca?"

"He's physically getting better every day."

"I hear a but."

"We are at a crossroads. I have everything that Carmine wanted me to have. Now I need to figure out what to do with it. My mom never wanted any of us to have anything to do with this life, yet now I've found I'm thrust in the middle of it."

"When it came down to it, I protected Frances from everything Carmine was doing. In the end, the very life she hated is what got her killed."

"If I leave here tomorrow, would you come with me?" I throw it out there not really wanting to know the answer. Maybe because I already know.

"Let me tell you a story. My life is a series of good things and bad things. There are things I've done that I'm not very proud of, but I did them all the same. If I was to go back in time, I would probably do them all again. Are you sure you really want to hear this?"

"Honestly, I know I don't have a choice. I need the truth, all of it. I can't make decisions without it."

"All Carmine ever wanted was a son to carry on the business he was building. My boys were slaughtered one by one on the streets of New York. Butchie told Carmine that Agosto was behind the murders. It wasn't true, but at the time Carmine believed him. He needed someone to blame. He retaliated, of course, but later he found out that Butchie was given bad information. It didn't matter; Salvatore was dead. Bad blood between the brothers kept mounting. After Agosto's wife Gisele died, he was in a really bad place. I tried to help him, remind him that his children needed him. Carmine accused him of all sorts of things, things that were mostly untrue." She pulls a handkerchief from her pocket and dabs her eyes.

"If it's too much, we can take a break."

"No, I'm fine. This story needs to finally come out. Anyway, Agosto came to me and asked me to marry him. I quickly said no, I couldn't. You were just a baby, and I was helping Frances raise you. Besides, at that time, Carmine was still alive. In my world, divorce was unthinkable. Agosto went out every night trying to drown his sorrows and forget about me. That's when he met Luca's mom, Sofia. It was not love, at least for him it wasn't. Sofia filled a need that I couldn't. Agosto did not want to marry her, and he told her that from the beginning. He told her he was waiting for the love of his life to come to her senses. She didn't care and quickly became pregnant with Luca. Maybe she thought that would change his mind, but it didn't. He was there for Luca, but not how a father should be. It was more of an obligation. I told him to marry Sofia and give his son the name he rightfully deserves. He wouldn't do it. That is until Sofia became ill. That's when he went to her with his hat in his hand and offered to marry her. She said no. However, she knew she had to do whatever she could to protect her son. She let Agosto legally adopt Luca as his own. That's when he had Mateo's name legally changed to Luca. The boy had no idea that any of this happened. All he knew was his mother was dead. In time, Agosto learned what a wonderful son he had, but by then, there was too much water under the bridge. I begged him to tell Luca the truth. He was too ashamed. Ashamed of everything that he should have done but didn't. Hindsight is always twenty-twenty. When Carmine pretended he died, Agosto asked me to marry him again. I thought about it, but Frances was so upset. She threatened to take you away. I don't hate her for that; I understood her fear. This way of life is scary and dangerous. The bad outweighs the good by a landslide." She stops and pours herself some water from the pitcher on the table.

"Then one day Frances hired some men to come and do work on the house. One of the men walked in with some boxes and I took one look at him, and I knew—Carmine. That's when he put the boxes up in the attic, the journals he put aside for you. He came up behind me and, at that moment, every hair on my body stood at attention." She's rubbing her arms like a chill just ran up her spine.

"What did he say?"

"Make sure Michelina gets them. That was it. He turned and walked out. I never saw or heard from him again. Right after that,

Agosto asked me to marry him again, and again I said no. I was having a few problems with my memory. Nothing much . . . you know, losing the keys or forgetting to close the garage door. He went to Frances with what he thought was a great idea. He wanted me to move in with him. Frances would have no part of it. She even tried to stop him from coming over to the house just for coffee. That's when Agosto came up with a brilliant plan. I was to make Frances believe I was more forgetful than I really was. Eventually, she would suggest the nursing home. Everything fell into place and once I moved in, Agosto purchased the business. Frances felt good about keeping me safe and away from Agosto. She never knew she was deceived. In the end, life is as it should be. If I would have said yes to Agosto all those years ago, Luca would have never been born."

"Why are you telling me all of this now?"

"I told you everything because you have some very hard roads ahead of you. Having all the information might make your decision easier. I know you have reservations about Agosto, but there is so much more to the man than you know. Remember the summer everything happened with you and Jessica? When you came to me for help? It was Agosto I turned to. He is the one that made it right for you and Jessica. He's kept that secret all these years. That should show you he is a man of honor."

I start to speak but stop. I can't believe how many lies there were. Like a tangled web, each lie working off each other. "You've laid so much at my feet. I have to talk to Luca about all of this. We have to figure out together what to do." I get up to leave but she grabs my arm.

"Please wait, Michelina. Let me finish."

"There's more?"

"I never wanted to deceive anyone, especially Frances. I felt it was the best for everyone if I kept my feelings to myself. As far as what you should do, the best advice I can give you is to be the change. This organization—and yes, it is a business organization—has been run by two sets of rules. The first set for people who are just coming into it: the rule of violence and secrets. The second set has been in place going back to Sicily long before even my parents were born. You can try to make the good outnumber the bad. It won't happen overnight, but it definitely won't happen if you and Luca run away. If the two of you can bring this fractured family together, that would be a great start. Be the good, Michelina. You have it in you to do it." As I let her words sink in, she leans in and kisses me on my cheek before getting up and going inside.

CHAPTER SIX

Luca

W E GET TO THE HOUSE, AND I GO IN SEARCH OF CHELLE. I find her sitting in the garden alone. The walk from the front to the garden bench is long. I'm thankful that I listened to my body and took my cane for support. I sit next to her on the bench and take her hand.

"Hey, why are you all alone out here? Is everything okay?" I bring her hand up to my lips and plant a kiss on the top of it.

"I thought you were home resting?"

"I fell asleep but when I woke up, you were gone. Do you want to share with me why you're out here all alone?"

"I just finished up a long talk with grandma," she says as she leans her head onto my shoulder.

"Is everything okay?"

"Okay? No, it will never be okay, Luca. However, I now have a better understanding as to why certain things happened. Agosto asked her to marry him several times over the years. For one reason or another she always said no. When she moved into assisted living, he bought the facility. It was part of their big plan to be together."

"Why? I mean why go through all of the cloak and dagger crap?"

"For my mom. I never realized how much she hated this life. In one of Carmine's journals, he talks about his children. He wished my mom would have been more like Sammy the Bull's kids. More accepting of the lifestyle. I didn't realize how much she hated it. I get why she hated it. She lost so many people. Rather than hate it to the point where you lose everything, including your future, why not make changes?"

"It's not as easy as you think it is. I know you think you are going to be the one to make changes. Have you figured out how?"

"I have all of Carmine's blackmail material. Why can't I use it for something good?" She lifts her head to look back up at me.

"You think you're going to turn this one-hundred-plus year organization around and actually make it legit?" I'm trying not to stare at her in total disbelief, but I can't help myself.

"You make it seem like it can't be done. Well, in my world can't means won't."

"You're a good person . . . a kind person. Hell, you have to be a saint to be teaching high school kids. I honestly don't believe you have an evil bone in your body. At least not what it's going to take to pull this off. Look, what about giving everything over to Agosto for a very fat chunk of cash and monthly dividends? We could go away and start over someplace where no one knows who we are."

"Back to farming in middle America again? Why are you so afraid?" she raises her voice.

"I'm not afraid for me, babe, I'm afraid for you. I don't want you to become something your mother never wanted you to be."

"And what's that?"

"A female Carmine." My words hang in the air like a dense fog that never goes away.

"You act like I have a choice?" she says in an almost defeated tone.

"In life there are always choices. Armed with everything you know about him, why would you choose to be like him? Don't say you have no choice, free will says you always have a choice." She gets quiet and for a moment, I think I might have gotten through to her. That is until Gianni comes running outside.

"Dad needs us all inside now. There is some sort of emergency," he declares almost out of breath. We all head inside. Gianni races ahead of us while Chelle and I go as fast as my body will allow.

When we get into Agosto's office, I quickly take a seat in one of the sofas while Chelle gets me water. I'm staring at Agosto and notice he's pasty white like a man living in fear. "Agosto, what's going on?" I ask him.

"Will I ever earn the title of dad?" He gives me a half of smile. Wow, I wasn't expecting that.

"Old habits die hard. Why don't you tell us what's going on."

"About ten minutes ago I received this message." He presses a remote and the screen on the wall comes to life. A video comes on showing Geno and Jessica in some sort of cell. There is a noose around Geno's neck, and he is standing on a chair. There is some blood running down the side of his face. His hands are tied behind him. Jessica is standing next to him wearing a white sleeveless dress with blood stains down the front. I'm not sure if it's hers or Geno's. Her hands are tied together in front of her. They are also bloody and she's crying. Into the frame steps Nick Jr. He takes a riding crop and runs it slowly down her cheek, trailing it around each breast before he quickly snaps it, making her body jerk. He stops and turns to face the camera.

"Hello, everyone. Yep, it's me, Nick. Gianni, you should have made sure I was dead instead of trying to save your bastard brother. Michelina, you have twenty-four hours to bring me everything good old Carmine left you. For every hour you are late, Geno's chair will get smaller and smaller until there is nothing left for him to stand on. When that happens, he dies a slow death." He waves to someone off camera who replaces Geno's chair with a round stool. His feet just fit on it. Anything smaller and he won't be able to hang on.

"Tick tock, Michelina, tick tock. Now Jessica and I have to go; we are getting married. Well, just as soon as I get this bloody dress off of her." With that he pulls out a pocketknife and cuts away her dress. She is left with only her panties on. The screen goes black.

"How did this happen?" Chelle's voice is just above a whisper.

"Does that matter, Michelina? We have to give Nick whatever he wants. I cannot lose another child, not in my lifetime."

"Yes, Agosto, it matters! You wanted us all under one roof so you could protect us. Look how well that worked out," she yells as she steps toward his desk. I can't get up fast enough to hold her back. Gianni steps in front of her, blocking her access.

"If you want to blame anyone, Chelle, blame me."

"Who told you he was dead? Why didn't you make sure yourself that he was dead?" she screams.

"Oh, I don't know, maybe because you were begging me to save Luca's life at the time," he tries to defend himself. She takes a step back and turns toward me. She had a look of desperation mixed with fear. Something I've never seen in her before.

"Luca, you're the professional, how do we get them back?" Finally, I get up, take the remote off the desk and hand it to Gianni.

"Agosto, how was this sent to you?"

"It was sent in an email," he answers. I can't help but smile.

"Mind sharing what's making you so happy?" Gianni glares at me.

"Yeah, email is the number one stupidest move a criminal can make. Do me a favor; run it very slow." I watch frame by frame hoping something will catch my eye.

"Luca, how good are you with computers?" Gianni asks me.

"Top of my class at the bureau. I could bring it to the office and rip it apart."

"Or you could look at it on Geno's system. He probably has a better system than the FBI does." He waves me on and leads us into Geno's office and one quick look around I can tell his setup is way beyond anything the bureau has. Gianni opens Agosto's email and loads the video.

It feels strange to sit at his desk—my brother's desk—a man I know very little about.

"First, I'm going to make a series of stills from the video. From there I'll take Geno and Jessica out of the pictures. Maybe we'll be able to figure out where they are." Working with such advanced software makes it much easier. I put a few different frames up on the massive computer screen on the wall. One in particular raises the hair on the back of my neck. I get rid of all of them except for that one and blow it up.

"Luca, what is it? Do you know where they are?" Chelle asks as she stays transfixed on the screen.

"I know exactly where this is. When I was a kid, I was obsessed with haunted buildings. My mom took me on a tour of the top five haunted jails in Arizona. That's 1910 Gila County Arizona Territorial Sheriff's Office and Jail. It was the absolute best place for ghost hunting. It's in Globe, Arizona." Everyone's eyes are on me except for Gianni. He opens a gun safe and starts pulling out enough stuff for World War three.

"I know I'm not able to back you up, Gianni, but at least let me take you there."

"We have a small private plane at the Scottsdale Airpark that's always on standby."

Chelle steps up to go but Gianni holds up his hand stopping her. "It's not that I don't think you can handle yourself, but there is not enough room. I need Luca to show me where the place is and my men to have my back. I promise as soon as we get them, I'll have Jessica call you."

"Please be careful, all of you."

Gianni holds out a Glock for me. "It doesn't look like you're carrying. Are you okay with this one?"

I take the gun and check the clip and chamber a round before putting it in my waist band. We head out a side door that leads us into the garage. A black SUV is waiting for us. Nick is a wild card; I pray that they are there and still alive.

CHAPTER SEVEN

Nick

"**G**ET HIM DOWN FROM THERE. I DON'T NEED HIM SLIPPING AND killing himself before I'm ready." Sometimes I have to tell my men everything in great detail. Why can't they think for themselves? As much as I love looking at this broad's tits, it's a distraction that I don't need right now. I free her hands and toss her a t-shirt to put on. "Put this on before I change my mind.

You see, Geno, I'm not a bad guy. I covered her up. I'm just playing with her—for now. What I really want is Michelina. I've got big plans for her, none of which she is going to like. Me on the other hand, I'm going to have a great time."

My crew is filled with men I know I can trust with my life. That's the first step in taking over this organization. Build from the bottom up until you get to the point when the only men around you are the ones that will always have your back. Danny and I have been friends since he was five years old. His mom moved to the neighborhood beyond poor. My mom took them in. We're as close as brothers.

"Danny, did you get it?" I ask. He tosses me a can of neon orange spray paint. I roll my eyes at his color choice.

"Let's get them loaded up in the van so we can get out of here. I'll take care of the wall." I look around at the place while barking orders. "Rocco, snap out of it, all that blow you're using is making you stunad. Get off your ass and help Danny with them. Make sure you give Geno more of that rohypnol shit; I want him drugged up for a while. I don't want him getting any ideas." Danny throws the broad over his shoulder and Rocco pushes Geno along. Staring at the walls, I need to decide which one is the best. I decide on the west wall. By the time they get here, words will be blazing in the setting sun.

Luca

It will take us longer to get from the house to the airpark then it does to fly by private plane from Scottsdale to Globe. It's a small plane with six of us and the pilot.

"Luca, what can you tell me about this place?" Gianni's voice has a savage edge to it.

"Growing up, I was into all that paranormal stuff. Every summer when school was out, Mom would take me on a tour of some well-known haunted places. This jail that we are going to was number one on my list."

"You know I don't believe in that shit, but I've got to ask; what made it number one?"

"All the stories about it. The sightings that were reported in such detail." He is looking at me like a deer in the headlights. "Okay, so for the record, I was like fifteen or something. I was also very into *X-Files*."

"Luca, do you have a life? If not, now would be a good time to work on that."

The pilot interrupts us with an announcement that we are landing. I'm silently thanking him for bailing me out of an awkward situation. I want to get to know my brother—hell—I took a bullet for him. I need to push the uneasy silence away. "It's amazing how quick it is when you're flying."

"Yeah, it takes longer to taxi, take off, and land then the time we've spent in the air."

"Gianni, what's your plan? You can't go in with all guns blazing, you need a plan."

"You stay with the car. I'll take my guys and go in the front and send some of them around the back. Don't worry. I don't plan on leaving here without the two of them alive and safe."

When we land, there are two SUVs waiting for us. Gianni heads to the first one and I follow suit. As we drive over, I quickly explain the layout from what I can remember. It's pretty basic. We pull up. There is no one in sight. Now I'm second-guessing myself. Everyone heads inside while I nervously wait by the car. I'm not sure how long they've been gone but it's too quiet. I can't wait any longer. With my gun drawn, I make my way toward the building. One of Gianni's men opens the door and waves me inside. When I finally step inside, everything is as I remember it except for a messaged that's been spray painted on the wall in the same room the video was filmed. I step closer to it, reach out and touch it. It's still tacky. We can't be that far behind them.

"I'm taking my soon-to-be bride away from all of this, maybe permanently. Geno's life is on the clock. You need to find him before he runs out of air. Tick tock."

Gianni picks up a nearby an old wooden chair and screams as he throws it towards the wall where it easily shatters. I pull my phone out and begin to take pictures—a lot of pictures.

"How the fuck is taking pictures of this shit going to help find my brother?" he yells at me. I'm just the closest thing to a whipping board right now, so I don't get upset about it.

"It can't hurt." I kick the can that was left on the ground. It rolls over a plastic Walmart bag. I use the bag to pick up the can, not that I don't know who left it. Creature of habit, I guess. That's when I notice the receipt in the bag.

"Does that help us in any way?" The self-assured man is gone. There is desperation in his voice that wasn't there before.

"We need to get the footage from the local Walmart. There is a time stamp on the receipt. I don't think Nick will be on the video, but whomever is helping him will be. Usually spray paint is locked up behind a gate. It's a start, Gianni, but I won't be able to get the footage without a warrant." This is where I hope he can step in and strong arm the manager to get the footage.

"My brother will be dead by the time we wait for that. I'll get it and anything else we might need."

"Great, let's go; every minute counts." We get to the SUV and speed off while I look at the pictures I took. There has to be some sort of clue that I'm just not seeing.

CHAPTER EIGHT

Geno

I'M FIGHTING TO OPEN MY EYES, BUT I CAN'T. THAT BASTARD GAVE me something and now my mind is foggy. Jess, dear God, I need to get to her. I slowly move my arms. They are numb but I remember when Nick's men grabbed us, I had the presence of mind to hit the action button on my watch, engaging the wayback service. My friend Daniella is a designer at Apple and sent me the new Ultra something or other watch to test out. I'm praying everything she said about it is true. Hopefully, it's still on my wrist. My arms are so numb it's hard to feel anything. What the fuck did Rocco give me?

It's dark. I close my eyes and open them again. It's really dark, not a sliver of light anywhere. I need to slow down my breathing and try to clear my head. This is when I'm thankful to my ex-girlfriend for dragging me to her Pilates classes. Slow, long breaths. Gianni was told that Nick was dead, which leads me to think we have a mole among us. The question is who? Who hates us that much to want to see me dead? I think I have a better shot at finding out who hated Carmine and along with Nick so much that they would take a chance going after a made-man's family.

My guess it would be that person who now wants to take revenge on his granddaughter. I can't fight off the need to close my eyes and rest. Slowly my mind gives into my body, and I drift off.

Gianni

Time seems to be moving so fast even though I don't want it to. In a matter of days, I find out I have another brother and I might lose the one I've known my whole life. I put those thoughts out of my head as we disembark the plane. Of course, the SUVs are waiting to take us back home. I don't know how I'm going to explain to Dad that I failed him. I look over at Luca and he's staring at his phone. "Hey, what are you doing?" I cringe, realizing I sound like a boss reprimanding an employee not a brother talking to a brother. "I'm sorry, Luca, I'm just worried about what this news will do to Dad," I quickly apologize hoping to take the sting out.

"I was looking at what Nick wrote, trying to read between the lines."

"Do you want to wait till we get home?"

"No, I want to be able to offer Chelle and Agosto some hope, even if it is a slim one at that."

"Okay, tell me what you see because, honestly, it sounds like childish nonsense."

"Of course, it's childish. Nick dropped out of school with pie in the sky hopes of being someone big in the family. When I was in charge of watching Carmine, he loved to talk. I always thought he was just full of himself. Yet as time went on, I realized he had a good read on people. He hated Nick Sr. He felt he was nothing more than a two-bit scammer trying to take shortcuts in life. He was right, of course. I asked him one day why he didn't kill Nick Jr. when he showed up with a gun, ready to use it on him. He said Nick was just a child trying to avenge his father's death. He related to the kid and thought he had potential."

"What do you think?" I lean in, making sure I don't miss anything.

"He's a wild cannon with nothing to lose. If we break up the riddle into two parts, then we have to pick one to follow. If we don't choose the correct one, then one of them can die. Die by our own mistake."

"This is not what I want to hear. How do we choose which direction to go in?"

"We don't; we split up. We can't leave anything to chance. I think Geno is in more danger right now than Jessica."

"What makes you say that?" My chest gets tight, and I just want to scream.

"Killing Geno will gut Agosto, but that's not who he really wants to destroy. It's Chelle he needs to destroy. He has her best friend. Aside from her grandmother, Jessica is all she has."

"Chelle seems to be very protective of Jessica, more than just a friendship. Do you know why?"

"No, and if I did, it wouldn't be up to me to say anything." I glance over at him from my phone and then back to the pictures.

"Look, I know I'm coming into this brother thing with you really late in the game, but I've got to ask, why don't you call him Dad?" He's staring at me with such an intensity, I feel it down to my bones.

"It's a long story for a much later date. Let's get through all of this and then I will tell you the story of my life, deal?"

"Deal. We're here. Let's get inside and tell everyone what's going on." I have to accept for now whatever he is willing to offer. Right now, I have no choice. We head inside to find everyone is sitting in the living room except Chelle. I can see her though the glass doors out back on the phone. She's pacing and yelling. Her movements are very animated. She finally turns and sees me. Whomever was on the receiving end of that call just got hung up on. The door swings open and she races in.

"What happened? You were supposed to call me. Where are they?"

"I'll let Luca bring everyone up to speed. I need to make a call." I head into Geno's office for some privacy. I get a beer out of the fridge and sit at his desk. I know there is a mole in our organization. That's the only way someone could have gotten to them. My phone pings with a new text message. It's from Luigi, my soldier. I texted him from the plane.

I don't know why I'm surprised he's already gotten back to me, after all, he is the best and digging up stuff that should stay hidden.

"You wanted to know who your mole is, well say hello to little miss Gemma. She is fucking Rocco. You know who he is. But just in case you forgot, he is one of the top guys in Nick's crew." I open the attached video and it's Gemma on her knees giving Rocco a blow job. He stops and pulls her up by her hair, pushes her back against the wall. In a very swift move, he opens her legs and shoves his cock into her pussy, so hard he lifts her off the wall. As he's pounding into her, he's yelling at her to tell him where Geno will be. There it is, with each pounding she is yelling out everything she knows. She's had open access to all of us for years. This is the way she pays us back for everything we've done for her. Everything inside of me, all the rage and betrayal is boiling to the surface. She will pay with her life. I fling my beer bottle across the room as I let out a roar. Luca chooses this moment to open the office door. The bottle just misses him.

"I take it you found out something and it's not good."

"Nothing was crazy around here until you and Chelle came knocking. I know none of this is your fault, but I just found out the mole is Gemma. Another one of Carmine's messes that I'm going to have to clean up. He should have taken care of all of this when the kid came to kill him."

"How do you know about that, Gianni?"

"You and Chelle think that everything that goes on in this organization is a well-kept secret. I have news for you; you wipe your ass and everyone in this world knows all about it. That's why keeping your existence a secret for so long is amazing."

"Other than throwing blame around, do you have a plan?"

"No, Luca, I just found out about this right before you came in. Do you have a plan?"

"Chelle's been trying to find Gemma since we left—nothing. I say pick up Rocco and let's try to get what we can out of him. Do you know anything about him?"

"Yeah, he's into the drugs, mainly coke. I'll have one of my men find him. In the meantime, what did the family say?"

"They are trying to decipher Nick's message." He's staring down at his phone, and he seems to be lost in thought.

"Luca, snap out of it, what is it?"

"Sorry, just a thought I had. Look at the message again." He hands me the phone and with a few clicks on the computer I'm able to pull it up on the big screen. I pass him back his phone as we both stare at the message. Dad steps into the room, his eyes fixated on the screen.

"Dad, where is Chelle?" Luca is paying neither of us any mind while he is messing around on the computer.

"She took Viviana back to her room. She keeps trying to call Gemma, but no answer."

"That's because Gemma is the mole." Dad's face pales as he stumbles back to one of the chairs. Chelle comes in just in time. She grabs a water bottle and gives it to Agosto.

"Why would she do that? I treated her like one of my own."

"Sex and possibly drugs. Although, I'm not one hundred percent sure about the drugs, yet."

"Gianni, so what you're saying is another one of my half siblings has turned out to be a monster."

"Yes, but we don't have time to wallow in self-pity. Geno's life is on a clock. None of that will change the fact that my brother might be dead already." I look at the screen and see Luca has pulled up a map of the area from Globe to Phoenix. "Luca, what are you thinking?"

"He buried him. It's the only thing that makes any sense. That tag on the wall was still wet when we got there. Agosto, when you were killing people and hiding the bodies, where did you put them?" Brother or no brother I can't let him talk to my father like that. I leap out of the chair ready to pounce on him.

"Gianni, stop," Dad bellows. "He needs the truth. Your brother's life depends on it. Lake Mead, but with all that global warming shit that's going on, he couldn't put him there. Besides, if what you're saying is true, he would not have had the time to get him to Lake Mead. It would have to be close to Globe."

"The mines. There are a lot in that area. Most are shut down until the price of copper goes up. They keep industrial machinery there, so it would be quick and easy to dig a hole."

Luca is staring at the map on the big screen. I walk up to Luca and stand next to him, looking at the map. "Aren't all those red marks mines?"

"Yes, which is why we need more information before we go off half-cocked. I remember from my training at the FBI, you have five and a half hours of air in a closed casket. Providing the conditions are just right, of course. The fastest way to find him is to find Rocco." Chelle grabs Luca by the arm and spins him around. She fists his shirt collar and pulls him closer. I think we are all in shock.

"What about Jessica? What are you doing to find her? She is left alone with a madman. I don't think she could survive anything like this again," her voice trails off and she begins to cry. What does she mean *again?*

"Gianni is going to work with his men finding Geno. You and I will do whatever we can to find Jessica. If we split up, we can cover more ground. Chelle, what did you mean when you said about her surviving anything like this again?" Luca asks.

"That has nothing to do with this. Right now, we need to find her and fast." I nod my head in agreement then turn my focus back to my brother.

"Okay, Gianni, I numbered the mines. There are three mines along that route that are not active right now. I'll take one, you take three, and we will meet at number two. Hopefully, Gemma is with Rocco and your men can find them. Give Chelle a weapon and let's get out of here."

I open the gun safe, pull some stuff out and put it on the table next to the safe. That's when it hits me. I grab the box and toss it to Luca.

"What is this?"

"It's Geno's new toy that his friend Daniella gave him. I know it's a long shot but if he still has it on and it's activated, we might be able to find him."

"Gianni, the Find a Friend app won't work if he's buried in one of those mines."

"This is some sort of new watch that has GPS, SOS, and God knows what else. Geno was bragging about it the other day. I wish to God I would have paid more attention."

"Do you know how to use any of the services?"

I pull my phone out and call the one person who can help us.

"Hey, Dani, Geno is in trouble, and I need your help to save him," I say as soon as she answers.

CHAPTER NINE

Jessica

I'M THE BOWELS OF HELL, STUCK WITH A MADMAN—AGAIN. WHY, God, why? I made my peace with you, but apparently that wasn't good enough. I'm finally able to focus on my whereabouts. Nick's got me in some sort of RV/Camper kind of thing. All he left me with is a thick collar around my neck that's attached to a very heavy chain. The chain is bolted to the floor. I have nothing on but my panties. This madman is my best friend's half-brother. How is that even possible. When I try to get up and walk around, the chain is so heavy that I can hardly move. I drag myself and the chain to one of the windows. When I pull the curtains back, I can see the widows are all boarded up. I want to scream at the top of my lungs, but who will hear me? I don't even know where I am. The doorknob jiggles and then it is pulled open. Nick climbs in carrying a wedding dress. *Oh no…*

"Well, look who's up, finally. Get cleaned up and get this dress on. We are getting married."

"Please, don't do this. Talk to Chelle, she will give you whatever you want. You don't have to do this to me," I beg.

"Where does she have Carmine's stuff? Don't say you don't know. Now think, Jessica, where did she say she has it. I know it's not in the house she was living in—been there, done that. I know it's not in her car and it wasn't in Frances's car, otherwise, I wouldn't have blown it up. Is it at Agosto's house? I could get in there and kill everyone, including your precious Michelina."

"I don't know, honestly. Why would I lie?"

"You would do anything to protect Michelina. How did she earn such loyalty?" Spit flies out with his words, spraying across my face. I stand there frozen, unable to form any words. In one quick move he punches me on the side of my head, and I drop to my knees.

"Get up and clean yourself up. When I come back you better be ready to go." He turns and walks out, locking the door behind him. I'm in the fetal position, my head pounding. I don't have what he wants, which means my life is worth nothing. I curl up making myself even smaller, just like before, except Chelle is not here to save me this time from the monster.

"Wake up, wake the fuck up!" I hear yelling, but I just want to die. I flutter my eyes open, and Nick's face is next to mine. I try to push back but his hand quickly wraps around my throat.

"Jessica, I told you to get cleaned up. We can't get married with you looking like this. Why is it so hard to follow directions?" With his hand still around my throat he lifts me off the floor along with himself.

"Why do you want to marry me?" I struggle to get the question out.

"I want everything my dear sister has."

"Where is Geno?" He looks at his watch and back at me with such a sinister smile, that it makes my blood run cold.

"Right about now, panic has probably set in. If my dear cousin Geno is as smart as people make him out to be, he might be thinking of ways to get out of his predicament. He's as good as dead, though. Unless, of course, he's Houdini." Now he's laughing so hard, he can hardly catch his breath.

"Oh my God, what did you do to him?" I ask as he takes his hand off my neck and pulls me close to him. Our faces only inches apart. I can feel the heat coming off of his body mixed with the rage I can see in his eyes. He is beyond frightening.

"You don't need to know that, yet. However, I suggest if you want to stay alive, you better get cleaned up and dressed for our wedding. Oh, and it will be filmed, so make sure you look your best."

He uncuffs me and turns to leave but stops at the door, looks over his shoulder at me, and smiles. "If you think you can escape, make sure you factor in my love of bombs." He turns back, opens the door and leaves. I can hear his laughter through the door—pure evil.

I'm frozen in place. If he was serious about the bomb, which I have no doubt he was, what will set it off? Why would he ever want to marry me? Why does he have so much hate inside of him for Chelle and her family. Wait . . . it's his family, too. At this moment, I'm thankful that Chelle never told me where she hid Carmine's things. Is it so valuable to him that he would kill for it or is it just revenge? Maybe it's both. I read all the journals. I have knowledge of what Carmine thought of him and his father. Maybe I could use this to my advantage.

When I step into the bathroom, there is a shower stall, a sink, and a commode. As I stare into the mirror, I'm taken aback by the reflection staring back at me, my reflection. How quickly this man destroyed me. How quickly I let him. In my mind, I'm getting flashbacks of me all those years ago. A prisoner by my uncle. If I close my eyes, I can still feel the weight of those chains. A month of dragging them around his basement. He raped me day after day. My parents thought they were leaving me in good hands with my father's brother while they went back to California to settle my grandmother's estate. I was a prisoner, until Chelle saved me when no one else could. She beat my uncle to death with a baseball bat. Swoosh, whack, swoosh, whack, over and over again. At the time, we didn't know he was dead. Once he was down, she found the key and unlocked my chains. We ran, my hand in hers, pulling me to safety. Chelle brought me to Viviana's house. She knew her grandmother could fix everything. After that, nothing was ever said about my uncle, or what Chelle did. I went home and life picked right back up where we left off. That is until I found out I was pregnant. Once again, I had to turn to Chelle for help. I was too far along to have an abortion. I was too young to have a child, much less raise a child. That's when Viviana stepped in again. She made arrangements for Chelle and me to spend the summer in Sicily with relatives. Before I came home, I gave birth to a healthy baby boy. I wanted no part of him, I couldn't. He was adopted by a local family, and I never saw him again. We came home and never spoke about what happened. I owe Chelle and her family so much. There is no way I would ever let someone hurt any one of them. Now, it's my turn to fight back. I can't let Nick destroy her, destroy us. I turn on the water and step in the shower letting the hot water run down my body until my skin is red. I have to formulate a plan before it's too late for all of us, especially Geno.

CHAPTER TEN

Geno

M Y HEAD IS POUNDING AND THERE IS AN AWFUL SMELL. I'M finally able to feel my hands and feet again. I try to move but I can't. It's so dark, no light whatsoever. I feel around and realize I'm in some sort of box. Natural instinct tells me to try and push the top off or yell until someone comes. However, I realize that's not going to help the situation. If anything, it will make it worse. I need to slow my breathing and try to conserve air. If this is what Nick did to me, what the hell is he doing to Jessica? I need to put that out of my mind and try to figure out where the hell I can be? When I try to feel around again, I find what feels to be a disposable lighter. It takes a few tries to flick it on, I'm exactly where I thought I was: in a casket. There is writing on the top. "Tick Tock… Time is running out. Thanks for Jessica."

Quickly I let the flame go out, so I'm not wasting air. I can feel my heart pounding in my chest. I want to scream but I know I can't waste air on stupid shit. All this started when Michelina came into the picture. I need someone to blame but it's not her. Her life was turned upside down right along with the rest of us. There was a feud between Carmine and my dad that should have been ended years ago, not left to stew. Now that evil has worked itself into all of us.

Jessica, sweet Jessica. She is an amazing woman. I thought I would get to spend the rest of my life with her. Now all I have are the few memories we made. For however long I have left, I will treasure them. Damn it, Geno, snap out of it. You're not dying, yet. Maybe I should try to set the box on fire. Desperate idea—stupid and desperate. That would mean I'm setting myself on fire. If I try to break the cheap pine, whatever is on top is coming down on me. What if I'm not that far down? What if I'm really six feet under? What ifs are not going to get me out of this box. My thoughts are foggy, but I remember my watch! I remember hitting the action button or whatever it's called. Now that my hands are no longer numb, I tap my watch and pray for the battery Daniella was bragging about still having a charge. It comes to life, and it still has sixty percent battery left. I know I told Gianni about the watch. I can't remember what else I told him. If he remembers I have it, there's no way he'll know how to use it. It took me almost a week to figure it out. I pray he realizes I have it on and calls Daniella. She is the only person who can find me now. I close my eyes and relax my breathing while I pray for help.

Gianni

I'm out by the garage pacing, watching the minutes tick by as I wait for Daniella. I feel like the waiting is hurting my brother, not helping him. Finally, she gets here, and I practically grab her out of her car and take off running into the office. She waves at everyone but darts over to the computer.

"While I'm activating the search for Geno, tell me exactly what happened."

Luca is standing behind Daniella, watching everything she is doing. He quickly gives her the run down on what's happened and where we think he might be.

"Exactly who are you?" That's Dani right to the point.

"I'm Luca, and Geno is my brother." The room goes silent. This is the first time I've heard him acknowledge that.

"Oh, long lost, I presume, since I've known Geno since the first grade."

"Something like that. Can you tell us what exactly you're doing?"

"Sure, in layman's terms, Geno activated the action button on his watch. What that does is drop compass waypoints everywhere he goes once it's activated. It also sends out the standard SOS. It also has a siren but if he is buried like you think he is, the siren could damage his hearing. It alternates the between the two. We use Backtrack, which takes the GPS data and shows where he could be."

"What if he's underground like we think he is?"

"It will still work. Okay, I've got him. It's not exact but it will be pretty close to where he was last actively moving." She pulls up a map of the mines and hits right around the Carlota Copper Co. Not exactly in that particular mine, but in that area.

"Gianni, you need to let me come with you. I have a new portable tracking device that might help in the search. It's still in the development stage but this could be a good test run."

"I'll call in a favor and have a bigger plane waiting for us. Dad as soon as we know something, I'll get in touch." We race out the door and head to the Scottsdale Airpark.

Geno

It's getting colder in here and my feet are starting to get numb. I don't think I'm running out of oxygen, yet. However, I know the desert can get really cold at night. That's assuming I'm even in the desert. I can't give up, yet. I know my brother won't quit until he finds me. My brother Gianni, that is. As far as Luca, I know nothing about him. I will always be in debt to him for saving Gianni's life. If I don't make it out of here, will

Luca take my place? I know I shouldn't think like that, but it's hard not to. That day when Gianni called me, all he would say is, "The shit hit the fan. Get Dad to the emergency room at Banner Heart Hospital." Never in my wildest dreams would I think the events of that day would change all of our lives forever. Till this day, my father has yet to explain anything to us about Luca. Viviana, the one person who knows all of his secrets, would never betray him. When I broached the subject with her about Luca, all she would say is, "I'm not his mother." That told us nothing. I don't want to die not knowing the truth. Gianni is the hot-headed one, just like our mom was. His emotions have always run wild. Dad always said Gianni might go off half-cocked, but Geno would plot revenge to his grave. Well Dad, take a guess where I am now.

CHAPTER ELEVEN

Jessica

A WEDDING IS SOMETHING MOST GIRLS DREAM ABOUT, AT SOME point, even me. After surviving the hell my uncle put me through, I didn't feel like it was even on my radar anymore. Chelle helped me not to be a victim of my circumstances. All I've ever wanted was to love someone and be loved in return. For a fleeting moment, I thought I had that with Geno. I should have known better. I've been broken for so long. I thought I was going in the right direction, but I need to face the facts: I'm defective. Nothing anyone tells me will ever change that.

I'm staring at myself in the mirror wrapped in only a towel and looking defeated, which confirms everything comes full circle. All those years ago, I told Viviana I was going to hell. She prayed and taught me to pray. I believed I was forgiven. Apparently, I was wrong. I was a part of a man losing his life. No matter how evil he was, he was still a child of God. I shouldn't have been his judge and jury, that was up to God. Please God, don't let Geno be another victim. When I glance in the mirror again, I jump back and yelp. I've been so lost in my own thoughts that I never heard him come in. He's in a fucking tux holding up a wedding gown. "You can't be serious."

"Yes, I'm very serious, and you should be too, if you want to stay alive."

I turn and walk out of the bathroom, brushing right past him and his ridiculous gown. "I'll marry you under one condition, you let Geno go." He throws his head back and laughs a dark sinister laugh.

"Bitch, you act like you have a choice. Everything is arranged. Now put the fucking dress on!"

"Where is Geno?"

"Your precious Geno is out of the picture—permanently."

I feel like all the air has left my lungs as I stumble backwards. "And Chelle?" my words barely a whisper.

"For now, she's alive and if you want to keep it that way, you'll put the fucking dress on."

I pull it from his hand and walk back into the bathroom to get dressed. When I step out of the bathroom, he gives me a cat-call whistle. I ignore him and head toward the door. When I step out of the trailer, I look around and know exactly where I am: the Superstition Mountain Range. Many people have gotten lost in here searching for the Lost Dutchman mine. Maybe that's where he's holding Geno. He pulls me along and practically tosses me into the Jeep. As we pull away from the trailer, he holds up a remote in his left hand and pushes a button. The trailer explodes with such force that the Jeep fishtails. He quickly gains control and laughs as we drive away.

"I told you I love bombs."

"Where are we going?"

"Vegas, baby. I always wanted to get married at the Elvis chapel."

"Nick, do you have a plan?" He stops laughing and shoots me an irritated look.

"If I do, I'm not about to tell you."

Maybe if I keep him talking, he will slip up. "How does any of this get you closer to Carmine's stuff?"

"You know I believed you when you said you didn't know where it is." A quick subject change, as if I wouldn't notice.

"Really? Why would you believe me?"

"For some unknown reason to me, Chelle is very protective of you. So, if I have to make a trade, it better be something good."

"You don't have to marry me to use me as bait." He slows down, grips his hand around my throat and pulls me in for a kiss. I try to pull away, but his grip gets tighter.

"I know that, but I want to have fun, so I figured why not get married."

Fun, this is fun? He's a fucking whack job. "Do you even know what Carmine had?"

"Everyone knew what Carmine had. Whomever finds it is sitting on top of the world. I plan on being that someone."

"What did Geno have to do with any of this?"

"Absolutely nothing. He's my means to an end. The distraction I needed to get to you and get out of town."

"Once you have Carmine's stuff, what makes you think someone else won't try to kill you for it?"

"Awe, you worried about me baby?" This time he grabs a fist full of my hair and pulls me back towards him, his kiss is ruff and sloppy just like the man.

"When can we stop to eat?" Maybe, I could get some help when we do.

"We're not stopping. There is a cooler behind your seat with drinks and snacks. It's only five hours; I'm sure you won't starve to death. Besides, do you think I'm an idiot? I know you will look for any opportunity to escape."

I turn the music up and stare out into nothing. My fate is sealed.

Agosto

They say that time waits for no one. As my son's life is slipping away, I still find myself begging God for more time. I head out back and find

Viviana sitting on the bench feeding the quail. I take a seat next to her and toss some bird seed.

"I'm assuming, Agosto, that you haven't heard anything."

"No. The silence is deafening. I sit and think about all I've done wrong and wish I could go back in time and change things."

"You'd go back and do the same things all over again. You made your choices with the information you had at the time. None of your choices were done with any ill will attached to it."

"Viv, I don't know what I will do if Geno doesn't make it back to me."

"We will cross that bridge when we get to it."

"I know we've never talked about this since everything happened. Does Michelina or Jessica know who cleaned up the mess they left behind?" I ask. She silently tosses some more bird seed.

"That was such a long time ago, Agosto. We did what we did together to protect the girls. Besides us, the only one who knew anything about what happened was Frances and now that died with her."

"What about Jessica's son?"

"What about him? Jessica was fourteen years old. What could she have possibly done other than what we helped her do? Her parents never knew about the baby, and they never questioned where the uncle was. I think in their minds, they knew he was a bad person, and realistically they never should have left her with him. The money they were due to inherit meant more to them than the child they left behind. I hope they carried that guilt with them to their graves."

"You know I had nothing to do with their car accident all those years ago."

"Yes, I know. Karma however works in strange ways sometimes."

"What do you know about Michelina's plans for Carmine's stuff?" She looks away from me and becomes very quiet. I can wait. When it comes to Viviana, I've been waiting a lifetime.

"I'm not sure what she plans on doing. Honestly, I don't want to know."

"Surely, you've advised her. I mean she is a babe in the woods when it comes to all of this. You can't expect her to take upon the entire organization and live to talk about it." I know I've raised my voice more than she is used to. I want to apologize, yet I'm compelled not to.

"I told her to be the change she wants to see. She is a very strong person and if she has Luca by her side, they just might make it out of this alive. Realistically, she doesn't have a choice. That was taken away from her when Frances left her everything."

"Frances knew about everything and look where that got her."

"That's because she didn't want any part of this life. No one walks away and lives to talk about it."

"I know her choices are limited but if she doesn't let me help her, guide her, it's over before it starts." I digress.

We go back to tossing the bird seed and waiting for the phone to ring.

CHAPTER TWELVE

Michelina

THE PLANE RIDE WAS SHORT, BUT MY FOCUS IS ON JESSICA. I know that everyone wants to know what I meant when I blurted out about Jessica not being able to survive this again. I never should have said it out loud. It was a secret that we've kept buried for years. I know that the focus has to be on Geno since he is in imminent physical danger, but what about Jess? Nick stated he is going to marry her. Who would marry anyone under such duress? Jess is not going to go along with it unless she thinks she can save Geno's life. Since they've met, it's been a whirlwind for both of them. He is the first person that she's even given the time of day to. It's always been one-night stands. So, for her, that's huge. Who knows if either one of them is going to make it out of this alive. Luca's nudge snaps me out of my thoughts.

"Chelle, I promise you I won't stop looking for Jessica."

"Thank you. I know the focus right now is on Geno. How much time do you think he has left?"

"There are too many factors to even hazard a guess."

The plane is already starting its descent. When we touch down, there are numerous cars waiting for us. "Gianni, how far is it from here to the mine?" I ask trying to calculate in my mind how much time we have and how much we've used already.

"It's about fifteen minutes or so. I just got a notification that the foreman of the mine that we think he is near is waiting for us. He also wanted to let me know that he has excavators on standby for us, along with an ambulance." For the first time since all of this happened, Gianni actually sounds hopeful.

I've never been to this area, but Luca has. He's nervous. He would never admit it but when he is nervous, he rubs his thumb knuckles. Everyone has some sort of sign, and that is his. The ride to the area only takes fifteen minutes. I feel like I'm always in the hurry up and wait mode. We hop out and Daniella takes the lead. At least Gianni is not opposed to taking directions from a woman. The local police are also there with cadaver dogs. If he is buried, then how will they be able to smell him. Luca takes my hand and pulls me close to him. His lips against my ear.

"Stay close to me," he whispers. Like, where the hell else would I be? I want him found just as much as the next person. He might lead me to Jessica and, right now, that's all that matters. They are spreading out in a grid search since his last known coordinates doesn't mean he is in that spot, it's only an estimate. They gave us all a long piece of rebar to poke the earth with. They also gave us a whistle to blow in case we find anything, along with a hand radio. I set my watch to vibrate every thirty minutes. Each time it does, it takes my breath away. Each time, I'm reminded that we are no closer to finding Geno or Jess. Each time is like another nail in the coffin, Geno's coffin.

"Gianni, maybe we are in the wrong place!" Luca shouts.

"Keep looking, Luca, for any disturbance in the earth. This mine has been closed for a while due to the price of copper. There shouldn't be any disturbance."

We continue with the grid. We can wish time could speed up or slow down, however, in the end, it goes as it's supposed to. The sun is fading into the background and soon it will be pitch black. Even with all the lights that were brought in, it's still getting dark. Luca is pulling me along while I try to look around in areas off the grid.

"Michelina, we need to focus on where we think he might be. You keep drifting off."

"I have a feeling we are going in the wrong direction. Look over to the left past where everyone has already gone. The earth looks disturbed. I don't know if it's new or old but maybe we should check it out." He turns his head and looks to where I'm pointing.

"Go poke it and I'll wait here for you, so we don't lose our spot." I run over and shine my light on the area and it's definitely recently-disturbed earth. My rebar goes all the way in but doesn't hit anything. All the other spots the rebar only goes in a little bit before it hits a hard ground. I wave Luca to come over.

"It didn't hit anything but that doesn't mean that nothing is here." He squats down and shines his light around the area. That's when he begins blowing his whistle. I'm jumping up and down yelling to attract anyone that can help. Gianni finally spots me and comes running.

"Chelle, what did you find." He's out of breath and can hardly get the words out.

"This earth has been recently disturbed and Luca found cigarette butts in the corner near the fence that don't look old. We tried putting our rebar in, but it doesn't hit anything. Unlike the other areas where it won't go more than a couple of inches. It could mean that the casket is deeper than our rods, or it could be nothing. I think it's worth a shot."

"Gianni, if you don't want to stop your search, Chelle and I can take one of the small excavators and start digging here."

"I think that would be the best way to go, this way we aren't putting all our hopes on this one spot." He waves his hand around as if he's dismissing us and walks away.

"Luca, get the excavator over here so we can get started. Gianni can go fuck himself for all I care. I need Geno found so we can concentrate on finding Jessica." I know I came across as demanding, but we all have skin in this game, including me. It doesn't take long for Luca to get one of the men to get started on the area we found. Unfortunately, it's not a fast process. Each bucket of dirt that is lifted out must be moved to a location away from where we are digging. We hear the whistles blowing in the distance. Maybe we were wrong, maybe this isn't where Geno is buried. Luca put the radio closer to his ear.

"What's going on, did they find him?"

"They found a spot they are going to start digging in. Gianni wants us to take up the grid search."

"What about here?" Before he can answer we hear a bang and a scrap from where the excavator is digging. The man operating the excavator stops and shuts off the engine.

"Gianni, we've got something, get here fast." Luca drops the radio and shines his light in the hole. There is still too much dirt to see what we hit. For all we know it could be a mineral vain. There is no way Luca can climb down and help with the dig. He's still recovering from a gunshot wound. In a matter of minutes, the crew are down in the hole digging. I don't want to blink for fear that I will miss something. Finally, they are standing on top of a casket. They are trying to get it open, but they can't.

"Gianni, there should be a slide on the side of the casket. That will unlock it." I'm looking at Luca like *how the hell do you know that?*

"You would be surprised how diversified my training was at the FBI."

Gianni gets the lid open, and Geno is staring at him. "I never thought you would find me alive. Where is Jessica?" He is shivering as they help him get to the top of the hole. The paramedics take over and begin checking his vitals. He tries to push them away, but Gianni will have no part of that.

"Bro, don't be stupid. Let them check you and then we can find Jessica."

Geno's eyes grow wide and fixed on me. "Listen to your brother."

"I want to blame you. Our lives were going along nicely until you came into the picture."

I stand up a little bit taller, ready to take on the world, if I must. If it means I find Jess, I will take on the entire fucking mob. "What's stopping you, Geno?"

"Obviously I had a lot of time to think, Chelle. None of this was your fault. From what Jess told me, you were minding your business, teaching science and loving life. The people that should be held responsible for all of this is my father and your grandfather. My dad always says he didn't want this life for us. If he really felt that way, he could have done something about it years ago. Now it's left to us to clean up this mess. I have no idea where that bastard took Jess, but he was hell bent on keeping her. A trophy wife to rub in your face. I need to find her."

"We need to find her, Geno. Going forward, we need to work together as a family. Agosto wanted change, well, we are going to be the ones to make that change. Now, let's find Jess."

CHAPTER THIRTEEN

Jessica

W E ARE FINALLY IN KINGMAN, ARIZONA. NICK PULLS OFF the highway and into a gas station to fill up. "I have to use the bathroom, Nick." He is totally ignoring me as he pumps the gas. He comes around my side of the Jeep and opens the door for me. I take a moment and look him up and down, not out of fear but out of disgust.

"If you have to go, then get out and go. If you pull any bullshit, not only will I kill you, but everyone inside. Oh, and if you behave, I might tell you what's going on with your boyfriend."

With those words, he just sealed the deal. We head into the convenience store hand in hand like some lovesick puppy dog. I wipe my tears and hold my head up high as he asks for the key to the restroom. He passes it to me and kisses me on the cheek. I want to puke, but what would that mean to Geno?

"Thank you, Nick." I head into the ladies' room knowing that the few people in there are staring at me. I mean it's the middle of the night and I'm walking around in a very skimpy wedding dress. I'm not the glowing bride. When I'm finished, I step out of the stall and a lady is standing in the corner staring at me. I head toward the sink and begin washing my hands.

"Are you okay? Do you need help? I can lock you in the back office and call the police. He won't be able to get in there."

"What makes you think I need help?" Stupid question, Jess.

"I've been here for thirty years, honey, I've seen it all. If you need help, I can help you."

"No, thank you. I'm fine. It's just been a very emotional day for me." With that I dry my hands and walk back into the store where I find him right outside the ladies' room door, waiting for me. He takes my hand and, with no words spoken, I head back to the Jeep.

"Did you talk to anyone?"

"No." Before I can say anything more, his fist lands into my stomach. I double over in pain.

"I know you spoke to the lady that went into the bathroom after you. You know I was outside the door listening."

"If that was the case, then you know I said I was fine," my words barely a whisper.

"Why couldn't you just tell me that Jessica? I don't want to hurt you. I mean after all, we are going to be married very soon."

The thought of marrying him makes the bile rise in my throat. "What about Geno? You promised you would give me an update on him."

"I do keep my promises. Geno has been rescued, which I figured he would be. I mean, I left clues and his brother is FBI. Burying him alive bought me some time to get out of town with you."

"Oh my God, you buried him alive? What kind of sick fuck are you?"

"The kind that you're going to marry, so watch your mouth."

"How do you know he was rescued?"

"Everyone has a price, Jessica." With that he pulls out of the station and back on to the highway. The desert night flies by as we head towards Vegas. All I can do is pray Chelle can figure out where I am and rescue me like she did all those years before.

Michelina

My little pep talk was nice but, in reality, I'm scared to death I won't find her.

"Geno, please try to remember every little detail," Luca pleads with Geno for something, anything.

"Luca, I've been laying in that hole, replaying the last forty-eight hours over and over again. I do know that the mole is Gemma and that she partnered with Rocco. They kept drugging me. I tried so hard to fight them, to fight the drugs. Nick kept me just out of reach of Jessica. He tormented me with stuff he was going to do to her. He fucking raped her right in front of me, and I couldn't move." His voice cracks as he begins to shake all over. Gianni wraps a blanket around him. The paramedics want to take him to the hospital but he's fighting them.

"Geno, there was nothing you could do for her at that time. Right now, you need to listen to the paramedics and go to the hospital. Let them check you out." I squeeze his hand and his face pales. "Find her, Chelle." As the ambulance takes him away, I feel the knot in my stomach get tighter.

"Luca, now that Geno has been found, we need to regroup and come up with a plan." Before he can answer, Gianni steps in front of me and wraps his hand around my wrist—tightly.

"Chelle, I think we need to focus on why he took her, and if you really want to find your friend, you need to tell us everything. We can't find her, if you don't help. I know all about having best friends that would have your back, but there is something you're not telling us. Something that I think Nick knows or figured out."

"When we were fourteen, Jessica's parents went to California to take care of family business. They left her with her uncle. He chained her in the basement and repeatedly raped her. Her parents never said anything about leaving. I searched and after a month I finally found her. I helped her escape that day and we've never left each other's side since. Nick has to know, if he raped her in front of Geno, he wants me to know. The same way he made it pretty easy to find Geno. I don't think he wanted him to die. He needed time to get away and formulate his plan."

The thought of everything Jess has been through and now it's started all over again makes me sick. I have to fight for Jess's sake.

Luca puts his hands on my shoulders and forces me to look him right in the eye.

"What happened to the uncle?" His voice is so deep, and his grip gets tighter. This is Luca the FBI agent not Luca the man I'm in love with.

"I killed him with a baseball bat. We went to my grandmother and told her everything that happened. I could never tell my mother; she would have flipped out. Jess and I were ready to go to the police but instead, Grandma told us to just go about our business and forget about it."

"Oh my God, my father. He had to know all of this. You know how close he is with Viviana." Gianni stops in mid thought. "There has to be more, isn't there, Chelle?"

"Jess's parents came back but we never told them anything. Grandma said if they could leave a fourteen-year-old to go take care of money, then that's all they cared about. By the time summer rolled around, Jess found out she was pregnant. She was too far gone for an abortion. Once again, we went to Grandma for help. She sent us both away to Sicily. Jess gave birth to a boy at the Catholic seminary where they helped pregnant single girls that got into trouble. The boy was adopted, and we came home. After that, we were inseparable. I know she would take a bullet for me, and she knows I would for her." My tears are finally falling. All those years of holding them in. Fear that what I did would be found out. All the hell Jess went through and now she is going down that road again. I don't think she can take it. Luca takes me in his arms and for the first time, I don't care who knows, I never want to leave them.

CHAPTER FOURTEEN

Nick

THE RIDE WAS LONGER THAN I EXPECTED BUT WE HIT SOME construction around Henderson. Jessica's curled up in a ball and fast asleep, either that or she's faking it. I didn't want to hit her but damn she pissed me off. Almost as much as Carmine did when he laughed at me all those years ago. Look who is laughing now, Carmine. I reach over and brush the hair away from her face. She is so beautiful. I really want to keep this one, unlike the others. This one is different, I'm not sure why. Maybe because my sister wants her. Agosto thought he buried everything that happened with Michelina and Jessica. He of all people should know nothing stays buried, not in this business. Now if I could just find the kid she dumped in Sicily, I would have real bargaining power. We pull onto the strip, and I nudge Jessica. "Hey, get up and look at all these lights." Her eyes flutter open and my cock instantly gets hard.

"Did you find out anything more about Geno?" And now my cock has deflated.

"I told you before he was rescued, what more do you want?"

"I want you to let me go and I'll forget about everything that happened. I just want to get back to my family."

I grab a fist full of her hair and pull her face close to mine. "The more you talk about this shit, the madder I'm going to get. You are mine now and that's the end of it." I give her a ruff kiss and then push her away.

"Can I at least ask where we are going?"

"The Elvis chapel to get married. It's always been a dream of mine to get married by Elvis. Doesn't that sound exciting?" She doesn't answer, instead she turns her head and stares out the window. We pull into the parking lot for the chapel, and she finally turns around and glares at me.

"Look, Nick, I'm not here of my own free will. I'm here because I was trying to save Geno's life. Now that you've said he's fine, there really is no reason for me to go along with this charade." She reaches for the door handle and I grab her arm, hard.

"Do you really think this is over now? My target has been and will always be Michelina. Do you get that I want her dead? Before that, though, I want her to suffer. If you want to keep your precious Chelle alive for now, you will march in that chapel with me and be thrilled when Elvis himself declares us husband and wife. Do you understand?"

She gets out of the Jeep and slams the door. "Fine, if that's what you want, that's what you will get. You think everything will be sunshine and roses but let me tell you, I will make you so miserable, you'll be begging for me to give you a divorce. When that day comes, the answer will be no."

"Why the sudden turn around?"

"You ruined it for me. Geno is not going to want me after you raped me. Chelle will never give you what you want, so that's it, asshole, you're stuck with me. Now, let's go meet Elvis." She stomps her feet all the way to the chapel door. She might think she has some sort of control, but she has no clue how far I'm willing to go. Before I open the door for her, I grip her arm and I watch her wince with pain. Her pain, my pleasure.

"You will behave and do exactly as I tell you to do. One wrong step could cause me to kill your precious Michelina. I have people everywhere and *I mean everywhere.*" I open the door and we head inside. Since

I had Rocco arrange everything ahead of time with our contact, Sharon Pagano, this shouldn't take too long. When we get inside the chapel, I look around and am surprised how nice everything has been arranged. The front door to the chapel opens and Sharon comes in with an Elvis impersonator. She heads down the aisle toward me with her arms open.

"Nick, you look great." Her embrace is strong and lasts a little too long.

"Thank you, Sharon. This is Jessica my fiancée." Under her breath, I hear her mumble which number is she? I let it go.

"If you're ready, we can get started. Now, Nick, you need to be up front and, Jessica, you need to wait outside with Elvis."

"No, Sharon, Jessica doesn't need Elvis to walk her down the aisle. We will walk together up to the alter. Elvis can stay in the back and sing something." Jessica looks away from me. Sharon has a smile plastered on her face that is not moving anytime soon. I take her to the back of the room and the music starts. With my arm tightly around her waist, we walk together up the aisle. There is a small table with a goblet filled with wine, a knife, a rope, two simple wedding bands, a small bowl, and a candle. Jessica's eyes widen as she takes it all in.

"What is all of this?" Her eyes never meet mine.

"We are having a very special type of ceremony, one that will bind us together in this life and in the afterlife. I told you I'm not giving you back, so get used to your new life, Jessica—our life. We're ready, Sharon."

"Nick, Jessica, we are here today to bind you together for this life and beyond." She lights the candles and holds up the rings.

"These rings are not just an outward symbol. Please take them in your hand and pass it slowly over the flame. May the heat of these rings burn into flesh as a reminder of the day you became one. Now place them in the bowl." Jessica opens her hand and the ring tumbles into the bowl. Sharon picks up the knife and takes my left hand in hers and slowly cuts the tip of my ring finger. She holds it over the bowl, and I watch as my blood drips over the rings. Next, she takes Jessica's hand.

"You need to stop trembling; I don't want to slip with the knife."

She makes the cut. As the blood drips down, Jessica looks away. Next, she holds both our fingers over the goblet. As the blood drips in, Sharon presses Jessica's finger to mine. Our blood mingling. Now she takes the goblet and holds it so we can both wrap our hands around it. Next, she takes the rope and loosely binds our hands together.

"As you both take a sip of this wine, remember it contains both your blood, blood that passed through both your hearts. This rope binds you both together and no one can break it, not even death." We each take a sip before Sharon takes the goblet and releases the ropes. They fall to the floor at our feet. She holds up the bowl swirling it around to mix up the blood and the rings.

"Please take your rings and repeat after me." We each take a ring and hold it up. The blood glistens in the light.

"These rings are a symbol of our binding blood. Wherever you go, I will follow from life to death." We repeat the vow and slip the rings on. At that moment, Elvis starts singing and I kiss Jessica. "We are one, babe, forever."

CHAPTER FIFTEEN

Agosto

THE ONE THING WE ALWAYS PRAY FOR IS MORE TIME. TIME TO heal. Time to fix things. Time to enjoy what we feel we missed. All the praying in the world won't get one minute back. When I tell Viviana that I wish I could go back in time and have a do-over. She always says we would go back and do the same thing and life would be exactly as it is, as it's supposed to be. She believes our path in life has already been chosen. I would like to think we always have freewill to choose our path in life. Her words don't make me feel better. I love her. I've loved her from the first day I laid eyes on her. Unfortunately, it was a love I could never have, so I settled for friendship. Now looking back on everything, I don't think I settled at all. As you get older, you realize the value of true friendship. That friendship carried me through some of life's most horrific times. At the request of Viviana, I cleaned up a big mess that the girls found themselves in, not once but twice. That's when I realized Michelina was really a younger version of Carmine. The brother I hated with my entire being. She beat a man to death with a baseball bat. Not that the bastard didn't deserve it, but she was a fourteen-year-old girl. She broke his back and crushed his head. She never had nightmares and never had a second thought about it. Yes, Carmine's granddaughter has so many of his ways. She drew the line in the sand. As far as she was concerned, he was wrong and deserved to die. I told Viviana that I would take care of everything, which I did. I only had my most trusted capos with me, yet someone found out. Nick has Jessica, and he is not about to let her go. I heard rumblings about someone looking for the boy, now it all makes sense. The question is: who is the snitch? I know about Gemma and Rocco, but they were never privy to any of my secrets. Whoever did leak this information has to pay the price. While I wait for everyone, I head outside to my bench. I find Viviana sitting there feeding the babies.

"Can I join you?"

"Of course, Agosto, it's your home. Why do you look so troubled? You got Geno back, now you can put all your focus on finding Jessica."

"I'm afraid everything is out in the open now. Someone is looking for the boy."

"Agosto, we did the right thing. We protected the boy. The girls got a chance to live a normal life."

"Normal until now. The very world that Frances tried to shield Michelina from has now taken her in and there is no going back. She killed a man, Viviana. There is no statute of limitation on murder."

"Murder with special circumstances, and since when are you worried about rules and laws?" I try to take her hand, but she pulls back.

"Right now, we need to put everything aside and focus on finding Jessica."

"Let's not forget the boy, Agosto, we need to keep him safe."

"Do you want to tell Michelina what we did, or do you want me to tell her?"

"How does telling anyone help find Jessica?"

"Tell me what?" We both jump at the sound of her voice.

"You shouldn't sneak up on a private conversation."

"I'm sorry, Agosto, I didn't realize you were having a private anything back here in the great outdoors. Now how about someone tell me what's going on? If you're thinking it's going to help Jessica, then you have to tell me."

Viviana nods her head and I know it's time to tell Michelina everything. "You might want to have a seat."

"I'm good, thanks. Just tell me."

"I'm the one who cleaned up the mess you and Jessica left behind."

"Mess?! Do you mean the murder of the pedophile that repeatedly raped Jessica? I'm the only one who looked for her, Agosto. I'm the one who rescued her when no one even missed her. I was only fourteen years old but given the chance, I would do it all over again only this time, I would make him hurt more before he dies, so much more. Make him hurt for every little girl he ever did that to. You and I both know that if he did it once, he did it before. It was too damn easy for him. She was chained to the fucking basement floor, for Christ's sake, naked and afraid. Is that the mess you're referring to, Agosto?"

Her yelling has brought everyone outside. "You are starting to sound more like Carmine every day. What's next, Michelina? Will you kick us all to the curb, so you can take over? Is that what was in Carmine's journal? Your path to power?"

"Agosto, how long have you had your hand in everything that has gone on in this family?"

"I've been a friend and a confidant since before you were born. You would do right by showing me the respect I've earned."

"What else are you hiding? How many more lives will you destroy?"

"Enough!" Viviana yells as she gets off of the bench.

"None of this is bringing Jessica back home. You need to work together for her safety and the safety of this family."

"You're right; we do. Now tell me what you are hiding?"

Viviana thinks Michelina is so innocent and fragile, this right here should show her how ruthless she can be. "The baby that you and Jessica think was adopted and sent away, is actually growing up with my cousin Lorenzo in Sperlinga Sicily. Nick somehow knows everything, and he is looking for the boy."

"Why would you do that to the boy, put him in that much danger? Grandma, did you know all of this? Is this what you meant when you said he helped you?"

"Yes. No one wanted the boy."

"Why?

"Because he was a product of rape. His father was a pedophile. No one wanted him. What were we supposed to do?"

"Is he okay?"

"Yes, he is happy and health. We need to protect him and just let him be. He doesn't know he was branded at birth by the evils of his father."

"How did Nick find out?"

"The only thing I can think is Gemma had full access to this house. She must have seen or heard something. Maybe she found something when I was not around. I do have a file in my office, but I never thought I had to hide stuff from family."

"She's not your family and now it's come back to bite us all in the ass. Let's go, Luca, we need to find Jessica. Hopefully, we can find her before Nick tells her about the boy."

They leave but Geno and Gianni are still here.

"Dad, I can't believe how much you kept from us, starting with Luca. How many more secrets do you have? How many more lives are you going to destroy?" He takes a step toward me, but Gianni grabs his arm. I've never been afraid of my children, but Geno is really upset, with good reason. I kept secrets for all the wrong reasons.

"Geno, stop. None of this is going to find Jessica. Let's go back into your office and try to help Luca and Chelle, so they are not spinning their wheels." They turn and leave Viviana and me to feed the quail.

CHAPTER SIXTEEN

Jessica

BEFORE WE LEFT THE CHAPEL, NICK HAD ME SIGN SOME PAPERS. Realistically, I had no choice. I was not ready for another beating. Besides, who really cares? Even if I get out of here, I'm damaged goods. I've always been, but now I'm on display for everyone to see. Maybe this is where I'm supposed to be—married to Nick: a sociopath, killer, tormentor, just a downright evil person. "Where are we going now?"

"I rented a hotel room for us. The honeymoon suite." He glances over at me with a wicked grin that's loaded with a lot of plans . . . plans for me.

He actually believes all of this is real. "Aren't you afraid I'll cause a scene and try to get away from you?" He throws his head back and laughs.

"You won't do any such thing. You have a sick obsession with Michelina, and you don't want me to kill her. You'll do whatever I ask you to."

We pull into the Bellagio Hotel. The valet is looking in the back of the Jeep.

"Our bags will be arriving later. See that they get sent up to our room." He tips the guy a hundred dollars like it's nothing.

"We have bags?" I question. He pulls me through the door where there is a man waiting for us.

"Good evening, sir. Everything is arranged as you requested. I'll show you to your suite."

"Thanks, but I'm fine. I'm sure my wife will want something to eat." He turns toward me but I'm so enthralled with everything I can't formulate an answer.

"Just keep it light for her and throw in my usual steak dinner. I can take it from here."

When we get inside the elevator, he slips the key in a slot for the penthouse. The elevator races past all the floors and doesn't stop until we reach the top. The doors open and we step directly into the living room of a beautiful penthouse. That's when I realize this is a private elevator.

"The only way for anyone to come up here is to have this key, the same for leaving." He holds it up like a prize possession. I'm frozen in place while he heads inside and pours himself a drink.

"What are you waiting for? Don't tell me you think I'm going to carry you in."

"No, I'm just taking it all in. As far as I'm concerned, you don't have to come anywhere near me for the rest of my life. How ever long that is." He puts his glass down and in the blink of an eye he's right in front of me. He scoops me up and heads into the bedroom. He gently puts me down and backs up.

"Have a nice long bath, you need it." He steps out of the room and closes the door behind him.

I begrudgingly get up and walk into the bathroom. The tub is massive. I run the water at a comfortable temperature and to my surprise, it's filling up pretty quickly. I slide out of my wedding gown and stand in front of the mirror naked. I have a bruise on my stomach where Nick punched me. The bruise I tried to cover with make-up on the side of my forehead is getting darker. As I stare into the mirror, the person staring back at me is hardly recognizable. Oh, it's the same face except with added bruises, but it's the person inside who is different. Even if Chelle was to find me now, I could never be the same again. I was brutalized at the age of fourteen and I never got over it even though I buried it and continued on with my life. When I found out I was pregnant, I begged God to take me, he never did. Instead, Viviana stepped in. She spoke to my parents and before I knew what was going on, Chelle and I were on our way to Sicily. At first, I thought my parents knew, but Viviana assured me that they were clueless. Chelle thought I wanted to keep the baby. She came up with a plan for us to raise him. I knew from the first day I didn't want to keep him. It's hard to explain the gamete of emotions I went through. Blaming myself, blaming my uncle, blaming my parents for leaving me with him. In the end, I blamed God. He should have protected me. I wash the make-up off my face and stare at the hollow person staring back. The only one to blame is me. I was a victim in the past. Maybe I should have listened to Chelle when she told me bad things could happen if I stayed with her. This is where my loyalty has taken me. I climb into the oversized tub and wish I could float away to another life, another time. Anywhere but here.

Michelina

After being buried alive, Geno doesn't miss a beat; he's back behind his computer with Dani trying to figure out where Jessica is. I pray that we find her and maybe there is a chance for them to have their happy ending. "Did you remember something? Do you have an idea where they are?"

"Dani is helping me piece together my memory. Nick kept talking about a wedding, his wedding to Jess. He kept thanking me for Jessica. He even wrote that on the lid to the coffin." A sudden look of disgust passes over Geno's face. Luca comes into the room. Agosto and Grandma must have stayed outside.

"Maybe we could check all the chapels near Globe," my voice trails off as I watch Geno close his eyes and continually rub his temples. Luca pulls Geno's chair around and crouches down in front of him.

"Are you trying to remember something? Something you think might be important?"

Geno slowly opens his eyes. "Yeah, but my head is pounding. It's right on the edge, but I can't pull it forward."

"I know you don't know me from Adam, but I need you to trust me. I can help you. You just have to trust me."

"I'll do whatever I have if it means I get Jess back safe."

"I'm going to use a form of hypnosis. It's going to help you relax enough to let the memory in. There are different forms of hypnosis, the traditional hypnosis will probably work best in this situation."

"How do you know all this shit?"

"My training at the FBI. I need you to take some deep breaths and slowly exhale. Focus on the clock on the wall. Listen only to my voice. You are back in the prison with Jessica and Nick. Tell me what you see?" His grip on the chair gets tight at the mention of Jessica's name.

"Nick is cutting away her top. I'm hung from the rafter. When I try to move, I nearly kick the chair out from under me."

"What is Nick saying?"

"Hold on there, little buddy, I need you alive for my plan to work."

"You're doing good. Relax, what else do you see?"

"Nothing."

"What do you feel."

"Rocco sticks me with a needle again. My body feels heavy and as I try to speak, I can't feel my tongue."

"What else do you hear?"

"I hear him raping her. I want to scream but I can't. I fight to open my eyes and he's on top of her. Jess is crying. She keeps saying 'not again, please not again.' Nick is laughing. He gets up and begins ordering his men on things he wants done." In my mind, I see the little girl chained to the floor all over again. I can't stop the tears.

"This is good, Geno, what else do you remember?"

"That crap that Rocco gave me is making my head pound and I can't fight it anymore. I'm falling asleep and the last thing I remember is Nick singing."

"What is he singing? Think, Geno, you're safe and no one can get to you now."

"An old song that I've heard before but not sure where I heard it. 'It's Now or Never.'"

"Okay, Geno, you did great. You can close your eyes, but when you open them again, I want you to remember what happened. You are totally relaxed and when you are ready you can open your eyes." He opens his eyes and looks around.

"The song, that has to be some sort of clue, right? I'll look it up." He turns to face his computer, but Luca stops him.

"Don't bother. I know the song and I know exactly where they are. My mom was a big Elvis fan. That's one of his songs. We are heading out to Vegas. He probably took her to the Elvis Chapel to get married."

Once again, we are racing out the door to follow the first solid lead we've got.

CHAPTER SEVENTEEN

Nick

JESS HAS BEEN IN THE BATHROOM FOR A COUPLE OF HOURS. WHEN I go to check on her, she's not in there. I know she couldn't escape. The master suite is through the bathroom, and I find her in a bathrobe fast asleep. I really need to convince her to stay with me, so I don't have to kill her. Besides, I think having her want to stay with me will really drive Michelina over the edge. I'm no fool; after the events of the past few days, I'm sure there is a bullseye on my back just as large as the one I have on Michelina's. I go back into the living room and find my bags waiting for me with the bellman quietly standing by.

"You can leave them there. My wife is sleeping, and I don't want to disturb her." I reach into my pocket and peel off a hundred dollar bill from my roll. He leaves with a smile. My phone chimes with a new text message.

> Rocco: What do you want me to do with Gemma?
>
> Nick: She served her purpose, get rid of her. Make it look like a drug overdose.
>
> Rocco: Do you need me to come to Vegas?

Nick: No, you need to lay low. I'll let you know if I need you.

I'm sure by now Rocco realizes his days are numbered. Once a mole always a mole. I need to get in touch with Bruno. He handles all my special needs and always takes my calls.

"Hey boss, what's up?"

"I have a special job for you. It's got to be fast and clean. I need you to take care of Rocco. He's been a thorn in my side for a long time. You know what Bruno; I want you to do that aquamation Rocco was talking about it last week. He had it done for one of his dogs. He was telling me all about it. The body goes into vat filled with some shit he was talking about, and everything dissolves except for the bones and fillings. Then give the bones to his dogs."

"I'll let you know when it's done." He hangs up and now I bring the suitcases into the bedroom. It looks like my instructions were followed to the T. There's a first for everything. I pull out the sleeping pills and nudge Jessica.

"I'm sorry, I was so tired I fell asleep."

"That's okay, you need your rest. Here take this."

"What is it?"

"Something to help you relax." She takes the pill and sips the water.

"Do you want me to get you something to eat or wait until later?"

She mumbles, "Later" and falls back to sleep. Now I can continue on with my business.

Luca

Agosto's plane gets us to Vegas in thirty minutes. I use my FBI creds to muscle my way inside the Elvis Chapel. Even though I'm on a medical leave, they are still active. Gianni and Geno go in like cowboys at the O.K. Corral. While they interrogate the Elvis impersonator, I take Chelle and head into the office. No one is in there, so I help myself to the ledgers sitting on the desk.

"Do you see anything?"

"Chelle, I just started looking. You pull apart the file cabinet." I go back to the books because this is where the money is, very old school but that's okay. A very large chested woman comes into the office and make a beeline to get the books away from me. When her back is to Chelle, she pulls out her gun and holds it to the woman's head.

"Look lady, we are with the FBI and we are trying to find a kidnapped victim. Get in my way and I won't think twice about blowing your fucking head off." My eyes grow wide and I'm trying not to laugh, she sounds like Dirty Harry.

"What do you want to know?"

I pull out my phone and show her a picture of Nick and then a picture of Jessica. I'm looking for these two people. Were they here today?"

"Yes, they came first thing this morning. I had to set up the special table for them."

Chelle finally lowers her gun and steps where the woman can see her. "What do you mean the special table?" Chelle's words barely above a whisper.

"The blood vow rituals. Very few people get them anymore. The thought is you are bound by blood, not just words. It means you are bound together beyond this lifetime."

Chelle grabs the corner of the desk to steady herself. She's unable to speak and seems to be in shock but I can't stop the questioning now.

"Did the girl seem to go along with this or was she being forced to do it?" She reaches for something on the desk and Chelle instantly pulls the gun up from her side and points it at the woman.

"Easy lady, I just want to show you something. I got no skin in this game, so I really don't care." Chelle lowers her gun. The woman reaches for a different journal that is tucked inside a magazine. She hands it to me. "That's every blood vow that has ever been done here. You'll notice some of the names are familiar."

"What exactly is a blood vow, and why do you keep them separate?"

"It's a ritual that is believed to bind the souls for the afterlife. This guy Nick has gotten married here a couple of times before, but not for a blood vow."

The realization of what she just said hits Chelle hard. She backs into a chair and slowly sits down. Her mouth is open, and she begins to cry.

"Where are the others . . . you know, the ones before the blood vows?"

"This is Vegas; what do you think?"

"You wouldn't happen to have heard where he was going?" I know it's a long shot, but Vegas is big and any help I can get is welcomed.

"Nick Ciccone is a big player. He always hangs at the Bellagio, but he's all over this town. He throws money around—a lot of it—and that's why people hang all over him."

"Why are you telling me all of this?"

"He married a friend of mine. It was all fun and games until it wasn't. Then one day she was gone, never to be heard from again. She was a stripper. Before you ask, I filed a police report, but they said she probably just ran off with someone. I was told that Nick has quite a few people in his back pocket, and I should probably leave it alone. I have a family that depends upon me. I don't want to end up missing one day, so please keep me out of it. Now, since that is all the information I have for you, I think you need to leave."

"Thank you, and I will leave you out of this." I take Chelle's hand and we head out the back door. The less we are seen, the better. We go around the back to the parking lot and find Geno and Gianni waiting for us.

"Where did you two disappear to?" Gianni's demands loudly.

"We were gathering information. I found out where Nick and Jessica are. I'll fill you in along the way. We need to get to the Bellagio before he finds out we're here."

"What makes you think he will find out we are here?" This time Gianni seems calmer.

"From what I heard, he has a lot of people here on the payroll, including local law enforcement. You know, I don't think he's as dumb as everyone has made him out to be."

"Do you mean to tell me the FBI has nothing on Nick?"

"I wouldn't know if they do or don't; I was in charge of Carmine." They might be my brothers, but after I said it, I can see disgust on both their faces. Like smelling a dead skunk.

"Look, that's what I did for a living. We need to put everything behind us and focus on getting Jessica home safely." That seems to appease them. We get in the car and head toward the Bellagio. I'm praying we are not too late.

CHAPTER EIGHTEEN

Nick

THIS HOTEL IS ROCKIN' TODAY, WHICH IS GREAT FOR ME. THE less eyes on me, the better. My seat at the poker table at the Bellagio's Club Privé was waiting for me. Two hours of play and I'm up sixty grand, which makes up for last month. My phone vibrates, letting me know my time is up here. When I get back to my room, Jessica is up and going through the clothes I had brought up for her.

"How are you feeling?"

"Do you care?"

"No, just get ready to leave. You have fifteen minutes." I head back into the living room and sit at the desk. I pull out the pad and pen to leave my darling sister a note.

Michelina,

Hello dear sister, sorry you couldn't make it to our wedding. It was everything a blood vow should be and more. The day I met Carmine, it changed my life. I went with the intention of blowing his fucking brains out. I was young and stupid. Thankfully, he made me see that. He also made me realize what I needed to do. If I wanted revenge, there was one way of getting it: learn the business inside and out. Let them think I'm a putz and swoop in at the end. That's when people are most vulnerable, when they think you're not capable of doing anything.

I have Jessica and I decided I'm keeping her. Either you come to your senses and split everything Carmine left with me, or all bets are off. Everyone's head is on the chopping block, even your beloved Viviana. I killed your mother and I have no qualms in killing Granny. Oh, and I got the kid, thanks. I'll be in touch soon.

Nick.

I fold the note and place it next to a bottle of bourbon on the bar with a couple of glasses. I figure once she reads it, she will need a shot. Just as Jessica comes out of the bedroom, a text comes through letting me know the chopper is ready.

"You look amazing." I pull her in close to me and give her a gentle kiss. She pulls back and looks at me like a lost little girl.

"Where are we going?"

"Home, baby, your new home."

"You promised if I went along with all of this you would leave Chelle alone."

"I said I wouldn't kill her. I'll never leave her alone." I take her hand and we head up to the roof just as the chopper touches down. Within minutes we are on our way.

Michelina

How could this man always be a step ahead of us? From everything I've learned about him, he is considered a middle of the pack flunky. "Gianni, is there something we are missing about Nick? I mean I thought he was a nobody."

"I'm working off the same information that you got. My understanding is he never even finished high school. He's more muscle than anything else."

Once again Luca's creds gets us upstairs, that's when I find the note addressed to me. As I read, I feel my heart shatter into a million pieces. I pass it to Luca and pour myself a Bourbon as Luca reads it out loud. Geno grabs the bottle and pours himself a shot.

"Chelle, why would she go along with this?"

"Geno, I'm sure she was doing it to protect me."

"After what we found out today, it's all starting to make sense. We need to find the boy and protect him from Nick. He said he has him but that could be just to rattle your cage. The boy's life matters no matter who his parents are."

"I agree, but where do we start? Luca, do you know anyone who can help us in Sicily?"

"No, but you don't need that. Agosto knows where the boy is. I say we need to get to the boy before Nick does." Gianni is on the phone barking out orders and then abruptly hangs up.

"The jet is ready to take us back to Arizona. Dad will have the information on the boy along with our passports waiting for us on the large jet at Phoenix Sky Harbor. We need to leave now." For now, I have to put all my feelings aside and help rescue an innocent boy.

Jessica

I'm being whisked from the hotel room to the roof top and then to a private jet. I couldn't stop this even if I tried. Nick went from a man who raped and tortured me to a gentle, kind man and now I don't know what he is. All I know is I'm scared, not just for me but for Chelle and Geno. Nick is out for blood, just not mine. I decide to try and broach the subject of where we are going. I turn in my seat to see his face, but he's busy on his iPad. I tap him on the arm and finally he stops and closes the iPad.

"Nick, can I ask you a few questions?"

"Make it quick; I've got work to do."

"Where are we going?"

"New York. I'm letting my sister do the leg work for me."

"Is that where we are going to be staying?"

"Jessica, until I tell you otherwise, Queens, New York will be your home. If there is something you need from Arizona let me know and I'll have one of my men pick it up."

"What about Chelle and Geno?"

"Right now, they are safe. Are you happy?" I don't answer, cause why bother? It wouldn't matter to him anyway. As long as I know that they are safe for now, it buys me time to figure out a plan. I've never been to New York. Right now, I feel like I'm fourteen all over again. At least I'm not chained to the basement floor, naked. I'm not sure what will happen down the road, but I will do whatever I have to stay alive.

"Jessica, I need to talk to you about something and remember, before you answer, I will know if you're lying. Tell me about the boy you gave away."

My head begins to pound, and I jump out of seat, race to the bathroom and throw up. How could he know? Viviana assured Chelle that no one will ever find him. Is that what he meant when he said he was letting his sister do the leg work? Is the boy still safe? I clean myself up and head back to my chair. He is staring at me for an answer.

"What would you like to know?"

"Let's start with why you gave him up rather than have an abortion?"

"When I found out I was pregnant, I was too far gone to have an abortion."

"Well then, why didn't you keep him?"

"If you know all of this, why do you have to bring it up? Does it give you pleasure that you're hurting me?"

"No, I want to know what you were thinking at the time, that's all."

"I spent a month in my uncle's basement chained to the floor, naked. He raped me every day, sometimes twice a day. At night, if he had too much to drink, he would try to rape me but couldn't, which would piss him off and he would beat me. Not unlike you did." I had to say it. If he hits me, then so be it.

"Please, continue on. What happened when Chelle found you?"

"When Chelle came down the basement to look for me, she found him on top of me. His hand was around my throat, and he was raping me. She picked up the baseball bat and swung as hard as she could. First, she hit him in the back and when he turned around, she hit him on the side of his head. I heard the bones crack and blood was everywhere. She pulled him off of me, got the key from his belt and set me free. We took off running towards Viviana's home. As we ran Chelle took off her t-shirt and had me put it on. She didn't care that she was running through the streets in her bra. All she cared about was me. Maybe now you'll understand why I would take a bullet for her."

"So now you found out you were pregnant. How far along were you?"

"Almost six months. I was never regular, so I didn't think about it until my body started to change. I couldn't go to my parents because I would have to tell them what happened, and I needed to protect Chelle. I went to Viviana, and she took care of everything. I gave birth at a Catholic home for girls. The baby was adopted, and I never saw him again. Why the interest in all of this?" My hands are shaking so bad, I clasp them together hoping it will help.

"Well, it was Agosto who took care of everything. Getting rid of the body and the adoption of the boy. You see, no one wanted him because of where he came from. No fault of yours. Agosto should have put him up for adoption in another country where nobody would find out. Now the boy is living only a town over from where he was born, and Agosto's cousin takes care of him."

"Is he safe? What are you going to do?" My head is spinning. I don't want to hear anymore, but I need answers.

"For now, he is safe. However, if I found out, then any one of Agosto's enemies can too."

I get up, go get a bottle of water along with a blanket and curl up in the chair across from Nick. I will myself to try and sleep, but it never comes.

CHAPTER NINETEEN

Michelina

IT'S SUCH A SHORT TRIP THAT BY THE TIME WE GET WHEELS UP, we're already preparing to land. Something is nagging me, but I can't figure out what. Everyone's been very quiet, focused on their phones. "Excuse me, can every one stop looking at their phones for a minute? I don't think we should go to Italy. I think it's a trap. You can't all believe that this boy is in trouble. What use would he be to Nick? Bait for me? He already has my attention. If we go, I think Nick goes after Agosto and Grandma. Carmine is dead and has not been replaced yet by the family. If Agosto is gone, that makes only three left. I think Nick is going to try and pick them off one by one, and he'll use us to do it."

Geno is shaking his head no. "Look, I want to rescue Jessica and I'll do whatever it takes. I'm not leaving her with a madman. Gianni, what do you think?"

"This could go either way. We could put extra protection around Agosto and Viviana. Luca, you're very quiet what's going through that head of yours?"

"If we go get the boy, then we are doing Nick's work for him. While we are gone, it gives him more time to plot his revenge against Chelle. The boy means nothing to him just as he means nothing to Jessica. She closed that part of her life and, with the help of Chelle, moved on. Nick is not going to stay in Arizona, it's not his home base—New York is."

"So, you think we need to go to New York, and do what?" Geno says with a distinct sarcasm.

"Yes, I think we need to go to New York. But before we do, we call a meeting of the families. We put them on notice that Chelle, with the backing of her family and Agosto's blessing, is taking over her grandfather's position. That's what Carmine wanted all along for his granddaughter is to take a stand."

"And you know this how?"

"Gianni, I spent months babysitting the guy. He put a lot in his journals, but there was an awful lot that he didn't." Luca's revelation about Carmine knocks me off guard.

"What about Jessica? I want her back no matter what that bastard did to her." Geno has a white-knuckle grip on the sides of his seat.

"Oh, don't worry, Geno, she is and always will be my number one priority. So how do we go about putting this plan in motion?"

"We have Agosto call a meeting. Chelle you will bring something from the stuff that Carmine left you as a good faith offering and proof that you mean business. We set the meeting place some place where we have total control. Nick will take the bait and when he shows up, we get Jessica."

"You make it sound so easy."

"Geno, it's not easy but we have more going for us than Nick does."

"What's that?"

"We are a family that will stick together no matter what. All he has are paid flunkies."

"In theory, what you're saying makes sense, but the reality is this is an old school organization, and they don't take well to change."

"Gianni has a point, Dad always said, 'woman are there for support and men are there to lead.' Michelina, how do you plan to get everyone to take you seriously?"

I take a moment to compose my thoughts. "Carmine left me a treasure trove. Not just the journals, but diamonds, pictures, and cash . . . lots of cash. All this time I kept wondering why would he leave it to me? Then I realized it's because he wanted change. From the beginning his journals talked about it. He wanted my mom to be more like Sammy the Bull's daughter. A daughter who was confident in her strength. Who was a born leader. My mom was not that person and I think her trying to live up to his dreams only put a wedge between them. What I got from Carmine is power, confidence, and determination. I am going to tell Agosto to set the meeting. I will not back down, and I will get Jessica back. I hope we can form a united front." I take a deep breath and slowly exhale while I wait for some sort of rebuttal. Gianni looks at Geno and then to Luca.

"Chelle, we are all in." With everyone's agreement, we can now move forward.

When we got back to the house, Agosto was not pleased that we canceled the trip to Italy. He was even less pleased when he found out why. I'm banking on Gianni and Geno to get Agosto on board. I honestly don't think he would listen to Luca, so why bother. What I need to do is get to the bank and pull out some of Carmine's stuff. The question is: what do I take? Maybe I should take Luca in with me. On second thought, until he is officially no longer attached to the FBI, I don't want to take any chances. I will, however, have him take me to the bank and watch my back. I head out the back way to the garage and find Luca waiting for me.

"Thank you for taking me and being understanding when I asked to go in alone."

"Chelle, I want you to know that after today, I'm turning in my papers."

"I was thinking about that and maybe you should wait." His eyes shift nervously.

"Why? I thought this is what you wanted?"

"First of all, it has to be what you want not me. I was thinking maybe you should hold on to your current status until after the meeting."

"No, I disagree. If I go into that meeting as a FED, it will never happen. I need to resign, and Agosto has to come out as my father, otherwise, none of this will work."

"In theory it sounds great, now let's hope it works. I do have a question for you. When you were taking care of Carmine, did he really talk a lot more than what he put in the journals?"

"I never read any of the earlier journals, but I did read the ones he wrote while he was with me. He insisted I read them."

"Didn't you find that odd?"

"At the time, yes, but thinking back now, no. He knew who my dad was. Yet, for some odd reason we got along."

"Do you know what everything is that he left me?" I had to ask and knowing Luca, he won't lie.

"I do. He told me what he was doing. I warned him that Frances could turn it over to the FBI or set it on fire. He said he didn't think she would do that. Especially when he gave her a detailed report of Nick Sr.'s dealings with other families along with the other children he had." My poor mom, all the crap she went through but never said a word. I only wish I could go back in time and tell her I understand and give her a hug. I take a few breaths fighting back the urge to cry.

"What do you think I should bring with us to the meeting?"

"Bring the first ledger. If I remember correctly that has a lot from the early days. I remember Carmine also had a lot of damaging photographs. And you have to bring something of significant value to show good faith." We pull up to the bank and I'm so nervous. I know my best friend's life is on the line and again, I'm the one that can save her.

"Please come into the lobby and wait for me there, just like the last time." He gets out, looks around and then opens my door. He shields me as I enter the bank. Mom's friend Emma greets me.

"Hi, Michelina, how are you doing?"

"I'm taking it day by day. I need to get into my box today."

"Of course." She has me sign the book, yet, the entire time she has her eyes on Luca.

"Will your friend be joining you?"

"No, thank you." I don't want to elaborate any more than I have to.

I follow her to the box and after that, she leads me into a room. The last time I was in this box I didn't take the time to go through it all. Now that I have the time, I begin to pull out stuff. There are five ledgers, one for each family. The sixth ledger is what Luca was talking about. It details stuff that Carmine and Agosto did in the early years. There are a lot of different size envelopes filled with photos. Most of the photos are of political people that could turn this country on its ass. There is the pouch of diamonds and emeralds. There is another pouch that has one very large Tanzanite blue/violet stone. It's so beautiful I can't take my eyes off of it. I shake my head and put it back in the pouch. I decide to take some of the emeralds and some of the diamonds. I put them in a plastic baggie that I took from the kitchen. I'm sure Carmine is shaking his head right about now. I open the ledgers and decide on the one that Luca suggested. I also take some of the photos as an added bonus. When I go to put everything back in the box a letter falls out of one of the ledgers. It's addressed to Carmine. When I open it up, I see it's from Agosto. Shit! What the hell am I supposed to do now? I want to read it, yet I don't. I'm torn between doing what's right and giving it back to Agosto or being nosey and reading it. I justify it by saying reading it might save my friend. It's a stretch but I'm taking it. I sit down and take it out. The paper is old and yellowed. It' is written in a beautiful penmanship. Why have I never noticed Agosto has such nice penmanship? That's when I realize it's not from Agosto but from Grandma. I think my heart sank a little. It is actually a letter that Grandma wrote to Agosto, yet it is among Carmine's papers—why? I fold it up and shove it in the bag. After putting everything else away, I let Emma know I'm ready. I take Luca's hand and we head out.

CHAPTER TWENTY

Michelina

THE DRIVE BACK TO AGOSTO'S HOUSE IS VERY QUIET. I KNOW Luca wants answers but so do I. The letter is burning a hole in my purse. Part of me wants to read it and part of me knows I shouldn't. I should respect their privacy. Maybe I should put it away until after they pass.

"Chelle, what's wrong?" His words snap me back to reality.

"Before we go inside, I need some advice." He leaves the car running so we don't roast with the desert heat.

"You have my undivided attention."

"The first time I went to the box, I didn't go through everything. Even now there is more stuff, but I was pressed for time. I did find a letter and I'm not sure what to do. It's a letter that Grandma wrote to Agosto. I'm thinking it's pretty personal. Why did Carmine have it? Should I read it? Should I give it to Grandma or Agosto? I don't need any more on my plate." He pops his seat belt off, turns and faces me. He strokes the side of my face. His touch is comforting.

"If Carmine had it, then the reason he did can't be good. I think you should give it back to Viviana. She was the original sender of the letter. Knowing Carmine, chances are it never made it to Agosto. It's the past, Chelle, and that's where it should stay. All of this crap that Carmine left you is the past. Sometimes the past should be buried and stay buried."

"We never had a chance to talk about the plan for this family, we're just diving right in. Are you prepared for what will happen? This is a lot to take on and very dangerous. Also, why didn't you ask me about the man I killed?" Might as well throw everything out there.

"Chelle, I love you. I'm putting it out there so you can hear the words that you seem to need right now. I'm prepared to do whatever it takes to secure our future together. As far as Jessica's uncle, you did what you had to do to rescue her. I applaud you for that."

"Luca, I love you. I don't care if I burn in Hell because we're second cousins. I know this has been a wild ride for both of us, but I wouldn't change a thing . . . well, maybe the part about you getting shot." He pops my seatbelt off and pulls me close. Gently he kisses me, and I swear my ovaries are about to explode, that's what this man does to me. I run my hands down his chest, but he grabs my wrists and pulls back.

"The first time I have you it will not be in the front seat of a car." Once again, I'm left hanging on a thread from this man. We head inside to start the process of calling a family meeting.

When we get inside, everyone is waiting. Everyone except Grandma. "Agosto where is Grandma?"

"She is resting. Do you want me to go get her?"

"No, let her rest. I'll go see her when we are done here. Where will we be doing the zoom call?" Geno gets up and pulls a chair out for me.

"Please, have a seat. Before we go into Dad's office, we wanted to discuss something with you." I sit down and Luca has that *what the fuck now* look.

"We were thinking we should do the meeting with Nick only. We can tell him you have everything, and you are prepared to make a trade. You will give him Carmine's stuff and he is to give you Jessica alive and unharmed. Once everything goes down, we take him out. I'll have some of our best men with us. After that, we arrange a sit-down with the family to discuss terms. What do you think?" I can't keep looking to Luca for answers. If I'm going to take command of this family, I need to trust my instincts.

"Okay, I brought a few items that we can show Nick."

I lay them out on the table and the room falls silent. Geno picks up one of the largest emeralds and whistles. "If that doesn't get his attention, I don't know what will."

I don't tell them about everything else. Some things need to be played close to the vest. "Let's get this over with." I get up and place everything back in the bag as we all head into Agosto's office.

"Geno, do you know how to get in touch with Nick?"

"I put out feelers to his crew. Once he took the bait, I set the call up for today."

"So, you knew I was going to go along with your plan?"

"Look, Chelle, I want Jessica back just as bad as you do." I pray we can get her back and hopefully, she won't be mentally and emotionally destroyed like the last time. She never trusted her parents again. The only one she trusted was Grandma, and that took months.

Geno places the call, and the screen comes to life. Jessica is sitting next to Nick. Her face is drawn, and her eyes are glassy. I let out a gasp. She lifts her eyes, and she finds mine. She mouths something but I can't figure it out.

"Hey, sis, what do you have for me?"

"I brought something with me today as a good faith offering." I get my hand closer to the camera and pour out the diamonds and emeralds. I then take out the ledger and flip through some pages. Finally, I pull out some disgusting pictures of movies stars and politicians. One is dressed like a Nazi and he's whipping naked women. It gets worse from there.

"Wow, that Carmine really knew what to keep. How many ledgers are there?"

"Not including this one, there is six. There are more gems and a box filled with gold religious medals."

"Why would he have them?"

Luca step forward so Nick can see him. "When I was babysitting Carmine, he talked about them. He was very superstitious as many Italians are. When he would grant favors to people in need, they would pray for him and give him a medal. He had no clue what to do with them, so he put them in the box."

"What else did he tell you, Mr. FBI guy?"

"You'll find out when we make the exchange. Where and when Nick, I want this over with." We all turn and look at Luca. He is dominating this exchange.

"We will be in town later tonight. I want it done in a public place. Michelina, you come alone and bring everything."

"Do you really believe that I would show up to an exchange with you and not have any back-up? Why don't you wake the fuck up and share whatever the hell you're on." I reach over to Geno's keyboard and hit delete, and just like that, he's gone.

"Before any of you say a word, I can't let him think he can walk all over me, especially since I'm a woman. He'll call back." At least I pray he does. It doesn't take long for him to call back.

"Okay, sis, I'll let you bring Agosto."

"No, he's an old man with a heart condition." All eyes turn toward Agosto as he gets up and walks closer to the computer.

"I will allow my son Gianni to accompany Michelina with my guarantee that he will not be the one to blow your brains out. That's the final offer."

"Okay, but I pick the place and time. I will have back-up with me. I'll text you the information." The screen goes black.

"For everyone's information, I do not have a heart condition." He turns and walks out of the room.

CHAPTER TWENTY-ONE

Luca

I NEED THIS WOMAN UNLIKE ANYONE I'VE EVER NEEDED BEFORE. My need to protect her is off the charts even though I know she can protect herself. I follow her into her bedroom and lock the door behind me.

"Luca, why did you try and rattle his cage?"

"He needs to understand that he's not dealing with a bunch of idiots who stumbled across a treasure in the desert."

"Okay. I need to go check on Grandma and I want to give her that letter." She turns to leave but I grab her around her waist and lift her into me. When I get to the bed, I place her on the edge. As I begin to take off my clothes, she gasps. "Holy Mary and all the saints above, you have a body that could stop the world from spinning."

"My cock has been ready to explode since the day I met you. I can't wait any longer. I want you. I need you. And I'm planning on having you over and over again." There's a knock on the door and I want to scream. Instead, I grab my clothes and head out on the balcony. While Chelle heads to the door and unlocks it. When she opens the door, Viviana is standing there.

"I didn't mean to bother you." She looks at the balcony and back toward Chelle and smiles.

"It's fine, what do you need?"

"I wanted to know what happened when you took a good look through the box?"

Chelle reaches into the bag and pull out the letter. She hands it to her and as she takes it, Chelle takes her hand to stop it from shaking.

"I didn't read it. It was written by you and sent to Agosto. I'm not sure why Carmine had it but it's your property and I have no business reading it."

"It was a very dark time in my life. I was committed to Carmine, however, I was in love with Agosto. I wanted to run away with him, but Carmine intercepted the letter. Agosto never knew how I felt and that's when he met Luca's mother. Sometimes things happen that are out of our control. I believe God has had control of my life and I need to open my eyes to see that."

"Maybe you are meant to be together now." She puts the letter in her pocket, kisses Chelle on the cheek and leaves. I'm about to rip my clothes off but there is another knock on the door. This time it's Gianni. I come in from the balcony knowing that what was to be will have to wait.

"We got the text from Nick. He wants to meet at the Barry Goldwater Memorial Park. There is a stone wall behind the statue. He wants to make the exchange there. The parking lot is very close so I'm guessing he's going to shoot, grab, and run. He fancies himself a cowboy and not a hitman. Which, by this choice, I have to agree."

"What time?"

"He wants to meet at 8:30. It's not fully dark and that park is really just a postage stamp. There are no gates; it's tiny. I don't think this was a good place."

"Actually, Gianni, maybe he will have people in the surrounding houses. It was a special marksman that pulled off the hit on Cody." Gianni is chewing on his bottom lip, no doubt processing everything I've said.

"Well, I'm going with Chelle, let's get others set up before time. Meet me in Geno's office and I'll have some idea for him on how we want to go forward." He leaves and Chelle kisses me. It's so soft at first but then with a passion that threatens to overtake us both.

"I know you'll have my back, you stay safe, too."

Geno has every map available of the park and the surrounding area. "I've pulled up every available angle to the meeting spot. How many guys do you think we should bring in?"

"Who is your best sharpshooter?"

"Luca, that would be you."

"Good, I rather it be me. Let's plot it out and then get over there. Chelle, I need you to grab one of those office boxes that you had the journals in. We will use that instead of the stuff that you got today." I give her a smirk like, did she really think I didn't know anything? Jesus, I helped Carmine pack the boxes and put them in Viviana's attic. Agosto chooses that moment to walk in the room wearing jeans, sneakers, and a gun on each hip. Dear God, what now?

"Before anyone says anything, I'm not that old and I can still pull off a hit, if I need too. At least let me be backup." Gianni jumps up to say something, but I stop him.

"Hold on, Agosto, I know that you are more than capable of holding your own out there. However, if you go with us that would leave Viviana home alone. Do you think that's a wise choice?" The power of manipulation and skilled negotiation.

"Yes, of course. What was I thinking? Luca, son, please bring everyone home safely." For a minute I feel a lump in my throat. He called me son—now. I shake it off and continue with the plan.

"The men that you are bringing in, are you sure about their loyalty?"

"Yes, most of them have been with the family for many years."

Chelle comes back in the room with the box. Gianni takes it from her, and I take her hand in mine. "Let's go, babe."

Nick

The plane is getting ready to touch down in Phoenix. Jessica seems happy, almost giddy. "Hey, why are you so happy?"

"You are going to trade me for the stuff today. Why wouldn't I be happy?"

"Oh, maybe because I'm not trading you. I hope my stupid sister believed all that crap, just like you did."

"You're going to get what you want; you don't need me." I don't understand how some people can go through life with no common sense.

"Let's think about this for a moment. We did a blood vow, Jessica. That means even if you die, we are bound together not just here but in the afterlife. My blood runs through you and your blood runs through me. My plan is to take out my sister, along with that bastard Luca. If it wasn't for him, I could have killed my sister weeks ago. I plan on taking over all the families. You and I will be sitting on top of the world." I shake my head at her stupidity and prepare for landing.

CHAPTER TWENTY-TWO

Michelina

I'VE NEVER BEEN TO BARRY GOLDWATER PARK. IT'S MORE LIKE A postage stamp. A small park surrounded by houses and busy streets. Why would anyone even call this a park? Gianni and I wait in the car while everyone else sets up.

"Chelle, I can't believe you went along with Luca's insistence that you wear a bullet proof vest. You must really love the guy, or you don't trust his shooting." He laughs, which I'm sure is to settle his nerves.

"If it makes him happy and it doesn't hurt anyone, why not?"

"So, you gonna marry him? Is that even legal?" He gets a weird look on his face like he's trying to figure that one out.

"We are second cousins, so yes, it's legal. As far as marrying him, I'd like to concentrate on getting through today." Our ear coms go off and it's Luca.

"You know I can hear everything you are talking about." I gasp and he laughs.

"We are ready for you guys to take your positions. Don't forget the box. Make it look heavy." Gianni takes the box and tosses some large river rocks in it. We head over to our spots and wait. I can see a car pull up in the distance. It's Nick with Jessica. I wish they could just shoot him now, but they can't take that chance with Jessica. Plus, who knows who Nick has meeting him here. He makes his way closer to us and my skin begins to prickle.

"Well hello, Michelina, it's about time I finally get to meet my sister."

"Let's just get this over with."

"Let me see what's in the box."

I open the lid and sitting on top are some of Carmine's journals. I was not about to give him the ledger. I also show him the gems. "I've kept my part of the bargain, now keep yours—let her go." He pulls out a gun and it's pointed right at my forehead.

"Did you really think I was going to give you Jessica and let you live? You're so stupid and you believe you're going to be able to run the family. That's right, sis, I have people everywhere. I know exactly what your plan is and sorry to say I'm not going along with it."

I hear Luca in my ear. "Take a small step to your left." Just as I do, I can hear the sound of the bullet whizzing past me. It goes right into the center of Nick's forehead. He's dead. I grab Jess and hold her in my arms while everyone comes running. I hear more gunshots and Gianni throws us down and blankets us with his body. A bullet bounces off the stone wall and I feel my heart in my throat. When Gianni finally gets off of us, it's Luca helping us up. I look around and see a sea of FBI agents.

"Luca, what's going on?"

"I spoke to Agosto about the plan, and he felt as I did, that we couldn't have a shoot-out in the middle of a busy area. That's why I called the bureau in and had you take the journals instead. Now, let's go home. We still have another meeting to handle."

Agosto

Luca had everything set up so that I could watch it on my phone. Modern technology is amazing. When they come through the door, I have champagne waiting for them.

"Congratulations, Jessica, welcome back." She nods her head but doesn't say much. I figure she is going to need a lot of counseling to get past all the horrors in her life. Geno tries to talk to her, but she doesn't say much. I fear my son's heart will get broken.

I have arranged the meeting at a private residence of a friend of mine. His place is in Paradise Valley, but he is traveling through Italy right now. I have made everyone aware of the circumstances of today. They agreed they want to do this quick and quietly. We leave in an hour."

"Do you want me to bring what I took out of vault with me?"

"Yes, Michelina, that is your good faith offer."

While she heads up stairs to get the stuff, everyone else goes to get cleaned up. Everyone except Luca. "What's troubling you?"

"Why did you call me son today?"

"That's what you are, my son. It was through my own fears that I didn't acknowledge you as I should have. For that, I will always carry a heavy burden of guilt and pain. I hope in time you can recognize me for who I am: Dad—your dad."

He stares at me for a bit and then reaches out his hand toward me. I'm grateful for whatever I get, even these baby steps. Everyone comes down and they are ready to go.

"May I make a suggestion? Jessica, will you do an old man a favor and stay here with Viviana. I don't really like to leave her, but I need to be at this meeting."

"Of course, I'd be happy to."

We head out the door to the limo. It's a short drive, so I need to tell them what to expect. "So, when we get there, I will introduce you to everyone at the table. After that, all of you will sit in the chairs that are set up behind me. If everything is agreed upon, we can take it to the next level." We pull up. Geno gets out first and opens the door. We are quickly ushered into the meeting room where everyone is waiting. It's a small group of four men and their bodyguards. I make the introductions and when I get to Michelina, it feels like all the air has left the room.

"Agosto, why is she here?" One of the men spats out.

"We are here with an offer. It is fair and the time has come for us to accept women into this organization."

"That's never going to happen. I'm out of here." As he pushes his chair back, I move to the side so Michelina can speak.

"Excuse me, sir, I don't think any of you have a choice. I took care of my half-brother Nick, so everyone in this room can breathe a little easier. Today I stand before you with a sample of what my grandfather Carmine Amato left me." I open the box and pass it around, everything but the jewels.

"Your grandfather was a rat bastard, and now you come here trying to blackmail your way into our organization. Agosto, this is a punishable offense. Have you no shame, no scruples?"

"Agosto is not responsible for what I do. I want peace. I want us to stay in our lane. No one touches upon anyone's territory. Understand I will not be pushed aside. If need be, I will go to war with all of you, however, I would rather have peace."

"So, what you are saying is we have no choice."

"You have a choice: peace or war. You are getting not only me, but our entire family."

"Agosto, will you be sponsoring her?"

"Yes, Michelina and my sons Luca, Geno and Gianni. As I said, the entire family."

"Is Luca a pure blood?"

"He is my son; his mom was from Naples. He is a pure blood."

"Then so be it. Did you bring everything with you?" I reach into my pocket and pull out my switchblade, four cards with a saint on them and a lighter. I spread them out in front of me and call each child up one by one.

"Do you agree to the following: You must never assist the authorities in crimes against the family. This is your family now; they are above your blood family. You will keep our secrets as your own." As each child says they do, I take the knife and prick the finger. I squeeze the blood onto one of the saints' cards, place it in their palm and set it on fire. When the ceremony is over, the four leaders get up and shake everyone's hand before they are escorted out to their car.

I look at everyone with hope that they can pull this off.

"It is done." I turn and leave with the family following behind me.

CHAPTER TWENTY-THREE

Michelina

I T'S BEEN TWO DAYS SINCE OUR INITIATION INTO THE MAFIA family. I thought I would feel something different, but all I feel is numb. I've spent the past two days with Jessica. I got her into a good program. Hopefully, in time, she will make a full recovery. At least Geno is not giving up on her. When I head downstairs to get my coffee, I find Grandma sitting at the table alone.

"Want some company?"

"I was hoping you would come down while everything is quiet. I wanted to talk to you about the letter you found."

"I promise you I didn't read it. Like I told you, maybe you're meant to be together now."

"In the beginning, I loved Carmine. He was charming and funny. In the end, he was cruel and vicious. If you love Luca like I think you do, don't let time pass you buy. Don't end up two old people feeding the birds and having an espresso. Grab life by whatever you can and live it to the fullest." She gets up, kisses me on the forehead, puts her cup in the sink, and heads outside. No doubt to feed the birds. I've been waiting for Luca to make a move, but he hasn't. Grandma is right, I'm not waiting any longer. I head upstairs and slip into his room. The light snore tells me he's still asleep.

I make my way in the dark to the edge of the bed leaving a trail of clothes behind me. I slip between the sheets and run my hand up his rock-hard cock, he's huge. I can feel the heat from his skin as I continue to explore. He's not moving so I let my fingers do the talking and find his nipples. They are hard like his cock. When I swipe the tip of my tongue around it, he laughs. "You're up? How long have you been up?"

"By the time you had your last piece of clothing off, I was ready. I didn't want to spoil your fun, but I'm ticklish. Now that's a weapon you could use against me."

"Your skin is amazing. It's an olive color that actually glistens, and it's so warm."

"I'm glad you like it because I'm going to blanket your whole body with it as I make love to you." True to his word he works his way on top of me, covering me with soft, gentle kisses. When he gets to my nipples I feel like I'm going to die.

"Harder, Luca, please. I won't break." That was all I had to say. He gave it all to me. When I feel like I'm about to come, I stop him and take his cock into my mouth. Slowly, I swirl my tongue from the tip to the base. Every time I give him a throat bump his body jerks.

"Please, stop. If you do that again, I won't be able to control myself. I need to feel myself inside of you." I slow down and climb on top of him. I'm about to take his cock deep inside of me when he flips me over.

"You had your fun, now I need mine." In one fluid motion his cock is so deep inside of me. He stops, closes his eyes and takes a few breaths.

"Luca, what about a condom?"

"I love you, Chelle. I'm going to marry you. Bareback for life, babe." With that he picks up his rhythm. He hits my g-spot and I lose all control. "Oooh my God, I need it harder." With my nails digging into his shoulders, he takes my cue and pounds into me. I can't control myself any longer. This man that I wanted for so long is exactly where I wanted him to be. We both find our release before he pulls the sheet over us and tightly holds on to me. I'm at peace, knowing I'm right where I was supposed to be.

The End
Or is it?

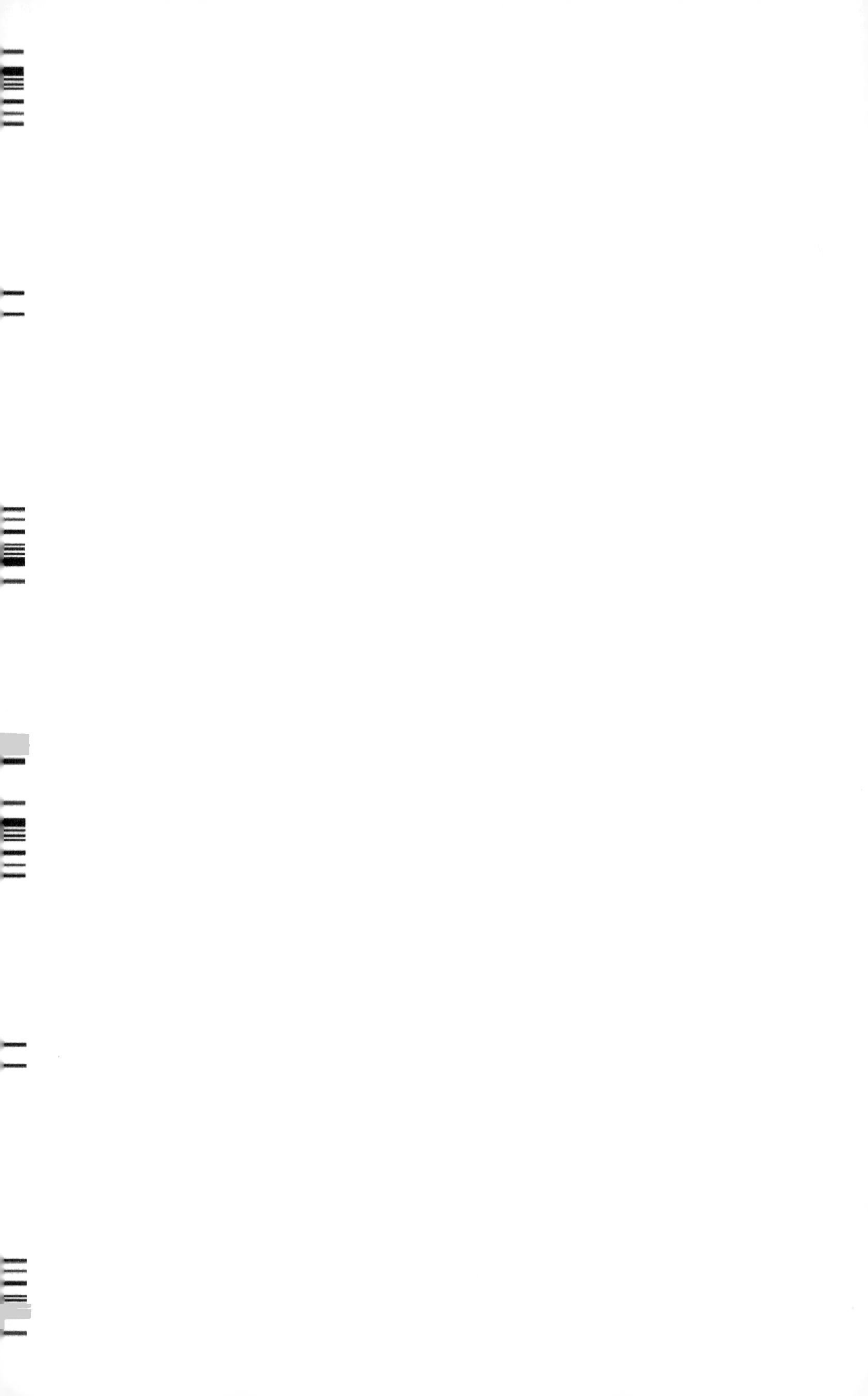

INFINITE
ABSOLUTION

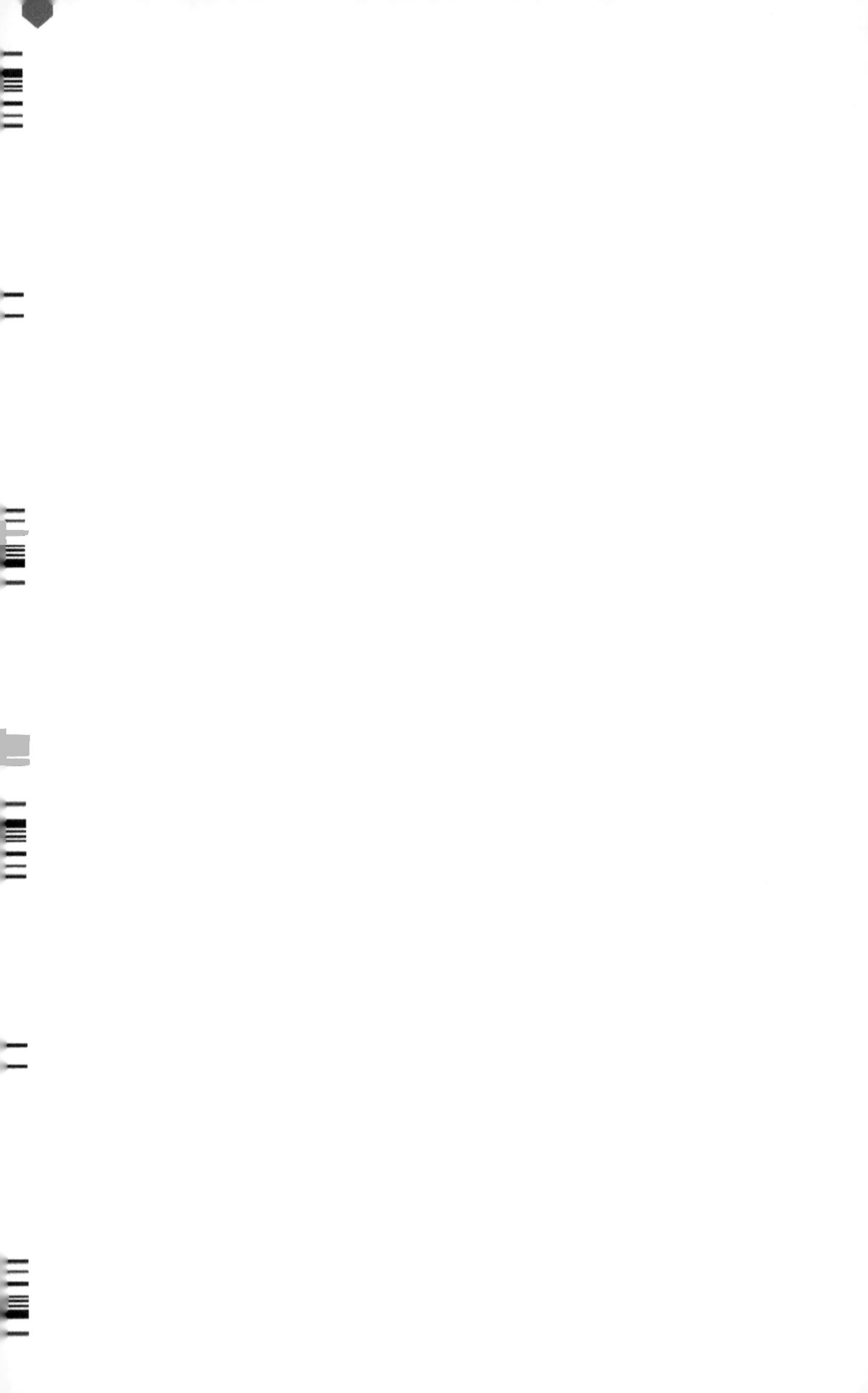

Melissa Kulis

This is by far one of the hardest things I've ever had to write. My best friend, my first Facebook friend, the keeper of all my hopes and fears has passed away. I wasn't ready, not that anyone ever is. This is not the way it was supposed to be. We helped each other through some dark times and celebrated the happy ones. I can't wrap my mind around the idea of not talking to you multiple times a day any more. I'll never hear that laugh again. There is a huge void in my heart, and I don't think I'll ever stop crying. The only peace I can find now is knowing you're sitting with your mom and telling her all the crazy antics that you've been up to. I know Carmine was one of your favorite characters, so I hope I did you proud with the way his story ended. Until we meet again my friend, rest easy and know I'll always look after the kids for you.

Love you more

CHAPTER ONE

Viviana

IT'S A BEAUTIFUL MORNING. THE BIRDS HAVE COME TO EXPECT ME at sunrise. I wonder what they will do when I'm no longer here. After all, I'm an old woman; they can't expect me to always be here. With the shuffling of his feet, I hear Agosto before I see him.

"Good morning, Viviana, do you mind if I join you?"

"I believe it is your house, so you can go wherever you want." I slide over and continue with the mindless tossing of the seeds.

"You seem very distracted today, is everything okay?"

"I was reminded by Michelina that no matter how much we think the past is buried, it will always find a way to rear its ugly head." I reach into the pocket of my house dress and pull out the folded envelope with the letter inside and press it into his hand. He doesn't move, he just stares at it.

"Agosto, I wrote this letter to you a very long time ago. I thought when I mailed it and you never responded, that was your way of telling me goodbye. I thought you didn't want me. I didn't know that Carmine intercepted it. Looking back, if you had gotten it, your relationship with

Sofia would not have happened. Luca would have never been born." He looks down at the envelope but never takes the letter out.

"Why give this to me now?"

"I didn't want another day to go by without you knowing what my true intentions were."

He puts it in his pocket, never giving it a second look.

"I was wondering if you would like to go on a trip with me. After everything that has gone down, I think we could use a break."

"Where would you like to go?"

He picks up some seeds and tosses them on the ground. The quails come running around him. "I would like to go back to Sicily, back where it all began."

"Are you sure? You know you can never go back, Agosto. Life was different then—we were different. As we get older, the bad memories soften and finally move to the back of our minds. It's our hearts way of protecting itself."

"I understand all of that. For me, it's a pilgrimage back to a time when life was simpler. I'm an old man, Viviana, who knows how much time I have left. When I left Sicily, I was a boy, but now, I'm returning as man. Will you make the journey with me?"

"Let me think about it."

"Please don't take too long. I'm getting older by the minute." I pass him some more seeds and we silently toss them about. My days should be getting simpler, instead, they are always changing, becoming more complicated.

Michelina

Today is my first official day of heading up the family. True we are all in this together, but it seems that everyone is looking to me for guidance. By nature, I'm a nurturer. I think that's why I went into teaching. However, I'm not sure where to begin. When Luca and I threw out the idea of running the family, we only knew from the FBI's side what the family was involved in. I thought maybe Agosto would show me the ropes, but he seems to be removing himself from everything, including his family. Maybe the distance makes it easier on him. His old way of doing things is dead and buried. That's something that can be very hard to face. This is what happens when you play on the wrong side of the law your whole life.

I decide to look to Gianni for some guidance. When I get to his office, I find him nearly buried behind a stack of papers on his desk. "Hey, I was coming to pick your brain, but you look like you are in this transition just as deep as I am."

"Pull up a chair; maybe we can get through some of this faster if we work together." I slide a chair next to him and take a folder off the top of the pile.

"What exactly am I looking at?"

"These are Dad's files. He kept everything on paper. As you can see, he wrote everything in pencil, which is crazy because it will fade over time. Geno has been automating everything but it's taking a very long time. I thought I could help by weeding out some of this old stuff that is no longer needed." Maybe that's what he wants, the old stuff that he did to fade away over time, like it never happened. Unlike his brother Carmine who documented everything he did and used it as a weapon against anyone he could. Quickly I put aside my wandering thoughts and turn my focus back to Gianni.

"Where did he keep all of this?"

"Come with me, and I'll show you everything." He gets up and I follow closely behind him. There are so many rooms in this house that I've yet to explore, especially the ones near Agosto's room. He stops and pulls a key down from the top of the door frame. I'm about to say something about the security, but I realize it's just for show. Who is going to get in here and how would they sneak anything out? When he swings the door open, I grab his arm to steady myself. It's floor to ceiling banker's boxes.

"There has to be at least a hundred boxes in here."

"Try two-hundred *and* fifty-eight, to be exact."

I know my mouth is hanging open, but I can't help it. "Why does he have all this here, and what exactly is it?"

"These are what Dad views as current files. He has a storage unit not too far from here that has more . . . lots more." I'm left staring in disbelief at the amount of paperwork that is contained within just this room.

"So are the files on your desk part of this pile?"

"Yes, as well as the stack in Geno's office. Chelle, can we go for a walk, away from anyone listening?" I step out of the room and wait for him to close it up.

"Lead the way." I wave my hand and follow after him into the garage. *Not exactly what I was thinking.* He opens the passenger side door of his Bentley. While the garage door opens, he flips a switch that makes the top go down. This is a car I can see Agosto driving, not a young guy like Gianni.

"Go ahead, Chelle, I know you are dying to ask about the car," he says as I slide into the seat.

"Well, it doesn't seem like something you would drive."

"It's not, it's Agosto's car." He shrugs, closing the door behind me before heading over to the driver's side. "Sometimes I like to cruise around in it. Just like sex, Chelle, it's not always about speed." I throw my head back and laugh as he gets in. It feels good to joke around for a change.

"What is it that you want to know?" I ask as we slowly pull out of the garage and make our way off the property.

"I'm worried about Geno. He thinks he can fix everything for Jessica, but it's going to take more than loving her to get her past the hell that she went through. I want to help but I don't know how."

"I found a therapist that I think might be good for her. She has an appointment tomorrow. She's not going to be fixed overnight, but this is a step in the right direction."

"Providing she tells the therapist the truth and not what she thinks she wants to hear."

"So, it sounds like you are familiar with therapy." He pulls over and finds a spot out of the sun.

"When my sister died, I was young and didn't really comprehend the gravity of it. She was always sick, so I kind of thought that would happen. When my brother Sal died, it tore my dad apart. By that time, my mom was already sick, and I needed an outlet. Geno internalizes everything—I don't. My dad took me to the church and had me sit with the priest. At first, I didn't take any of it seriously. I told the priest what he wanted to hear. Not too long after that, my mom died. That's when I started opening up to him."

"So, Geno never spoke to anyone?"

"No, the only one he's ever confided in is Daniella. They've been friends since kindergarten. Everyone thought they would end up together, but they remained just friends. What about you? You've been through so much, have you spoken to anyone?"

"I've always turned to my grandma for everything. She is the one who can help me maintain calmness and clarity."

"Yeah, but her and my dad really pulled one over on your mom with the whole nursing home thing."

"I think there are a lot of things we still don't know about but, in time, it will all come out. Gianni, the secrets we want to stay hidden usually find their way out."

"I agree. Why were you looking for me?"

"I wanted to work with you on formulating a plan to handle the transition."

"I know we talked about taking everything above board but, honestly, that might be a stretch, even for the four of us. We better get back before Dad sends out a posse to find us. When we get back to the house, we can bring the others together and get started."

We head back toward home. The longer I'm here, the better understanding I'm getting of the family dynamics.

CHAPTER TWO

Jessica

S LEEP HARDLY COMES, YET I STILL TRY. GENO HAS BEEN DOING everything to make me forget but, in reality, I think nothing will ever make me forget the hell that has been my life for so long. When I thought Nick was going to keep me forever, I told him everything Chelle did for me. In that one moment it seemed he grew a heart . . . maybe even a moral compass, but then the wall came crashing down and I knew it was never going to end well. I roll over and tuck myself into Geno's side. His beating heart has a way of calming me.

"Jessica, what can I do for you? Please just tell me. I will never judge you for anything you had to do to survive."

"Just hold me and be patient with me. Chelle wants me to see a therapist she found. I've been on the fence about it, but maybe it's a good idea." His arm squeezes me tighter to him as he kisses my forehead.

"Babe, I think it's a great idea. Speaking to someone who is not in the mix might really help you. I will do whatever you need me to do."

"What if nothing works? What if I'm left like this? I feel so empty,

empty and void of all feelings. Sometimes the broken pieces can't be put back together again."

"Jess, you have to fight. You can't spend the rest of your life living on the sidelines because of fear."

"Chelle told me about the vow that you all took. That was your opportunity to get out—for us to get out—why didn't you take it?"

"I won't leave my family, and I'm sure you would never leave Chelle. We have to stand united and fight for change. I need you to get better and stand beside me."

"I promise I will try. Right now, that's really all I can offer." He says nothing more and begins stroking my arm. I know where this is leading and I'm not ready. Hell, I don't know if I'll ever be ready. I try to pull back but his grip on me tightens.

"Babe, you are not going anywhere. We can take everything at your pace. Right now, all I want to do is hold you tight. You know you'll always be safe in my arms."

As I drift off to sleep, I whisper, "Thank you." But I'm not even sure he heard it.

Luca

I knew when we took upon the role of leaders it would mean more work, but I wasn't aware how much more. Chelle is always busy and when she's not, her mind is on Jessica.

I'm sitting outside the FBI's main office in Phoenix. I know I'm supposed to turn in my papers today, which includes my gun and my badge. As I look down at them sitting in my lap, a whirlwind of emotions come back to me. Why I joined and why I'm quitting has actually come full circle. It's ironic: I joined to spite my father and now I have to quit to help my father. I wonder what my mom would say if she could see me now. Would she be happy about my life choices? I know she would love Chelle, if for nothing else, for how happy she makes me. I knew when I first met her there was something amazing about her, but I also thought it was forbidden. I rub my thumb over my badge one last time and head inside. Waiting for me is the new director for the Phoenix office, Madeline Gray.

"Hello, Ms. Gray. Thank you for seeing me on such short notice."

"Don't thank me just yet, Mr. Gill. Let's go into my office where we can talk freely."

The hair on the back of my neck stands up. I follow her into Peter's old office. Not much has changed. I skip the niceties and get right to the point. "Is there some sort of exit interview I need to do?" I glance at my watch long enough to let her know my time is my own.

"Do you think that is necessary given the situation you've found yourself in?"

"By situation do you mean my family dynamics?"

"Yes, that situation."

"Well, I really thought we could focus on how the director of the Phoenix branch of the FBI, along with a top field agent, tried to kill me regardless of the fact that I'm fellow agent. Let's not forget that last part, Ms. Gray." As I slowly stretch out her name, she stares at me for a bit longer than I feel comfortable with.

"Luca, what are your plans once you leave here?"

"I plan on enjoying the rest of my life, not that it's any of your business." She doesn't smile, instead, her lips seem to tighten more in their straight line.

"I have a proposition for you. What do you think about working for us undercover? Think of yourself as the Whitey Bulger of the Arizona branch of the organization."

"The only one out here that is of any importance is my father, and he retired. Yes, believe it or not, you can retire from the organization. You need to maintain your vow of silence, and get the blessing from the other families, which he did. So, I think you are barking up the wrong tree. Now, I would like to file my papers and leave."

"Keep in mind, Luca, I didn't get where I am today on my back or my knees. I know a lot more than you think. It's okay if you want to leave, but just know this is far from over. Agosto doesn't get to peacefully ride off into the sunset with Viviana by his side."

That's it—I'm done. At her mention of my father and Viviana, I realize she is never going to let this go. I get up and place my credentials, along with my gun, on her desk before turning to leave. I won't give her the satisfaction of a reply, and there is no way in hell I'm looking back. When I get outside, I climb into Gianni's car that I borrowed, taking off and never looking back.

As I pull up to the house Gianni is standing outside.

"Hey, I left a note that I needed a car until I find one I like that won't blow up." I get out of the car realizing that as much as I hate to admit it, my body is still not healed.

"That's not why I'm out here waiting for you, but what did you think of the ride?"

"I didn't get to go far, but I bet it would be nice on the open road. A Lamborghini on the streets in Phoenix isn't much fun. So, what do you need to talk to me about?"

"Dad has been talking about going away and he wants to take Viviana with him."

"Did he say where?"

"The old country: Sicily."

"Why are you concerned? He can take care of himself. It might be good for both of them."

"I worry he won't come back. What if one of the other families decides on a revenge kill. He's harder to protect being so far away. You know they weren't exactly thrilled about the new reign."

"Do we have someone we can send with them?"

"Maybe. I'll run it by Geno and see who he thinks would be good for the job. I showed Chelle all the boxes that Dad has stored, along with the ones that Geno has been working on. She is overwhelmed—we all are."

"We can tackle it together. I'll get Chelle and we'll meet you in Geno's office." I hit the remote for the garage as we head inside.

CHAPTER THREE

Michelina

A FTER SEEING EVERYTHING THAT AGOSTO HAS KEPT, I'M GLAD I'm not alone trying to make these life altering changes. I head back to Agosto's office, dragging a whiteboard along with me that I found shoved in the closet with all the banker's boxes. Finding a spot to hang it was difficult, however, in the end, I removed some of Agosto's paintings from the wall. I'll be sure to have them put in his room. I divide the board into four columns. Each of us gets a column. Once I begin breaking up the business, it actually plays out pretty easy, at least, I think so. I can feel him before I even see him. When I spin around, Luca is standing in the doorway. The suit and tie he left with this morning is gone. He's now donning shorts and a tight tank top. His arms are crossed, and he is leaning against the door jam. My heart skips a beat just looking at him. My eyes slowly travel up and down his body, taking in every inch of him. His body is so ripped, like a guy that spends hours working on it, yet he's so casual about it.

"You look delicious, Luca. How long were you watching me?"

"Long enough to know you need a break, or more like you need me,

Chelle." He steps inside the room and kicks the door closed behind him. He pulls his shirt off and as he takes a few more steps toward me, he unbuckles his belt and quickly he whips it off. The closer he gets to me, the more I can feel the heat rising in my cheeks. He drops his shorts. *Sweet Baby Jesus—he's commando.* As he steps out of his shorts, I could swear my ovaries just exploded. When he's only inches from me, I can feel the heat radiating off of his body, and it's off the charts. He takes his thumb and presses it to my lips. Right about now, I'm fighting the urge to climb him like a tree. Instead, I wait, letting him take the lead.

"Oh, Chelle, you are so easy to read." He runs his thumb down my throat. He traces my nipples through my shirt, and they instantly stand at attention. I want to try to resist him, but my body is betraying me.

"You know we have a lot of work to do, Luca. Besides, what if there is a camera in here?" His eyes dart around the room and then he graces me with a big smile.

"As long as I'm happy, I'm pretty sure my father probably doesn't care what I do. My brothers, on the other hand, might need some lessons." Suddenly, there is a loud buzzing noise. There is a land line in every room, along with an intercom on the wall. I'm pretty sure that was the intercom that just buzzed. Luca ignores it as he slowly kisses my neck.

"Luca, we need to go over everything for the changes we are implementing. This meeting will require clothing. Please be in Geno's office in five minutes." I can hear Gianni laughing as he disconnects the call. Luca pulls back and glances around the room, laughing as he retrieves his shorts.

"Luca, I think the first order of business is to find out which rooms have cameras."

"No, Chelle, the first order of business is to decide if we are even going to stay here."

"Let's table that for when we are alone." I pick up his shirt and toss it to him as we head to Geno's office.

The closer we get to his office the more I feel my body starting to flush. He takes my hand before lightly tapping on the door but doesn't wait for an answer. He swings the door open, squeezes my hand and pulls me inside with him.

Luca takes the lead. "Okay, get all your snide remarks out now." Both brothers are laughing so hard, they can't catch their breath.

"Of all the rooms you chose to have wild sex in, you picked Dad's office." They are laughing again and if there was a hole big enough, I would crawl into it.

I pull away from Luca, step in front of the desk. "How about you both stop laughing and tell us which rooms have cameras."

Gianni nudges Geno. "Geno, put them out of their misery and tell them."

"Dad's office, the back yard, and the garage. There are intercoms in every room. As Dad gets older, we were thinking we would have to add more. They are for his benefit, Chelle. I swear we don't spy on him. He falls a lot, so we put them in the rooms he spends the most time in. We also got him a smart watch that will alert us if he falls someplace where there are no cameras."

"Gianni, how far were you going to let Chelle and I go before alerting us?"

"Luca, we stopped it before anything happened with Chelle. After all, we are gentlemen." I roll my eyes at the thought of them as gentlemen.

"Okay, guys you had your laugh. Let's put all that aside and finish formulating a plan." Geno gets up from behind the desk and comes closer to all of us. He looks around and I'm getting an uneasy feeling. He heads to the door and closes it. Now, I'm beyond uneasy.

"Chelle, before we get into that, we need to discuss Dad and the trip he is planning."

"Wait, what trip is he planning and why am I just finding out about this now?"

"He wanted to ask Viviana before he said anything. He only told me this morning. I was in the kitchen getting coffee and I heard him mumbling something. When I asked if he was okay, he said he was rehearsing what he wanted to say to Viviana. Chelle, I thought he was talking about marriage. Probably by the look on my face he must have realized what I was thinking. He laughed and said, *"Close your mouth, son, I want to take her on vacation."* I probed him a little bit, but all he said was he wanted to go back to Sicily as an accomplished man with a beautiful woman on his arm, not the scared little boy who fled to the States."

I let Geno's words sink in while I try to wrap my mind around the fact that my grandmother will most likely go on a European vacation with Agosto. "Geno, maybe it would be for the best that they are both out of the country while the four of us dismantle the business that he built up. If he's not here, then he can't readily object to the decisions that we make. The question is, will they be safe?"

"After he told me, I pulled the files on some of our security personnel. We won't be able to stop them from going, but we could make sure they have security with them twenty-four-seven."

Luca takes my hand and gently squeezes it. "Chelle, do you think Viviana will go?" he asks me.

"A year ago, I would have said no way. However, after everything that has happened, I can honestly say I have no clue what she will do. I think I want to talk to her first before you guys start making arrangements." I pull my hand from Luca's. "Alone," I whisper as I head out of the room.

CHAPTER FOUR

Michelina

I HEAD OUTSIDE TO SEE IF SHE IS AT HER FAVORITE SPOT ON THE bench. She's not, but Agosto is. "Chelle, I'm glad I've got you alone. Can you sit with me for a bit?" He knows I can't say no, it would be disrespectful.

"Of course, Agosto. What can I do for you?" I ask as I sit next to him.

"I wanted to let you know that I've asked Viviana to accompany me to Sicily. What I haven't said is that I want her to marry me. My plan is to take her to San Vito lo Capo, which is one of Sicily's most romantic places, and there I will propose. I made reservations at the Hotel Piccolo Mondo. It will be very romantic. I want to do this for her, since she's never had anything like this before. Hell, Carmine's idea of a vacation was a day trip to Coney Island."

"It sounds like you already made your mind up, so why are you telling me all of this?"

"I want your blessing. Truthfully, it means nothing to me, but I know it would mean the world to Viviana." He casually grabs my hand and palms it between his, looking straight in my eyes. I can see the sincerity in them, but it doesn't make me any more on board with this idea. It's not safe. But . . . they are not children.

I try to remember all my teacher training that taught me patience and restraint. "When will you be leaving?"

"I want to leave in two days. Neither one of us is getting any younger." He smiles with a little shrug, trying to make light of what he is trying to do.

"I will go talk to her now. If she decides she wants to go, I won't stop her. As far as my blessing, if she wants to marry you, I won't stand in your way." I pull my hand back gently before getting up to leave before he can question me further.

I'm still navigating my way around this massive home. I'm so preoccupied with everything going on that I realize I'm standing in front of a carved door with stained glass inserts that I've never seen before. My curiosity gets the better of me. I knock and slightly push the door open just a little and the familiar smell of frankincense and myrrh hits me. Oh my, Agosto has made a small Catholic church right inside his home! When I open the door a little further, I see Grandma sitting in the front pew. There are only five rows, so I make my way up to the front pew, taking in everything around me with such wonder. When I get to her pew, I kneel and make the sign of the cross. The rituals of the Catholic church have been ingrained into my memory from when I was a child in Catholic school. It's a place that brings me comfort when I'm feeling lost. I take a seat next to her, kneel down and pray.

After a bit, I sit back and wait. Waiting is so hard when you have something on your mind. I just want to blurt it out, but I say nothing. She has her rosary out and I know she is praying. When she is ready, she will let me know. Finally, she sits back, turns toward me and smiles.

"I'm sorry, Grandma, I didn't want to disturb you."

"I knew you would come looking for me. Agosto can't keep a secret to save his life. I venture to say he told you about the trip." She gives me a warm, knowing smile.

"Yes, he did. I was surprised that he wanted to go so far away while we are making so many changes," I confess.

She stares down at the rosary beads between her hands and says nothing. I rest my hand on hers and gently squeeze them.

"Agosto is pushing me to go but I don't know what to do. Part of me wants to but you know I worry about you, and in all honesty, I worry, if at my age, I can even make the trip." And now I know what she was praying about.

I let her words sink in. Truthfully, I don't look at her aging. To me, she is always Grandma. "If you think you can't physically do it, that's a valid reason not to go, but if you think you have to worry about me, that's a hard no, Grandma. I have survived gun shots, bombs, and hell, I've even survived teaching high school science. So, I think a can survive you going on vacation." She looks at me and laughs, which I haven't seen in a while.

"Michelina, those aren't the things I worry about, it's your affairs of the heart." She nudges my shoulder with hers, her face still full of mirth.

"Luca?! You're worried about him? Believe me, you have nothing to worry about." I push the nonsense away with my free hand.

"Never take anything for granted, Michelina, in an instant, it can be gone. You never want to watch love slip through your fingers like grains of sand."

"I have a question, and you can take your time and think about it. Would you want to marry Agosto?" If she says yes, then I won't ruin his surprise.

"I don't know, Michelina. I'm old, and past all the hearts and flowers in life. Now, it's exciting to wake up; I'm still here and no one is throwing dirt on my grave. Why are you asking me this?"

"After all the years of putting everyone else first, maybe now it's your time," I suggest. She laughs, which is not what I was expecting.

"Oh, Michelina, don't look so serious. When you think about it . . . we are the last ones standing. So, I guess we would have nothing to lose if we got married," she states astonishingly as her eyes light up at the thought.

"Well, when you put it that way, I guess we better get back to your room so I can help you pack." I nudge her back before getting up and stepping into the aisle. When she steps out, I hook my arm into hers and we make our way out of the church.

"How crazy is it that Agosto built a Catholic church in his home. Did he ever say why?"

"No, but maybe it's the only one he feels welcome in." Wow, what do you say when someone says that to you? I decide to leave it at that as we head to her room. Maybe it's for the best that they take this trip.

Luca

I wish I felt more comfortable with my brothers. No matter how hard I try, I can't seem to put away my FBI training, even now that I'm no longer an agent. After this morning with my boss or ex-boss, I don't think she is going to let that go, either. Besides that, I still haven't found the right time to give Chelle the final piece of the Carmine puzzle that I've had tucked away for years. It's very easy to say we will work together as a family, but it's very hard to do, especially when there is no trust. I can't blame any of them, well, maybe Agosto. He should have come clean a long time ago. Hell, there is a lot that we all should have come clean about. Eventually, life bites you in the ass.

When I check my watch, I realize Chelle has been gone for almost an hour. Geno and Gianni are going through files and I'm doing nothing. They won't say it, but it's that trust factor. "Hey guys, while we wait for Chelle, I'm going to run an errand. I shouldn't be too long." Gianni grumbles out an *okay* and Geno waves. I quickly leave and when I get to the garage, I look around and decide to take the Ducati. I'm sure it must be Gianni's, and I know it has to have a tracker on it. Arizona does not have a helmet law if you are over the age of eighteen, however, I would be a fool if I jumped on one of the most powerful bikes without one. Thankfully, my brother has a few of them on the shelf in the garage. It's weird thinking of him as my brother. I'm sure I'm not thought of with the same fondness. When I find one that fits, I start her up. *Yes, all bikes are of the female persuasion.* The feel of all that power under my ass is amazing. I take off knowing the problems will still be there when I get back, but for a few hours, I don't want to think about them.

CHAPTER FIVE

Luca

W EAVING MY WAY THROUGH THE STREETS OF SCOTTSDALE on the Ducati is challenging. However, it doesn't take long for me to find myself entering Cave Creek. I thought once I turned in my papers, life would just fall into place. Instead, it's done anything but fall into place. Agosto taking off for Sicily right now is crazy. I think there is more to it than he is letting on. There is so much change within his own organization, so why now? What is he planning? Why take Viviana with him? They are both too old to be making this pilgrimage back to their homeland. Something isn't right, but it doesn't look like anyone has any intention of stopping them. My brothers will just send them off with extra security. I thought Chelle and I would have more time together if I moved into Agosto's house. We have even less time together and we are never alone.

I pull into the Roadhouse parking lot, which is filled with so many different bikes. I guess I wasn't the only one with this idea. When I look at the menu, I realize I'm a lot hungrier than I thought. I order a burger and fries along with a local craft beer. The music is loud, and the sights are plenty. The service is quick, and the food is amazing. I'm messing around on my phone when I hear someone calling my name. When I look up from my phone I see Ms. Gray. "Are you following me, Ms. Gray?" I cock my head to the side, trying to figure her out.

"Luca, please call me Madeline. Actually, I'm with a couple of other agents. Once a month we get together and forget about everyone and everything. We get on our bikes and just ride."

I lift my beer and toast her. "Well, here is to not following me around and just feeling the desert wind on your face."

"Have you given any thought to our conversation?"

"You mean the one about me being a snitch? Yeah, never going to happen. Now, I would like to finish my lunch in peace." I pick up my phone and continue to scroll through social media. She walks away without another word, but I don't think she is done with me. I also don't think she just happened to be here. I'll figure it out, I always do.

I miss the days I spent with Carmine. The endless conversations. There was so much to learn from him about life and living. He figured out who I was very quickly. He said it's the reason he requested that I be the one to do the intake interview. What was supposed to be two days of interviews turned out to be more, so much more. I know I need to tell Chelle everything, however, it could be the secret that will tear us apart. I push away my plate and toss four twenties down for the tab. I'm sure the waitress will be really happy with her tip. When I get outside, I look around hoping I can figure out how Gray knew where I was, but nothing. I would think if I had a tail, I would have seen it. I mean, after all, I haven't been out of work that long. I climb on the bike and slowly make my way onto the highway. When I glance up, I see it—a drone. I don't know why I'm surprised, but I am. I head to my apartment more determined than ever to protect what little I have left that is just mine.

The beauty of having a bike is being able to weave in and out of traffic. When I get to my apartment door, I check the top of the door to see if anyone went inside. The strand of hair that I taped across the top of the door with clear tape was split in half. Something that simple—no one would think to look for. Instinctively, I reach for my gun but realize I turned my service weapon in. Slowly, I step inside and begin to look around. Nothing seems to be out of place. I'm a minimalist by choice, so there is not much that could have been moved or taken without me noticing.

I quickly pull up my home security app on my phone. It's not a big apartment, so the three cameras pretty much cover it all. The video comes on and I can't believe what I'm seeing—Agosto. What the fuck? When did he do this? Why? Hasn't he caused enough damage in my life? He's clearly looking for something. I would think if he knew about my tapes with Carmine he would have questioned me about them a long time ago. Maybe he thinks I'm a snitch. I go into my bedroom, and everything is just as it was when I left. When I open my closet, I see the only thing that has been moved is my gun safe. To the untrained eye, that is the only thing worth anything in the closet. I pull out the box with my hiking boots, open it up and pull out the sock that is inside the right boot. I reach in and pull out a micro-cassette recorder. There are also some tapes in the boot. I pull the sock out of the left boot and dump out the rest of the tapes. They are just as I left them. I look at all the tapes and can't help but laugh; Carmine hated anything that he couldn't understand. That's why he wrote everything down in his little black books. The books that Chelle has hidden in the bank deposit box. He insisted his writings would be very valuable someday. I insisted that my tapes would be just as valuable. That's when we agreed to disagree, and he let me tape our conversations. He knew who I was from the first day we met. I was a junior agent, but he would only talk to me. Carmine turning states evidence put me on the map. Look at where I am now, sitting on the floor of my bedroom with a pile of tapes in front of me. Tapes that made me understand the inner workings of the Mafia but, most of all, these conversations helped me understand my father and the choices he made. I remember one day I asked him why he hated Agosto so much, his only living brother.

"Luca, it didn't start out that way, but over time he wanted what I had, starting with my wife. He tried to kill me and, of course, he screwed that up

and killed a capo instead. I begged the counsel not to kill him. I vouched for him, Luca. What did that get me? At the end of the day, you have to rely on only yourself and your gut." When I asked him why he would go to the counsel and plead for them not to kill Agosto, all he could say was, *"He's my brother; blood is thicker than water."* At least, he had a brother. I might have them now, but I don't know anything about them—the real them—not what I read in the FBI briefings or internet. I grab a backpack from the closet and put everything inside. After taking one last look around, I lock up and head out. I need to find my own vehicle, but first I need to stop at the bank to add these tapes to my safety deposit box. When the time is right, I'll share everything with Chelle.

CHAPTER SIX

Michelina

I help Grandma to her room. She isn't even in her recliner for ten minutes before she's sound asleep. As much as I want her to do what makes her happy, I also have to be the one that makes sure she doesn't do too much. If this is how tired she gets just from sitting in the yard and going to church, there is no way she will have the energy to go abroad. If it was her dream, that would be a different story, you would always find the energy to go. But this is Agosto's dream. When Jess and I went, we were young, and it took everything out of us. They are both too old to be traipsing all over the countryside. Maybe I need to talk to Luca about it. I drape a thin blanket over her legs and head out to find him.

I find Geno and Gianni still in Geno's office and arguing, but no Luca. "Hey, where is Luca?" They stop yelling and look over toward me.

"Hell, you weren't gone five minutes, and he took off on my Ducati. If he puts one scratch on her, I will kill him myself." Gianni's face turns beet red as he's trying to rein in his temper.

"Gianni, I'm sure he will be very careful with your bike."

"Look, Chelle, I don't mind, but he could have asked me first. Plus, aren't we supposed to be working on the transition?"

I decide to just steer away from the conversation. "I checked on Grandma and I don't see how she is going to make this trip. I also spoke to Agosto, and he makes me feel like she has no choice. Has he always been my *way or the highway* kind of guy?"

"When we were little, we didn't have a choice. I guess in some way, it's still the same. Do you think the trip is too much for her?" Gianni's voice has softened after his outburst about his bike.

"Yes, I do. I'm not sure how to approach him about it?"

"What did Viviana say? Does she think she has no choice?"

"Before she fell asleep, we talked a little and I don't think she is taking any of this seriously. Her answer to me was '*as long as no one is throwing dirt on her, then all is good.*' I took her back to her room and she fell asleep. Why did Agosto build a church in his home and does a priest come to perform Mass?" At that moment, Luca strides into the room.

"What did I miss?"

"I don't mind you borrowing a vehicle but, the next time you decide to take my Ducati out, I want to know. That's my baby and I'm pretty protective of her."

"Sure, Gianni, I'm sorry; I didn't think it would be a problem. I plan on going car shopping anyway."

The tension in the room is so thick you could cut it with a knife. "For now, let's table the car and Agosto's trip. I think we should make some decisions about the business, mainly drugs. I really want to get out of that. What does everyone else think?" No one is saying anything. "Geno, you know all the aspects of the business the best, help me out here." He gets up and walks over to the wall behind me and flips a switch on the wall. Slowly a giant computer screen comes down. I've never seen anything that large before. With a clicker in his hand the screen comes to life.

"Chelle, it's easy to say you want out, but it's hard to walk away from the cash cow. I saw that you dragged out Dad's old white board. Not to sound rude, but you're not teaching class anymore. If we can all turn our attention back to the screen. The first page of the spreadsheet is the drug business broken down by territory. As you can see, the profitability is amazing. This is just a sample, Chelle. I think before we make any changes you should think about what you want to change and why."

I can feel that all eyes are on me as I stare at the screen. "At the end of the day, I want to run a legit business that I know that we can all be proud of, including our children someday." Luca wraps his arms around my waist as he pulls my back up against his chest.

"Babe, however honorable that is, it's also not realistic. Those things only happen in the mob movies on television. Let's not forget when Carmine turned, his crew scattered and joined other families that would take them. They had to or they would have been labeled a snitch and then their days would be numbered."

"Did any of them come to work for Agosto?" Gianni looked at Geno and then Luca, as if they all knew the answer and I should have.

"None of them came to Agosto," Gianni informs me.

"Was there that much hatred between the brothers that they couldn't come to an agreement?"

"Chelle, Carmine threw Dad under the bus every chance he had. There was really a lot of bad blood between them," Gianni informs me.

"So, is it too hard to back out of the drug business because of the danger it poses on us, or is it too costly?" My mind flashes back to one of Carmine's books when he talks about drugs and how he really wanted nothing to do with them, but he only had so much control over what happened when he wasn't around.

"Both, Chelle. And you would be busting up crews, along with taking away the crews' livelihood. Geno, pull up the spreadsheet on how the money flow works. I think that would really help her." Geno gives Gianni a nod and pulls up a flow chart on the different crews. It shows the areas that they run. "It's nothing more than a pyramid scheme. Jesus, I had no idea this was still going on. So, you're saying this is still profitable enough that all the families continue to sell drugs and move the money up the pyramid?"

"Sadly, The United States is the largest user of illegal drugs. It's a cash cow even with the danger it poses. Once the money starts moving up the pyramid, it's clear sailing for the higher ups. It's the soldiers and the associates that take the risks."

"I don't want to be a part of drugs or prostitution. Carmine looked the other way on so much of that, why can't we do the same?" Luca's arms tighten around me while Geno and Gianni are looking at me like I have just grown a third eye.

Geno comes from around the desk and steps in front of me. "Chelle, Luca, I'm the one who handles all the financial business. The best thing I can tell you is: if you really feel this way, then you need to walk away from all of this. For your safety and the safety of this family. You can change a lot of things, but when you come between men and women and the potential amount of money they will make, your head will spin. Carmine might have said he wanted no part of it, but when his capos came to pay him, he didn't think twice about taking the money. Besides, if you did that, you would probably be dead sooner rather than later. That's the God's honest truth."

Luca lets go of me and steps closer toward his brother. "I have no problem walking away, but Chelle would never leave Jessica and Viviana. Have you thought about that when you came up with this little scenario of yours?"

"That choice would be up to Jessica and Viviana, not Chelle," Geno states angrily. I need to stop this before it escalates into a fight that they won't be able to come back from.

I grab Luca's arm. "Stop! I need to think all of this through. When the decisions were made, it was to stop everyone trying to find Carmine's books, books that would lead to so much destruction. Give me twenty-four hours to come to some decisions. Geno, can you please send those charts to my email, and I will put the whiteboard away. Thank you." I don't wait for an answer; I walk out holding tightly onto Luca's arm.

CHAPTER SEVEN

Luca

"CHELLE, I NEED TO GO BUY MY OWN VEHICLE TODAY. WHY don't we go together and get out of this house for a while," I suggest, knowing we desperately need some alone time.

"Do you even know what you want?"

"As a matter of fact, I do, and I checked with the dealership before I came home to see if they have one in stock."

"Well, don't leave me hanging, what are you getting?" She smiles up at me.

"Mercedes-Benz G-Class Wagon. Black on black with heavy tinted windows. They had it in stock. It needed to be tinted, and I got a message that it's ready. Now, let's go pick that baby up." At this point, no is not an option. We head outside and our assigned detail drive us to the dealership. I'm sure when we are done, they will closely follow behind us. Not everything about this lifestyle is fun and games. Hell, I've yet to find anything about my current situation exciting, well, except for Chelle. It's not a long drive and there is no better feeling in the world than picking up a brand-new kick-ass vehicle.

"It won't take long. When you are paying cash, the entire transaction should take about thirty minutes." I hold the door open for her and we head inside. She is looking around at all the different vehicles while I make my way to the manager's office. A few more signatures, turning over the cashier's check and, just like that, this baby is mine. I find Chelle in the showroom checking out all the new vehicles. I slip my hand in hers and we head out to the curb where my new baby is waiting for me. I open the door for her and get hit with that amazing new car smell mixed with the scent of leather. I open the driver's side door and get in tossing my backpack on the back seat. When I went to the bank to lock up the tapes, I got distracted getting the cashier's check. I'll have to drop them off tomorrow. Right now, they will stay safe with me. I notice there are two water bottles in the front cup holders. They thought of everything. For what I just spent, they should.

"Luca, where did you get this kind of money?" It didn't take long for her to get suspicious.

"You've seen how modestly I've been living. That made it easy to stash cash. And since my last car blew up, I added the settlement to the pile. Can we just enjoy the drive and not worry about anything for a while?" The look on her face is all I need to realize I've hurt her feelings.

"I didn't mean for that to come out so harsh, Chelle. I'm not used to justifying my spending habits or anything, for that matter, to anyone." That seems to smooth things over, at least, for now. Once I tell her about everything else, I'm sure things will change.

"Luca, do you think it's necessary to go through all of Agosto's papers?"

"Are you having second thoughts about taking over? No one would blame you if you were." I glance over at her. She mindlessly sinks her teeth into her bottom lip and it's like a direct line to my cock.

"Look at the hold Agosto has on my grandmother. That's why walking away was never an option, and now that he wants to marry her." I hit the brakes and nearly give us both whiplash.

"He wants to get married? When did this happen and why the fuck am I just finding out about it now?" I can't help but raise my voice.

"I just found out this morning. I went to talk to Agosto about his trip to Sicily and that's when he dropped this bombshell. He said he was asking my permission but, in reality, he couldn't care less what I think. He was asking me out of respect for my grandma."

"Wow, did you talk to Viviana about any of this?"

"I did this morning while you were gone. I didn't come right out and say Agosto wants to marry her. I asked her if she was up to the trip and how she felt about marrying him."

"What did she say?"

"She kind of laughed about it, and she said she would think about the trip, but it sounds like her mind is already made up." It now makes sense that she has been on edge since I saw her this morning.

"Chelle, she will have plenty of protection and I don't think Agosto would force her into anything she didn't want to do," I try to calm her nerves. She stares out the window seemingly lost in thought. "Talk to me, Chelle, are you having second thoughts about the business?"

"I don't know a way out of this that wouldn't hurt so many people. I guess I thought the business had evolved and things like drugs, prostitution, and gambling were part of the past, not the future going forward. The look on Gianni and Geno's faces when I gave some of my suggestions told me things were never going to really change." Hearing her say all of this out loud makes me think a farm in the middle of Iowa is not such a bad idea after all.

"You have an out, Chelle, you always have an out. Use everything Carmine left you for your protection." I start driving again to find a location where we can safely park and talk.

"I thought of that, but what about my grandmother and Jess? Most of all, what about you . . . us?" her voice trails off as we pull into the Scottsdale McDowell Sonoran Preserve. It's perfect, no motorized vehicles allowed. I reach for my backpack but stop. I've already missed the bank, but it will be safe to leave it in the car. I grab the two bottles of water and get out and head around the other side to let Chelle out.

"Where are we going?"

"This is a beautiful preserve with all kinds of different trails." Her eyes grow wide at the mention of this. "Don't worry; we are going to do a simple trail for now. I just wanted to be away from that house and everyone in it for a bit." Before we can even move, our detail is right behind us.

"Guys, we are just taking a walk. You can follow but please keep your distance." They nod their heads in agreement as I take Chelle's hand and we head off to the trail.

"This place is beautiful. I never knew it was here."

"I always come here when I need time to think."

"What's bothering you, Luca, I mean besides the obvious?"

"I wish I could turn back the clock to before my mom died. I know anyone who ever lost someone feels that way, but there are so many lies that Agosto has told and I have so many questions, questions I'll never get answers to." My fingers are locked in hers so tight, I'm praying she doesn't disappear.

"Where is this coming from? You seem to be dealing with the changes in your life just fine."

"Anything but, Chelle. I'm a guy who was raised to do the right thing. Then right before my mom dies, I find out who my father is. In my mind and my heart, I think I can be better than him. Just because his blood runs through me doesn't mean I have to be like him. So, I head off to the FBI and that's when my world turned upside down."

"Is it because of me that your world turned upside down?"

"Yes and no." She tries to loosen the grip I have on her hand, and I realize that I unintentionally hurt her.

"Please don't pull away. Give me a chance to explain." We keep walking down the trail.

"I'm listening."

"My father made sure that when I joined the FBI, no one knew who I was. Part of me knew he did that to protect me, but the other part of me felt like he didn't want me. I didn't fit into his world. That's why I put everything I had into the bureau. When I met Carmine, I was right out of the academy. The thing is, Chelle, he knew exactly who I was from day one. He refused to talk to anyone but me. Most of all, even though Carmine hated my father, he knew I had integrity. Carmine understood that the man I am was so unlike my father. Today when I turned in my papers, I realized the FBI also knew who I was from the very beginning. Carmine told me so many times that they knew who I was, but I didn't believe him."

"What happened today that made you realize this?"

"It's small things that were said, add on to that, the new director, Ms. Gray asked me to be a snitch." She doesn't ask me if it's something I was considering. Maybe Carmine was right about her.

"I know you could never live with yourself if you did that, the same way I couldn't. When you talk about Carmine your whole face lights up. How well did you know him?" This is my chance to tell her about the tapes, about everything. Her phone rings. In my mind, I'm pleading with her not to answer it. However, it's Jess and I know she's worried about her—hell—we all are. Maybe I should put all this on the back burner, or maybe we just aren't meant to be together.

CHAPTER EIGHT

Michelina

J ESS'S TIMING IS HORRIBLE, BUT I CAN'T BE MAD AT HER. SHE HAD no way of knowing what was going on between Luca and me. After taking a few steps away from Luca, I answer the call.

"Hey, Jess, is everything okay?"

"I wanted to remind you about my appointment today with the therapist. Are you still able to go with me?"

"Yes, of course. I'll be home soon. Is everything okay?"

"I'm scared, Chelle. I'm so broken. What if Geno doesn't want to deal with my baggage?" I kick a few pebbles on the ground trying to stay calm.

"Did he say something to you that would make you think he doesn't want a relationship with you?"

"No, just the opposite, but what if he's saying that because he's afraid if he dumps me, I'll go off the deep end?"

"Stop overthinking everything. If he didn't want to be with you, you would know it. Now, get ready; I'll be home shortly." I hang up and head back over toward Luca.

"Is everything okay?"

"Yeah, I have to start heading back home. I have to take Jess to her therapy appointment. I'm sorry, Luca, we can go out for a nice quiet dinner tonight." He just nods, takes my hand and we head back to his car.

"Chelle, as much as I know you want this to all work out, I think we might have taken on way too much. You believe you can change things, maybe even make part or all of the business legitimate. After today and seeing the mountain in front of us that will need to be changed, do you really believe that is still a possibility?"

"What other option do we have? I get that you are not close with your family and leaving is floating around out there, constantly tempting you. If you really feel you want or need to leave, I won't stop you. All I want is for you to be happy and safe—always." My heart is in my throat, but I don't want him to feel trapped because of me.

He stops abruptly before reaching to open the door for me and turns sharply to face me. "Get this through your head, Chelle, I'm not going anywhere without you! We didn't come this far just to come this far. We have to find a quick and painless way to tie this all up. While you go with Jess to the therapist, I'll work with my brothers on what options we have. Deal?" I lean up and kiss his cheek. They instantly flush and I can't help but smile.

"Deal," I say before getting in. He closes my door and walks around to the other side, climbing in himself and starting up the engine. We hold hands in silence, enjoying the quiet and scenery of the drive back.

When we make the turn into the driveway, Geno, Jess, and Gianni are waiting for us. It doesn't take long for Gianni and Luca to bond over his new SUV.

"Wow, Luca, she is a sweet ride. Now you need to name her."

"I'll work on that. In the meantime, while Chelle takes Jess to her appointment, I think the three of us have a lot of work to do." He heads inside and the others quickly follow. Seeing Luca take charge is different and *hot*. The door closes and just like that I'm back to reality. I decide to let our guards drive us to our appointment rather than follow us in another car. When we get into the car the divider between the front seats and the back goes up. I don't believe they can't hear us, and I want to keep my mouth shut for the duration. Jessica has other plans.

"What's going on with you and Luca?" she begins to grill me.

"What do you mean, nothing has changed."

"Lately, it seems like there is a lot of tension between everyone. Chelle, do you miss the days when we taught school, and the only thing we worried about was what we were going to do for summer break?"

"Those days are a lifetime ago. Now my days are spent keeping everyone safe." I let out an aggressive sigh. Her face turns pale, and her body stiffens as my words hang in the air. I realize her experiences are still so raw. I need to be more aware of what I say. Just another thing on my plate.

"We're here, Jess. I'll go upstairs with you, but I'll stay in the waiting room in case you need me." The office is on the second floor, and we decide to take the stairs. I need to get my steps in any way I can. When we get to the office door, Jess's hand hovers over the doorknob. Fear is crippling her. I reach for the doorknob, but she pushes my hand away.

"I got it, Chelle. I just needed a moment." How someone could have so much fear yet be so brave at the same time just blows my mind. I step to the side and then follow her lead. While she checks in, I have a seat. Jess already filled out everything online a few days ago but of course there is always one more form that needs to be filled out. Since Jess and I are no longer employed, I took it upon myself to get us both COBRA insurance. Jess was surprised when I told her, but we could wake up tomorrow and the government could seize everything we have. Then again maybe I'm watching one too many crime shows. Just as Jess finishes filling out the form, the office assistant calls her back. Her fingers are wrapped around the arm of the chair so tight that her knuckles are white. As I pull her hand free, she realizes that she has a death grip and let's go. The office assistant calls her name again, this time she gets up and heads toward her, but not before she turns and looks back at me.

"I'll still be here when you get out, Jess, promise." I give her a smile of encouragement.

She disappears behind the door, and I finally let out the breath I was holding. She is in such a fragile state right now. It would only take one thing to put her over the edge. I know Luca wants out and, after today, I'm thinking he might be right. However. I can't leave Jess or my grandmother. If I go talk to the FBI about walking away, everyone will know. If anyone gets wind of what I'm even thinking of doing, everyone's life will be in danger. How the hell did my grandfather do it? When Luca took me to the preserve earlier, I really thought he was going to propose. Now I think that was the furthest thing from his mind. I'm finding it harder and harder to have any kind of alone time with him and, when I do, I can't shut my mind off. Maybe I need some therapy, then again, I can't even etch out time to mourn my mom let alone talk to someone about the crazy life I've found myself in.

I check my watch and discover that Jess has been back there for thirty minutes. This is a good sign, considering I had to push her to even seek out therapy. Sometimes the person who protests the most is the one who needs it the most. I've been through so much this year, and it's only May. Knowing I need someone to talk to is not enough. Finding someone I can trust is huge. With everything on my shoulders and Grandma going to Sicily, I don't know when I can find the time. My phone vibrates; it's Agosto. *"When you get home, please come and see me."* I close my eyes and pray that I'm not going to be entrusted with more secrets and lies.

CHAPTER NINE

Jessica

THE NURSE TAKES ME TO DR. BANNING'S ROOM. AS I WALK IN the room, I feel a shiver run up my spine, like I just entered a commercial walk-in freezer. The room looks very sterile, void of any personal items until I look see a photo on the corner of her desk. I strain my neck to try and see the whole photo. She turns it toward me, and it's a photo of a young girl holding up a ribbon next to a very large horse. "Is that your daughter?" I ask as I sit across from her, my eyes fixated on the photo. I'm not sure why I would care.

"Actually, that is me. That is the last time I rode my horse, before I had a freak accident and broke my back." She pushes back from the desk and that's when I notice she is in a wheelchair. It's not the common type of wheelchair you would see. This one has no arms, which is why I didn't notice it when I first came in.

"I'm sorry, I didn't mean to pry."

"Don't be sorry. I keep the photo so my clients can see how young I was when I had my accident and that I was still able to carry on with my life."

"What about now, do you still ride?" I don't know why I'm so curious, but I still can't take my eyes off of the photograph.

"When I first had my accident, I didn't want to. I closed myself off from the world. However, time really does heal, Jessica. Now I ride at least twice a month. Why don't you tell me your story, not what's on the forms you filled out before coming here." I ball my fists in my lap and take a deep breath. Some things are still so raw, and yet some stuff I've buried so deep, hoping it never sees the light of day.

"I was a victim when I was very young, as you know from those forms I had to fill out. I was held a prisoner by my uncle for months while my parents went to California to pick up their inheritance. My uncle chained me to the basement floor and raped me on a daily basis. Chelle saved me from that madman. After that, I vowed I would never be a victim again. However, sometimes life is out of your hands. Then again, maybe I was always meant to be the victim. A few months ago, I was kidnapped and raped. I became the very thing I vowed I would never be again: a victim." As she puts her pencil to paper, I can't help but become fixated on the movement.

"No one is ever meant to be a victim, Jessica. After you were rescued from your uncle, what steps did you take to protect yourself?"

"I was in shock. My parents had no idea what happened and when they were told, they didn't believe me. It was my best friend Chelle and her family that took care of me."

"How did they take care of you?"

"They made me feel safe." My chest begins to feel tight, and I can barely get the words out.

"So, at that point you were no longer Jessica *the victim*, you were Jessica *the survivor*. That's something to be proud of."

"Except, I found out I was pregnant. Once again, I had to turn to Chelle for help. I was too far along to have an abortion. I was too young to have a child, much less raise a child. That's when Viviana, Chelle's grandmother, stepped in again to help. She made arrangements for Chelle and me to spend the summer in Sicily with relatives. Before I came home,

I gave birth to a healthy baby boy. I wanted no part of him, I couldn't. He was adopted by a local family, and I never saw him again. We came home and never spoke about what happened. I owe Chelle and her family so much.

"What happened next?"

"Like I said, we came home, and life went on as usual. My parents basically checked out of my life."

"No therapy?" she questions. I squeeze my eyes shut to block out the memories.

"No, their way of dealing with everything is to act as if it never happened."

"Jessica, you survived, again." She looks up from her paper and smiles. It's warm and calming. The chill is slowly going away.

"Everything was going great, but Chelle's life turned upside down, and I had to be there for her like she was for me. Unfortunately, it was her half-brother that she didn't know she even had who kidnapped me. He raped me and threatened to kill me and Chelle. I did whatever he wanted; I had no choice. Finally, the FBI stepped in, and they saved me."

"So, you not only survived some horrific times you also offered comfort and support to your best friend. I would say you're pretty amazing."

"But it didn't last . . . nothing good ever does. I'm waiting for the other shoe to drop. Day in and day out, I know it's going to eventually happen. I'm not meant to be a survivor."

"You are meant to be whatever you want to be. What happens next is in your control. You have to take steps to protect yourself. Even if it's baby steps. Did you get a complete exam after you were rescued?"

"Yes, Chelle made sure of it. I thank God I didn't end up pregnant again. I don't think I could have survived it. I was also tested for all communicable diseases. Everything came back clear. I have to be checked again in six months. So, it's not easy to forget all of this when there will always be a reminder."

"Are you in a relationship?"

"I'm trying, but I'm so scared to give him my all."

"You need to focus on you and if this relationship is meant to be, it will be. Over the next couple of days, I want you to work on your plan. The plan will be how you are going to protect yourself going forward. You need to name it and own it."

"Self-preservation."

"That's a great start, Jessica. Now I want to see you back here in one week with a start to your plan. Give this paper to the check out and they will make the appointment for you. I look forward to seeing you again."

I look at my watch and realize an hour flew by. I get up and take the paper. When I came in it felt so sterile, but now I have hope. "Thank you, I'll see you soon." I say before letting myself out. After making my appointment, I head out of the waiting room and Chelle is gone. I feel instant panic: my heart races, my palms getting sweaty, a weird white aura appears around everything I look at, and I feel like I can't breathe. It's at this moment, I realize I don't think I can go on without Chelle. She quiets the fear inside of me. I stand in the middle of the room, not knowing what to do. Suddenly, the door to the ladies' room opens and Chelle steps out. She is instantly by my side.

"I panicked when I didn't see you. I'm sorry, Chelle." I start to cry as everything inside me crashes. Chelle sits me and I put my head between my legs, trying to control my breathing. Chelle gets me a cup of cold water from the cooler and has me drink it. The cold calms my nerves and my breathing normalizes.

"Don't be sorry. Let's go home. If you want, you can tell me all about your session when we get to the car." I nod my head and stand up with her. She slips her arm through mine, and we head home. For the first time I might have some hope for a normal future, but it's obviously going to take a lot of work.

CHAPTER TEN

Michelina

O N THE CAR RIDE BACK, JESS SEEMS TO BE A LITTLE different. She's smiling and that's something I haven't seen in a while. "So, tell me what you thought of Dr. Banning?"

"She is so real, you know she's been through some difficult times herself, so she can relate to what I've been through. Thank you, Chelle, for finding her for me."

"I'm just glad you're comfortable with her. We both need to get back to a somewhat normal life. Moving forward and moving on." She instantly stiffens at the mention of this.

"Chelle, what does that look like to you, you know . . . normal and moving on?"

Words are very powerful. I know I have to choose my words wisely, so she doesn't lose the progress she has made. "That's what we have to figure out, and we will. One day at a time. Right now, I need to deal with Agosto and Grandma leaving for Sicily."

"Maybe it will be good for them to be away from everything. You know, give the dust a chance to settle. I'm sure she will be very safe there, like we were," her voice trails off as we both sit in silence. A melancholy look quickly washes over her face. Yes, we were safe during our time in Sicily, however, it was also a very sad time.

"We're here. I need to find Agosto, are you okay?"

"Of course, I'm going to let Geno know what happened today."

We get out and I go in search of Agosto. I thought I would find him in his usual place in the garden, but no one was there. My gut is telling me to head toward the little church he built in this enormous house. When I get there, I peek inside and find him sitting in the back pew. I study him for a bit. I'm always trying to figure him out. However, I don't think I ever will. That makes me a little sad. I mean, after all, he is Luca's dad. I shrug off my uneasy feeling, open the door and slowly head inside. He lifts his head when he hears me but doesn't turn around. I dip my finger in the holy water, make the sign of the cross, and bow to the altar before stepping inside the pew next to him. He doesn't acknowledge me; he just stares straight ahead.

"Thank you, Michelina, for meeting me alone."

"Why did you build this place?" my voice, barely a whisper.

"It's the only place I know of where the truth can't be hidden. God knows what's in our hearts."

I shift uncomfortably in my seat. "Is that why you brought me here?"

"What has you so uneasy about me? Is it my relationship with Viviana or my lack of a relationship with Luca?" If there was ever a time for me to let my feelings out, it's now.

"Actually, both. You make yourself out to be a God-fearing Catholic when, in reality, you have done some awful things. Yet, you expect forgiveness. It's like every Saturday you come in here to confession and that wipes the slate clean. Sunday, you rest. Come Monday morning, you're back at it again. Granted, you now have your children doing your bidding for you, but your hand is in it, always. I don't want to see Luca's reputation get tainted by yours. I don't want my grandmother hurt, emotionally. I really believe you could be the one to break her." He holds his hands tightly together and I watch as his knuckles turn white.

"This from a woman who beat a man to death at the age of fourteen, but who am I to judge you?" I feel the bile rise in my throat.

"I have lived with that decision my whole life. It was in self-defense, and you know that."

"I don't want to fight with you. I just want you to understand I mean no harm to Viviana or Luca. I'm an old man now. I'm tired and reflecting on the past doesn't help any of us—least of all—me. I will seek infinite absolution from my God on his terms when the time comes. I want Viviana to have some lasting happy memories of what little time we will have left together. Thanks to Carmine, I couldn't do that before. If you don't give your approval, she won't go." There it is, the other shoe dropping.

"What about Luca?"

"I don't think that relationship will ever be what either of us wants it to be." I slowly turn and it takes so much of me to not just smack him across his face. How is it possible that this man can bring out the worst in me? Is that what he did to my grandfather?

"How will you know that if you don't try? Why would you think it's okay to just give up on any kind of relationship with Luca?"

"Michelina, the trust between us was broken when his mother died. Some things in life you can't come back from."

"You're not even willing to try and mend the relationship. That is so sad and a total copout. When things get tough, you run away? That's a class act, Agosto." I can't control how pissed off he is making me.

"Maybe you should ask him why he showed more respect to Carmine than to his own father?" The hair on the back of my neck stands up and a shiver runs down my spine.

"He was only doing his job, Agosto. What makes you think it was anything more than that?"

"That's a conversation for the two of you. Viviana and I are leaving today. I would like you to try and be happy for us. At least, for her sake." With that, he stands up and the conversation is over. As he makes his way out of the pew his words about Carmine and Luca are front and center in my mind. Why do I feel that he knows something that I don't. Secrets are deadly, especially when it comes to this family. I take a few minutes to compose myself before I go in search of Luca.

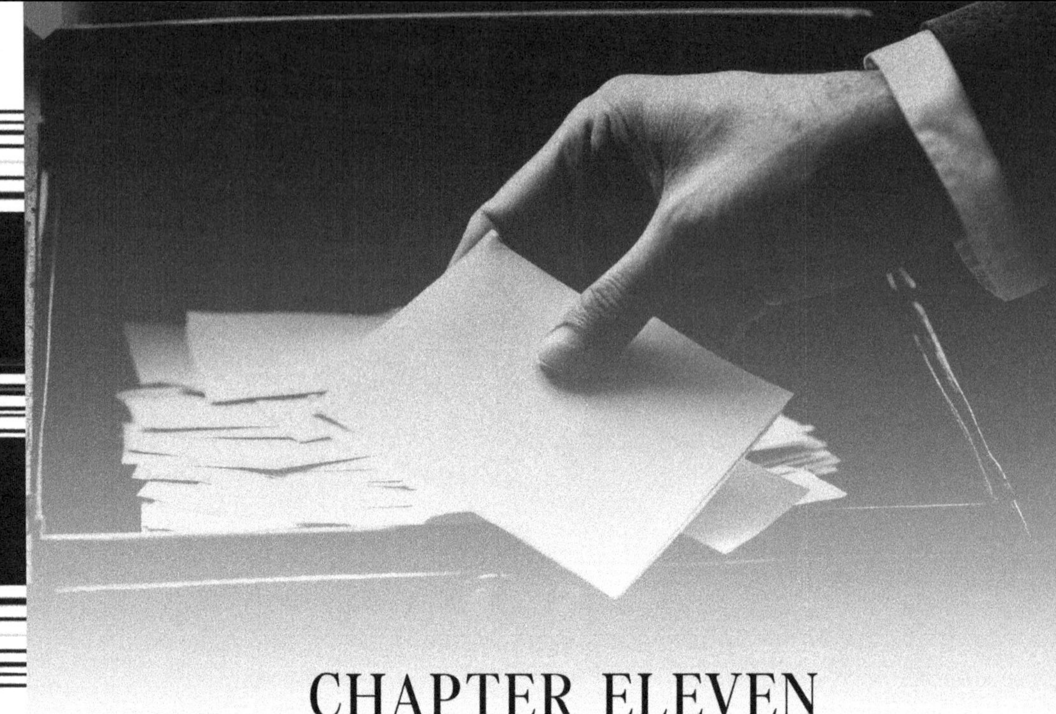

CHAPTER ELEVEN

Michelina

Today I saw the darker side of Agosto. The side he rarely shows anyone Was it me? Did I bring out the worst in him like Carmine did? Instead of searching for Luca, I head to my grandmother's room. Just as I get to her door, I hear voices come from inside. I'm not sure who it is. I knock on the door before entering. I find Luca and Grandma sitting on the balcony. They stop talking when they realize I'm here.

"I didn't mean to interrupt. I thought I would be back earlier. My eyes catch sight of the suitcases, and I guess I have all my answers. "It looks like you're all packed and ready to go." Luca gets up and pulls out a chair for me.

"Unless you have a really good reason why I shouldn't go."

I steer clear of that subject. "Do you know how long you'll be gone?"

Luca takes my hand and gently squeezes it. "Chelle, it looks like Agosto only booked a one-way ticket, which is why I came in here to talk to Viviana." I now have a death grip on his hand.

"Grandma, did you agree to all of this?"

"Honestly, we never talked about it."

"Are you sure you even want to go?" my voice, almost a squeal.

"I don't know why both of you seem so apprehensive about this trip. We are two very old people wanting to enjoy whatever time we have left before our traveling days come to an end."

"Why do you have to go so far away, and why now? Things with this family are so unsettling to the point of being dangerous."

"My dear, I'm not getting any younger. I'm tired of sitting around waiting for the Grim Reaper to come around the corner." I give her words a moment to sink in, which leaves me wondering what it is that's really eating away at me.

"Why one way?" Before she can answer, there is a knock on the open door. When I look up, I see Agosto. It's like he's always there, lurking in the background. *Maybe he's the Grim Reaper.*

"The door was open, and I didn't want to interrupt."

"How long have you been standing there?"

"If you have questions, Michelina, you can always ask me. I promise, I won't bite." He has a smirk on his face that some might find charming, I don't.

"Okay, why one way? Most people that book a vacation know when they are coming and going."

"I didn't want to have any added pressure. We are up in years, and I know this trip might well be our last one. That being said, I want to take my time and show Viviana all the beauty of Sicily. See, Michelina, nothing sinister at all. We will be leaving soon. The plan is to fly through the night. We will arrive in the midafternoon tomorrow. Geno has arranged for extra security. I think we have everything covered. I promise to keep you updated every step of the way. I hope that will make you feel at ease about the trip. Now, I have a few last-minute details I need to go over with Luca before we leave."

Luca gets up and heads out with Agosto, making sure the door is closed behind him.

"Michelina, please stop carrying the world on your shoulders. It's going to be okay. I mean how much trouble can two older-than-dirt people get into?" She laughs. However, I don't find any of this amusing.

"Nothing surprises me anymore. Can I ask you something?"

"Of course."

"You know Luca practically his whole life. Why do you think Luca seems to hold back when he's around Agosto? More importantly, why does Agosto treat him differently than he treats Geno and Gianni?"

"As you know Luca's mother Sophia insisted that Agosto remain silent about being Luca's dad. She hated the life and didn't want her son to be a part of it. When she became ill, Luca was still in high school. She had no other family and knew she had to make arrangements for him. You know the devil you know verses the devil you don't. When Luca found out, he had a lot of resentment. When you see the dynamics between Agosto and his other sons, it's very different. He's been their dad their whole lives. I can only imagine in Luca's eyes Agosto was his mother's friend first and then his father. There is a trust missing, and I'm not sure if that will ever change."

"If she didn't want her son in that lifestyle, then why get involved with Agosto?" I throw my hands out.

"Michelina," she smiles, "the heart wants what the heart wants. Sometimes life doesn't give us a choice."

"Shouldn't Agosto try to maybe do more with all three of his sons? Being more inclusive might bridge that gap."

"He wanted to do that but when Luca decided to join the FBI, Agosto saw it as a smack in the face. For Agosto, that relationship is a dead end."

"Is that why he never told his kids about Luca?"

"Put yourself in their shoes. With the business they are in, I don't think they would have been so welcoming or trusting to a half-brother in the FBI. However, Luca saving Gianni's life was a game changer. They had to accept him."

"Sadly, there is a big difference between accepting and trusting."

"Michelina, you have to have faith that things will fall into place for them. Maybe without Agosto around they will have no choice but to work together to become the family you think they should be."

I get up and give her a kiss on the cheek. "I'll let you rest before you have to leave. Have fun and don't overdo it. If you want to come back sooner or if you run into anything that makes you uncomfortable, call me and I'll come and get you. I love you, Grandma."

"I love you, too."

I pray that this is not the last time I will see her.

CHAPTER TWELVE

Luca

I'M SITTING IN GENO'S OFFICE TRYING MY HARDEST TO SHOW SOME interest in what he and Gianni are talking about. However, fighting the urge to nod off is very strong. Agosto had little to say to me when we left Viviana's room. He was more or less advising me to keep Michelina out of his affairs of the heart. I tried not to laugh when he said it, like I would have any say in that. I focus my attention on the conversation in the room.

"So do we have enough security on Viviana and Agosto while they are in Sicily?" I ask, trying not to show that I'm more concerned about Viviana than Agosto.

"Luca, can I ask you a question?"

"Gianni, you don't need permission to ask me anything. If I don't want to answer, I won't."

"Why don't you call Agosto Dad?"

I let the question roll around in my head trying to think what the best way to answer this would be. Finally, I opt for the truth. "Agosto didn't acknowledge me as is son until right after my mom died. All I ever knew him as was Mom's boyfriend. I know it was at my mom's request that he didn't acknowledge me, but by the time he did, it was really too late. Don't get me wrong; I did try, but it never felt right . . . more like forced. You both grew up with him as your dad, I didn't."

"Okay, but when you did find out, why didn't you try to offer an olive branch, since it wasn't him who wanted it kept a secret." In my mind, I'm instantly that teenage boy again, desperate to fit in, to be wanted.

"He went along with keeping the secret."

"Why did you join the FBI? At that point, you knew who your dad was, don't you think that maybe you doing that made it hard for Dad to trust you?"

I take a minute to answer this. I don't know how much they know, but they deserve to know everything, not just what Agosto told them. "Honestly, I did it to piss him off. You need to understand, I was a teenager whose mom just died. The responsibility for me was forced on a man who already had his own family in place. He let it be known that he didn't want to marry my mom and he didn't want any more children. Before he shipped me off to boarding school, he made me change my name and have plastic surgery. I had no choice or a say in anything. I had to do what he said. I lost my mom, all my friends, and my identity. He took away every piece of me," I unload it all, holding nothing back. Gianni sits down next to Geno on the sofa. Both men are quiet. No doubt they had no idea what Agosto did.

"He made you change your name and have plastic surgery? Why?" Geno asks.

"He said it was for my protection. He had the papers ready for me to sign the same day my mom died. I felt like I died that day, too." This is the first time I've said this out loud, and it still enrages me.

"Did you question him about it?" Gianni asks while Geno is staring at me with disbelief.

"His standard answer to all my questions were always the same: *'It's for your safety, son. In time I will bring you into the fold.'* In the blink of an eye, he took me away from my life and created a whole new one for me. That's when I realized Matteo, and anything about him, was gone forever."

Gianni gets up and steps closer towards me. "Luca, look at it from our side. We knew nothing about your existence until the day you took a bullet meant for me. He sent you away which, in our eyes, makes no sense. We were homeschooled for our safety, not sent away, which is what he should have done. He should have brought you here. Maybe it would have been easier for all of us, including him. We had a brother who was murdered and a sister that died from cancer. He knew first-hand what all of that did to this family, so him doing what he did to you makes no sense."

"You're asking me for answers that I don't have, when it's Agosto you should be asking. It's not that I don't want to talk about it, I just don't have the answers you're looking for." Geno opens his mouth to speak but stops suddenly. I turn around and see Agosto in the doorway. I'm not sure what he heard and, honestly, I don't care. Gianni quickly gets up and heads to the door.

"Viviana and I are leaving now. Do you need anything from me before I go?"

Gianni is quick to answer for all of us. "Safe travels, Dad. We have everything under control." He turns and leaves, probably happy to be away from the mess he's created. Geno quickly goes back to his desk and shuts down his computer. He declares he's done for the day. He's taking Jessica on a moonlight picnic. Funny how when they want alone time, it happens. When I try to get alone time with Chelle, there is always some sort of crisis. I know the longer I keep her in the dark, the worse it's going to be for us. Gianni pulls a chair directly across from me and sits down. This must be what it feels like to be on the other side of an interrogation.

"Luca, it's just us now, so tell me the truth. You were spotted at The Roadhouse eating with the Feds after you supposedly resigned your position. You need to talk to me and tell me what's really going on with you."

"You're spying on me?!"

"No, I was tracking my damn bike that you took without asking first. When I saw where you were, I called a friend who is a waitress there and asked for the lowdown. You know that place is a known Fed hangout." I'm staring at him in disbelief.

"I had no idea it was an FBI hotspot. Look, I resigned and, instead of having a standard exit interview, I was asked to stay on and become a snitch." He cocks his head and raises one eyebrow. I've come to understand that he usually does this when he has doubts about what he's being told.

"You can rest easy, Gianni. Never in my life would I do such a thing."

"So, then what's eating away at you? Don't insult my intelligence by saying nothing."

"I honestly don't know if this is what I want to do with the rest of my life. This lifestyle is not anything that was on my radar. Sometimes I feel like I'm a teenager all over again. Choices are being made for me and my only option is to follow along."

"What about Chelle? What does she want?"

"I don't know. Every time I try to talk to her, we get interrupted. Besides, she would never walk away from Jessica or her grandmother." I sigh and run my hand through my hair. He's bouncing his leg at a record speed while chewing on his bottom lip. Finally, he stops and now I see genuine concern.

"Luca, Geno is not going to let Jessica walk away. In fact, he's proposing to her tonight."

"This has become one big cluster fuck from the day Carmine died." I state casually. He's staring at me and now I wonder if he knows everything Agosto did. How much was hidden from his sons?

"Exactly how close were you and Carmine?" he asks quickly. Now, I'm weighing my answer. I don't want to give away too much, but I don't want him to think I'm clueless.

"Apparently, close enough that Agosto thinks he should break into my apartment earlier today and search through my personal things." I let the words hang in the air, waiting to see his reaction. If he knew, he doesn't show it.

"Why would he do that? Do you have something to hide?"

"So, Agosto does something so heinous, and it must mean I have something to hide." My voice raises and I fight the urge to get up and walk out.

"No, it's just that he's an old man. Carmine is dead. You resigned. So, why would he bother?"

"Exactly, Gianni, why?" The only thing I can think of is maybe Agosto knows about the tapes. I can't see how, since there is only two people who know, and one is dead. "Maybe now you get why I won't give him a chance to be a father when he looks at me like I'm his enemy."

"You should have confronted him as soon as you knew. Now, he's on his way to Sicily. He plans on proposing to Viviana while they are there. So, I don't think you'll ever get Chelle to leave. Can you live like this . . . you know, someplace you don't want to be because the woman you love is not leaving?" He shuffles his hand out for emphasis.

Suddenly, I feel her eyes on me. We both turn toward the doorway to find Chelle standing there. Gianni gets up, puts his hand on my shoulder. "I'm going to leave the two of you alone. Oh, and there are no cameras or audio recordings in this room." Chelle steps aside to let him out of the room. He closes the door behind him. I get up and slowly make my way toward her. When I finally touch her, I can feel her body quiver.

"Chelle, we need to talk."

CHAPTER THIRTEEN

Luca

"LUCA, WHAT'S GOING ON?"

"Gianni wanted to know about my past, and why I never gave Agosto a chance at being a real father to me."

"Wow, what did you tell him?"

"The truth." I take her hand and take her to the sofa.

"What did he say?"

"He doesn't understand, since he's never had to deal with Agosto the same way I had to. Did you know they were homeschooled? I got stripped of my identity and shipped away, while they were homeschooled," I say with a mixture of anger and disbelief.

"I'm sorry, Luca, I've been so wrapped up in everyone else's problems that I let our relationship slip through the cracks. I'm thinking it's time we all put the past behind us and focus on the future."

"I told you Ms. Gray wanted me to be a snitch, but what I didn't tell you is that Carmine asked me to do the same thing. He wanted me to become his right-hand man but stay at the FBI to keep him informed." Her eyes grow wide.

"What do you mean Carmine asked you?"

"Carmine turning himself in to me, the rookie right out of the academy, was no accident. He knew from day one who I was."

"I read his journals and what he thought of you when he first met you. Why are you telling me this now? Carmine is dead, you resigned, and life has moved forward. Why haven't you?" Her voice quavers, which is not like her. I think this is really hitting home. However, as much as I want to protect her, she needs to know everything.

"I can't move forward until I understand why events happened in my life. Was I a pawn in the game of chess between Carmine and Agosto? I have questions that need to be answered. But I doubt they ever will."

"Why would he turn himself in to only you? How close were you with my grandfather?"

"At first, I thought I was one lucky guy. I was young and cocky. Hell, I was bringing in the leader of the largest New York City crime family. When I was finally able to talk to him alone, I realized it was a set-up—by him. He knew exactly who I was, and he tried every day to get me to go to work for him. I swear I must have been the most clueless FBI agent ever." My grip on her hand tightens.

"Why would he go through all of this?"

"It took time but, eventually, he told me. He knew your mom hated the business and wanted nothing to do with any of it. All of his other children died. He thought you were going to be the one who could elevate his family to the level he always dreamed it would be. However, he knew the gatekeepers of the old reign would never let a woman have that kind of power. He begged me to protect you, probably because he knew I would fall in love with you. Plus, sticking it to Agosto was a bonus."

"You could have transferred, so why did you stay?"

"At first, that's what I wanted to do but, as time went on, a friendship grew between us." Her face pales at this information.

"What do you mean a friendship?"

"We gained a mutual respect for each other. He used to joke that someday they will make a movie about us. He told me about the journals and all the other stuff that he was leaving to you. That's when I told him I wanted to record our meetings. At first, he said never, but as time went on, he understood it wasn't for the FBI or the news hacks. The tapes were for me to never forget his voice, his laugh, and how he made me feel that this world was my birthright. He made me feel wanted, something Agosto never did."

"Why are you telling me this now? I mean, it's all water under the bridge."

"Today I went to my apartment to get the tapes so I could share them with you. I wanted you to hear another side of Carmine. The good side. I wanted you to hear what's not in those journals. I wanted no secrets between us."

"Why do I hear a *but* coming?"

"I have cameras in my apartment, Chelle. Plus, I have a little setup that tells me if someone goes in without my knowledge. You know, just in case the cameras went out for some reason. Today, Agosto broke into my apartment and looked around. He moved some stuff and left empty-handed."

"Are you kidding me? Why?"

"I have no idea. All I can think of is maybe he found out about the tapes. I planned on confronting him about it, but he already left." She lets go of my hand and jumps up.

"I didn't want them to go but he basically said he couldn't care less what I want. Luca, he is planning on getting engaged while they are there. Is this why you keep telling me we should run away from all of this?"

"Like I told Carmine, being the head of a high-level crime family was never on my radar."

"What did he say?"

"Basically, I might not have a choice," is what I say, however, his response was actually a lot more explicit. She drops to her knees in front of me.

"Jesus, Luca, what the hell did we get ourselves into and are we ever going to get out of it?"

I get up and pull her up into my arms. "We will figure this out together—promise."

"Do you think my grandmother is safe?"

"She is the ultimate prize, Chelle. From the day he met her, everything Agosto did was to get Viviana. Unless Carmine can come back from the dead, I think she is safe."

"What about Jess? Do you think she is safe with Geno?"

"He's going to ask her to marry him tonight." She pulls back and nearly falls backwards.

"What? When did all this happen? Why didn't you tell me?"

"I just found out about five minutes before you walked in the door. Do you think she will say yes?"

"I have no doubt that she will. I mean, why wouldn't she? She's safe here with Geno. That means everything to Jess."

"What about your friendship and everything you did for her?"

"When I spoke to Agosto earlier, he tried to throw guilt in my face for saving Jess's life. He actually tried to compare what I did to the killing he's done his whole life."

"Wow, how the hell did you keep it together, I don't think I could have."

"Well, we were sitting in church, so that helped. I told him God will forgive me because I was saving a life. When I asked him why he thinks God will forgive him, he made it sound like God will give him infinite absolution because he goes to confession on Saturday and church on Sunday. What else could I possibly say to him? I don't want my grandmother hurt but if it means I have to go toe-to-toe with him, I will. Luca, when you said Grandma is the ultimate prize, was that Carmine talking?"

I take a minute to formulate exactly how to say this, but then it hits me. "Rather than hearing it from me, why don't you listen to what Carmine thought about the Viviana/ Agosto story."

"You would share that with me?"

"Some secrets are meant to be shared. I think Carmine wouldn't have a problem with it." I get up taking her with me.

"Where are we going?"

"Someplace I know it will be just you and me."

CHAPTER FOURTEEN

Agosto

Finally, I have my Viviana, and we are headed out of the country. I've waited so many years for this moment. I've finally outsmarted the one bastard who always stood in my way—Carmine. Even dead he became an obstacle. I pull the champagne bottle out of the bucket and pour us each a glass. I hold up my glass toward her and she slowly lifts her glass toward mine.

"Viviana, today you made me a very happy man, thank you." She clinks her glass with mine as her cheeks flush. I might be on a plane, but I lift my eyes towards the heavens and silently thank God. I smile as I picture Carmine burning in hell.

"Agosto, you wouldn't tell me your plans, but now that we are in the air, will you share them with me?" My smile slowly fades.

"That would ruin all the surprises I have for you. I promise you'll enjoy everything. Honestly, we should have done this a long time ago. We let too many people dictate what we should and shouldn't do. No more." She doesn't say anything, there's only that smile that grabbed my heart all those years ago. As she slowly lifts the glass to her lips, I picture those lips all over my body. Oh, how I wish I was a younger man.

"Will we ever go back to the States?"

The feeling of euphoria that I waited so long to feel again with her slowly disappears like a ballon slowly losing its air. "Eventually, if you want to, we can. Viviana, we just left, how about focusing on us and what lies ahead of us, not behind us."

"Behind us is family. I told you years ago that the family I have left would always be the center of my universe."

"What about me? From the day we met, all I ever wanted was to be the center of your universe." She becomes incredibly quiet, running her fingers up and down the worry bracelet she wears. Did I push too much?

"You knew from the beginning we could only have a friendship."

"Why don't we put all of this talk about the past away and eat some dinner? I had a chef prepare some of your favorite foods."

"I'm not hungry, Agosto. Since we are alone, I would rather talk."

"Always with the questions. What would you like to talk about?" I sip my champagne and try not to show how angry I am.

"Michelina came to me today with some questions about Luca. Mainly the lack of your relationship with him. I guess now that we are all under the same roof, she sees how you interact with your other boys. I know all these years you've had your reasons, but do you think now that everything is in the open you would maybe try to have a better relationship with him?"

"I spoke to her before we left, and we will see what happens when the dust settles. There is still so much that needs to be done." What I really want to say is *the bitch should mind her own business*. Then again, maybe it's better that she's meddling into my relationship with Luca, that keeps her from looking so closely into my relationship with Viviana. We've had a lot of years together that Michelina doesn't need to know about.

"You've said that a lot through the years, *'when the dust settles.'* Sometimes, I think they should get in the car and just drive out of town. You know, like we tried to do. That is, of course, until Carmine stopped us," her voice trails off. The memories instantly bring us to that horrible day. A day filled with so many dreams and what ifs.

"Viviana, so many times we tried, but somehow either Carmine or fate stepped in."

"You chose to live a dangerous life on the edge, but these kids didn't. Hell, not that being a schoolteacher is a walk in the park these days, but I want Michelina and Luca to be happy and live a safe life."

"Let's put everything away for now and enjoy the trip. There will be plenty of time later to figure out what's best for both of them."

Luca

I wanted to take Chelle some place quiet but, given our current circumstances, along with the security that is always flanking us, I opt for the safety of my apartment. I made sure I put together something to take with us to eat, along with a few bottles of wine. I grab my backpack filled with the tapes and we head out. The ride is short but when I look over, I see her hands clasped together, and her eyes are closed. She is taking in slow, deep breaths. Maybe this wasn't a good idea. I stroke the back of my hand down her arm, and she nearly jumps out of her skin.

"I'm sorry, Luca, I'm nervous and worried. I know I shouldn't be, but I can't help what I feel." She takes my hand and squeezes it.

"Never apologize for telling me your feelings. Why are you so nervous? Is there anything I can do to ease your fears?"

"Change, so much is changing so quickly. I'm not sure all of it is for the good." I'm sure when she hears Carmine's spin on the different events over the years, her opinion might change. I know mine did.

"Believe me, Chelle, I understand. When my mom died and my world was turned upside down, I didn't think I would ever be able to have a normal life again. We have to trust each other and be totally honest. We can make it work, one day at a time." I pull into my assigned covered parking space, get the stuff out of the backseat and we head up to my apartment. Before I open the apartment door, I look up and notice the string is still in place. I've been putting that string up every day from the first day I moved in here. Only one time it was breached, and that was today by Agosto. Maybe Chelle is right, maybe I should have confronted him before he left the country. Would he question what I have that required me to even have all this security? Probably. My mom always said more is less and less is more. Our security is waiting outside the apartment, so while Chelle pours the wine and sets up my makeshift picnic that I brought for us, I bring them two folding chairs and a couple of bottles of water. I know how boring it is waiting around for something to happen that usually doesn't. Most things happen when it's least expected. When I head inside, Chelle is on the balcony with everything spread out for us. I grab my backpack off the chair and head outside.

"Hey, I hope there is enough food. I just grabbed stuff and threw it in the bag."

"Luca, why are you nervous?" she asks as I crawl onto the chaise next to her.

"This has always been very private for me. He was my unexpected friend and then he was gone. Honestly, I miss him. I know everyone has their own interpretation of who Carmine was, but to me, he was an assignment that turned into a friendship that I thought wouldn't end. He was real, brutally honest, funny, frustrating, and that's just the tip of the iceberg." I hand her a glass of wine and clink it with mine before we take a sip. I pull out the tape recorder and a small box filled with tapes. Her eyes grow wide as they focus in on all the tapes.

"Oh my God, Luca, how many tapes are there?"

"There are three boxes like this one. The funny thing is, Carmine didn't want to be taped. I refused to continue on unless he let me. Our agreement was, when the time was right, you'd be the only person he said I could share them with."

"But I have all his journals, what makes these different?"

"The journals are his thoughts, an accounting of things he's done or mainly stuff he had on other people. These tapes are conversations with

Carmine. We fought, laughed, drank, and gossiped about the world and the people in it. They are real and spontaneous. That's not something you'll find on paper." They are all numbered. I pick up number one, pop it in and press play.

"*So, Matteo, now that I've agreed to let you record me, what exactly do you want to talk about?*"

"*Why do you insist on calling me Matteo? You know I only go by Luca.*"

"*You let that bastard take away your birthright. Every day that he stifles you is a day that he wins. You need to stand up for yourself. Agosto will smell fear and pounce like a lion in heat. He really is an evil bastard. I'm sorry you drew the short straw, kid.*"

"*What are you saying . . . that you would have been a better father? Look at your relationship, or lack of one, with Frances.*"

"*I tried with her, but she wouldn't believe anything I had to say. I figured Viviana was filling her head with nonsense. At least she did something right and gave me a wonderful granddaughter.*" I stop the tape and look back at Chelle. She has a blank stare and now I'm worried.

"Are all the tapes like this?"

"Depending upon his mood; they varied every day."

"He had absolutely no respect for my mother or my grandmother, yet it seems you think he is wonderful. Your face lights up when you hear his voice." A deep frown creases her forehead. Her words sting.

"I understand the way you feel but you need to understand there are many sides to this story. Agosto tried to take Viviana away from Carmine, and in the process, he tried to take you, too. Everything Agosto failed to do for me as a father. He failed my mother, Chelle; she was young and vulnerable. When she was diagnosed, why didn't he insist she get the best care possible? It's not like he couldn't afford it. Maybe Carmine was not a wonderful dad, husband, or friend. Was Carmine the end all for me? No, but he was very educational. I learned to look at a problem from many different angles. Believe nothing you hear and only part of what you see. The only thing I learned from Agosto is how to deceive." My words are a little harsher than I expected. I begin to put the tapes away and she puts her hand on mine, stopping me.

"I didn't say I didn't want to listen to them. I need to understand what you were thinking when all this was going on, that's all. Please don't read anything more into it."

I take a deep breath and press play again. I'm watching her face. I know what's coming next and wait for her to react. *"You keep telling me about your wonderful granddaughter, why?"*

"Why, because even though your father is a dog, you are a good man and you'd be perfect for my Michelina. When I'm gone, I'm leaving everything to her. It will be overwhelming for her. Frances won't want anything to do with my business and she will try to talk Michelina out of her birthright. That's where you come in."

"Carmine, she's my cousin. Besides that, I don't want or need anyone in my life."

"Matteo, she is your second cousin, and in Arizona, it doesn't matter. Why do you think I insisted on coming to this God forsaken desert. Although, the golf has been surprisingly good. You can protect her. You will love her with that tender heart of yours. Just give it a chance." I stop the tape again and watch as Chelle with a shaking hand pours some more wine. This is only the beginning.

CHAPTER FIFTEEN

Michelina

I watch my hands shake as I pour some more wine. I'm so parched, I don't think I can form any kind of words that will make any sense. "He had an agenda the whole time. He wanted us together. What if that didn't work out? What would you have done?"

"When I was growing up, my mom told me that a bad decision in a split moment can't be undone. She would say *'Matteo, take the time to think things through. Look at all the possibilities.'* Because of her words, I research everything until there is nothing left to discover. After that, I make my decision, and don't look back. I didn't just say, *'okay I'll get with Michelina.'* I pumped Carmine for as much information about my father and his kids as possible. Then, I turned my research on you. Once I learned that I would be protecting you, all that research helped keep you safe. Look, Chelle, no one is perfect. It comes down to what you are willing to accept. I knew Carmine was a killer, but so was my own father. It wasn't for me to judge either of them. I live by the morals that my mother taught me. Carmine started out as just a job, but then it was more. I never told Agosto that Carmine knew from the beginning who I was. All I said was I think Carmine figured it out because I look like your brother, and not even having plastic surgery helped." I let his words sink in, but it's hard not to think of myself as a project.

"If there was no me and you. Where would you be today?"

"Probably still at the FBI, still trying to protect you. When I told Agosto about my assignment, he was pissed. He demanded that I quit the FBI. I refused and he didn't talk to me for months. I wasn't going to let him take anything else from me. Eventually, he came around again, acting like nothing ever happened. When I was working, I enjoyed my job. Helping other people, who can't help themselves, it's a rush you can't get doing a nine to five office job. Although, once I learned about the corruption on both sides of the playing field, I really wanted to step back and figure out my life. You know, become a farmer in the middle of Iowa type of thing."

"Do you still think that's what we should do?"

"I love you, Chelle, and I will stand with you no matter what you decide. You have a grandmother and a friend that are your whole world, I get it. I think you need to figure out what you want to do. You know what's best for you." I reach over and press play.

"Why do you hate Agosto so much? I mean I know your brothers and there will always be that push and pull between siblings, not that I would know, since I'm an only child, but there has to be more."

"The first thing you need to understand, kid, is there's always more. More hate, more love, more competition, more trust, and more lies. It's like the story of Cain and Able. Our older brothers were reckless, and the times we grew up in had no rules and no boundaries. By the time Agosto and I were old enough to head out into the world, I learned from our brothers' mistakes. I learned what to do to stay alive. Agosto took way too many chances, always trying to best me. He was very jealous, and you know what that got him?"

"I'm assuming arrested since he's not dead."

"Bingo, kid. He at least kept his mouth shut, but the damage was done. I never trusted him again. Did I forgive him—yeah. At the end of the day, blood is thicker than water, but I never trusted him again."

"What did Agosto do to get arrested? I tried to look it up, but those records were nowhere to be found. The answer I got is when the system went automated those records were put into a warehouse that eventually flooded."

"You believed that line of crap?"

"No, but it didn't seem worth my time trying to figure out."

"Agosto made his money on the backs of hookers and drug addicts. In the process, he killed a Capo. When he got pinched, he wanted out of the mess he created. So, Agosto did what he always did, he went to the higher-ups for a way out. They gave him a hit to do that, of course, no one wanted. He did it, made his bones and got out of a very messy situation. Except, one police officer wouldn't look the other way, and off to jail he went."

"Who did he kill?"

"None of my business."

"What happened to the cop who arrested him?"

"No one knows. Kid, the more you know, the more involved you are."

"One more question for today, Again, Carmine, who did Agosto kill to make his bones?"

"Save that for another day."

"No, I need to know. I already gave you my word even though there is no statute of limitations on murder, I would not use anything we speak about to go after him or anyone for that matter."

"A priest, Matteo. That's why he is always seeking absolution. It was a hit that no one wanted for a reason. We are already going to burn in hell, but that seals the deal. Now, I'm tired."

I hit stop, and stare at Luca in disbelief.

"You mean to tell me the very thing I said I didn't want to be a part of—drugs and prostitution—is how Agosto got started? Then, he wanted out and now he's knee deep in it all over again. A priest?! Are you kidding me? Does Carmine talk about this anymore?"

"I was assigned to him from day one. I think we were together for almost a year. A lot was talked about, not just the past but his hopes for the future. Yes, if you continue to listen to the tapes, Carmine said Agosto stayed out of that line of business for less than thirty days. He just couldn't stay away from it; the money was too good."

"I try to never use the word hate. However, I can honestly say I hate Agosto. He is nothing more than a snake in the grass." I feel my face flush and I try to remind myself that he is still Luca's father. He takes my shaking hand in his and brings it to his lips.

"I get it, Chelle. To me, he is nothing more than a sperm donor. I wanted to try and get to know my brothers, but I don't see that ending well, either. Look, I don't think you need to listen to all these tapes. I wanted you to hear this one, so you understand why Carmine felt the way he did. I also want you to listen to the one when he talks about Viviana. Down the road, if you feel you want to listen to more of them, then I have no objections." I reach for the wine to refill my glass and I realize it's already gone. Luca goes inside and comes back with another bottle. I take a few sips of the cool, refreshing wine.

"Please let me hear what he has to say about my grandmother." He puts in a new tape and presses play.

CHAPTER SIXTEEN

Luca

I KNEW IT WOULD BE HARD TO SHARE THESE TAPES WITH CHELLE, I just didn't realize how much it would hurt her. I've accepted my father for who he is, and yet I'm still surprised by some of the hurtful things he does.

"*Hey, kid, you know the FBI knows who your father is, and yet they still hired you and agreed to have you, for lack of a better word, guard me. Why do you think that is?*"

"*Maybe they don't know who my father is. I mean, Agosto staged a car accident and sent me for plastic surgery. I would like to think that it wasn't all for nothing.*"

"*Pipe dreams, kid. I'm surprised your father didn't push for you to become a lawyer. He could have had his own in-house consigliere.*"

"*Get all your laughs out now, Carmine. There is plenty to talk about and my career choice is not one of them.*"

"*Seriously, kid, what did Agosto say when you told him you were joining the FBI? Oh, how I wish I could have been a fly on the wall for that one.*"

"*There was nothing to say. My mind was made up. Now, we've talk about Michelina, and we've talk about Frances, but you hardly ever talk about Viviana, why is that, Carmine?"* I pause the tape.

"I was always trying to push back, but just when I thought I was getting the upper hand, he would come back with something that would make me question everything I thought I knew."

"Out of curiosity, what did Agosto say when you told him your plans?"

"He said take some time to think it through. Looking back, I think he was more worried about himself and his other sons." Before I press play again, I get a couple bottles of water. The last thing I need is too much wine distorting why we are here.

"You want to know about Viviana. Well, kid, here is the best advice I can ever give you. Some days you lie in bed, look over at the woman next to you and think, wow I'm one lucky bastard. Then there are days you look over and think, what the fuck was I thinking? That's marriage, kid. I don't care who you are, it's all the same. I loved her and I was faithful to her. She made no bones about the fact that she would have much rather been with Agosto. You know there are many different kinds of infidelities. Your body can stay faithful, but your heart and mind doesn't. That was Viviana's problem. She stayed faithful with her body, but her heart was elsewhere. I don't think a marriage can come back from that, especially when that other person is your own brother." I hit stop and cast my gaze on Chelle.

"Do you want to continue?"

"Why does he keep calling you kid? I mean I get why he said it, but didn't it drive you crazy?"

"I think he continued to do it just to drive his point home."

"Which is?"

"We are who we are. All the name changing and plastic surgery wouldn't change what's in the heart."

"You're showing me a different side to him that I really didn't think existed," she states almost like she's not sure how she feels about that . . . almost. I slowly exhale and my eyes meet hers. Maybe this is going to work out after all.

"Should I play more?" She nods her head, and I hit play.

"When did you know that Viviana wanted Agosto?"

"He kept trying to weasel his way around her whenever he could. He used his grief as an excuse. First, it was his daughter Daniella that became ill. After that, his wife Gisele was never the same. When you lose a child, it takes something from you that you can never get back. After Gisele died, he kept doing everything he could to find ways to be around Viviana. It didn't matter that we were not on speaking terms. Hell, he was lucky I didn't slit his throat! Anyway, Viviana came to me and told me she was leaving me for him. I told her if that was what she really wanted then she should go. She was all smiles and then I let the other shoe drop. If she wanted to go, she could, but she was to leave with just the clothes on her back—no Frances and no Michelina. A marriage cannot work if there is a third person in the mix."

"Carmine, why would you want someone if they didn't want you?"

"I am a man of my word, Matteo, and you should be, too. It's very easy to walk away, but it's harder to stay and be true to yourself."

"Did she ever talk about Agosto again?"

"No. I know she kept a relationship with him. She didn't hide it, but she didn't put it out in the open. I'm sure once she thinks I'm dead, she will go running to him."

"Carmine, you claim you don't care, yet the somber look on your face says otherwise."

"That's it for today, kid." I stop the tape, eject it, and put it in the case.

"Chelle, every day was like that. So much information. No way I could have remembered it all. That's why I pushed to tape the sessions with him. This was the day that I felt I got behind the brave front he put up. I saw a vulnerable side to him that made me question so much more. After that day, I never took anything he said at face value. Going forward, I knew he was an extraordinarily complex man, a man that could move mountains if he wanted to. Not only did I question everything, but I also listened to what he said and why he said it. He was brutally honest, but always with a smile on his face."

"What about my grandmother? I think she is safe, but am I doing the right thing letting her stay in Sicily with him?"

"I don't think you have any other options. She is cognitive, healthy, and doing what she wants to do. I think if you force her to come back home, it will age her very quickly. You can't choose what or, for that matter, who makes her happy, only she can do that."

The Arizona night air can get very chilly. I pull her into my arms and wrap a blanket around us. Staring into the night sky, both of us very lost in our thoughts.

"How about we table this for now. I think I've given you a different look into the man you called your grandfather."

"Why do you think Agosto broke in here today? I mean you said only you and Carmine knew about the tapes."

"Something Gianni said to me today stuck in my head. Apparently, the place I stopped for lunch today is an FBI hotspot. Gianni knew where I was because of him tracking his bike. Instead of trusting me, he called a friend of his who was waitressing there and asked her what I was doing and who I was with. Maybe he spoke to Agosto about it. Do you think that could be why Agosto broke in here?" I throw the question back at her because, honestly, I'm at a loss.

"I love that you think I have all the answers. Unfortunately, the more we dig into things, the more I think this family is crazy."

"Does that include me?"

"Luca, at this point, I think you and I are the only ones without an agenda. I will tell you that when I spoke to Agosto earlier, he said you showed more respect to Carmine than to him, your own father. How did he know that?"

"He must've found out about the tapes, but I have no idea how."

"I do think that as long as my grandmother is alive, Agosto will not do anything to hurt me."

"I agree, but I'm not so sure about me. Yeah, I'm his son—I get that—but there is no trust between us. I feel like he's always lurking around the corner, waiting for that moment when he can drop the other shoe. That's not a normal father/son relationship on any level." I pull the blanket tighter around us, thinking that will ward off the chill. However, I don't think the night air has anything to do with the chill.

"Do you think if your mother had lived, that the relationship you have with Agosto today would be any different?"

"I don't know. It was only right before she died that she told me he was my father. Some days I wonder what my mother was thinking. Maybe she would have never told me. Always more questions than answers."

"Luca, Agosto is a charmer for sure. As much as neither one of us wants to think of him that way, look how long he's been charming my grandmother. I mean she's done some questionable things when it comes to him."

"I wish you would've known my mom. She didn't fit into this lifestyle at all. That's what makes this even harder."

"What was she like?" I grab my phone from the table next to us and pull up my favorite picture of my mom. I pass my phone to Chelle.

"This is my favorite photo of her. It was a fall day, and I didn't want to go to school. Instead of forcing me to go, she packed lunch for us and took me to Topsmead State Forest. It's in Litchfield, Connecticut, where I grew up. It was a day I will never forget. We had the best time ever. That is until we got home, and she got the results from her biopsy. I know it's silly, but I've never gone back there since."

"I didn't know that's where you grew up. She was beautiful. How did she meet Agosto?"

"She was a parish administrator for the Catholic church in our hometown. My understanding was he was in town on business, and he stopped at the church for confession. You know how he is with that. Afterwards he went into the parish office and wanted to make a sizable donation, and that's when they met."

"So, even back then he was seeking absolution."

"Chelle, that's out of our hands. I'm just trying to figure out what is best for us. We have the means and the knowledge to walk away from all of this and stay safe. I get that it's a hard decision. Somewhere along the line, someone will get hurt. But if they are safe, then maybe it's worth it."

"You're talking about Jess. We made a pact, when we were fourteen, that we would always be there for each other, no matter what. What am I supposed to do?" She turns in my arms to face me.

"How can we have so much power, yet so little freedom? I have no doubt that Jess is going to marry Geno. He can and will protect her no matter what. Viviana is with the person that she always thought she should be with. She's in Sicily, no doubt having the time of her life. She couldn't do this when Carmine or Frances was alive. This is her time. If you're that worried about her, let's go to Sicily and see for ourselves that she is okay. We use what Carmine left you to secure our safety. When I was still with the FBI, I looked at life much differently."

"What do you mean?"

"Chelle, the past couple of days, I've realized that the lines are becoming more blurred. I've been thinking a lot about my mom. I know this is not the life she would have wanted for me. If I stay here, what will I become, a snitch for the FBI? A flunky for my brothers? Or perhaps help run a business that I never wanted to be a part of. You and I, Chelle, we're not like them. I don't want us to become just like them. They are all very bitter people. They act like the life they are living is, in some way, owed to them."

"Maybe you're right, maybe we should go to Sicily, and this way I can see for myself that my grandmother is happy."

"If you see she is happy, are you prepared to walk away? I mean, honestly, I don't think Agosto has any intentions on coming back to the states."

"Well, Luca, it's not like I have a choice. I think that's what's bothering me the most. In a short span of time, I lost my mom, and my best friend is probably going to marry into a mob family. I mean, we were teachers, living our best life and now we are in a whirlwind of danger and lies. I just want all of this to end. Hopefully, with no one getting hurt."

I want to ask her, what about us, but I'm not sure I'm ready for the answer.

"Okay, let's go back to the house and I'll make all the arrangements. On the way to the airport, I want to stop at the bank and put these tapes in my safety deposit box." She puts a hand on each side of my face, looks into my eyes and then gives me the most tender kiss ever. Maybe this is her way of letting me know that there will always be an *us*. I pray to God that I'm right. I pack everything up, and we head back to Agosto's house.

CHAPTER SEVENTEEN

Agosto

WE ARE NOT EVEN OUT OF THE STATES FOR TWENTY-FOUR hours and Geno is trying to contact me. Thankfully, this jet has a bedroom suite with two twin beds. Viviana is fast asleep, so as to not disturb her, I take my phone and go into the main cabin. I call Geno back. He answers on the first ring.

"Son, what is so important that you needed to talk to me right now?"

"I'm sorry, Dad, but there are some things going on here that I thought you should know about. First, I asked Jessica to marry me, and she said yes."

"That's nice, but couldn't that wait until we got settled in at our hotel?"

"That's not why I called, Dad. Chelle and Luca are leaving in a little bit, they are headed to Sicily, to be precise."

"Why the hell are they coming here? We just left; what could they possibly want to see us about?"

"Look Gianni and I tried to get it out of them, but they are being very mysterious."

"Do you know when they are going to be here?"

"No, but you have a good head start on them. Besides, what could they possibly want from you?" His question is more like a declaration of my old age and how useless they think I've become.

"This can't be good, Geno. I have a good mind to turn this plane around, but I've waited years for this time with Viviana. I'm not about to let anyone come between us, including that self-righteous granddaughter of hers. Thanks for the heads up, Geno. I will adjust my plans. Oh, and congratulations on your engagement." I quickly hang up and formulate a plan.

I love my son because the world says I have to. The church says I'm supposed to love him and nurture him. I've tried—God knows I've tried, but something with Luca is missing. It's always been different from the day he was born. I didn't want him, and that's one of the many things I pray to God for forgiveness over. Sadly, that list keeps growing. Luca took a bullet that would have killed my Gianni and, for that, I'm grateful, nothing more. I sat by his bedside because of the guilt I felt, not because of the love a parent has for a child. The longer he was under the influence of Carmine, the more he became just like him. I loathe Carmine and curse him to Hell every day. I fear that's what's going to happen with Luca. If that happens, I will never have absolution. God will never forgive a man for hating his child. I might have been able to be with Viviana sooner if he wasn't born.

I pour myself a cognac and contemplate my next move. The amber liquid burns as it goes down but then a warm flush comes and clears my mind. After a second drink, the memories that I've locked away start to come back. *Is it guilt?* That is not something that comes easy for me . . . guilt, that is. Guilt is reserved for the weak. I feel like I've been living the past fifty years in a slow-motion movie. I take one step forward and two steps back. How is that even possible? After Carmine gave Viviana the ultimatum that changed all our lives, I knew I would have my work cut out for me. When Luca came to me and told me about his new assignment to protect Carmine, I knew he would be lost to me forever. Carmine would get his claws in him, and Luca would never be the same again.

Viviana and I set things up so that we could be together. We ignored Carmine's warnings, and we were discreet. When we thought he was finally dead, I purchased the assisted living facility and Viviana convinced Frances that she needed to be in there. Still, Frances put up roadblocks. I thought if Frances knew what it was like to lose a child, then maybe she would understand. If she knew real pain and real betrayal, then maybe she would leave us alone. Viviana and I needed each other to heal.

That day I set my plan in motion. I never said anything to Viviana for fear she would leave me. Instead, I decided to take Nick jr. and Gemma under my protection. I had to take Gemma or Nick wouldn't come. Nick was an idiot and a hot head. The perfect combination for a killer. I could nurture him and turn him into the killer I needed. All those years ago, I was given the same task. I had to do a hit no one wanted. It was the only way to redeem myself in the eyes of the elders. That's the only reason why I'm still alive today. That's when I started seeking absolution. I had Nick plant a bomb in Michelina's car. The idiot got it wrong and blew up Frances's car with her in it.

I pour myself another drink, slowly sipping this one while I wait out the turbulence. Nick begged me for a second chance. He even went so far as to offer up his sister Gemma for collateral. Piece of work, that boy. By this time, Luca had told me that he was in love with Michelina. She's his damn cousin, but he said he didn't care. I decided to give Nick a second chance. Hate can fuel so much if you let it. He planted the bomb in Luca's car. I knew I was sacrificing my son, but I didn't care. He chose Carmine over me a long time ago. Nick promised to get it done fast and provide proof it was finally over. I was hoping Viviana and I would be in Italy when it happened. I would comfort her and there would be no reason for her to go back to Arizona. Unfortunately, the dumbass couldn't even get that right. Oh, he blew up the right car this time, but Luca and Michelina weren't in it. So, what did dumbass do next? After his big screw up, he grabbed Jessica and my beloved son Geno. With that move, he signed his own death certificate and Gemma's, too.

Now, I get the phone call that not only is Geno marrying Jessica, but Luca and Michelina are on their way to Italy! I can't catch a break. I can't imagine why they are coming here and, truthfully, I don't care. Gianni has put four guards on this trip to protect Viviana and me. Joseph has been the only protection I ever had until Viviana came to live with me. He always shows respect, and he only takes orders from me. I wave him over from the front of the plane. "Joseph, come sit with me," my voice barely above a whisper.

"Sir, do you need something?"

"Have a seat, please. Apparently, Luca, and Michelina, are on their way to Italy. They are going to try and meet up with us. I need you to stop that from happening."

"For how long?"

"At least until I slip that ring on Viviana's finger and the priest says we are married. After that, there is nothing anyone can do."

"What if Viviana finds out . . . or anyone else, for that matter."

"I need discretion, Joseph, and I need a diversion. You do that, and I can handle the rest." He nods his head and checks his watch.

"Don't worry, Joseph, we should be landing in an hour. We have plenty of time. I'm going to slowly wake up Viviana. When we land, I want to be ready to bolt."

I stop by the galley kitchen and take a pot of coffee along with a pastry to wake up Viviana.

CHAPTER EIGHTEEN

Michelina

LUCA'S APARTMENT IS ONLY FIFTEEN MINUTES FROM AGOSTO'S home. He told me when he first took me there that Agosto had picked it out. Did he pick such a simple place because he knew that's what his son wanted or was it because he couldn't care less about him? Maybe it was the location, or maybe I'm just reading something into nothing. Although, every day, littles things are starting to make sense. The one thing I've learned is: everything with Agosto is smoke and mirrors. I thought we would be able to take this family out of the dark ages and bring them into the future. How stupid am I to think we could actually turn this family into a legitimate business? When Agosto got busted, he couldn't even last thirty days on the straight and narrow. What made me think all of them could do this today? When I saw Geno's spread sheet, I knew in my heart that this is never going to work out. This family is a well-oiled machine on all things illegal. They are all the things I am not. It's not what was sold to me when Luca and I made the decision to run this family. How much of this did Luca know? How much did my grandmother know? Today, I saw the struggle in Luca's eyes. Whether he knew or not, he clearly doesn't want to be a part of this, and I'm forcing him to be. Ten years from now, will he resent me? Hate me for my choices? Or worse, will he become like Gianni, Geno, or God forbid, Agosto. In my heart, I know I couldn't live with that. Maybe the best thing I can do is let him go. I can use some of what Carmine left me to guarantee his safety. He can start over in the middle of nowhere. At least I can keep him safe. He deserves that and so much more.

I stop at Jess's room before I head to mine to pack. Her door is open. I knock and head inside. She's sitting in front of the window. She looks up and smiles when she sees me.

"Chelle, guess what? Oh, you don't have to guess—here." She sticks her hand out and shows me her ring.

"Wow, that's some diamond. It's beautiful. Tell me everything." I give her the brightest smile I can manage.

"Geno took me on a picnic, and it was so beautiful. He talked about the future, a future with me. Oh, Chelle, I'll be safe with him, and I do love him. Just think, we will be one big, happy family." My heart sinks, leaving me with a giant hole in my chest.

"Jess, what if things were different? I mean, what if Luca and I decided to walk away from the business? We could still talk every day and see each other, we just wouldn't live here, or be part of the day-to-day business."

"Is something wrong? Why would you do that? We are all together and safe, finally. It's been a long time coming. I don't understand." As her smile faded, her lips trembled around her words.

"There are a lot of changes, some I'm not so comfortable with. I need time, Jess. I have questions that only my grandmother can answer. Luca and I are going to catch a flight out and try to meet up with her and Agosto."

"Well, Agosto doesn't seem like the type that is going to like that, so be prepared for some pushback. I'll be here if you need me, Chelle." Before I can say anything more, she throws her arms around me and gives me a hug.

I head to my room and begin pulling clothes out of the closet while I formulate some sort of plan. I'm not sure how much time passes before I look up and see Luca in the doorway. I tend to talk out loud to myself. It would drive my mom crazy. She blamed it on my being an only child. Something else she blamed Carmine for.

"How long have you been lurking in the doorway?" I pray he didn't hear much of what I said.

"First of all, I wasn't lurking, and, secondly, I was getting ready to knock but thought maybe you had your earbuds in, and you were talking on the phone. I didn't want to disturb you. Do you always mumble to yourself out loud?" I ignore his question and quickly change the subject.

"I have no idea what to pack? How long are we staying?"

"Well by the looks of what you're packing, a hell of a lot longer than I thought." He holds up a duffle bag as if to make a point.

"You're a guy, they always pack less."

"We can get whatever we need when we are there. I'm trying to book a private jet for us. It's leaving in two hours. I don't know if we got it yet, but finish up here, just in case."

"Two hours! Did you tell everyone that we are leaving and where we are going?"

"Jessica wasn't around, but I did speak to Gianni and Geno. I let them know we were heading out. As much as I didn't want to tell them anything, in this family it is very hard to keep big things like this a secret. Let's not forget we also have guards watching our every move."

"How much do they know?"

"We are headed out to Greece for a much-needed vacation." I slide down onto the foot of the bed and just stare at him.

"Chelle, are you okay?" He crouches down by me.

"I always wanted to go to Greece, how did you know?" I whisper.

"Well, that was just a cover story but if you really want to shoot over there for a couple of days, we can do it."

"You're distracting me. I need to find my passport."

"I have it already. Where is your bag? I can help you pack." I reach under the bed and pull out my new bag that is still in the plastic. It's flat but folds into a duffle bag. I try not to laugh as Luca is trying to figure out how it all zips together.

"The ad for the bag popped up on one of my social media sites. I'm a sucker for a pink bag." I open it up and show him how it starts flat and then folds into a duffle bag. It holds so much stuff with room to spare. I should probably write a review for it.

"Chelle, are you stalling or are you that in love with this crazy bag?"

"Honestly, both." I hand it to him, and we head out. When we get to the garage, only Gianni is waiting for us. Just once I would like to think my every move is not being watched.

"What is the big secret? Why couldn't you just say why you were heading to Sicily? Why do you have to leave everyone guessing? If you wonder why I don't trust you, Luca, this is why." Before I can say a word, Luca's arm slips around my waist and pulls me closer towards him.

"Gianni, maybe, just maybe we would like a little bit of privacy. Since I got shot, this whole family has been up my ass twenty-four-seven. I've had to quit my job, move out of my apartment, my car has blown up, and I have guards on me all the time. I was an FBI agent who is more than capable of taking care of myself and my girl."

"I get all of that but, since we took an oath to run this family together, you better get used to all this togetherness shit. Now, why are you going to Sicily?"

"I have some things—personal things—that I want to talk to my grandmother about. Agosto hightailed it out of here so fast, I didn't get to finish talking to her."

"I think Dad has had his plan in the works for years. It's only now that he was able to make it a reality."

I want to nail Gianni to the wall and find out how much he knows about Agosto's plan, but that would reveal the existence of Carmine's tapes. They are Luca's, not mine. Only he can decide if he wants to tell anyone about them. Instead, I have to stand here and take his bullshit, for now.

"Gianni, we don't have time for this. Chelle and I have a flight to catch. You need to save this pissing match for another day."

"I called in a favor; you have a private jet waiting for you. The pilot has an envelope you will need. Now we are even." With that we get in Luca's car and head to the airpark. He has a tight grip on my hand. When we are far enough from the house, he eases up.

"Luca, that was hot." We both begin to laugh, and I swear it's like a giant weight has been lifted off of us, at least, for now. I have the plane ride to figure out what I'm going to say to my grandmother, and what I'm not going to say to Agosto. For now, I just want to enjoy my time with Luca.

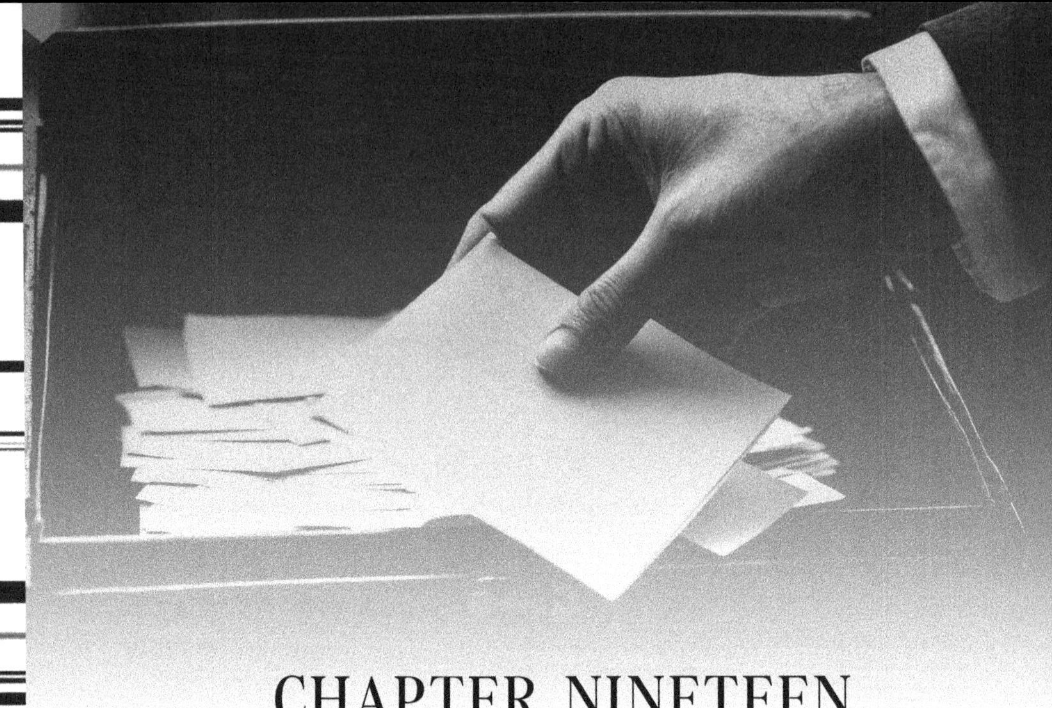

CHAPTER NINETEEN

Jessica

I NEVER THOUGHT THAT CHELLE WOULD LEAVE ME, IF ANYTHING, I always thought I would be the one to make that first move. There is a knock on the door and when I look up, Geno is standing there. Just the sight of him takes my breath away.

"Come in. You just missed Chelle."

"So, she told you they are off to Sicily. Do you know why?" I take a seat on the chaise and move so when he sits down, my feet are in his lap. He knows I love when he massages them, and his hands begin working their magic.

"I suppose she has more questions for Viviana. You need to understand that Chelle was kept in the dark about a lot of stuff. It's only when she was given Carmine's journals that she found out about her grandfather's business and all this extended family that she has." I don't think talking about Carmine's journals is spilling any secrets; everyone knows she has them.

"Jessica, I don't like secrets, so please promise we will be open and honest with each other."

"I agree, babe. I see what all the secrets, which are now coming to light, are doing to my best friend. It makes me sad."

"Why did Frances and, for that matter, Viviana keep so much from Chelle?"

"She has been looking for answers her whole life. When she finally got the courage to talk to Frances about her father, Frances shut her down. It was like the blame game, except this was happening with someone's feelings. Frances blamed Carmine for everything that went wrong in her life. She was a very bitter woman. That bitterness spread through everything in her life. I remember one summer Chelle and I went to Sea World. They had the most amazing jellyfish exhibit. Chelle stood there staring at them with tears running down her cheeks. When I asked her what was wrong, she said they reminded her of her mother with their stinging tentacles. At first, I didn't get it. All I could do was be there to support my friend. Later, she explained that her mother was so bitter that no matter what she would ask her about her father or grandfather, her answers would sting and wound her. She finally stopped asking."

"Wow, it's hard for me to see this through her eyes. I thought she knew everything. I guess it's no different than my dad keeping Gianni and I in the dark about Luca."

"Do you know why he did that? I mean it's not like he cheated on your mom, he was a widow finding comfort with someone. Why the big secret?"

"Gianni tried talking to Dad about it and he shut him down. Then he went to Luca and asked him about it. However, he knows just as little as we do. The way that generation operates—secrets and lies—it's a wonder that they got anything done."

"Luca joining the FBI probably didn't help the cause any. At the end of the day, it was a respectable job. I wonder what he is going to do now?"

"What do you mean? He is part of this business."

"What if Chelle and Luca decide to walk away from all of this, what would happen?" I wave my hand for emphasis.

"Do you know something?"

"Nothing concrete, Geno. I think that might be what she wants to talk to Viviana about. You know none of this was ever in Chelle or, for that matter, Luca's wheelhouse. Who knows; maybe it has become overwhelming for them." He stops rubbing my feet, seemingly lost in his own thoughts.

"Maybe, Jessica, it's overwhelming for all of us. I mean, a brother who is—was—an FBI agent. We were brought up to hate any kind of law enforcement. We were always taught to never trust law enforcement, never rat out anyone, and, no matter what, keep your mouth shut. The family will always protect you and your family. You go to jail, if you have to, and the family will make sure everything is taken care of. So, knowing we have a half-brother that was FBI . . . this is not easy for any of us."

"Do you think that maybe it would be best for everyone if Luca and Chelle walk away from the business? If they did that, could they be safe?" He pulls me into his lap, leans in and gently kisses me. His lips are so soft. He pulls back and runs his fingers down my cheeks.

"I wish I had the answers, babe. I know Chelle has enough of stuff from Carmine to keep them safe, but what kind of life would they have?"

"Maybe, like in the movies, they move to the middle of nowhere and change their names. I can't imagine moving someplace and not knowing anyone. Chelle and I always thought we would have each other, and we had no intention of leaving the valley. We always thought we would buy houses next to each other and raise our families together. Now, I'm wondering if that is just a pipe dream."

"I'm sorry. I don't think that will be a reality for you."

"After we get married, where will we live?"

"What do you mean? We will live here with the rest of the family." My whole-body tenses and I'm sure he can feel it.

"Why? Can't we have our own place? It doesn't have to be far from here, just some place separate to call our home. This is Agosto's home, and it always will be."

"I'll talk to Dad about it. I know he likes everyone under one roof for safety reasons." I'm thinking more like a control freak, but I will let this play out.

"Have you thought about what kind of wedding we are going to have and when?"

"Jessica, I'll have whatever you want. I was thinking we can have it here. As far as when, the sooner the better."

"Okay, Geno, let me see if I got this right. You don't care what kind of wedding, as long as it's here. You don't care when, only that it's soon. On top of that, we have to live under Agosto's roof, which means we live by his rules. This is sounding more like a prison; not much different than the hell you rescued me from." I wiggle out of his lap, get up and head out on the balcony. What the hell have I gotten myself into? He doesn't follow me outside, instead, he gets up and leaves. Now I'm left with more questions than I started with.

CHAPTER TWENTY

Geno

I HEAD INTO THE KITCHEN TO GRAB A BEER AND FIND GIANNI eating a pizza he must have just had delivered. I grab a slice and sit down next to him. We eat our pizza and drink our beer in silence. When I finish my pizza, I get up and grab two more beers. He takes one and finally looks at me. "Spill it; what did you screw up, little brother?"

"What makes you think I screwed up?"

"Well, you just got engaged to a beautiful lady and you're sitting here with me, so what did you screw up?"

"Everything."

"You've got to be a little more forthcoming than that."

"She asked me where we will live, and I said here. She asked what kind of wedding I wanted, and I said I didn't care. I thought we could just have it here, sooner rather than later. She wasn't happy. She asked why we have to live here under Agosto's roof and by Agosto's rules. Honestly, I never thought of it that way."

"Geno, for such a smart guy, sometimes you are such an idiot. She's an only child. She has no concept of having any family up your ass morning, noon, and night. She was kept a prisoner by a madman. Do you think she wants to feel like a prisoner all over again? Don't let Dad force you into living here. Give her the life she deserves. Look at Luca and Chelle; neither of them wants any of this, they just can't see their way clearly to do anything else. Chelle is here because of an obligation to Viviana and, in some part, Jess. I love Dad but, sadly, he is aging quickly. When I talk to him, he thinks he's still in the past dealing with Carmine. He screwed up royally with Luca. I mean he forced the guy, his own son, to have plastic surgery. What the hell is he going to do next? This trip with Viviana is more for him than for her. I think she's going along with it because she really has nothing else better to do."

"I came to you for some advice on my situation and you gave me anything but that."

"You want advice? Well, here you go. This is a no brainer, Geno. Don't have a quickie wedding because she will always compare it to the wedding at the Elvis chapel she was forced into. Do something different. As far as your living arrangements are concerned, why the hell don't you move out? Buy her a house nearby as a wedding gift. The Bruins up on Canyon drive are getting ready to list their house. They came by last week to let Dad know. It would be perfect for you and Jess. By staying nearby, you're making her happy that she's not under the same roof as Dad, but she can still have easy access to Chelle and Viviana, and you will be close to Dad. Plus, your commute to work is a simple walk down the road. Like I said, it's a no brainer." He gets up, clears the table and heads out back. He makes it sound so easy. I get up to get another beer and find Jess standing in the doorway.

"Hey, Jess, we need to talk."

"That's why I came looking for you. Geno, I don't want to live here after the wedding." I walk toward her and take her into my arms.

"I agree; we need to be on our own. Gianni gave me a lead on a house right here in Eco Canyon that I think would be perfect for us. The owner contacted Dad first to let him know he was listing it in case he was interested. I will give the owner a call in the morning. We can look at it and, if you like it, it's ours. As far as the wedding is concerned, Jess, I know the hell you've been through; I thought I was making it easier for you. We can have whatever type of wedding you feel comfortable with. I promise I will never let anything bad happen to you ever again." I run my fingers through her hair and gently kiss her.

"Thank you," she whispers as her lips touch mine again. I lift her up into my arms and carry her back to her room.

CHAPTER TWENTY-ONE

Luca

I was shocked when Gianni made the travel arrangements for us. I was even more surprised when the pilot handed me the envelope that Gianni mentioned because it says *Agosto's itinerary*. I pass it to Chelle. She looks at it and passes it back to me.

"Why do you think he did all of this for you?"

"For us, Chelle. I think he was more affected by everything that Agosto did to me than anything else. Plus, technically, I'm the baby brother and he is the oldest. If something were to happen to Agosto, he would be in charge."

"That's very old school, Luca."

"Like it or not, that's the way most families work. Given what this family does for a living, he can have all of it."

"So, your mind is made up?"

"For now, I'm keeping an open mind, but I need to be able to sleep at night, which is a problem right now."

"I'm going to try and get some sleep before we land. Are you coming?"

"I'll be in shortly. I'm going to have a nightcap before I turn in." I watch her leave me and the two guards that Gianni insisted tag along with us. I wonder how much they really know. It reminds me of a conversation I had with Carmine.

"Only trust yourself, kid. If you screw up, it's on you. If you take help from other people, that opens up a can of worms that you won't be able to close."

At some point in our conversations, I told him he should write fortune cookies or greeting cards. We both got a good laugh out of that. Without a doubt, if he was still alive, I would have somehow managed to free him and, ultimately, would work with him. However, we are not always given the life we want. I get up and pour myself a bourbon and that's when I remember the envelope Gianni gave me. I grab it and the bottle of bourbon before stretching out on the sofa.

I'm not sure what Chelle thinks she needs to hear from Viviana that would make whatever her next decision easier. I wish there was something I could say to make her see that staying where we are is a bad decision. I don't think Chelle understands how much of her soul this business will take from her. I realize as much as I love her, it's not a choice I'm willing to make.

I open the envelope and pull out the papers inside. I thought it would just be the itinerary, however, there is more. Apparently, the first few pages consist of everything about my mother. From where she was born to all the schools she went to and every job she had. The next page was her medical information. I feel a clutch of panic in the pit of my stomach as I begin reading. Apparently, my mom was adopted and knew nothing of her birth parents' medical history. The report is pretty cut and dry until it gets to me. The report on me starts when he shipped me off to boarding school at the lovely age of fifteen. There are pictures of every girl I ever went out with. Pictures of me playing Rugby. My position was a winger because of my speed. My mom was a sports junkie but, when I first took up Rugby, she was very nervous. After a while, she was okay with it. The only way I would agree to go to boarding school is if I got to continue playing Rugby. Agosto agreed. Who knows, maybe I should have asked for more, like an introduction to my brothers. But realistically, that was never going to happen. I pour myself another bourbon and flip the page. Next is the complete report on Chelle and how she rescued Jessica. *I don't understand why Gianni gave me this.* Suddenly, the next thing I read has me sitting up real fast. The child that Jessica had was never put up for adoption. He was given to Lorenzo to pay for a debt that he held over Agosto's head. His name is Valorous, and he has no clue about any of this. How could someone just give away a child to pay a debt—a child that isn't even his? I flip the page and I get to Agosto's itinerary. He plans on marrying Viviana tomorrow. Why the rush? It's not like anyone is going anywhere. The next page is a note from Gianni.

Hey Luca,

When you saved my life and Agosto wouldn't tell me anything about you, I took matters into my own hands. I hired someone to dig it all up. The next part of the report is very disturbing, even for me. I knew my father was capable of so much, but this is where I draw the line. You saved my life once, and I think this will make us even. This was a very hard thing for me to do, but I don't even know this man anymore. At this point, everyone's safety is my only concern. Oh, and I know you're not headed to Greece. You can't lie to save your life."

Gianni

I flip the page and begin to read all about Agosto's arrangement with Nick Jr. On Agosto's orders Nick killed Frances. That bomb was meant for Chelle. He then ordered Nick to kill me and Chelle. *Me*—his flesh and blood! No wonder he made sure I was the one who would take the shot that would kill Nick. He knew I would never miss. He knew what was at stake. The rush to marry Viviana is because when she finds out he killed her daughter, he's knows she won't want him. No one wants him. He *has to* marry Viviana to beat Carmine. In his mind, it's all about Carmine. It's always been about Carmine. How the hell am I going to explain all of this to Chelle when I can't even wrap my head around it? I put everything back in the envelope, finish my drink, and head into the bedroom to talk to Chelle.

CHAPTER TWENTY-TWO

Michelina

I'VE TRIED TO SLEEP BUT I CAN'T SHUT MY MIND OFF. LUCA FINALLY comes in and I can feel an ease come over me. Maybe I'll finally be able to get some rest. He crawls into bed and turns on the light.

"Hey, what's with the light?"

"We need to talk."

"You sound ominous."

"That's because I am. Remember that envelope the pilot handed me, you know the one with Agosto's itinerary? Well, it wasn't just his itinerary, it's so much more. I'm not going to bore you with all the details. Let's start with the fact that Agosto never put Jessica's son up for adoption. Instead, he used him to pay off a debt." I'm watching Luca's face and as bad as this sounds, I don't think this is the worst part.

"There's more, isn't there?"

"Yeah, apparently, he hired your brother Nick to plant a bomb in your car. Nick screwed up and put it in your mother's car. It wasn't Frances that he wanted dead; it was you." I jump out of the bed and race to the bathroom to throw up. I feel him behind me stroking my back and holding my hair up. Finally, I compose myself, grab my toiletries bag, retrieve the mouthwash and rinse out my mouth. When I'm done, I stare at him in total disbelief.

"There's more, isn't there?"

"Yeah, he gave Nick a second chance to kill you but that time, he added me into the equation. I'm barely able to say it, Chelle. My father wanted *me* dead. That's just surreal. He made sure I was the one who would shoot Nick because I don't miss, and he was counting on that. Apparently, he is marrying Viviana tomorrow before she can find any of this out." We head back to the bed and sit on the edge. Both of us staring into space like we are in a bad movie.

"Why did Gianni give you all of this?"

"He said when I saved his life, he went to Agosto with questions, but he wouldn't answer them, so he hired someone to look into me."

"What happens if he marries her before we get there to stop it?"

"All we can do is give Viviana all the information and let her decide. We will support her and help get her the hell out of Sicily."

"I think it's safe to say I won't be getting any rest. When do we land?" I check my watch, grateful that it automatically adjusts to the time change.

"Two hours until we land. According to Agosto's itinerary, they have already landed."

"This is not something I'm about to tell her over the phone. What about Jessica? Did Geno play any part in all of this?"

"According to the report, he was in the dark like everyone else."

"What should we do about Jess's kid?"

"His name is Valorous and, according to Gianni's investigators, he has no clue about any of this. I say leave him alone. Why disrupt his life only to make it a living hell? For all we know, he could be happy right where he is." I get up, head into the bathroom, and brush my teeth again before packing up my toiletries bag.

"As soon as we land, we need to get to Grandma and finally confront Agosto with everything we know. I know he's your father, but I don't want her anywhere near him, or any of us, for that matter." He doesn't say anything.

Finally, the pilot buzzes us to let us know we are getting ready to land. The faster you want time to go, the slower it moves. I pull out my rosary beads and begin to pray. I haven't prayed this much in a long time. It seems, lately, I keep asking God for one thing or another. Tonight, I realize the only thing I'm asking him for is safety for my grandmother.

From what I can see of the countryside, it looks beautiful, however, I can't focus on anything other than my grandmother. Luca squeezes my hand.

"Chelle, I've been thinking, I don't want Gianni's name brought into the conversation at all. He put his life on the line for us when he really didn't have to."

"I agree. If Agosto asks where we got our information, what will you say?" He pulls out Gianni's letter from the envelope and lights it up with a match before throwing it out the window.

"I got it from the FBI when they asked me to be a snitch."

"You're quick on your feet when you have to be."

"Lives are at stake, Chelle. I'm sure there is still a bounty on both our heads."

"I remember Agosto said they were going to head to San Vito lo Capo. He got reservations at the Hotel Piccolo Mondo. Is that still the plan?" He looks down at his phone and shakes his head yes.

We stay in silence, and for just a moment, I believe I'm prepared for what lies ahead of me . . . of all of us. Then, reality hits me like a ton of bricks. Will I be the one to break up this dysfunctional family? Will any of us be able to lead a normal life after this? As far as the business is concerned, I don't want it. It's a pipe dream to think that this business could have been run legitimately. I don't want all this evil around me.

The car comes to a stop, and I see the most magnificent hotel on the hill. I'm sure none of these things matter to Grandma. She just wants to live whatever life she has left with no worries.

"It's beautiful, Luca," I say as we climb out of the car.

"I'm sure they are checked in by now. I'll find out what room they are in and get us a room, too."

I wrap my arm in his and smile. "I'll come with you."

Luca is quick to get answers. It helps that he is very generous with his tips. He slips his arm around my waist, and we take the elevator up to the penthouse. With a knock on the door, it opens, and Agosto is standing there.

"I thought you both would be here sooner. Please, come in." He opens the door wide and with his other hand waves us in. "Viviana will be right out; can I get you a drink?"

"No, I just want to talk to my grandmother." With that, the bedroom door opens, and she steps out.

CHAPTER TWENTY-THREE

Michelina

S EEING THE LOOK OF JOY ON HER FACE ONLY MAKES THIS HARDER. Agosto is quick to put his arm around Viviana's waist. He takes her left hand in his and that's when I notice the wedding bands. The bands that he made sure I noticed.

"Well, it looks like we missed the wedding, Luca. Agosto, you knew we were coming, why didn't you wait for us?" I ask. His face never loses its smile. The face I've wanted to smack on more than one occasion.

"We waited so long for this, and we just didn't want to wait another minute, right Viviana?" She smiles but says nothing.

"Well, I hate to break up this little party but there are some things I need to talk to you about, Grandma. I'll start with Agosto ordering Nick to put a bomb in, what he thought was, my car but instead, was my mother's. That's right, Grandma, he killed your daughter, my mother. Then, the sweet and innocent Agosto ordered Nick to put a bomb in Luca's car, hoping to kill Luca and me. That's some great fatherly love you got going there. Oh, and please don't let me forget that you never put Jessica's baby up for adoption; you gave him to your cousin Lorenzo to repay a debt. You are a class act. How the hell do you live with yourself? Oh wait, I know. You go to confession on Saturday for absolution and you start all over again on Sunday." I don't even recognize my own voice that is shaking with fury. The next few minutes, everything moves in slow motion. My grandmother pulls away from Agosto, walks up to the bar to get a drink and, when she turns around, she has a gun in her hand. She places the muzzle up against her throat. I try to run to her, but Luca holds me back.

"Any sudden movement and that gun can go off. It's a revolver, so there is no safety. Viviana, why don't you put the gun down and we can talk about all of this." Luca's voice is extremely low and steady.

"The time to talk was before all of this happened. Michelina, I'm so sorry you got dragged into all of this. I found out about a week ago everything that this bastard did. I agreed to this trip and sham of a wedding, if only to enact my own revenge. I didn't expect you to show up without warning," she says to me with tears slowly streaming down her face. "Why, Agosto, why? Did you think you needed to do all of this just to get my attention?" She brings her focus back to him.

"I did all this because I love you. I needed to make up for everything Carmine did to you."

"Carmine didn't do anything near as horrific as you have. You killed my daughter!" Her voice cracks, and I'm not sure how much more I can take.

"Please, Grandma, put the gun down. We can go home and get this annulled. You never have to see him again." As Agosto takes a step toward her, she turns the gun on him and fires three times. Each bullet hitting their mark in his chest. Then she turns the gun on herself and fires. I race to her, and Luca pushes the gun away. I'm applying pressure, trying to stop the bleeding.

"Please hang on, please."

"No, Michelina, I know God forbids this, but I brought that evil into our lives. Now I too must pay the price. I lived a long life. I'm very tired and I want to talk to Frances . . . to apologize. I love you, sweetheart." And with that, she is gone. I'm frozen in place. The guards are trying to help us get out of here. They keep saying they will take care of everything. What is there to take care of? *—my grandmother is dead!*

After the police came, it took them a week to figure out what to do with us. Eventually, Lorenzo came and spoke to them, and we were released. As we were getting ready to head to the airport, Lorenzo pulled Luca aside and let him know that the debt was settled. We have no idea what he was talking about and, honestly, I don't want to know. He was able to make the arrangements for their bodies to travel back to the States with us. As we head to the airport, I look back and see Lorenzo standing there, just another old man with his hat in his hands. A man who now doesn't have to hold onto Agosto's secrets. The car is filled with silence. I look at Luca as he stares out the window. I wonder how the death of his father will change him, change all of Agosto's son's. How could one man do so much damage to his own family, all in the name of love?

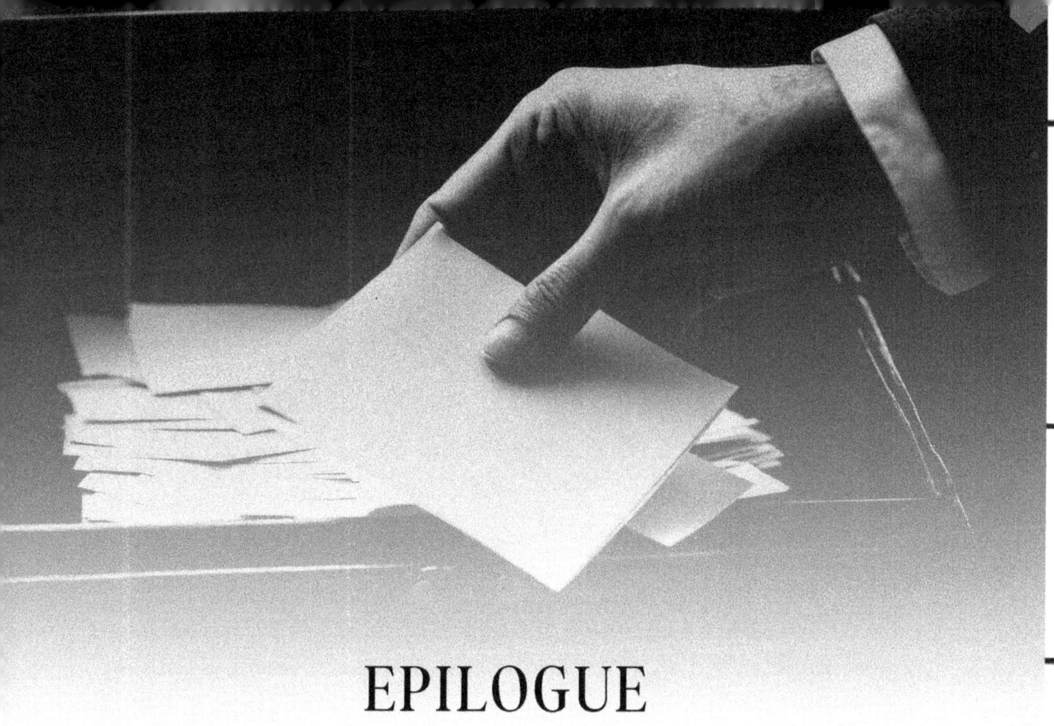

EPILOGUE

Michelina

WHEN WE TOUCHED DOWN IN ARIZONA, IT WAS GLOOMY and rainy. Those days are so rare in the desert. We were met at the airport by Gianni, Geno, and Jessica. It was not a warm welcome for the brothers; however, Jess pulled me into a hug, and I let her. When we got back to the house, there were so many questions. I was the one who told Jess about her son. How he was used to pay a debt. A debt that till this day, no one knows what it was. She took it a lot better than I thought she would. Maybe having Geno in her life will be good for her.

When it came time to tell them what happened right before the shooting, it was Gianni who started with the questions.

"Where did Viviana get a gun?"

"Apparently, it came from one of her guards," Luca states.

"Did you tell her about the bombs?" Gianni's voice sounds unsteady, knowing it was all in the report that he gave Luca.

"No, Gianni, she already knew. She said she found out a week earlier. She held onto that information until she decided what she wanted to do."

Geno looks at Luca and back to Gianni. That's when the realization that Gianni knew becomes apparent. "You knew and you didn't tell me, why? Gianni, we are brothers. After Mom died, you said we will never have secrets. You lied; you are just like him."

Gianni jumps up, his face only inches from Geno's. "I am nothing like him!" he yells.

"Why did you keep this from me, your own brother?"

"You always saw the good in him . . . in everyone. There was no need to taint your vision with the reality that our father, Agosto Amaro, was a very evil man and a killer."

"When did you find out? How long have you been keeping this secret?"

"When Luca saved my life and Dad refused to answer any questions about him, I started digging into the past. It was like opening Pandora's box."

"What happens now?" Luca looks to me for the answers. We talked about it privately, but I wanted to see how Jess was before doing anything. Seeing her today and how happy she is, I have my answers.

"We will all go before the heads of the family and let them know that Luca and I are stepping back. I can't be a part of all of this, and I won't raise a family around all the danger and lies. We have enough stuff from Carmine to keep us safe."

"Where will you go?" Jess asks, her voice trailing off.

The room falls silent. For a moment, I'm reminded of something Luca said his mom told him, "*A bad decision in a split moment can't be undone.'*

"Wherever we go, we will be happy and at peace."

The End

Coming Soon

The Amato family's story continues as the newer generation begins to piece together the past, so they can build a better future.

OTHER BOOKS

ABOUT THE AUTHOR

Theresa Sederholt was born and raised in Brooklyn New York. She is a graduate of Campbell University in North Carolina, with a degree in Criminal Justice. Theresa now calls Florida home, with her husband, a professional chef, and her two dogs.

Experiencing life first hand is what she does best. Believing she can do anything has put her in many crazy situations. Whether it's babysitting a pig farm or cutting the top off of a mini truck; nothing is ever out of reach. Her list is endless, A to Z.

Theresa's beliefs are pretty simple. There isn't a luggage rack on the hearse, and give a girl Nutella and espresso and she can change the world.

Theresa enjoys connecting with her fans. She can always be reached through her website at:

www.theresasederholt.com

www.ingramcontent.com/pod-product-compliance
Lightning Source LLC
Chambersburg PA
CBHW061113100726
47911CB00013B/517